THE ALPHABET KILLER

KERI BEEVIS

Boldwood

First published in 2013 as *M for Murder* and *Dead Letter Day*. This edition published in Great Britain in 2026 by Boldwood Books Ltd.

Cover Design by Head Design Ltd

Cover Images: iStock

Every effort has been made to obtain the necessary permissions with reference to copyright material, both illustrative and quoted. We apologise for any omissions in this respect and will be pleased to make the appropriate acknowledgements in any future edition.

A CIP catalogue record for this book is available from the British Library.

Paperback ISBN 978-1-80658-861-9

Large Print ISBN 978-1-80658-863-3

Hardback ISBN 978-1-80658-860-2

Trade Paperback ISBN 978-1-80658-862-6

Ebook ISBN 978-1-80658-864-0

Kindle ISBN 978-1-80658-865-7

Audio CD ISBN 978-1-80658-855-8

MP3 CD ISBN 978-1-80658-856-5

Digital audio download ISBN 978-1-80658-857-2

This book is printed on certified sustainable paper. Boldwood Books is dedicated to putting sustainability at the heart of our business. For more information please visit https://www.boldwoodbooks.com/about-us/sustainability/

Boldwood Books Ltd, 23 Bowerdean Street, London, SW6 3TN

www.boldwoodbooks.com

To Mum, Paul and Holly, thank you for always being there, and to Dad, who would have been so proud

PROLOGUE

He had known from the beginning that they would come for him eventually and, in a way, he guessed he was lucky that it had taken them so long to find him.

Almost eight years. Seven years, ten months and twenty-seven days, if you wanted to be exact. He knew of course, because he had counted those days in thick black marker pen on the white emulsion wall, each one that had passed denoted with a red circle, there in plain view for anyone who entered the room to see.

Of course, nobody ever had seen. But that was the beauty of hiding; no one was supposed to know where you were.

A twisted smile tugged at the corners of his mouth. It was over now, and they would take him away, but it didn't really matter. Gripping tightly at the arms of his chair, it struck him with bitter irony that he had been living in his own private prison anyway. How would a cell with bars on the window be any different?

It wouldn't take his jailers long to realise that the force of what he had created could not be stopped.

Footsteps echoed on the stairs below, growing louder as they neared the attic. Glancing in the dresser mirror, he watched as the door opened behind him, and smiled in reassurance at the familiar face that entered the room; at the one person who had been there for him, who had helped and believed in him, and who was now studying him with a concerned look on his face.

'They're coming for you.'

It wasn't a question, but he nodded at the reflection, raising his finger to his lips. 'We both knew that they would sooner or later,' he said softly. 'But it doesn't matter any longer, does it?'

Although his question went unanswered, he knew that they were both thinking the same thing.

Rodney Boone had been caught, but the game was far from over. There was someone new to fill his shoes now. Someone who didn't want to see what he had started go to waste. And that someone had a new name and a new face, and new hands with which to kill.

1

It was their second doughnut stop of the day. Rebecca Angell, waiting in the patrol car for her partner, stole a glance at her watch and noted that it was only ten thirty. Letting out a sigh, she leant back against the headrest and muttered a curse under her breath. All the time though, her eyes remained alert, watching the crowded city street around her.

This was not what she had expected or wanted.

The move to Juniper had been planned as an escape from small-town life; a chance to get away from her home in Swallow Falls.

Sure, she loved the place. She had lived there all of her life, and it held many fond memories, but it would have been a lousy place to be a cop.

Her parents loved the town, and it was unlikely they would ever leave. Her dad was minister of the parish, while her mom worked part-time at the high school and, now her daughters were grown up, served on the local committee.

Rebecca, at twenty-six, was the youngest of her siblings. After high school she had attended college for two years, during which time her rather old-fashioned parents had extolled the virtues of a nice, safe secretarial job, and sure enough, after graduating, she had found herself fetching coffee, answering the phone and performing other mundane duties for a local law firm. She hated the work, stuck it out for a couple of years, but eventually realised she couldn't spend her life pleasing her parents. A part of her had always hankered to be a cop, probably because she had grown up on a diet of *Starsky & Hutch* and *Charlie's Angels*. While her oldest sister, Jess, made out with boys, and middle sister, Wendy, played with her dolls, Rebecca, much to her mother's chagrin, had hung out with the Brady twins, playing cops and robbers. Back then, when she had told her parents that when she grew up she was going to put away bad guys, they had laughed her ideas off, putting them down to a childish whim.

How disappointed they had been then, to discover that all these years later she still had her heart set on a career in law enforcement, and shock followed that disappointment when, after graduating from the academy, she had applied to join Juniper Police Department.

It hadn't even been a decision for Rebecca, who knew that if she stayed in her hometown, the job would amount to little more than writing out parking tickets and breaking up the odd barroom brawl. Juniper, meanwhile, was a big enough city to offer the excitement that she craved, while still close enough to home that she could visit regularly.

Her mother had predictably begged her to reconsider, over-exaggerating the situation to the extent that anyone would think her youngest daughter was heading off to war, but Rebecca's mind was already made up.

Now she was here in Juniper though, niggling doubts were starting to creep in. Maybe she was expecting more than the city had to offer.

But then again, maybe she wasn't being given a fair chance to prove her worth.

Although she had only been here a little over three weeks, she already had the distinct impression her new colleagues didn't think she was up to the job. She suspected that it had a lot to do with the fact that she came from a small town and, it seemed, they thought working in the city was going to be too much for her, and that was no doubt why she had been partnered with Victor Boaz.

A couple of months of putting up with his lazy, sexist attitude would be enough for her. Let her think that city life was too much trouble and she would soon go running back to the safety of her small town, tail between her legs.

It might have worked if Rebecca had been a different person, but she wasn't, and if Vic and his buddies intended to scare her away then they had a surprise coming, because she didn't give up easily. Her mother called it her stubborn streak, never letting up until she got her own way, while Rebecca preferred to think of it as dogged determination. She was good at digging her heels in and had no intention of quitting when she had worked so hard to get here.

The car door opening broke her from her thoughts, and she glanced up as Vic climbed into the driver's seat, half a doughnut in his hand, the other half wedged in his mouth. In his free hand he held a greasy paper bag, which he offered to Rebecca.

'Want one?' he mumbled through his mouthful.

She screwed up her nose. 'Thanks, but I think I'll pass.'

Taking the bag from him, she added it to the growing collection already in the glovebox, making a mental note to clear it out when they next stopped, and thinking that if Vic kept eating doughnuts at this rate, he would end up looking like one.

Not a pleasant thought.

That wasn't to say he was ugly, or even overweight. Even features, close-cropped dark hair and grey-blue eyes, tall, and with a bulk that, at the moment, was mostly still muscle, thanks to the few hours a week he did bother to put in at the gym. But he would be piling on the pounds soon if he wasn't careful. And if he did pork out, he didn't exactly have a personality to carry him.

The man wasn't just a pig when it came to his food either. He was lazy, had little respect for women, and it had quickly become apparent to Rebecca that he would rather spend his day with his feet propped up in front of the TV with a six pack of beer at hand than behind the wheel of a patrol car.

At first, she had wondered why he decided to become a cop. It took just a week of working with him though to realise he was in it solely for the perks. Not punching a clock, and with no one constantly looking over his shoulder, he was able to make as many social stops as he liked, and he frequently abused the siren whenever he didn't feel like sitting in traffic or wanted to get somewhere fast.

As a rookie, Rebecca was sure she could learn a lot from this man.

Finishing his doughnut, Vic used his pants to wipe the sugar from his fingers and started the engine. As he edged away from the curb, Rebecca had one eye casually trained on the crowded street. She watched as a middle-aged woman pushing a baby stroller paused by a bus stop to fuss over the infant inside.

The boy ran from an alleyway, slowing to a jog as he approached them. He looked young, probably only about fourteen, and had straggly blond hair and a pair of jeans that hung down to the backs of his knees. He made a grab for the woman's purse and, though the two of them struggled briefly, the boy gained control easily, succeeding in knocking the woman into a crowd of disgruntled pensioners who were waiting for the bus.

Rebecca glanced at Vic, who appeared oblivious to the commotion going on across the street. 'Didn't you see that?' she snapped, thumping him hard on the arm.

He turned to her in irritation. 'Do you mind?'

Rebecca barely heard him, already out of the patrol car and heading across the street towards the alleyway she had seen the kid disappear down.

'Stop! Police!'

The boy paused momentarily, glancing over his shoulder long enough to flash a quick mocking grin, before disappearing from sight. Rebecca charged in after him.

The alleyway was long and narrow, the entrance to it flanked by the kitchens of restaurants. Steam and smoke billowed from various pipes and vents, and the strong aroma of Chinese food filled her nostrils. The buildings on either side were tall, and both had fire escapes. The kid was no longer in sight, and she glanced briefly at the metal staircases wondering if he had used one as an escape route, before dismissing the idea. He had only had a few seconds' head start on her and she would easily have seen him before he'd had time to reach the rooftop.

She paused to catch her breath and, in that moment, caught sight of him darting from the doorway where he had been hiding, making a mad dash for the metal fence that blocked the end of the alleyway. As she gave chase, Rebecca picked up speed, glad that she'd persevered with her early morning runs. She wasn't naturally athletic and didn't enjoy exercise, viewing the daily running and her visits to the gym as punishment rather than recreation. Now, though, as she closed the gap between herself and the kid, satisfaction kicked in that her efforts were paying off.

Behind her came the wail of a police siren; evidently Vic had finally decided to get his ass in gear.

She didn't stop to wait for him. The kid was already scaling the fence and if he got to the other side, chances were, she would lose him. Her adrenalin was pumping and there was no way in hell she planned on letting some snot-nosed little purse thief get the better of her.

Reaching the fence, she made a grab for his leg. Catching hold of his sneaker, she pulled hard. Struggling and squealing, the kid kicked out hard, knocking her in the face. Rebecca fell back, landing inelegantly on her ass, the sneaker still in her hand.

Laughing, the kid pushed himself over the fence, dropping easily to the other side. Peering through the bars and waving the red purse he'd snatched as a trophy, he grinned at her.

'Sorry. Gotta run!'

Feeling cheated, Rebecca picked herself up from the ground and flew for the bars. He was already disappearing around a corner, but she climbed the fence anyway. Behind her Vic pulled the patrol car to a stop, killing the siren.

'Hey, Angell, he's gone. Let it go.'

Ignoring him, she swung her leg over the top of the fence. As she dropped to the ground on the other side, she realised that Vic had left the car and was approaching.

He scowled at her through the bars. 'This had better not be a wild goose chase. I don't like running.'

Rebecca brushed down the seat of her pants, fully believing him. She didn't doubt for a second that Vic tried to get away with as little exercise as possible.

'He has to be around here somewhere,' she muttered, ignoring him. 'I mean, where could he go?'

Vic swung a leg clumsily across the top of the fence and jumped down, landing heavily beside her.

'Believe me, sweetheart, the possibilities are endless.'

Following in the kid's footsteps, they found themselves in a longer alleyway, this one wider and littered with several large dumpsters. Another fence separated them from the only apparent exit, which meant he was probably hiding somewhere.

Her eyes trying to cover all possible hiding places, Rebecca removed her baton from her belt.

Behind her, Vic was trying to sound disappointed. 'Oh, well. Looks like he got away.'

'I don't think so.'

He looked at her incredulously. 'Are you crazy? So where the hell is he then?'

'I think he's hiding.'

'Sure he is, Angell. Like he wants to hang around and play games with his cop friends.'

Rebecca ignored the sarcastic comment. 'He didn't have time to get away, and we'd have heard him if he'd climbed the fence. If we check the dumpsters...'

'Hey! Wait a minute, wait a minute. What's all this *we*?'

'We're partners, right?'

'Yeah, sweetheart, except I'm the senior officer here and I say we go back to the car.'

'We can't just give up without checking,' Rebecca rationalised, feeling her temper rise a notch. She didn't take kindly to being called sweetheart.

'Okay. You want to look? Go ahead. I'll stay here and supervise.' Giving her a broad grin, he leaned back against the wall and folded his arms.

Rebecca glared at him, refusing to give in. 'Okay, fine.'

Baton in hand, she defiantly made her way towards the nearest dumpster, her temper close to snapping.

Keep it together, Angell.

She was the newest recruit in the department and couldn't afford to start making enemies. Vic was popular with many of the officers on her shift and she didn't doubt that, if he chose to, he could make her life a living hell.

Just bide your time, Angell. Keep him sweet for now and sooner or later you'll get your chance for revenge.

Her father wouldn't approve of her thought process. He was a firm believer that two wrongs never made a right.

Remember, Rebecca. Forgive those who trespass against us.

Maybe he was right, but the thought of somehow getting even with Vic Boaz was the only thing keeping her temper in check right now.

She approached the first dumpster cautiously, half expecting the boy to leap out at her with a gun or something. Maybe she should un-holster her own weapon.

Yeah, sure, you idiot. He's just a kid, just a pickpocketing kid.

Although she scolded herself, she held on tightly to her baton. Just in case.

The dumpster stank of rotting eggs and cabbage. He wasn't hiding down the side and, although she couldn't imagine anyone choosing to get inside it, she checked, just to be certain.

As she suspected, the kid wasn't there.

Moving on to the second dumpster, she hoped to hell that her hunch was right. She could just imagine the stick she would get from Vic if she was wrong.

The second dumpster also proved to be a futile search.

She could picture it now: Vic back at the precinct with his buddies, having a good laugh at the new girl's expense.

As though guessing her thoughts, he called out to her, 'You ready to call it a day yet?'

Never a quitter, Rebecca turned and started to tell him no.

Vic lurched forward, interrupting her mid-sentence. 'Angell! Move!'

Rebecca turned as the kid ran at her from behind the third

dumpster, a large wooden club raised above his head. Raising her baton to protect herself, she had it knocked from her grip as he brought the club down hard.

She raised her hands, expecting a second blow. It didn't come, as the kid dropped the wood and made a mad dash past a reeling Vic towards the fence he had originally assailed.

Back on her feet, Rebecca again gave chase, this time just seconds behind him as she jumped down from the fence. The end of the alleyway was littered with shopping carts and the kid paused long enough to push one in her path.

Triumphant that he had made his escape, he waved the bag he had snatched in the air. 'Catch me if you can.' He grinned.

Rebecca growled angrily, scooting around the cart. 'You little shit.'

He disappeared into the busy street; reaching the end of the alleyway and she paused for a moment to catch her breath, wondering how the hell she was going to get him now.

Vic arrived beside her. 'You okay?' he asked.

She glanced at him, a little surprised that he cared. 'Yeah, I'm fine. Looks like we've lost him, though.'

Vic scanned the street. 'No we haven't. Quick, there he is.'

Following the line of his finger, she saw first the red handbag then the kid. He had managed to weave his way through the lanes of traffic and had just reached the sidewalk.

'Come on!' Vic yelled, this time taking the lead.

Rebecca followed him across the road, ignoring the beeping cars that screeched to a halt to avoid hitting them. One guy started yelling a blue streak out of his window.

Hearing the commotion, the kid turned around.

As he did, a manhole cover opened and he walked headlong into it, losing his balance. A head appeared from the hole, male, maybe mid-fifties, wearing a hard hat.

'Game over, son,' Vic told the kid, grabbing him by his collar.

'I didn't do anything.'

'Sure you didn't.'

Rebecca glanced at the man clambering from the hole in the road and noticed he was completely drained of colour. 'Sir, are you okay?'

He shook his head and she saw he was trembling. 'He's down there.' He was struggling to get his breath. 'He's down there in the sewer.'

'Who is?'

He pointed back to the manhole. 'I tell you, he's down there. I saw him. I walked right into him.'

Rebecca glanced at Vic who was still struggling with the now cuffed kid. She'd assumed the guy was a sewer worker, but maybe he was just some crazy.

Vic grinned. 'Let me guess. "He" is a thirty-foot alligator, right?'

The man didn't find his joke amusing. 'This isn't funny. I don't know what the hell happened, but he's dead all right. He was all cold and stiff and he smelt of death.'

Vic's face hardened. 'Sir, have you been smoking an illegal substance?'

'If you people don't believe me, go down there and check it out.' The man stared first at Vic and then at Rebecca, his eyes full of fear, his skin pale and sickly. 'Like it or not, you people have got a real problem on your hands. There's a dead body floating around in the sewer and I don't think it got there by accident.'

2

The hole was dark and bottomless.

A stale smell rose through the air and, deep below, the sound of rushing water could be heard. Not that it could really be called water. It was more a kind of acidic, gungy substance, splashing against the walls, waiting to devour.

They didn't want to go down there. None of them did. But someone had to.

As the fat, greasy, pizza-covered fingers delved deep into the cardboard carton, the fries tried to back away, burrowing deep into the box. Two weren't quick enough to make an escape and, kicking and struggling to free themselves, they were carried through the air, their silent screams going unheard, towards the gaping black hole and the yellow crooked teeth that would crush them to pulp and then spit them down into the filthy sewer of his stomach.

Chad Mitchell finished reading and took a bow.

Many of the students in the room started clapping. A few of the guys whooped and several of them giggled. Justine Orton watched impassively from her desk at the front of the room, her head turned just enough to ensure she did not miss anything. She stole a quick glance at Mr Parker. He was leaning against the front of his desk, arms folded, eyes watching and the faintest hint of a smile upon his lips.

She wondered what was going on in his mind. Was he annoyed with Chad for trying to make a mockery of his class? Or did he, like the students, find the essay amusing? It was so difficult to tell what he was thinking. The mask of calm composure he wore never slipped and his black eyes seldom gave anything away. He just sat there, week after week, watching intently, his smouldering dark looks oozing sex appeal from every pore, like some Greek god.

Like Adonis. That was it. He was just like Adonis. *Her Adonis.* Justine watched as he nodded for Chad to sit down.

'Very interesting, Mr Mitchell. And the title of your work?'

A wide grin spread across Chad's face. 'It's called "Stu Hutchinson eats lunch".'

More clapping and laughter from the students. Stu Hutchinson, a fat kid with a low IQ, sat at a desk on the other side of the room. He stood up, his face bright red, and pointed a chubby finger at Chad. 'You're dead, Mitchell. I'm gonna kick your ass.'

Chad didn't bat an eyelid, even though at six foot four and over three hundred pounds, Stu dwarfed him. 'It was a joke, man. Laugh.'

'*Me* laugh? We'll see who's laughing when I kick—'

'Sit down, Mr Hutchinson.'

All eyes turned to the front of the class.

Stu looked at Mr Parker, a little uncertain of whether or not he should obey. Justine guessed he probably didn't want to look an idiot in front of the others. Mr Parker wasn't angry. He didn't get angry. He had this way of making people realise he was in charge. Even though his voice was calm, when he spoke it had authority.

Stu, deciding that he didn't want to cause a scene, sat down. In the opposite corner of the room, Chad grinned triumphantly. He was the class clown and part of the college in-crowd: a raucous, egotistical group of students who drew great delight from tormenting others. There were twelve of them, seven guys and five girls. All of the guys liked to talk hard and act with their fists, usually together and usually on less confident, defenceless students. The girls were all catty and had a reputation as an easy lay.

Justine did not belong to the crowd and didn't want to be part of it. She considered herself too mature to get involved with such petty individuals and had no desire to be known as just another notch on Chad Mitchell's bedpost.

A little annoyed that Mr Parker seemed to be letting Chad off scot-free, she was pleased by his next comment.

'Perhaps, Mr Mitchell, you would now like to give us an insight into how you eat lunch,' he suggested, his black eyes fixed intently on Chad's face.

Justine smiled; she had a feeling that this could prove interesting.

* * *

After fetching the squad car, Vic radioed for backup.

It took less than four minutes for a second car to arrive and, after handing over custody of the kid, he instructed the officers to get the sewage worker back to the precinct and take a full statement. The guy was still in shock, and they hadn't been able to get information that made any sense out of him, other than he had been separated from his co-workers and allegedly stumbled across a dead body.

Vic joined Angell by the manhole and shone his flashlight down into the darkness.

'See anything?' Angell asked.

'Are you kidding? It's blacker than soot down there.' He screwed up his nose. 'Stinks pretty bad too.'

'Great.'

Vic clicked off his light and grinned. 'Well, ladies first.'

Angell raised her eyebrows in surprise, looked as though she was about to say something, then evidently changing her mind, pulled out her own flashlight. As he watched her climb onto the ladder and disappear into the manhole, Vic's grin spread. He had a feeling that he was going to like his new partner. Several of the guys in the department had complained when they'd thought they might be saddled with the hick in a dress. Vic, though, hadn't minded. He had seen Rebecca Angell when she'd first arrived at the precinct, and his mind had immediately gone into overdrive as he imagined what he'd like to do with her.

He realised, of course, that she probably wouldn't be much fun on duty. Unlike the guys, she wasn't going to want to talk about football or have a laugh with him over his *Playboy* mags, but with her silky dark hair and small pert breasts, she was the best-looking woman they'd had on the force in the last five years and being her partner would definitely better his chances of getting inside her pants.

Of course, he hadn't counted on her being so damn feisty. He'd always assumed that women from hick towns knew how to treat men with a little respect. Boy, had he got that one wrong. While she had so far failed to succumb to his charms, it had already become apparent that Rebecca Angell was desperate to be accepted as one of the lads, and therefore it seemed that she'd do almost any damn thing he told her.

Which is fine, just as long as she doesn't make you run again, hey, Vic buddy?

He peered down the manhole. Aside from the faint beam of the flashlight, it appeared empty, with Angell's dark hair and navy uniform camouflaged against the walls.

'Are you at the bottom yet?' he yelled.

'Nearly.' Her voice was just a distant echo. 'You can come on down now.'

Vic glanced around at the second patrol car. He had been hoping to persuade Brown and Sanchez to take sewer duty, but they were having none of it. Kind of a shame, as he didn't fancy the idea of having to trudge around in other people's shit in his one clean uniform. Tempting though it was, he guessed that he couldn't leave Angell down there all alone. If the Chief found out he'd let his rookie partner go down into the sewer by herself, there would be hell to pay.

He looked at the sewer worker, now sitting in the back seat of the squad car next to the kid. The boots he had on came to just above the knee.

'I'll be down in just a second,' he yelled down the manhole.

'Okay.' Angell sounded slightly pissed off. 'Just don't take all day about it.'

Vic made his way back to the car. 'Give me those boots, will you?'

The sewer worker looked a little surprised, but didn't argue.

Vic removed his own shoes and put them in the car, then slipped on the boots, being careful to avoid touching where they were already wet. He made a mental note not to touch any of the doughnuts when he came out – at least not until he'd had the chance for a proper wash down. Climbing onto the rungs of the ladder in the manhole, he drew in a deep breath and screwed up his nose in preparation for the awful stench that was about to hit him.

'Oh well, buddy,' he muttered under his breath, silently cursing himself for being in the wrong place at the wrong time. 'Here goes nothing.'

* * *

Class let out at eleven thirty.

Mr Parker dismissed them all with a casual wave of the hand and almost immediately buried his head in the paperwork on his desk.

Justine gathered her books slowly, waiting for the other students to disperse. When the classroom was practically empty, she made her way up to the front. For a moment Mr Parker didn't even seem to be aware of her presence. Eventually he looked up, his black eyes on her questioningly. 'Hello, Justine.'

Justine hugged her books to her chest and smiled. Mr Parker had been their substitute lecturer for the past four weeks now and she had been trying to pluck up the courage to stay behind and find an excuse to talk to him. Now she was here, though, her well-rehearsed speech had completely vanished from her mind. She had done her research well. Mr Parker, Christian name Lawrence, but known as Lawrie to his friends (she thought that was cute), originated from California. He was thirty years old. Justine knew that because she'd overheard some of the other professors talking about the party his wife had thrown him last month.

His wife. That was the other thing. He was married, a thought that Justine preferred to push to the back of her mind. Mr Parker didn't look like he should be married. In fact, he didn't look like he should be lecturing in a college. He seemed too dark, too intense and too mysterious. It was silly really, but Justine couldn't help comparing him to Heathcliff from *Wuthering Heights*: passionate, intense and brooding. Right now, those intense and brooding eyes were watching her patiently, waiting for her to speak. Justine's cheeks heated.

'I'm sorry to trouble you,' she stammered.

Mr Parker arched his eyebrows very slightly; his eyes didn't stray from her face. 'What may I do for you?'

'I was wondering if... I was wondering, could you recommend any books that might help me with this course.'

'Are you struggling with the work?'

'Well, not exactly.' Justine managed a weak smile. 'I just like to be thorough.'

Mr Parker nodded, the hint of a smile touching his lips. He continued to watch her for a moment, and Justine felt her cheeks turn darker.

Oh my God! He knows why I stayed behind. He knows I fancy him.

She tried her best to hold his stare and failed miserably. As soon as she broke away, Mr Parker took a pen and began to scribble on a jotter pad on his desk.

He's just like a cat.

Justine couldn't help but wonder if he had done it on purpose, determined to stare her out, as if he was playing a game with her. Her mind still swimming and her heart thumping loudly against the inside of her chest, she took the piece of paper that Mr Parker was holding out to her.

'I've written down the titles of two books that should help. You'll find both of them in the college library.'

'Thanks. Thanks a lot.' Justine kicked herself for sounding like such a goofball. Things hadn't exactly worked out as she'd planned. What had happened to the cool, calm and seductive approach that she had hoped would result in him offering to buy her a cup of coffee? She was wondering if maybe she should give it a second go, when the door creaked open and Kylan Parker entered the room.

Justine knew her, though not to speak to. She had seen her around campus now and again, but it was only since she'd found out Kylan was married to Mr Parker that she had taken such an interest in her. And wished she hadn't. Kylan was stunning to look at, with pale-blonde hair that fell onto her shoulders, large dark brown eyes, porcelain skin and prominent cheekbones. Even now, dressed only in faded jeans and a baggy checked shirt, she still managed to look a knockout.

Justine pushed a hand through her own cropped hair, and wished it was longer, blonder. She coughed, feeling a little uncomfortable. As though she'd been caught doing something she shouldn't.

Like you wish.

Kylan glanced up at her and smiled. 'Hi.'

'Hi,' Justine mumbled back, hating Kylan all the more for being friendly. She glanced at Mr Parker. 'Well, thanks for your help. I'd better be on my way.'

She pushed past Kylan and made her way out into the corridor, stopping just outside the door to draw a couple of deep breaths. Back inside the classroom, she heard Kylan say in a joking voice, 'So, Mr Parker, does one of your students have a crush on you?'

Justine burned with humiliation. Was she that obvious? Clutching her books tightly to her chest, she swallowed hard trying to rid herself of the sick feeling welling in the bottom of her stomach. She took a step away from the door so as not to be seen and waited intently to hear what was said next.

* * *

Always in the wrong place at the wrong time!

Victor Boaz cursed himself while descending the ladder into the sewer, hardly able to believe the chain of events that had led him to this point. The doughnut stop, the kid with the purse, Angell stubbornly chasing him, and the sewer worker appearing out of the manhole at the exact moment they were passing.

Always in the wrong place at the wrong time!

'Boots?' Angell questioned, watching him climbing the final few rungs, her flashlight trained on him.

'I didn't want to get a load of shit on my pants.'

Angell glanced down at her own trousers soaked up to the knee. 'Well gee, Vic,' she grumbled sardonically, 'thanks for thinking about me.'

'The guy only had one pair, and I doubt they'd even fit you,' Vic argued, thinking that she had a smart mouth for a hick. He allowed his eyes to roam her body. 'Of course, if you really want the boots, I'm sure we could come to some kind of arrangement,' he said, smiling suggestively.

Angell gave a derisive laugh. 'You are kidding me, right?'

Vic glanced round the sewer, taking in the long narrow tunnel. For some reason the sewers always reminded him of the subway, only much smaller and wetter.

'Why not, Angell? It's nice and dark down here, just the two of us.'

He watched her as she rolled her eyes, looking disgusted by the idea.

'You think I want to fuck you?' she asked incredulously. 'Give me a break. I don't know what would be more repulsive. Doing it in the sewer or doing it with you.'

'Hey!' Vic snapped angrily, catching hold of her wrist. Rage swelled up inside him at her blunt rejection.

Damn bitch, talking to him that way.

Angell fixed him with a scathing look that warned him he was pushing his luck. He loosened his grip, and she snatched her wrist away, continuing to stare coldly at him for a few moments. Eventually she pushed her way past him, shaking her head.

'Come on,' she grumbled. 'I suppose you want me to lead the way?'

Vic collected himself quickly. 'Well, if you're volunteering, be my guest.'

Angell turned and smiled at him. It looked forced and sarcastic. Without a word, she started wading up the tunnel.

'Hey, wait a minute!' Vic called, wondering how come she seemed so sure of where she was going. 'What makes you so sure that this alleged body is in this direction?'

Angell turned and shone her flashlight on him. 'I guess I kind of figured it might be flowing with the direction of the water.' She rolled her eyes again, then shaking her head she continued up the tunnel.

Vic glanced down at the water rushing past his boots and felt himself redden. He was glad it was dark so Angell couldn't see. Christ, what an idiot. Why hadn't he thought of that? It had never occurred to him before that things could drift in a sewer, and he guessed that it was similar to the sea where the tide drifted in and out. Only the sea didn't smell so foul. He remembered how the sewer worker had said the body had smelt really bad and he wondered how the guy had been able to tell. After all, everything down here smelt really bad. Like a hundred dead bodies. Maybe a hundred dead rats. He knew plenty of them that frequented the sewers. Probably quite a few of the little furry rodents had snuffed it down here. Perhaps they might even see a few.

Vic grinned. That would no doubt give Angell a fright. Women always freaked out over things like that.

Oh well, Vic. Live and hope.

The tunnel came to a fork. Angell glanced over her shoulder. 'Which way?'

'How the hell do I know?' Vic moaned, wishing for the hundredth time that he'd never gotten into this situation.

Shrugging her shoulders, Angell took the left fork.

Vic checked this time that the water was flowing down both forks before he asked, 'Hey, why that one?'

'Why not this one?'

'Well, what if this body is down the right-hand fork?'

'We could always split up,' Angell suggested.

'Are you kidding?'

'No.'

'We can't split up.'

'Why not?' she challenged him. 'Are you scared?'

'Don't be stupid. I just don't think it's a good idea splitting up in the sewer.'

'We'd probably get out of here sooner if we did.'

Vic guessed that she had a point.

'Okay, we'll split up. But we meet back here in ten minutes.'

'Fine. Ten minutes.'

Angell didn't wait to discuss the finer details. Vic watched her wade across into the tunnel of the left-hand fork, the beam of her flashlight growing smaller. He trained his own light up the right-hand fork.

'Okay, buddy, where are you now? Come to Papa.'

A loud yell made him jump. He lost his footing and landed with a loud splash on his ass. The flashlight slipped out of his hand and he found himself sitting in darkness as filthy water sloshed around his chest, filling his boots. It was cold and foul smelling, and it made him gag.

'Shit!' he yelled, very much aware that there was plenty of it floating around him. 'Angell? Was that you?'

There was no answer.

Scrambling to his feet, Vic started to feel his way along the left-hand fork of the tunnel, towards where Angell had disappeared.

His heart was thumping loudly in his chest. What was going on? Had Angell found the body?

'Angell?'

This time he got an answer.

'Vic? Vic? Come here!' The tone in her voice was urgent.

'Where are you?' he called back, about ready to kill her if this was a false alarm. 'Shine the light, will you? I dropped mine and I can't see where I'm going.'

'I found the body, Vic.' She sounded almost excited.

'You did?' He swallowed hard, not sure that he was looking forward to this.

'Yeah, it must have got wedged somehow. I damn near tripped over it.'

'You sure it's a body?'

'Well, I guess it could be a giant rat.' Even though he wasn't yet close enough to see her face, he could tell by the tone of her voice that she was mocking him. 'Of course it's a body, you idiot.'

'A dead one?'

'Well, he's sure as hell not moving.'

He could see her now, about seven feet away, bent down, gripping hold of a large object.

The body?

'Give me the damn flashlight,' he demanded, feeling the need to take charge of the situation.

She threw it to him, and he missed. The second light went out, leaving them in total darkness.

'Damn, fuck, Angell!'

'Hey, you were the one who dropped it, idiot,' she fought back.

Her voice was close, and Vic reached out his hand. Feeling an arm, he took hold of it and pulled. 'Okay, I got the stiff.'

The arm struggled, and he fought to hold on to it. 'Hey! He ain't dead.'

'That's my arm, you jerk,' Angell snapped, pulling herself free.

Vic reached down for the body. A foul stench filled his nostrils. 'Boy, he smells worse than all the crap he's floating around in.'

'I wonder how he got down here.'

'He's probably some drunk who tripped down an open manhole.'

'You reckon?'

'Hell, I don't know, sweetheart. I can't even see what he looks like.'

Grabbing hold of the body by its torso, he tried to hold it steady. He glanced in Angell's direction, still unable to see her face in the darkness. 'So, Wonder Woman, what's your plan now?'

*   *   *

When Kylan left the classroom, Justine quickly turned away and tried to make out she was looking for her locker. Kylan didn't look her way; her head was tilted towards the floor, and she headed off in the opposite direction.

From what Justine had heard through the open door, it sounded as though Mr and Mrs Parker had been having a fight. A trivial fight, maybe, but still a chink in the armour. Kylan had wanted them to spend lunch together. Lawrie – Mr Parker seemed so formal – had told her he didn't have time as he had papers to mark. Therefore, Justine was surprised when, two minutes later, he too left the classroom.

He headed in the opposite direction to his wife and, feeling there were enough students around for it not to look obvious, Justine followed him, keeping a safe distance. When they reached the phone booths at the end of the corridor, Lawrie stopped. As he fished in his pocket for some loose change, he glanced over his shoulder, as though worried he was being watched. Seeming satisfied he wasn't, he headed to an empty phone.

Justine walked past him, towards the stairs to the left of the booths. Once certain he couldn't see her, she stopped and listened.

Lawrie spoke quietly and due to the noise going on around her she had trouble hearing much of his conversation. 'Yes... I only have an hour... Okay, I'll be there in five minutes.'

Justine's heartbeat quickened.

Did he have a mistress? Was he seeing someone behind Kylan's back?

She watched him walk away from the phone booth and head down towards the main foyer that led to the parking lot.

So dark, so brooding and so mysterious.

A surge of confidence swept over her. If Lawrie could cheat on Kylan once, chances were if the right girl came along, he would do it again. Justine decided that whatever it took, she was going to be that girl.

3
FRIDAY 18 APRIL 1997

Rumours had been circulating the department for much of the day that the FBI was to be involved with the 'Body in the sewer' murder. Rebecca had tried not to take it too seriously; rumours often amounted to nothing more than that. Besides, she couldn't think of any possible interest that the Feds would have in the case. As far as she was aware, this was a standard homicide investigation and, although the police of course wanted to apprehend the killer, it did appear to be a one-off murder, so she was more surprised than anyone when two suited men entered the office late on Friday afternoon.

Vic had been bitching about the Feds being involved ever since the story had started to spread. Rebecca had learned during the last couple of days that he had been forced to work with the FBI on a case down in California five years ago and he made it sound an unpleasant experience. She didn't doubt that Vic's main problem though had been that he'd been made to do some actual work.

He was getting coffee when the men entered the office,

Rebecca doing paperwork. They didn't stop to make small talk but headed straight into Captain Krigg's office.

One of the men looked to be in his mid-fifties, the other closer to her own age and, of the two, the older one seemed the most approachable. Despite the fact that he was dressed in a charcoal suit and tie, Rebecca couldn't help thinking that he looked a little out of place. His thick, straw-blond hair, ruddy complexion and heavily built frame would be better suited to more casual attire – she could easily picture him driving a rig or working on a farm, dressed in scruffy overalls or loose-fitting denims.

His partner, a tall guy with unruly dark hair, glanced briefly in her direction before entering Krigg's office, and she took an immediate dislike to him.

She wasn't sure exactly why. Maybe it was the air of arrogance that he seemed to carry with him in the way he walked, or perhaps it was the way he narrowed his eyes and half smiled, half sneered at her. She kind of hoped that maybe he'd walk into the door or trip on the step on his way in, thinking he needed to be brought down a peg or two.

Unfortunately, he did neither.

Krigg's door remained closed for the next two hours until eventually Stanley Blake, one of the department's veterans and also the detective in charge of the 'Sewer' murder, was summoned, renewing all suspicions as to why the Feds were there.

Blake was in the room for fifteen minutes, during which time raised voices could be heard. When he left, his face was flushed, and he looked annoyed. He glanced round the room, his dark eyes landing on Vic and Rebecca.

'Krigg wants to see you two, now.'

He didn't offer them an explanation as to why, nor stop long enough for them to ask.

Rebecca looked at Vic, eyebrows raised questioningly. The blue in his eyes had turned a stormy grey. Giving an exaggerated sigh, he got up from his chair.

'Just what I need, to get stuck in the middle of another fucking Federal investigation.'

Rebecca declined to comment. She was curious to know what was going on. Were the two guys with Krigg really FBI? And why did they want to see her and Vic? A sudden thought struck her. Maybe they had screwed up.

Getting up from her desk, she followed Vic into Krigg's office, her heart beating faster than usual, feeling a mixture of intrigue and apprehension.

Captain Krigg glanced up as they entered. He was a pleasant man, fast approaching retirement, and Rebecca had found him, in her brief time working under him, to be both personally and professionally meticulous. His thick white hair was neatly clipped and combed in a presentable style and the collars of his shirts always looked freshly laundered. His office was never untidy, no matter how busy he was. Paperwork was always in a tray, coffee cups were not allowed unless a coaster was used and the room had a personal feel to it, with pot plants on the window ledge and pictures of his many grandchildren on display.

Right now, the captain was smiling at them both, but Rebecca noticed it was with no warmth. She guessed the smile was forced: an effort, perhaps, on behalf of the Feds? As Captain Krigg was the only person in the department who seemed to support her joining the force, and the only one who so far had made her feel genuinely welcome, this left her with a strong sense of unease. What was going on?

He raised a hand.

'Why don't you both pull up a chair?' Then turning to the two alleged Federal Agents who were already seated, 'These are the two officers who found the body, Vic Boaz and Rebecca Angell.'

Rebecca, still feeling apprehensive, took a seat on one of the empty hard-backed chairs in front of the captain's desk. She nodded towards the two men and smiled politely. Vic was more forthcoming.

'Feds, right?'

The older man answered him with a nod and, in a grainy voice, introduced them both.

'I'm Special Agent Max Sutton and this is my partner, Special Agent Joel Hickok.'

A thin smile formed on Vic's lips. 'Hickok, hey? Any relation to Wild Bill?'

'Yeah, he was my great-granddaddy,' the younger man quickly retorted, a hint of sarcasm in his voice. Rebecca noticed that he had an East Coast accent. New York, possibly.

Vic raised his eyebrows in mock offence. 'Hey, buddy, lighten up. I was just kidding around.'

'Don't.'

The two of them exchanged a heated glance and Rebecca was glad that Krigg was in the room. She had a feeling that otherwise things might have turned nasty.

'So, what are the FBI doing in town?' she asked lightly, trying to change the subject.

'Business,' Sutton told her. 'We're thinking that the guy you found in the sewer was the victim of a serial killer.'

'Really? How come?'

Sutton gestured to Krigg, who passed him a pile of photographs from his desk. He in turn handed them to Rebecca. The top photograph was of Scott Jagger, the guy they had found in the sewer. He was alive in the picture and she guessed that it had probably been taken from his high school yearbook or driver's licence. The following three pictures were of his body, taken by the coroner.

It was the last one of the three that caught Rebecca's attention. Scott Jagger's long hair had been cut away and the picture showed the back of his neck. The letter J had been roughly cut into his skin. She looked up at the two agents.

'We never noticed this.'

Hickok raised his eyebrows in mock surprise. 'We didn't expect you would,' he said bluntly.

Rebecca stared at him, a little taken aback. Evidently Special Agent Hickok didn't have a very high opinion of the police force. She found it hard to believe, though, that he was rude enough to show it. Determined to remain professional and not sink to his level, she declined to comment and instead fixed him with an icy smile.

Sutton produced another photograph. This time he didn't hand it to Rebecca but held it up for Vic to see as well.

'Recognise this guy?' he asked.

The picture was of a man in a suit. He looked to be in his mid-forties, a few years younger than Sutton, but much better groomed. His auburn hair was combed back neatly; his thin lips half smiling, half taunting; his eyes were stone-grey, and they held no warmth. He looked vaguely familiar to Rebecca, but she couldn't quite place him.

Vic was also studying the picture intently. He looked up at Sutton. 'Another victim?' he guessed.

Sutton shook his head. 'I'm surprised you don't remember him, Officer Boaz. This is Professor Rodney Boone. Back in the summer of '89 he killed eight students at Juniper College; would have made it nine if the victim hadn't fought back.' He glanced at Rebecca.

'Do you remember the Alphabet Killings, Officer Angell?'

Rebecca nodded. 'Yeah, I remember them,' she said, stealing another glance at the picture of Boone, secretly pleased that Vic had just made himself look stupid.

She cast her mind back. The Alphabet Killings had happened just after she'd graduated high school. She could remember learning bits and pieces of information from the news. Boone had been a college professor and had picked his victims from the student register, killing them in alphabetical order of their surnames. Had it really happened only eight years ago?

Vic looked at Sutton. 'You never got that guy, right?'

Sutton smiled thinly. 'Correction, we never got what was left of him. The vic got away and called the cops; said she thought she'd killed him. When they got there, the house was in flames and there was no sign of the body.'

'So you think he's still alive?'

'It's possible. There was a huge manhunt, and the case is still open. It was a bad fire, so if he did get away there's no telling what kind of state he'd have been in.'

Rebecca was thoughtful for a moment, trying to make sense of what Sutton was saying. 'But you don't consider him a viable suspect for Scott Jagger's murder?'

'No, we don't,' Sutton told her. 'Admittedly there are a lot of similarities between the killings that we can't ignore. Jagger's body was found stripped naked, as were Boone's victims. He was strangled. Boone's victims were either strangled or suffocated. He was killed in one place and his body dumped in another. Same pattern again. And then of course there's the initial carved in the back of his neck.'

'J for Jagger,' Rebecca said quietly.

'Exactly. But like I said, the guy we're looking for isn't Rodney Boone.'

'How can you be so sure if you never found his body?'

Sutton shook his head. 'Well, for starters, while there are plenty of similarities, there are also a couple of things that this killer has done differently. Boone wrapped all of his victims up in a sheet of plastic before dropping them in the sewer. Like I already said, Jagger was found naked, but he wasn't wrapped in anything. Then there were the pills and alcohol found in his system.'

Rebecca raised her eyebrows. 'Pills and alcohol?'

'That's right. I know that our vic was a healthy twenty-year-old male who probably liked to party, but the mixture of vodka and sleeping pills found in his bloodstream suggests that he had someone with him who wanted to get him that way. Boone never drugged his victims. He was a thrill killer who fed off the pleasure of watching his victims die. The guy who murdered Scott Jagger seems to have been acting as more of a missionary, a clean-up killer. If we're right, he's not doing this to get pleasure; he just wants to finish up Boone's dirty work.'

'Why would anyone want to do that?' Rebecca asked, shaking her head disbelievingly. 'Surely the only person who'd want the Alphabet Killings to continue would be Rodney Boone.'

Sutton flashed a toothy grin, looking amused that she was challenging his theory.

'If Boone is out there, Officer Angell, do you really believe that he would have waited eight years before deciding to kill again? You know the rules with serial killers. They each have their own pattern, their own regime, and they stick to it rigidly. Rodney Boone would never have managed to go for so long without a kill.'

'He'd want to finish his alphabet, though,' Rebecca pushed.

'True,' Sutton conceded. 'But, like I've already said, it's not him. Our killer dumped Scott Jagger's body in the beach entrance of the sewer about half a mile back from where you guys found him. We know because the crime scene boys found an empty bottle of vodka back there that contained two sets of prints. One set of prints belonged to the vic, the other to his killer. We compared the second set to those of Rodney Boone's and guess what? They didn't match.

'You can forget about Boone, Officer Angell, he's got nothing to do with this murder. I know we never caught him, but I promise you the man is dead. The vic got him pretty bad with a knife and that was before the house burnt to the ground.

'No, I think it's more than likely that the guy who killed Scott Jagger is a sick, son of a bitch copycat who's read about Boone and decided to finish the alphabet for him.'

Rebecca nodded, deep in thought as her brain sifted through everything that Sutton had told her.

'The thing I don't get,' she said, 'is why start on J? If Scott Jagger's murder is in some way connected to the original murders, then the killer wants to complete the alphabet, right? If, as you say, the ninth victim got away, why hasn't the letter "I" been re-accounted for?'

Sutton exchanged a glance with Hickok before turning his attention back to Rebecca.

'To be perfectly honest, we're still not—'

'We do have a theory,' Hickok said, interrupting.

Rebecca looked at him, waiting to hear what he had to say. Instead of answering her, he coughed, clearing his throat, and shifted to a more comfortable position in his chair. He glanced briefly at Vic and then back at Rebecca, an expectant look on his face.

'Which is?' Rebecca said stiffly, annoyed that he was making her ask.

'Well, if you think about it, Boone did actually get victim I. I know he didn't kill her, but he pretty much went through the motions. It was only by pure luck that the vic left the house on her feet and not in a body bag.'

'So your theory is that whoever killed Scott Jagger didn't feel it necessary to go back for a new victim I?'

Hickok's dark eyes looked her up and down. He gave her a quick flash of his cynical smile. 'You're catching on quick, Angell. I'm impressed.'

Rebecca narrowed her own eyes, glaring at him. 'I'm a fast learner.'

'So it seems.'

'Your theory's a bit weak though, isn't it?' she challenged.

To her left, Rebecca heard Vic stifle a laugh. She glanced at Captain Krigg and received a warning look and cursed herself for not being able to keep her temper in check.

'I'm sorry,' she apologised quickly. 'I'm not trying to be difficult. It's just that if somebody is going to go to the trouble of completing another killer's murders, I would have thought they'd have made a point of getting the technicalities right.'

Hickok stared at her for a long moment before answering. Eventually, he shrugged his shoulders in a nonchalant manner. 'Like you say, they're just technicalities.'

'But...' Rebecca began, happy to sit and argue her point all day. Remembering the look she'd received from the captain, she caught herself. Maybe it would be best if she just sat still and kept her mouth shut like Vic, before she got into trouble.

Hickok continued to stare at her. 'I don't think you realise quite how many people idolise serial killers, Officer Angell,' he said in a taunting voice. 'Do you have any idea how many people there are who would love to finish off what Rodney Boone started? On the other hand, it could just be some sick fuck looking for his fifteen minutes of fame. Now they're two theories that definitely need investigating.'

'Which is why you're here,' Vic said, scowling.

Hickok grinned and sat back in his chair. 'Which is why we're here, Officer Boaz.' He glanced at Krigg. 'Captain?'

Krigg, who had been sitting quietly listening to them explain, now sat up straight in his chair. 'Special Agents Hickok and Sutton are going to be leading this investigation now, so I want you both to give them your fullest co-operation.'

'What about Blake?' Vic asked.

'Detective Blake has been assigned to another case.'

'Great. The suits come marching in and screw everything up.'

'You're not going to have a problem with this, are you, Vic?' Krigg spoke sharply.

'Hell, no, I can't wait. I'm sure we'll have a ball.'

Rebecca watched Hickok and Sutton exchange a knowing glance. From the looks on their faces, they couldn't wait either. As for herself, she wasn't sure what she felt. Any thought of parking tickets and barroom brawls were right out of the window now and that was good. This was a real murder investigation, with real dead bodies and a real killer ready to strike again at any time. And she was involved. This was everything she'd ever dreamt about and more. Still, she had feelings of apprehension.

Maybe because she wasn't looking forward to working with the FBI either. Particularly Special Agent Joel Hickok. Deep down, though, Rebecca knew it was more than that. Murder seemed so much more fun on the TV, when there were great minds like Sherlock Holmes and Columbo on hand to solve the case. This time it was different. This time it was real life and there were no geniuses around to count on.

Screw up now and you'll be right back on your ass in Swallow Falls.

Swallow Falls. The place had never seemed so inviting.

4

Rebecca's shift finished at six, and not wanting to hang around the precinct she stopped only long enough to change from her uniform into her jeans and T-shirt, before heading out to the parking lot.

She reflected on the day's events, still finding it hard to believe that a few hours ago she had been out on patrol with Vic, handing out traffic citations and taking down the witness statements from a bungled jewellery store robbery, and now she was involved in a murder investigation. Of course, it was more than likely that Sutton and Hickok just wanted a couple of errand boys to fetch their coffee and carry their files. It would be interesting, though, to see first-hand how a murder investigation worked. She didn't plan on being a street cop forever and hoped that once she had a few years' experience she might be promoted to detective.

Although she had already made up her mind to hate Hickok, Rebecca had a feeling she could grow to like Max Sutton. His rumpled appearance and laid-back charm reminded her of her favourite uncle, her father's younger brother, Louis. With the exception of Jess, he was the only one in the family who hadn't disapproved of her tomboy ways, had encouraged her to climb trees and play football then endure her mother's wrath when she came home with her clothes dirty and covered in cuts and bruises. She had fractured her arm on three occasions, each time falling from the large oak tree that stood at the foot of Uncle Lou's garden; after the third time she had been banned from visiting him unless her mother was present.

Rebecca wondered whether or not it would be a good idea to tell her parents about the murder investigation. In the three weeks that she'd been in the city her mother had called her at least once a day to check on her well-being, convinced that the next time her daughter came home it would be in a body bag. The mention of the word 'murder' would probably be enough to send her into one of her fits.

The fits amounted to no more than tears, headaches and dizzy spells, but they were often enough to keep Sarah Angell in bed for a couple of days and, although Rebecca didn't doubt for a second that her mother exaggerated and sometimes invented the symptoms, she didn't feel it fair to leave her father and sisters with the burden of looking after her.

She decided that it would be better if she didn't tell them anything.

Approaching her Jeep, parked at the far end of the lot, Rebecca reached into her pocket for her keys. She had bought it with savings from her first job five years ago and it was one of her most prized possessions.

She had learned to drive in Uncle Lou's almost identical one. Her mother complained that she had picked up all Lou's bad habits, taking corners too fast and braking at the last minute, but Rebecca had still learned enough from him to pass her test first time. The one thing she hadn't been able to get the hang of was parking. No matter where she was or how many times she tried, she never failed to get a wheel stuck on the curb or the nose of the Jeep poking into someone else's parking space.

Looking at how she had left it this morning, parked haphazardly across two spaces, she groaned loudly, her attention immediately drawn to the front flat tyre.

'Shit!' she muttered under her breath.

She had been looking forward to getting home and having a relaxing shower while she decided what to with her evening, but it looked as though her plans were going to be delayed. Unlocking the driver's door, Rebecca dropped her sports bag onto the seat and went around the back to fetch the spare wheel.

She glanced up at the sound of footsteps and saw Special Agents Hickok and Sutton heading across the parking lot. Sutton raised a hand in greeting. He looked at the wheel and the crowbar she was holding and frowned.

'Car trouble, Officer Angell?'

Rebecca pulled a face.

'Flat tyre,' she grumbled. 'Had to happen on a Friday night.'

She saw Hickok smirk at her. 'You need a hand to change it?' Although he was offering, there was something patronising in his tone.

Rebecca glared at him. 'I can manage, thank you.'

'Really?'

'Yes, really.'

Defiantly dropping the wheel and crowbar on the ground near the front wheel of the Jeep, she went back to get the jack. Sutton slapped Hickok on the shoulder.

'Come on, buddy, let's go.'

Rebecca watched him cross the lot to where a black Lincoln

was parked. Instead of following him, Hickok remained where he was, arms folded and an amused expression on his face as he continued to watch her. Ignoring him, she set about changing the wheel, glad that Uncle Lou had insisted on giving her basic lessons in vehicle maintenance. It had been one of the many things he'd taught her. Jess had been too busy partying to be interested in his lessons and Wendy far too girly, so Rebecca had been the only willing candidate. By the age of sixteen, aside from learning the basics of vehicle maintenance, she had also been taught self-defence and shown how to properly use a firearm.

It irritated the hell out of her that Special Agent Hickok didn't seem to think her capable of changing a wheel. He was probably one of those sexist stone-age men like Vic, who seemed to believe that women should be kept at home baking and cleaning and raising their children. A role Rebecca couldn't see herself ever filling.

With the front of the Jeep jacked up, she glared at him. 'Don't you have anything better to do?'

Hickok grinned at her. 'We've got a hotel to check into, but there's no rush.'

'Shame,' Rebecca muttered under her breath. Using the crowbar, she set about loosening the wheel bolts.

The Lincoln pulled up in front of the Jeep and Max Sutton poked his head out of the open window. 'Ready to go, Joel?'

Yes, go, Joel.

Hickok glanced at his partner and then back at Rebecca. 'You're sure you can cope?' he asked her, a half-smile on his face.

'Like I've already told you, I can manage perfectly fine,' Rebecca said sweetly, fighting the urge to take her crowbar and stick it up his ass.

He raised his eyebrows disbelievingly. 'Okay, then. We'll see you in the morning.'

'Unfortunately,' Rebecca mumbled darkly, watching him climb into the passenger seat of the Lincoln.

She finished changing the wheel and was loading the jack and the crowbar into the back of the Jeep when she caught sight of Vic and a couple of his buddies, Hal Peterson and Wayne Hankins. Vic glanced across the parking lot and waved a hand in her direction.

'Hey, Angell,' he called in a mocking tone. 'Have a good ride home.'

Rebecca watched his face crumple into a wide grin. Wayne Hankins slapped him on the back and the three of them started laughing as they headed across to Vic's car. Furiously, she slammed the back door of the Jeep shut. She hadn't considered that someone might have let the air out of her tyre on purpose, but it was just the kind of puerile thing Vic Boaz would do.

She tried to think what she had done to provoke him, and a dozen separate incidents immediately sprang to mind. The bottom line was that Vic was pissed at her because she had somehow managed to resist his irresistible charm and hadn't jumped into bed with him.

Rebecca realised that she hadn't helped herself either, by running off her mouth at him. She thought back to how she had rejected him in the sewer and how, for a moment, he had been pretty mad. That didn't give him the excuse to let the air out of her tyre though and she fully intended to see to it that he didn't get away with the act. She just wasn't sure how. Swearing about her partner under her breath, she climbed into the driver's seat of the Jeep and started the engine.

As she neared her apartment block, Rebecca caught sight of the sign for the Blue Moose Tavern just ahead and toyed with the idea of stopping off for a drink. She knew the place well and Ed the bartender was already familiar with her fondness for

Bourbon straight from the bottle – the one really bad habit she had picked up from Uncle Lou.

Deciding that her soak in the tub could wait, Rebecca signalled left and pulled off the road into the parking lot of the tavern. She had a feeling that tonight was going to be a double shots night.

5

Max Sutton placed the receiver down on the telephone and glanced at Joel Hickok, confirming what he knew his younger partner was already thinking.

'Looks like we may have our next victim.'

Joel accepted the news in his usual nonchalant manner. 'Female?' he asked impassively.

'Emma Keeley, second-year English student. Her roommate says she hasn't seen her since Thursday evening.'

'Maybe she went home to visit her folks.'

Max shook his head.

'No. Roommate says she would have called. Besides, she's already checked it out and she's not there.'

They were in one of the empty offices down the end of the corridor that had been cleared out for them and the call from Emma Keeley's roommate over at Juniper College had been patched through five minutes earlier. As soon as they knew it was regarding a missing student, both agents were able to hazard a pretty good guess that their killer had struck again. Joel got up from his chair behind the desk. 'Guess I'd better go find our cop friends.'

'Why? It's not going to take four of us to go over and interview the roomie.'

'No, only two.' Joel shook his head. 'I was thinking you could head down to the sewer.'

'The sewer?'

'Missing student. Initial K. We have to check it out, Max.' Joel gave him a sombre look, and Max knew they were both thinking the same thing. The fate of the students at Juniper College had become their responsibility. The number of casualties would depend on how well they did their job.

'So how come I get to go down in the sewer?' he challenged, eager to shake the thought.

Joel grinned. 'Because I know how much you like to do all the dirty work.'

Max screwed up his nose, already repulsed at the thought. He guessed he should have seen it coming. In the two years since he and Joel Hickok had been partners, somehow Joel had always managed to con him into doing all the shitty stuff. Not that Max was complaining. Of the partners he'd had during his years with the bureau, he liked working with Joel the most. Sure, the guy had a cocky attitude and yes, there were times when he could be a little insensitive, but he had a good head on his shoulders and a sense of integrity that most of the younger guys didn't have. He didn't always work by the book and sometimes he pulled his wise guy act a little too often, but Max knew that when the shit hit the fan he could always rely on Joel to be there to back him up.

He guessed that maybe it had something to do with his law enforcement background. His father, Don Hickok, had been a respected agent with the bureau until he had been injured in the line of duty and had to take early retirement; and of Joel's four brothers, three were cops serving with the NYPD. Not that most people would ever guess, the way Joel spoke to some of the officers they had to work with.

Max personally didn't have a problem with Hickok Junior. They both had a similar sense of humour and the age difference – Max was almost fifty-five and Joel had just turned twenty-eight – had never been an issue. Like Joel had four brothers, Max had four sons and the two of them had always managed to maintain a kind of father–son working relationship, which suited both of them fine.

'Tell you what, we'll flip for it.'

'You want to flip for it?'

Max pulled a coin from his pocket. 'Heads I go, tails you go.'

Joel nodded, looking amused at the idea. 'Okay, you're on.'

Max flipped the coin into the air. As it came to rest, Joel raised an eyebrow. 'So?'

Max glanced at the coin. It was heads. He let out a groan, knowing he was getting too old for this shit. 'Okay, you win, I'll go. Next time, though, you get sewer duty.'

Joel gave a wry smile. 'If there is a next time.'

Max pulled a face behind his back and followed him out of the door.

Rebecca Angell and Vic Boaz were both sitting at the double desk they shared out in the main part of the precinct, working through various reports. Joel rapped his knuckles loudly on the edge of Angell's desk.

'Come on, people, we're ready to roll.'

Angell looked up and Max thought he could detect a hint of derision in her eyes. He guessed she hadn't yet come to appreciate the sharper side of Joel's personality. Funny how he always seemed to create the wrong kind of impression with people when he first met them.

'Where are we going?' she asked, her voice lacking enthusiasm.

Joel grinned at her, either oblivious to or choosing to ignore her cool attitude towards him. 'Now, this is the good bit. You get to decide. Sewer or college?'

'You've got another body?' This time she sounded interested.

'Maybe.'

Boaz threw down his pen, looking somewhat vexed. 'Hey, man, come on. I'm not going back in that hellhole again.'

'I didn't know you went to college, Officer Boaz,' Joel wise cracked.

Boaz scowled, not getting the joke. 'I'm not talking about college. I'm talking about the sewer. I'm not going back down there again.'

Joel threw a side glance at Max. 'I think he's just saying that. I bet he wants to go back down there really.'

Max nodded and grinned, finding the situation amusing. Vic Boaz struck him as a lazy cop. One who was in dire need of a wake-up call.

'Oh, I'd say he definitely wants to go back down there.' He slapped the bulky officer on the shoulder. 'Come on, buddy, let's go.'

Boaz, already climbing to his feet, still protested like a child. 'Why do I have to go down in the sewer? I was stuck down there most of last Wednesday.'

'Good, then you have experience.'

'This sucks.'

'Sure it does, pal. But once you get down there again, it won't seem so bad.'

Joel smirked. 'Yeah, you'll probably feel right at home.'

Boaz opened his mouth to respond, but evidently deciding

against it, closed it again. Joel turned to face Angell, who had been watching the ensuing scene with a half-smile on her lips.

'Well, officer. Looks like it's you and me.' He grinned at her, and Max watched the smile drop off her face.

'Lucky me,' she muttered.

Joel nodded in agreement. 'Yeah, lucky you.'

* * *

Instead of the normal twenty, it took them just twelve minutes to get to the college. The campus was on the outskirts of the city, which meant either a bus ride or a long walk for the students without cars who lived off-site. Joel drove and, as ever, he drove fast.

Angell glanced disapprovingly at the speedometer. 'We're not in a race, you know.'

Joel shot her an irritated look. 'I do know. But thanks for pointing it out, though.'

She glared at him through cool green eyes. 'Just because you have a badge, it doesn't give you the right to break all the rules.'

'I never said it did.'

'So are you going to slow down then?'

'No.' To irritate her more, Joel stepped harder on the gas pedal.

Little Miss Uptight Law and Order. He couldn't believe she had the gall to criticise his driving. Was she planning to write him a ticket next?

Angell scowled, her mouth drawn in a tight line, and he grinned to himself, knowing from the stony expression on her face that he had succeeded in ticking her off.

'Tell me something, Officer Angell. Are you always this uptight?'

She scowled at him. 'I'm not uptight.'

'No, you're definitely uptight.'

'Yeah? Well you're an arrogant jerk.'

She shouldn't have said it. He had seniority over her and could easily get her in trouble. He could see she realised that the moment the words were out of her mouth.

'You know what, Angell? Flattery will get you everywhere.'

She turned to face him; her face flushed with anger. 'Do you really think that just because you work for the government it's your God-given right to belittle everyone around you?'

'Feisty too,' Joel said, ignoring her question. 'Feisty and uptight.' Rather than being annoyed with her, he found he was amused, and he was enjoying getting her to bite. 'Keep this up and I might just let you cook me dinner while I'm in town.'

'Sorry, I'm all out of pigswill.'

'Well, I'm sure there must be something else you like.'

He grinned broadly at her, and she glared back, seeming unsure how seriously she should take him. Eventually, deciding that she would be better off ignoring him, she turned her back to him and looked out of the window.

She was still a rookie, that had been obvious from the outset: wet behind the ears and a little over eager. Joel had checked her file and found out that she'd only been in the city a few weeks, which was probably why she was trying so hard to follow all the rules. It had to be hard for her coming from a small town like Swallow Falls and he guessed that he really should cut her some slack.

Should, but wouldn't.

Rebecca Angell had already proved somewhat of a contradiction to his preconceptions of her and, whilst he suspected that he was right about her wanting to be a good cop, he hadn't expected her to have a fiery temper. As long as she continued to rise to the bait, he knew that he wouldn't be able to resist the urge to torment her.

He guessed that at least she had the right attitude. Unlike Boaz, her idiot partner. Joel couldn't quite figure out why he was a cop. For law and order? To serve and protect? No, he didn't think so.

Although Juniper College had accommodation for over five thousand students, less than three thousand of them chose to live on campus; the vast majority instead lived locally and attended on a day basis. It was the same as every other college in the country in many ways, with its own football team, acres of recreation and park ground, and courses on offer for over two hundred and fifty different subjects. The one thing that singled out Juniper College was its grisly history.

The campus parking lot was busy. Aside from the faculty, most of the students had cars and with no other place to park, Joel pulled to a halt outside the front entrance of the administration block, behind a silver Ford.

Angell raised her eyebrows.

'You can't park here, you'll block that car in.'

They hadn't spoken since fighting in the car.

'There weren't any spots,' Joel said pointedly.

'It's probably the Dean's car.'

'So? What, you want to go clear it with him first?'

'No.'

'Then shut up.'

Angell gave him a quick flash of her icy smile.

Joel was beginning to hate it when she did that. Although they'd known each other less than a week, he'd been on the receiving end of that smile at least a dozen times. As they walked across the parking lot, a cold silence hanging in the warm air, she kept a few paces ahead of him. Joel looked her over, taking in her swinging black ponytail and her tall svelte figure. His gaze slipped down to her ass, snug in the navy pants of her uniform.

Cute butt.

Not that he would ever let on that he thought that.

On first appearances, his impression of Rebecca Angell had been that, although she was pretty in an understated way, there was nothing special about her. Unfortunately, and much as he hated to admit it, his opinion of her had changed drastically following that first meeting when she had challenged everything that he and Max had said.

He didn't want to find himself drawn to her and he didn't want to notice that she had a cute ass. But, like it or not, each time she got mad at him, and he found himself on the receiving end of one of her scathing looks, he realised that he was starting to like her more and more.

Of course, he would never do anything about it. Pigs might fly, but the day would never come when he admitted to Rebecca Angell that he found her attractive.

* * *

Dean Richard Edwards was waiting for them when they arrived. Joel had called ahead to let him know they were coming. Both he and Max had spoken with the Dean following the murder of Scott Jagger and the man seemed only too willing to help. Edwards was in his forties and married with kids. He had only transferred to Juniper in the last couple of years, brought in to help boost the college's flagging reputation. Aware that a second spate of murders on campus would probably destroy his career, he had made it known how eager he was to help.

Joel was pleased. It always made things so much easier when people were willing to co-operate.

Edwards stood as they entered his office. 'Hello again, Agent Hickok.' He nodded briefly in Angell's direction. 'Would either of you like tea or coffee?'

'No, thank you,' Joel answered for the both of them.

He saw Angell glare at him from the corner of his eye and focused his attention on the Dean.

As part of a routine check, Edwards had already been run through the FBI computers. He had turned up clean. Not that it proved anything in particular. Serial killers always had to begin somewhere. At this stage, everyone was a suspect.

'I take it that Miss Keeley hasn't turned up?' Joel asked.

The Dean shook his head. 'Not to my knowledge.'

Joel pulled a notebook from his pocket and started to leaf through the pages.

'We received a call from her roommate.' He found the page with the girl's name on it and glanced up. 'Mindy Tyson. She said she hasn't seen Emma since last Thursday.'

'Yes. Miss Tyson came to see us this morning. I've checked Miss Keeley's records and the last class she attended was on Thursday afternoon.'

'That class would be?'

'English literature.'

Taking a pen from his jacket, Joel began to make notes.

'What was the name of the professor?'

'Lawrence Parker, I believe.' Dean Edwards flicked briefly through some files on his desk to confirm this fact. 'Yes, Lawrence Parker.'

Joel nodded. 'Interesting. Isn't he the same professor that Scott Jagger had his last lecture with?'

'I believe so.'

'I'd like to speak with him.'

'That's not a problem. I'll arrange it.'

'Thank you.'

Leaning back in his chair, Edwards let out a frustrated sigh. His eyes met Joel's. 'So, what do you think, Agent Hickok? Do you think Emma Keeley is dead?'

Joel glanced briefly at Angell and then back at the Dean. Slowly he nodded. 'To be perfectly honest, yes, sir, I think she probably is.'

* * *

Mindy Tyson was the kind of girl that Rebecca would have described as fluffy. Not beautiful, but certainly cute enough to get a guy's attention with her wide eyes, button nose and long blonde hair. She came in a small package, probably not much taller than five foot, but what she lacked in height she made up for in flesh. Chubby cheeks, large hips and generous breasts.

Blonde and pretty, and definitely fluffy.

The room that she shared on campus with Emma Keeley was simply furnished with two beds, two desks, and a closet, and Rebecca was immediately struck by how different the two sides seemed to be, appearing to reflect each of the girls' personalities.

Everything on the left-hand side of the room was pink. The bedclothes were floral, the cushions frilly and a large brown teddy bear sat on the pumped-up pillow. On the wall above the bed was a picture of a muscular guy wearing a thong.

Hickok nudged Rebecca when he saw it and grinned.

'Oh, nice picture. Bet you've got a poster like this on your bedroom wall, eh, Angell?'

Rebecca ignored his remark, having already come to the conclusion that Joel Hickok was prepared to stoop to any level to get a laugh, and she turned to look at the other side of the room.

In complete contrast, there were no frills, no bears and

nothing was pink. The bedding was plain navy blue and a shelf running the length of the bed was cluttered with books, some fiction, some non-fiction. On the end of the shelf sat a thin blue vase containing five long-stemmed red tulips. Though both beds had a picture above them, this one was not of a naked man, but instead an expensive looking print of a group of ballerinas.

Rebecca guessed that the left-hand side of the room must belong to Mindy and the right-hand side to Emma. Her suspicions were confirmed a few moments later when Mindy Tyson crossed the room and sat herself down on the edge of the pink bed. She clutched one of the frilly cushions and stared up at the two of them through large hazel eyes.

'So, do you think Emma's okay?' she asked, her voice nervous.

'We're not sure at the moment,' Rebecca answered quickly, getting in before Hickok. She knew he was blunt and would probably upset the girl.

She needn't have worried. Hickok, apparently not hearing Mindy's question, was already over on Emma's side of the room, rooting through the top drawer of her desk.

Mindy's bottom lip wobbled, and she looked uncomfortable.

'You know, Emma doesn't like people going through her things.'

Hickok glanced over his shoulder. 'Yeah? Well, I'm sure she won't mind on this occasion.'

Without giving her the opportunity to object, he turned back to the drawer and continued pulling out textbooks, an unused writing set, a random joker playing card, and odd items of make-up.

Rebecca found that, even though she hadn't seen a picture of Emma Keeley yet, she was beginning to get a mental image of how she would look. The books indicated that she was studious; the make-up all seemed dark – black eye pencil and mascara, blood-red lipstick – the kind of colours you needed to have a perfect complexion to wear. Taking into account the difference in taste between Mindy and Emma, she pictured her to be tall and willowy, with dark hair and impeccable taste.

She watched as Hickok pulled a small blue velvet jewellery box from the drawer. He opened it and held up the dainty silver bracelet that was inside.

'Gift?' he asked Mindy.

'Her dad bought it for her birthday last week.' Mindy sniffed and hugged her cushion tighter.

Finally, Hickok finished his search. Finding nothing of any relevance, he put everything back and closed the drawer, then turned to give Mindy his full attention.

'So, the last time you saw Emma was on Thursday?'

'That's right,' the girl answered.

'Thursday. That's almost a week ago. How come you didn't report her missing before, Mindy?'

'I went home for a long weekend.' Mindy chewed on her bottom lip. 'I knew she hadn't come back on Friday morning before I left, but it's not unusual for her to stay out all night. I just didn't think anything of it.'

'When did you get back to campus?'

'Not until last night.' She glanced up at Hickok. 'That's when I started to get worried about her. When I came up to the room it looked as though she hadn't been in here since I'd left. I asked around, but no one could remember seeing her at all, so this morning I reported her missing.'

Hickok nodded. 'Okay. So, last Thursday when you last saw her, where was she?'

His questioning was blunt and to the point. Not exactly the way Rebecca would have approached the situation, but she watched with interest.

'We were here, in the room,' Mindy told them. 'I was packing, and Emma was getting ready to go out.'

'She had a date?'

'I'm not sure if it was a date or not. She said she had to go meet someone.'

Hickok glanced fleetingly at Rebecca. 'Was it a guy?'

'I don't know.' Mindy was thoughtful for a moment. 'She's been seeing a guy for the past few weeks,' she said eventually. 'Maybe it was him.'

'Who is this guy?'

'I don't know.'

'You've never met him?'

'No.'

'And Emma has never told you anything about him?'

Mindy shook her head, a blank look on her face.

'Not really. I know that she really liked him, though.'

'Did she mention if he went to college?' Rebecca asked.

'No, she said he was older.'

'Older as in middle-aged?'

'No, just older than us. Emma likes older guys and, like I said, she told me that she really liked this guy.'

Hickok had his notebook out and was busy scribbling. 'Do you know where Emma was planning to go on Thursday night?' he asked.

'She wouldn't tell me.'

Hickok rolled his eyes, looking agitated. 'Seems to me that Emma doesn't like to tell you much considering that you two are supposed to be best friends.'

Tears started to well in Mindy's eyes. She looked hurt by the comment. 'We are best friends.'

Rebecca scowled at Hickok, wondering if he actually had a sensitive side. Somehow, she doubted it.

She turned to Mindy. 'The guy that Emma has been seeing, do you have any idea where she met him?' she asked gently.

'She said that she first got together with him at The Coven,' the girl answered, wiping the tears from her eyes with the back of her hand. 'Though I think she might have already known him before that.'

'The Coven?' Hickok repeated.

'Yeah, that's where we go most evenings.'

'What is that, a bar?'

'It's a nightclub, a few blocks away,' Rebecca elaborated.

She had been there once, on her first weekend in the city, not realising until she was inside that the loud music, strobe lighting and smoky atmosphere wasn't really her scene.

Hickok nodded, grinning. 'The Coven, oh, I like that. I'll bet it's where you and your broomstick like to hang out, isn't it, Officer Angell?'

Rebecca felt herself redden, embarrassed that Hickok had chosen to try and humiliate her in front of Mindy. She made a mental note to make sure she got her own back on him at some point.

Vic and Hickok. Two wrongs to right. My, you are making enemies fast.

Fortunately, Mindy hadn't picked up on his quip.

'No, it's got nothing to do with witches,' she told him, looking confused. 'It's just a nightclub that a lot of the students go to.'

A smile spread across Hickok's face and Rebecca stepped in quick before he had a chance to explain his little joke in detail. 'Do you know if anyone else might have seen her there with this guy?'

Mindy shook her head.

'Not that I know of. You could try checking with the bar staff, though. A few of them know Emma.'

A knock came at the door, and all three of them looked up. Dean Edwards stepped into the room. He cleared his throat. 'Agent Hickok, might I have a word?'

Hickok nodded and got up from the bed. He paused, close by Rebecca, his eyes locking intently onto hers.

'Why don't you go buy her a cup of coffee or something?' he suggested, keeping his voice low, so Mindy couldn't hear. 'See what else you can find out.'

'Sure, okay.' Rebecca took a step back, uncomfortable at sharing personal space with him. She watched him leave the room before turning to Mindy. 'Why don't we go get something to drink and you can tell me a bit more about Emma?'

Mindy smiled, not at all convincingly. 'Sure, why not?'

6

Why of all places did it have to be the goddamn sewer?

Victor Boaz asked himself the question a hundred times as he trudged through the knee-deep polluted water.

Usually, victims' bodies were found in a field or a ditch, or even the damn river, but oh no, this killer had to be different.

And then of course there was the other question that just begged to be asked. Why him?

Of all the cops in the city who could have been stuck in this situation, he'd managed to pull the short straw twice. The odds of that happening had to be a billion to one. If there was someone upstairs, they must sure have it in for him.

Maybe it was payback time for all the shit he'd pulled in the past twelve years. For the number of times he'd used his badge for his own personal advantage. Or perhaps his ex-wives had banded together and pulled off some elaborate scheme to get him back for cheating on them. He grinned at the thought. Monogamy had never been his strongest point.

Vic Boaz loved women. It was just unfortunate that he had a

problem making any kind of commitment to them. But try explaining that to exes. They would probably love to see him now, knee deep in sewage, with the trickle of more water pouring into the sewer from the various pipes and drains around him. He wished he could push the sound from his mind. Frankly, it was starting to give him the urge to urinate.

Well, Vic, buddy. You're in the right place. You might just as well go ahead and pull your pants down.

The thought of unzipping his fly and exposing himself to all this crap was nauseating.

Why? It's no different to being in your own john at home.

Maybe not. But it sure felt different.

Trying to push the thought to the back of his mind, Vic shone his flashlight down the tunnel ahead and continued to search. He couldn't figure out why the hell they had to be down here in the first place. Surely it would be easier to just wait for the sewer workers to turn up what they were looking for.

The stupid Feds and their dumb ideas. His bladder started to ache.

Gotta pee. Gotta pee.

He tried to focus his mind on other things. He thought of Rebecca Angell over at the college and felt a pinch of jealousy knowing that he should be in her place.

Goddamn rookie. Boy, had she lucked out on that one.

Well, almost. She did still have to put up with that idiot Fed, Hickok. A small price to pay, though, to be in a nice, warm, dry building, chitchatting and probably drinking coffee.

Coffee!

Gotta pee. Gotta pee.

His bladder was starting to feel as though it might burst. It was no good. He was going to have to go.

What if someone sees you?

Vic glanced over his shoulder and swung the flashlight around. The tunnel was empty, and Sutton was hopefully a distance away, so not likely to stumble upon him. All he really had to worry about was running into the odd sewer worker. But right now, it looked as though he was pretty much alone.

Not that he would be likely to hear anyone approaching with all that damn water trickling in the background.

Trickling.

It was no good. He couldn't hold it in any longer. Vic clicked off the flashlight and slipped it into his belt. He didn't need to see what he was doing, and he felt safer in the darkness. Less exposed. He fumbled with his zipper, eager to get the dirty deed out of the way.

Come on, buddy. Out you come.

Warm fluid splashed onto the running water below and he moaned with relief. Something heavy ran into him, wedging itself between his legs. Vic jumped and let out a yelp. Still in full flow, he released one hand and reached for the flashlight.

He tried to widen his legs to allow whatever it was room to pass through, but it didn't budge. Pulling the flashlight from his belt, he clicked on the switch. The beam shone down on a face just below the surface of the water. A guy who had bright red hair and bulging eyes, whose mouth was open in a wide crooked grin, catching the fall of his pee.

Lurching forward, Vic barfed on the guy's face. Then he started screaming.

* * *

The coffee sold in the machine at the police precinct had never seemed particularly good, until today. Now, sitting in the large, clinical-looking cafeteria of the college, sipping acidic-tasting black liquid from a plastic mug, Rebecca found herself longing for a cup.

Mindy had wisely avoided the coffee, choosing instead to have tea, so it was probable that she already knew how bad it was. She was preoccupied, and Rebecca knew it was with worry about Emma.

She tried to place herself in the girl's position. Emma and Mindy were roommates and, according to Mindy, best friends. Half an hour chatting with her had Rebecca understanding that Emma had the bolder personality, and it would be fair to say that Mindy probably looked up to her, possibly even idolised her a little.

Emma was the one with good-looking boyfriends. Mindy, whilst dating a lot, never seemed to pick guys in the same league as her friend. Emma, studying piano, was top of her class. Mindy, on a real estate course, was struggling to maintain average grades. Mindy was cute, but Emma was perfect, with pale skin, ice-blue eyes and chic, shiny black hair. Rebecca had now seen the pictures and could imagine her up on stage, haunting and evocative, dressed in black and playing to a hypnotised audience.

Emma was the one everybody loved, the one with the bubbly personality and the brilliant social life. Mindy was her shadow, and now without Emma she seemed lost. Rebecca hoped for her sake that Emma would turn up okay. She knew that Hickok already had her down as dead, but there was nothing wrong with being optimistic. After all, it wasn't as if they'd found a body. At least, not yet.

Several of the students in the cafeteria had glanced over at Rebecca when she had walked in; a few of them started whispering. She knew it was the uniform. They were curious to know what a cop was doing at college and probably wondering what the girl sitting with her had done wrong. Chances were that Mindy Tyson was going to find herself very popular once she had left.

At the moment, Scott Jagger's murder was being kept under wraps. Even so, Rebecca didn't doubt for a second that the majority of the students knew, or at least suspected, what had happened to him. If Emma Keeley turned up dead, she barely dared imagine what kind of chaotic turmoil the college would be thrown into.

It had been less than eight years since Rodney Boone's reign of terror had taken place and it was only in the last couple of years that attendance figures at the college had started to rise. People weren't eager to spend time on a campus where one of the professors had killed eight of his students and it had taken a lot of convincing to make them return. With Scott, and possibly Emma, dead, the future reputation of the college was likely to be beyond repair.

Rebecca had pushed Mindy for further information about the person Emma was supposed to have met on the Thursday night she disappeared, but the girl hadn't been able to offer any more details. It was the same story with the mystery man Emma had been dating. Rebecca had taken half a page of notes, though she wasn't too sure that they would be of any help. They'd established that the guy was older. Though older, Mindy had pointed out, could be anything from twenty-five to forty-five, which didn't really eliminate very many people. The only other thing Emma had told Mindy was that they liked to make love to classical music.

Would a classical-music-loving killer choose the sewer as his dumping ground? It didn't really work in Rebecca's head, and she hoped that Hickok was wrong about Emma, that maybe she had just holed up with her mystery boyfriend and wasn't dead after all.

Hoped, but wasn't too sure that she believed it to be true.

* * *

Smooth, secretive and unpredictable. These were the first three words that sprang to mind when Joel Hickok met Lawrence Parker.

Dean Edwards had arranged the introduction. Parker had been only too willing and immediately Joel smelt a rat. This guy didn't belong in college. There was a sly self-serving cockiness about him, and he looked as though he should be on a billboard selling cologne or satisfying rich women, cash in hand – a regular Don Juan.

The two of them met in Parker's classroom. His mid-morning lecture had just finished, and a few students were still lingering when Joel entered the room. One of them, a young girl with short mousy-blonde hair, seemed to be purposely taking a long time to gather her books together. Finally, she made her way across the room, her walk slow and exaggerated, her hips swaying, and her head thrust back. Joel watched her sneak a look at Parker before turning on her heel and leaving the room, and he wondered how many more of the pupils had crushes on him.

Emma Keeley, perhaps?

The Romeo professor with hypnotic black eyes: was it a case of straightforward infatuation? Or did he play with the emotions of his students and return their advances? Not a strong enough motive to make him a murderer, Joel knew, especially since the victims they were dealing with weren't only female.

He was surprised upon shaking Parker's hand to notice he wore a wedding ring. This guy didn't look like the married type.

Didn't look like the married type and didn't look like he should be tutoring in college. One thing was for sure; Lawrence Parker was not the kind of person who could be read like a book.

'How may I help you, Agent Hickok?' he asked, fixing Joel with those black eyes, gesturing with his hand for him to take a seat.

Joel pulled up one of the wooden chairs from the front row of the class and sat down, noticing just how softly spoken Parker was. The lecturer remained standing, his back against his desk as he studied Joel. The teacher and the student. It was an authority thing, Joel realised. Parker wanted to have the upper hand and was trying to establish it by making him feel as though he was on a lower level. Although he understood the professor's intentions, Joel chose to remain seated. Let Lawrence Parker think he had the upper hand. If he thought he was in control, he was more likely to let something slip. *If he does have something to hide.*

Joel was certain he did. He fixed Parker with his most intense stare. 'What can you tell me about Scott Jagger?'

Parker thought about the question for only the briefest of seconds, slowly shaking his head.

'Smart kid, very popular. Could have gone a lot further if he had applied himself.'

Joel arched an eyebrow. 'Further? What held him back?'

'Scott was too busy chasing after girls and footballs to take his studying seriously. He had potential, though.'

'His last class before he went missing was with you, two weeks ago Friday. Did he seem okay? Was his behaviour normal?'

'Pretty much so. He was quieter than usual. I understand he'd had a fight with his girlfriend.'

'Her name is?'

'Joanna Daly.'

'She goes to this college?'

'Yes. She's in my fourth period class on Wednesdays.'

Joel pulled his notebook out and started scribbling. 'So they had a fight. Any idea what about?'

A hint of a smile touched Parker's lips. 'I try to stay out of my students' lives as much as possible. Too complicated.'

'I guess you have enough problems of your own.'

The black eyes bore into Joel's. 'Don't we all, Agent Hickok?'

Sensing he'd hit a nerve, Joel abruptly changed tack. 'What do you know about Emma Keeley?'

The question threw Parker and his expression changed to one of surprise.

'Emma Keeley?'

'She was in your class last Thursday afternoon, wasn't she?'

'Yes, she was. What does Emma Keeley have to do with Scott Jagger?'

'Emma disappeared on Thursday evening and hasn't been seen since.'

'You're kidding!' Parker looked visibly shocked.

Either the guy wasn't involved in her disappearance, or he was a very good actor. Either way, it was uncanny how he'd taken both Emma and Scott for their last lectures.

'Do you know if Emma had a boyfriend?'

Parker shrugged. 'She had a lot of boyfriends.'

'Meaning she slept around?'

'I didn't say that.'

Joel tapped his pen impatiently against the side of his notebook. 'But you just said she had a lot of boyfriends.'

'By which I meant she was a popular student.' Parker narrowed his black eyes defensively. 'She had a lot of friends of the opposite sex.'

'But not any one in particular?'

'I wouldn't know.'

Joel studied the professor, almost certain that he was hiding something. Was it possible that he was somehow involved in Emma Keeley's disappearance? But then, what about the secret boyfriend, and the person she had gone to meet on Thursday night? Were they one and the same? And was it possible that person was Lawrence Parker?

One thing was for certain; they needed to establish the identity of Emma Keeley's boyfriend, and quick, because at the moment it seemed he was the only one who held any of the answers.

Joel had spent another half hour firing questions at Parker, hoping to push the right buttons and get him wound up. It hadn't worked. Parker had remained calm and impassive, and it had been Joel who ended up getting irritated.

* * *

Angell got the brunt of his temper when they later met up, Joel flicking through the notes she had made, barely looking at them before he handed the notebook back.

'Is that all you got?' he stormed. 'Dammit, Angell, you were with her for over an hour. What the hell did you talk about? Your favourite shade of lipstick?'

Angell glared at him, her face red with fury.

'I did exactly as you asked. I questioned Mindy and I made notes. I wrote down every damn thing she told me. What the hell did you want me to do? Make it up?'

Joel scowled. 'I wanted you to do your goddamn job.'

'And I did.'

'You did not.'

Angell threw the notebook back at him. 'You think you can do better, Special Agent Hickok? Well, be my guest.'

She started to walk away.

Joel watched her for a moment, a little taken aback by her reaction. Although very aware that he was the one in the wrong, he was too stubborn to admit it.

'Hey, Angell? Where the hell do you think you're going?' he yelled after her.

She glared over her shoulder. 'As far away from you as possible,' she snapped.

'Yeah? Well get back here. We're not done yet.'

She paused, her back tensing, and Joel guessed she was debating whether or not to continue walking. He knew that he didn't have to remind her of the delicate position she was in. The Jagger murder was now part of an FBI investigation, which meant that she was working under him. By not co-operating she would be putting her job in jeopardy, and he knew that she didn't want to do that.

He watched her as, realising this, she reluctantly turned and made her way back towards him.

You're an asshole, Hickok.

Ignoring the voice, aware he was clearly in the wrong, he turned on his heel and walked away. Footsteps echoed behind him as Angell caught him up, but she refused to look at him, and together they walked down the hallway, a stony silence between them.

During the afternoon they spoke with Dean Edwards again, arranging to have the security on campus doubled, then they questioned Joanna Daly and a couple of other friends of Scott Jagger.

Joanna wasn't able to help much. She and Scott had broken up a few days before he disappeared. It had been her idea, one which Scott hadn't taken well, and he had made a couple of attempts to get her back that had resulted in fights. The last time she had seen him had been Thursday two weeks ago. A whole twenty-four hours before he vanished.

Jim Booker and Pete Harrison, who both lived on campus and had the rooms either side of Scott, were able to offer a little more information, though none that seemed of any use.

Scott, they said, had spent many nights drowning his sorrows down at The Coven following his breakup with Joanna. Could there have been a possible connection there with Emma Keeley, who, it seemed likely, had also been heading for the popular student club on the night she went missing?

The only thing that didn't add up was that both Jim and Pete were certain that Scott hadn't left his room on the evening of his disappearance. The two of them had been in the dorm until almost half ten and, when they'd called on Scott and asked him if he wanted to go for a drink with them, he'd answered the door dressed only in his boxer shorts, claiming he felt too hungover to bother. His hangover must have passed because he had left the campus at some point. It did seem strange though how no one had seen him.

Lots of questions, but no answers, Joel was thinking as they left the college later that afternoon. As they crossed the parking lot, the cellular phone inside the car started to beep. Joel unlocked the door and picked it up.

'Hickok.'

He recognised Max's voice, 'Hey, buddy, it's me.'

'What's up? Did you find anything?'

When Max finished talking, Joel hung up the phone. He glanced at Angell. 'Looks like they've got a body,' he said quietly.

Her eyes widened. 'Emma Keeley?'

Joel shook his head. 'No. It was another guy.'

She looked almost relieved. 'Another student?'

'Probably. He had the initial.'

'K?'

'No. L.'

Angell looked confused. 'But what about K?'

Joel gave a humourless smile. 'Well, I guess either we haven't found her yet, or we're dealing with a killer who doesn't know his alphabet.'

7

Justine waited in the cafeteria until the cop left Lawrie's classroom. Although he didn't wear a uniform, she knew he was a cop because of his officious manner and the way he watched everything. He had watched her too. She knew it. Back in the classroom when she had been collecting her books, wishing that the lesson hadn't passed so quickly and damning the cop for being there, because if he wasn't she could find an excuse to stay, she had felt his eyes on her, and they had stayed on her right up until the moment she had left the room.

She wondered why he was there. Was Lawrie in some kind of trouble? Her heartbeat had quickened with horror at the very thought. What if he was arrested and couldn't tutor her English class any more?

In the back of her mind she knew that she was panicking unnecessarily. The cop was likely there about Scott Jagger's murder. The whole campus had been buzzing with gossip for much of the past week. From various sources, Justine had heard that he'd been shot by a drug dealer to whom he owed money, that he'd been beaten to death by a gang who'd been trying to mug him and that some weird sex killer had strangled him. There were so many rumours flying around that no one knew quite what to believe.

The second cop, this one in uniform, pretty much confirmed her suspicions of why they were there. She was sitting in the larger of the two college cafeterias talking with a second-year student, Mandy, or something, Tyson. Her last name was always easy to remember because it was the same as the boxer.

Feeling curious, Justine bought a hot chocolate and pulled up a chair at the next table.

The cop was young enough that she could possibly pass as a senior, and she was pretty with long dark hair pulled back in a ponytail and a friendly face. Her attention was completely focused on Mandy Tyson, who was talking as the cop took notes.

Justine wasn't sure what Mandy had to do with Scott Jagger's death that would warrant her being questioned. Maybe they knew each other, though she couldn't recall ever having seen them together. She strained to hear what Mandy was saying, but the girl was talking quietly, obviously not wanting to be over-heard, and she was only able to pick up on odd words and sentences. After a few minutes had passed, she realised they were talking about Emma Keeley.

Now that was a name Justine was familiar with; in fact it was a name probably every student in the college knew. To say Emma Keeley was popular would be an understatement.

She was clever, confident and very pretty. Even prettier than Kylan Parker, and that was saying something. Although she wasn't a part of the childish in-crowd, she did have a lot of boyfriends and was always surrounded by a large group of friends.

Justine knew that if she was as pretty and popular as Emma

Keeley, she wouldn't have any trouble whatsoever getting Lawrie Parker's attention.

She wondered how come Mandy and the cop were talking about Emma. Did she have something to do with Scott Jagger's death? Come to think of it, she couldn't recall having seen Emma around campus over the past couple of days. Maybe she and Scott had been secret lovers and she had gone home to mourn him. Or perhaps she had something to do with his murder and had left town to avoid the police. Both possibilities, although far-fetched, were pretty intriguing: one of the most popular students on the campus involved in the sordid murder of a college football player.

Her mind working overtime, Justine didn't hear Luke Williams approaching. It wasn't until he actually sat down in the seat opposite her that she became aware of his presence.

'Daydreaming?' he asked with a smile, as he attacked the ring pull on his can of Coke.

Luke Williams was Justine's on-off boyfriend, had been for the past six months. Justine had met him at one of the first student parties she had attended, and she had to admit they did get on well. She liked him, he made her laugh, and he was fun to hang out with. Best of all, he didn't put any pressure on her for a heavy relationship.

He wasn't Lawrie, though, and over the past couple of weeks Lawrie had been the only guy on Justine's mind.

If it hadn't been for Kylan, getting Lawrie wouldn't have seemed such a daunting task. Justine was reasonably popular with both students and professors alike, she knew she was capable of holding an interesting and intelligent conversation – except of course with Lawrie, in front of whom she had trouble stringing together a single sentence – and, although she wasn't as pretty as Kylan or Emma, she hadn't ever had any problems attracting boyfriends.

Fairly attractive and an interesting conversationalist weren't going to be enough to rid Kylan Parker from Lawrie's life. If she wanted him, and Justine knew she did, she was going to have to come up with a master plan. She was going to have to try harder.

Not able to keep track of the conversation going on at the table next to her, Justine made small talk with Luke for five minutes before deciding to take a wander down the corridor outside Lawrie's classroom. Just to see if the other cop had finished whatever business he had been there to discuss.

It passed through her mind for just a brief second that maybe Lawrie was being questioned about Scott Jagger's death. She immediately dismissed the thought, unable to believe that Lawrie was capable of evil deeds, with the exception of cheating on his wife, of course, and realising that, as with Mandy Tyson, it was probably all just routine questioning. Besides, if the cops were really suspicious, they would have questioned him down at the police precinct, not in his classroom at the college.

Not wanting to make it obvious to those around her, Justine adopted the plan of passing the door and heading over to the lockers that were situated on the opposite wall. She noticed that the classroom door was open and allowed herself a quick peek inside. The room appeared empty and her heart sank as she realised she had missed them. Cursing Luke Williams under her breath, she continued on her way to the lockers.

Shifting her books under her arm, she adjusted her sleeve and checked the time on her wristwatch. Her next class started in just under half an hour. She could hang around and wait for twenty minutes, see if Lawrie returned to the room to prepare for his afternoon class. It was a long shot though and she might attract suspicion if she lingered around outside the classroom for too long. She could just imagine the kind of comments she would get if any of her fellow students found out about her infatuation, especially from the in-crowd.

Oh look, Mr Parker's gone and found himself a stray puppy dog. How sweet.

Justine blushed furiously at the thought.

She was debating what to do when the sound of a door slamming behind her made her jump. She swung around to see Lawrie leaving the room. Her heart skipped a beat; she hadn't missed him after all. Not wanting him to see her standing there, she quickly turned back to face the lockers.

Like he really can't tell you from the back view, Justine.

She counted to ten before peeking over her shoulder. It seemed that she'd gotten lucky and he apparently hadn't seen her – or at least if he had he'd decided not to say anything. Justine caught a glimpse of his back as he turned at the end of the corridor and disappeared. A little too eagerly, she left the safety of the lockers and turned to follow him.

Trying to keep a discreet distance, she followed him out of the halls and across the campus grounds, past the football pitch and into the library.

Juniper College had a great library, the best in the city, and although Justine wasn't the most voracious reader, she had to admit that when doing research for her classes she had always had luck in finding exactly what she needed. The building was on the older part of the campus and dated back over two hundred years to when it had originally been a church. The belfry still remained, though the bell was no longer in use, and inside the place was large and airy with a high-beamed ceiling and heaps of character. Although it had been greatly modernised over the past century, much of the old-fashioned aura had been retained. The distinctive patterned windows, delicately stained in hues of red, blue, green and yellow were still in place and the hundreds of bookshelves and large reading tables in the centre of the room were all carved from traditional oak.

Justine loitered behind a row of bookshelves and watched as Lawrie headed straight to the crime section, gathered a collection of books and made his way over to an empty table. She remained hidden behind the shelves, though moved a row closer to the desk he had chosen. It didn't take her long though to realise there was no need to hide. She could have taken her clothes off and lain naked across the table and Lawrie wouldn't have noticed, he was so engrossed in his reading. Not willing to take any chances, she chose to remain hidden and spent fifteen minutes watching him reading and making notes.

It didn't bother her that her feet were aching or that the book she held upside down, in an attempt to blend in, was about the birth of the shipping industry. She was close to Lawrie and could see his furrowed brow, could watch him when on occasion he ran the tip of his tongue over the top corner of his lip, and could hear the soft sounds of his breathing.

Eventually he glanced up at the clock. She heard him mutter 'Shit' under his breath and watched, disappointed, as he quickly got to his feet. It was probable that, like her, he had lost track of time and had work to prepare for his afternoon class.

Miss Grimwood, the matronly library assistant, who was possibly older than the building itself, and who had on more than one occasion strictly reprimanded Justine for returning books late, came to his aid.

In a butter-wouldn't-melt-in-her-mouth voice, she patted Lawrie on the arm and told him not to worry about replacing the books. 'You just run along to your class, Mr Parker. Leave the books on the table and I'll return them to the shelf for you.'

Justine gaped, wondering if she'd heard the old hag right. Lawrie's charm clearly worked on women of all ages. She watched as he thanked Miss Grimwood and asked her if she could keep the books to one side for him to collect later, before hurrying out of the library.

Her own afternoon class was in the building next door, so Justine still had a few minutes to kill. Seeing old Grimwood disappear behind a bookshelf, she hastily returned her own book and stepped hesitantly over to the desk where Lawrie had been sitting, intrigued to see exactly what kind of reading material he got his kicks from.

There were three books on the desktop, all heavy hardback and all non-fiction. The top book was a scientific dictionary of forensic evidence; the second an encyclopaedia of America's most horrific serial killers.

'Nice subjects, Mr P,' she muttered under her breath, lifting the encyclopaedia to reveal the sleeve of the third book.

The title that met her eyes caused her to let out a small gasp. She read the words over and over.

How to Commit the Perfect Murder.

A hand touched her shoulder making her jump. Justine yelped and swung around to face Miss Grimwood. The older woman's beady eyes glared at her over the top of wire rimmed spectacles.

'Are you using these books, Miss Orton?' she questioned, her tone crisp with authority and more than a little patronising.

Justine backed away from the desk, aware that the half-smile she had on her face was probably making her look stupid.

'No, I'm done.'

Her face flushing scarlet, she turned and walked quickly from the library, uncertain about the books she had seen, yet all the more eager to get to know the true Lawrence Parker.

8

Although Rebecca had decided not to mention anything about the incident with her Jeep, Vic had wisely kept a low profile around her ever since. With the FBI investigation it hadn't been difficult for him to stay out of her way, and, even when they were working at their shared desk together, there had been other people about, making it difficult for her to say anything.

She hadn't forgiven him and fully intended to get her own back at some point, and she suspected he probably knew that. Therefore, she was surprised to find him leaning against her Jeep when she left work on Wednesday evening. She made a point of studying both front tyres to check they were still full of air before looking up at him, her eyebrows raised questioningly.

'What do you want, Vic?' she asked bluntly.

Vic stared at the ground, looking a little uncomfortable as he shuffled his feet.

'My car's in the repair shop. I was hoping you might give me a ride home.'

Rebecca bit her bottom lip to stop it from dropping open. 'You're kidding, right?'

'Well, it is on your way.' He looked at her with a pleading expression on his face that she supposed he hoped would make her feel sorry for him. In truth, it only succeeded in making him look more pathetic.

Jeez! She couldn't believe this guy.

One night he was letting the air out of her tyres because he couldn't handle the idea of a rejection and now here he was, hoping to catch a ride home. She was about to tell him exactly what she thought of him when it struck her that maybe she could turn the situation to her advantage. It would be interesting to see just how badly Victor Boaz wanted his ride.

'So, you want me to take you home, do you, Vic?' she asked in her sweetest voice.

He seemed to take her question as a yes, edging toward the passenger door of the Jeep as he answered.

'I'd really appreciate it if you could, Rebecca. Thanks.'

Rebecca shook her head and forced a pained expression. 'Well, I don't know. I guess it all depends on whether my tyres are up for it.'

'Oh, that.' Vic turned to face her, caught a little off guard. He gave a guilty grin. 'Look, Rebecca, I'm sorry about what happened the other night. We were just joking around.'

'Joking? Is that what you were doing?' She fixed him with a frosty look. 'Sorry, Vic, I hadn't realised I was supposed to be laughing while I was changing my tyre.'

Vic pulled a sullen face. 'Look, come on, Angell, I've said I'm sorry. Why don't you quit fooling around and just give me a ride home? I've already had a shitty enough day.'

'So I heard.' Although she wanted to stay angry with him, Rebecca couldn't stop the grin from breaking out on her face.

By the time she and Hickok had returned from the college, the rumours had circulated the precinct about how Sutton and a couple of other officers had found Vic on all fours in the sewer, his pants down and a corpse wedged between his legs. Of course, he had angrily denied everything, but Rebecca had enjoyed watching him suffer for a change.

'I hope that's a clean uniform you're wearing,' she told him, screwing up her nose in mock disdain.

'Of course it is,' Vic started angrily before realising she was joking. He pulled the pleading face again. 'So what do you say, then? Are you going give me a ride home or what?'

'Honestly, Vic. I'm not sure I really want to.'

'Come on, please. I'll make it up to you.'

'You will?' She looked at him expectantly. 'How?'

Vic shrugged his shoulders. 'I'll buy you a beer.'

'A beer? Whoa, that's generous of you.'

'Well, what do you want?'

Rebecca thought for a moment, knowing that if she wanted anything out of Vic she was going to have to get it before she dropped him off. She didn't trust him to keep his word.

'Do you have your credit card on you?' she asked eventually, an idea coming to mind.

'Yeah,' Vic answered, sounding dubious. 'Why?'

Rebecca stepped around to the driver's side of the Jeep and unlocked the door.

'Come on,' she said, climbing inside and reaching across to open the passenger door for him. 'My refrigerator was looking pretty empty when I left this morning. You can help me fill it up.'

* * *

Kylan stared at the red sticky mess as more and more of it oozed out on to the floor.

Boy, talk about a splatter.

Glancing down at her feet she noticed that some of the goo had splashed onto the toe of her shoe. Screwing up her nose she took a step back. The guy in front of her, the one who had dropped the bottle of sauce, reddened slightly. He gave her an apologetic grin.

'Don't you just hate glass bottles?'

Kylan smiled politely and side-stepped around the mess.

Trust you to be in the wrong place at the wrong time.

She turned her mind back to the shopping list in front of her. Pasta, onions, tomatoes…

She hunted the shelf for the cans of tomatoes, certain they had been near the artichokes and black beans the last time she had come shopping, whilst absent-mindedly rubbing the toe of her shoe against the white linoleum floor. Manoeuvring her shopping cart into the next aisle, she found what she was looking for.

Typical, they always wait for me to come shopping on my own before they start moving stuff around.

Hurrying across, she collected a couple of cans of her preferred brand and deposited them in the cart. Scanning the list, she was certain that she had got everything.

Thank God!

She hated shopping. Usually, she and Lawrie did it together. At the moment, though, Lawrie had double his normal classes and it didn't seem fair to burden him with grocery shopping. Knowing that he had papers to mark, she had this evening come by herself, certain that he would return the favour in a couple of months when she had to study for exams. After all, it had been his idea that she go back to college; something she hadn't been at all sure about doing. Lawrie had promised her that he would prove her doubts wrong, so for his sake she was trying to give it a go.

She would admit it helped living off campus. The student buildings gave her the creeps, and she avoided going in them whenever possible. Having her own place was definitely better.

Lost in her thoughts, she absent-mindedly pushed the shopping cart to the end of the aisle and joined the line for the checkout. There were three people in front of her, a bald guy with a tattoo of a dragon on the back of his neck and two young women who appeared to know each other. She could see that both women had large loads of groceries, their carts piled. Kylan guessed she was probably going to have a long wait to pay.

Idly she began to browse the magazines tacked up in front of the cashier's till. As she selected a copy of *Cosmopolitan*, her eyes brushed past the mirror positioned above the rack. There was a man in the queue behind her. He had short, pale blond hair and bad acne, and he was staring at her.

Impulsively, Kylan turned around to face him. It was the same guy who had dropped the catsup bottle. He smiled at her, seeming pleased that she recognised him.

'Hello, again.'

'Hi.' Kylan gave him a tentative smile. There was something about this guy that she didn't like. Something about his eyes.

Even as the thought passed through her mind, she noticed that his eyes were passing over her body, slowly, lingering, until eventually they stopped on her feet.

'How is your shoe?'

'What?'

His eyes came back up to meet her face. 'Your shoe. I spilt catsup on it, remember?'

'Yeah, I remember. It's fine, thanks.'

He nodded and there was a brief uncomfortable silence.

Kylan seized the opportunity to turn away. One of the women had passed through the checkout, but there was still her friend and tattoo guy to go. She willed them to hurry up. Although the man hadn't threatened her, hadn't made any comment that could be taken the wrong way, she longed to be out of the store and away from him. Funny how she felt so unsafe when there were all these people around her. Her back was to him, but she could still feel his presence. How close was he standing to her? Close enough to touch her? Close enough for her to feel his breath on the back of her neck?

She tried to occupy her mind by flicking through the magazine. The words didn't register though, and the pictures seemed no more than a collage of bland images. Slowly, her eyes lifted up to meet the mirror. He was still watching her. He saw that she was looking at him and smiled. Kylan felt colour rush to her cheeks. Quickly she looked away.

Possibilities flooded her mind. She could move to another checkout. She could dump her cart and leave the store, maybe come back later. She could turn around and tell him to get lost.

All of the possibilities seemed stupid, she knew that.

Christ, Kylan, pull yourself together.

She drew a couple of deep breaths, avoided the mirror, and tried to focus on the magazine.

'Kylan?'

Hearing her name, she looked up.

Vic Boaz stood at the checkout next to her, a wide grin on his face.

Relieved to see someone she knew, Kylan greeted him a little too emphatically. 'Hi there. How's it going?'

Vic nodded. 'Great, thanks. Really good.'

He was in uniform, though he didn't appear to be on duty, and looked as though he'd put on weight since she'd last seen him. Beside him stood a tall, attractive woman of around her own age, with dark hair pulled back into a ponytail. Kylan wondered if perhaps she was Vic's girlfriend.

As though guessing what she was thinking, Vic introduced her. 'Hey, Kylan, you haven't met Rebecca, have you?'

'No, I haven't.'

'Rebecca's my new partner.' He turned and gave her a swat on the ass. 'We've been together now, what, about three weeks?'

Rebecca nodded, looking unimpressed. 'Seems like much longer, though, doesn't it?'

Kylan picked up on the sarcasm in her tone. Maybe the two of them weren't getting on quite as well as Vic would have her believe.

'It's nice to meet you.'

Rebecca returned her smile. 'Same. So how do you know Vic?'

'Oh, family connections.'

'I dated Kylan's sister, Tania, for a while,' Vic elaborated.

Dated and then cheated on, Kylan thought, though didn't say. 'So how are you doing, Vic?' she asked, unable to resist a dig. 'Any new girlfriends or wives on the scene?'

'Wives?' Rebecca raised her eyebrows, genuinely surprised. 'I didn't know Vic had been married.'

'Oh yeah, sure he has,' Kylan told her. 'Twice.'

'Really? A regular ladies' man, hey?'

Vic seemed pleased with the comment. 'I know how to show a woman a good time.'

'Yeah, I guess that's why you're single now.'

He narrowed his eyes. 'Very funny, Rebecca. You're a laugh a minute.' He turned to Kylan, eager to change the subject. 'So, how's that hubby of yours? What's his name? Larry?'

'Lawrie,' Kylan corrected. 'We're doing great.'

'Good to hear it. Are you both still at the college?'

She nodded. 'Yeah, we're still there.' It had been due to Lawrie getting the teaching position in the English Department that they had moved to Juniper. 'Things are working out well.'

'Good, good. Well make sure you say hi to him, okay?'

'I will.'

* * *

The run in with Vic and Rebecca provided Kylan with a brief diversion from Mr Creepy, but now they were gone she realised she hadn't come any closer to resolving her predicament. A quick glance in the mirror confirmed her suspicion that the man was still there.

Of course he's still there, you idiot. Where the hell did you expect him to go?

Yes, still there. Still watching her.

Seeing Vic and Rebecca leave the store, Kylan wished she had thought of some pretence so they could have all left together. Maybe she should have suggested they get together for a cup of coffee or something.

But you didn't, which leaves you right back here with Mr Creepy.

Fortunately, now there was only the tattoo guy ahead of her in the line, and he was already paying for his goods. Kylan felt a small surge of relief. She would hopefully be out of here in a couple of minutes. Quickly, she started to unload her cart, careful not to let her eyes wander in the direction of the man. The last thing she wanted was him trying to strike up conversation again.

Fortunately, he didn't.

* * *

Kylan packed and paid for her goods, leaving the store without further incident. It wasn't until she was loading her shopping into the trunk of her Volkswagen, that she saw the man again. He was sitting behind the wheel of a brown Buick, his face partially hidden by a newspaper, but his eyes were so obviously watching her.

She felt her stomach knot, forcing herself to finish loading the car then, slamming the door of the trunk shut, she made her way round to the driver's door, careful to avoid eye contact. This guy didn't need any encouragement.

Her hand shook as she tried to get her key in the door lock.

'Hey, Kylan!' a voice shouted to her and the keys slipped from her grasp, crashing to the floor. Quickly she retrieved them and glanced up to see who had called her. It was Vic, sitting in the passenger seat of a blue Jeep which had pulled up on the lane just behind her Volkswagen.

He looked amused. 'Kind of jumpy, aren't you?'

Kylan forced a smile. 'You surprised me.'

'You don't say,' he grinned. 'Anyhow, I was thinking. We haven't seen each other in a while, so maybe we should all go out to dinner this weekend. You and Lawrie, and I'll bring a friend of mine, Jill. We can have a few beers and catch up on old times. What do you say?'

'Yeah, that sounds great.'

Vic had been the only person, other than Lawrie and Tania, she'd known when they first moved to Juniper. Although she found him a little irritating, Kylan guessed it wouldn't hurt to go out for a meal. Plus, he had just saved her from an uncomfortable situation.

'I'll give you a call,' Vic suggested. 'You're in the book, right?'

'Under Parker.'

'I know.' He gave her a wink.

In the driver's seat beside him, Rebecca smiled and raised a hand.

'See you later, then,' he called.

'Yeah, see you later.' Kylan didn't wait to watch them pull away; her thoughts having returned to the guy in the Buick. Already she was busy with her door lock, her hand still shaking badly, and it took her three attempts to get the key in. When the door was eventually unlocked, she allowed herself a final glance at the Buick.

It was gone.

She stared at the empty space feeling a mixture of surprise and relief. The guy had really spooked her, and it had to be more than coincidence that she had run into him first in the store and then the parking lot. So, in that case, where the hell had he suddenly disappeared to?

* * *

Sitting alone in his attic room, Rodney Boone flicked through the pages of the cheap cardboard scrapbook in which he kept the newspaper clippings that told of his reign of terror. As he glanced at the pictures of the victims, each of their stories headed by a different letter of the alphabet, he noticed that the clippings were starting to yellow with age. He turned to the last used page, headed by the letter J, and carefully reread the one recent story in the book.

The story of the murdered football player, Scott Jagger.

He had known that, eventually, the time would be right for the killings to restart. They had to in order for his alphabet to be completed. And in order for him to fulfil the promise that he had made to his family. Closing his eyes, he leaned back in his chair and started to remember.

9

SAN PALIMO, CALIFORNIA. NOVEMBER 1963

'You're making a big mistake, Mr Kusack.'

Myron White stared at the boy standing below him, fully aware that his words had not sounded as threatening as he had hoped they would.

Bobby Kusack glanced up and met his eyes. The corners of his mouth creased slightly as a smile threatened to break out across his face. Reaching into the inside pocket of his black leather jacket, he pulled out a matchbook and a packet of Marlboro and observed the professor as he leant against his desk and lit the cigarette.

Myron licked at his dry lips, realising that his threats were not going to work. He decided to adopt a more genial approach.

'Come on, Bobby, this is silly. Why don't you cut me down and we can talk about this rationally.'

'Rationally?' Bobby nodded slowly, taking a drag on his cigarette as he appeared to mull the idea over. 'You want to talk about this rationally, do you, Professor?'

He got up from the desk, and Myron felt his heartbeat quicken as he watched the boy take a couple of deliberate steps towards him, his dark eyes never faltering from his face. Was he going to let him down?

Bobby stopped directly in front of him and sighed deeply. Rings of pale grey smoke billowed from his nostrils.

Myron forced a smile for him. 'We're all adults here,' he said in a joking voice, aware that his tone had a false ring to it. 'There's nothing that can't be resolved by talking.'

'Oh, we can talk, Professor, if that's what you want,' Bobby agreed, scratching the side of his head. 'But, you're staying exactly where you are.' Cigarette hanging between his lips, he slowly started to circle the desk, like a shark closing in on its prey.

Myron swallowed hard, feeling the rope cut into his throat as his mind worked overtime searching for a solution to his situation. Right now, he was trapped and at Bobby Kusack's mercy. Even if he were somehow able to untie his hands and remove the noose from his neck, he still had to get away from Bobby and his two buddies, who were standing guard outside the classroom door. He had spent enough Thursday evenings working alone, marking test papers, to know that nobody was going to come to his rescue. All the other professors in the English Department had long gone home, and security rarely ventured over to the building when they knew he was still here.

He watched Bobby carefully, trying to work out what his intentions were. Each time the boy disappeared behind him, a grip of fear knotted in his chest, as he imagined the chair on which he stood suddenly being wrenched from beneath him. He tried hard to keep his feet still, knowing that even if Bobby didn't pull the chair, it was still balanced precariously on the desktop and needed only the slightest movement to send it tumbling.

Staring down at the floor, Myron realised the drop was more than four feet. Probably enough to break his neck. The thought made him start to panic.

'Come on, Bobby, please let me down,' he begged, as the boy wandered back into his sight. He could feel his fear beading in sweat on his forehead, and he fought hard to bite back the feeling of nausea that was rising in his throat. For a moment the two of them stood staring at each other.

Bobby's black eyes were scowling, and Myron could see the hatred behind them. He watched as the boy dropped his cigarette end to the floor, stamped it out and took a step forward. The room was deadly silent, and he felt his legs begin to shake.

Oh God, no! Oh God, no!

Beneath him the rickety chair creaked and scraped against the surface of the desk.

Bobby smiled coldly. 'Careful, Professor. You wouldn't want to fall.'

'Don't do this, Bobby. Please!'

The classroom door suddenly jerked open, cutting through the tension, and Doug Colney poked his head into the room. He avoided Myron's eyes, instead focusing on Bobby.

'Hey, Kusack, come here a minute.'

Bobby turned and glared at Doug. 'I'm busy,' he hissed through clenched teeth. 'Get back outside.'

Doug stood his ground. 'I really think you should come out here for a minute.'

Bobby looked uncertainly at the classroom door, and then back at Myron.

'I'll be right back, Professor. Don't go anywhere,' he quipped, giving a deep-throated laugh.

Myron watched him cross the room with long, purposeful strides, grabbing hold of Doug Colney by his shirt collar when he reached him.

'This had better be good, Dougie boy,' he threatened, pushing him into the hallway and pulling the door shut behind them.

Myron could hear his heart thumping loudly in his chest. He glanced around the empty classroom, his relief at being left alone mingled with fear in case the chair and table suddenly collapsed. This was his chance. His one chance of escape. While logic told him that Bobby Kusack planned to do no more than frighten him, something he had already succeeded in doing, the irrational part of his mind kept reminding him that he barely knew the boy and what he did know about him was that he had a bad reputation. What if he really was crazy enough to kill him?

Frantically, Myron strained against the rope binding his wrists. The only way he could be guaranteed safety was to escape and he knew that he had precious little time left in which to do it. Slowly he twisted his head, feeling the bite of the noose around his neck as he tried to glance over his shoulder to see how his wrists were tied. Beneath him, the chair wobbled dangerously, and he froze for a long second, terrified it would give way completely.

He could hear hushed voices out in the hallway, and he wondered what the three boys were talking about. Did they have other plans for him? Perhaps they intended to leave him stuck there. Panic seared through his veins as he realised that by leaving him, they would be condemning him to death. It was useless to believe that he could get out of the noose by himself, and he would never be able to remain standing like this until the morning.

'Bobby?' His voice echoed across the classroom towards the closed door. 'Bobby! Please get me down from here.'

Glancing down at his feet, he noticed that the two front legs of the chair were perilously close to tumbling off the edge of the desktop.

Oh my God! Oh my God! I'm going to fall.

A second, stronger wave of nausea hit Myron, causing his

head to spin. Black dots appeared before his eyes and he felt his legs quake beneath him, threatening to collapse with weakness.

He fought to control his breathing, to get past the dizziness, dimly aware that the creaking chair was moving closer to the edge of the desk.

The door opened and Bobby Kusack stepped back into the classroom. His eyes slowly came up to meet Myron's through the cloud of smoke created by his freshly lit cigarette.

Bobby! Please! The chair!

Myron wasn't sure if he had spoken the words aloud or not, but he noticed Bobby glance down at the desk, and saw his eyes widen in horror as the cigarette dropped from his mouth. The scene played in slow motion as the boy took a step towards him. Myron heard a final creak, feeling the chair slip forward, pushing him with it, and a half scream tore from his lips as his kicking legs struggled to find a foothold.

He didn't hear the crash as the chair landed against the floor. The pull of the rope had snapped his neck a moment earlier, the pain lasting for just a split second before nothingness hit him.

As Bobby Kusack pulled frantically at the noose, trying to free his body, Myron White stared down at him with accusing eyes that no longer saw the face of his killer, but instead the white mask of death.

10

SAN PALIMO, CALIFORNIA. JULY 1964

His mother had blamed the students.

The policemen who had been sent round to explain what had happened told her it had been an accident. He remembered how they had said it was a joke that had gone wrong.

Nobody was to blame.

His mother hadn't believed them, and she had started crying. Shouting and screaming at them and hitting out with her fists.

Rodney could remember the night clearly.

He had been in bed when the doorbell rang and, wanting to know who was there, he had crept across the landing and hidden in the alcove at the top of the stairs. He had listened to the policemen as they talked, wondering where his daddy was and wanting to know what they had said to his mother to make her cry.

His mother never cried. She had always told him that tears were a sign of weakness and that if he were to cry then he should expect to be treated as a fool. He wondered why she had told him this when she now stood there, crying herself.

After the policemen had left, he had gone to her and asked, and not for the first time in his ten years she had hit him.

This time was different. This time, his daddy hadn't come and stopped her. It was shortly afterwards that he learned his daddy would never stop her again.

The pain of that night was etched in his memory more clearly than any Christmas or birthday. Daddy had gone. He would never come back. There were just the four of them now: Rodney, his mother, Clifford and the baby.

Things had changed quickly following Daddy's death. They had moved to a smaller house with no garden, where the wallpaper was peeling off the walls and the windows didn't open properly. He and Clifford had been made to change schools and the kids in his new class laughed at him because he couldn't read as well as them. They stole his lunch money and called him bad words, and they taunted him about the men his mother brought back to the house.

That was the worst thing: the men. A few of them were friendly, but most of them didn't speak. They were all nameless strangers who went into his mother's bedroom, one after the other. Sometimes they made her laugh, other times they made her cry, but nearly always after they'd gone, she would come out of the bedroom mad, and looking for someone to shout at. That person usually ended up being Rodney.

He never dared to ask her who the men were. The kids at school called her a slut and a whore, and he wondered what they meant. He knew that if he asked her, she would probably start hitting him. It seemed that these days all she did was either hit him or ignore him. She got especially mad when his teacher started sending letters to her, asking that she go in and see him about Rodney's poor grades.

'*Don't you think I have enough to do already?*'

'*I'm too busy to visit teachers, Rodney. You'll just have to try harder.*'

'*What kind of useless, stupid child are you? Can't you manage to do anything by yourself?*'

'*I have my own problems to deal with, Rodney. Stop wasting my time!*'

She wasn't well, he knew it. He could remember back to when Daddy had been alive, and they had been a real family. She had loved him then. Now she had to cope alone and the worries and responsibilities and her sadness at losing Daddy had made her ill. There were times when she wandered around the house in a daze, her hair all messy and dark circles under her eyes. She would often be sick, and Rodney would have to fetch the medicine that she kept in the box under the bed and help her put the needle in her arm.

He tried to do as much as possible for her, hoping she would get better and perhaps one day love him the way his daddy had loved him. He remembered how Daddy had helped him with his schoolwork, and he wished his father was still alive. He knew though that he couldn't rely on wishes. He had to be brave. The baby and Clifford were his responsibility now and he comforted them both, changing the baby's diapers and heating up his bottles, while listening to them cry tears he would no longer let fall. Rodney was their older brother, and it was his job to look after them now. His mother had told him never to give in to tears and he had seen how she had become weak that night with the policemen; that night when she had cried.

She was now too weak to look after them and so it was his job to make sure that everything was taken care of. He would work harder at school and help more around the house, and as soon as he was old enough, he would try to get a job so they could buy more food for the table and more medicines for his mother to help make her better.

Although he was still only ten years old, Rodney White realised that he was now the man of the house, and he was determined to make sure that nothing and no one ever hurt his family again.

11

JUNIPER, OREGON. SATURDAY 26 APRIL 1997

Saturday was normally their one day together.

In the summer they would go to the beach or the park, and, when the weather was colder, they often spent the afternoon at a craft fair or museum, or in an old movie theatre.

Today, though, was different. Lawrie had work to do at college and insisted that it couldn't wait until after the weekend. He'd refused to bring it home with him, telling Kylan that she would be too much of a distraction. Kylan guessed she should be flattered that he couldn't concentrate on work while she was around, and she knew that with the extra classes he had taken on he was being worked into the ground.

Still, she felt disappointed and a little annoyed, and spent the entire day at a loss for what to do.

At least she had the evening to look forward to. Tonight, they had arranged to go out for dinner with Vic Boaz and his girl-friend, Jill. Vic had called and made reservations for Angelo's, a classy, uptown Italian restaurant, one that both she and Lawrie were very familiar with and was coming to pick them up at eight.

Glancing at the hands of the kitchen clock, Kylan saw she had nine and a half hours to go.

The first two hours she spent doing household chores: dusting, polishing and vacuuming. They were all jobs she tended to put off for as long as possible, finding it difficult to fit them in with being at college full time. Today she had no excuse and, as she cleaned, she was reminded of the saying, *When you have time to kill, make sure you don't murder a good opportunity.* An amusing saying, maybe, but the words *kill*, and *murder* always sent a chill through her heart.

Her mind went to Scott Jagger, the student who had recently been found dead, and she quickly tried to shake the thoughts.

When her work was finished, she made herself comfortable on the large couch in the living room and read for a while. A couple of weeks back when she and Lawrie had been at a craft fair, they had discovered a quaint little stall full of second-hand books, most of which she hadn't read since she was a child. She'd bought *Jamaica Inn* and *Tender is the Night* and was currently halfway through Fitzgerald's tragic love story.

Thinking about Lawrie, hard at work, and looking forward to the evening, Kylan found that she couldn't concentrate on the book and, after turning half a dozen pages and realising that she hadn't actually read the words, she gave up on the idea. She returned her bookmark to where she'd originally picked the story up, placed the book back on the shelf and went through to the kitchen to put on a pot of coffee, deciding that that she needed to get a life and think of things she could do when by herself.

Shopping was a possibility. She was miserable and spending money always cheered her up. The idea was appealing, but not realistic, as she and Lawrie were struggling to get by on one salary. Lawrie had financed her return to college, and it wasn't fair to expect him to buy her a new wardrobe that she didn't need.

She wished Tania were here. She would know what to do. Now that her sister had moved again and she only saw her a few times a year, Kylan realised just how much she missed her.

She thought of calling Donna and Ally, her two best friends from college, to see if they wanted to do something, but then she remembered that they would be spending the day with their boyfriends, the way that she normally spent her Saturdays with Lawrie. Her mind still preoccupied with thoughts of Lawrie, she gazed absently through the rising stream of the coffee pot out of the kitchen window.

At first, she didn't notice the man, and initially he didn't see her at the window looking at him. Their eyes met at the same time and, recognising the pale features and pimply skin, Kylan felt her heart lunge into her mouth.

Quickly, she took a step back.

It took a second for her mind to register where she knew the man from and, as soon as that second had passed and she had placed him in the checkout queue and parking lot, an icy hand clamped over the pit of her stomach.

'Oh my God!' she half whispered to herself, barely aware that she had spoken aloud. Her legs shaking, her head fuzzy, she rushed to bolt the lock on the front door, unaware that he was no longer standing there.

* * *

It had been a close call. He shouldn't have let himself get so close. He was certain that she had recognised him from the grocery store, but how much she had read into it and whether or not she understood he was there because of her, he wasn't sure. He guessed he'd been asking for trouble, standing in the street in broad view for everyone to see. He should have kept to the shadows like he had been doing for the past couple of weeks. The last he had known; she had been reading in the living room at the back of the house. He had watched her for a while, thinking how lovely she looked dressed simply in a pair of denim shorts and a navy T-shirt, her tanned bare legs crossed at the ankles and dropping casually over the end of the couch. Her pale-blonde hair caught the light of the sun reflecting on the window and her eyes, big and brown, looked up every now and then to glance idly round the room.

It pained him to know that he held her life in his hands.

She wasn't the only one, though, he reminded himself. There would be others first; others who still had to be selected; others who needed to be watched.

* * *

After checking that every door and window in the house was locked, Kylan ran back through to the kitchen and over to the phone that hung on the wall. She grabbed the receiver and was relieved to hear the familiar dialling tone. She didn't know why, but she had half imagined finding the phone line dead. That was what always happened in the movies, wasn't it?

This isn't the movies though. This is real life.

Real life can be just as scary, she reminded herself. With shaking fingers, she punched in the number of the college.

The phone rang ten times, each ring in unison with the thrashing beat of her heart, before it was answered by a surly-sounding receptionist. Kylan asked to speak to Lawrie and was then left on hold, listening to the melodious sound of Chopin, as the receptionist paged through her call. While she waited, she glanced cautiously around the kitchen, half expecting the man to appear in the doorway, or come crashing through the window.

Eventually the call was answered, though not by Lawrie. Instead, it was the surly receptionist again.

'There's no answer in the English Department. Would you like me to leave a message?'

No answer? Where was Lawrie?

Kylan declined the offer, thanked the receptionist and hung up the phone. She contemplated calling the police.

And tell them what? That the man who stood behind you in the grocery store a couple of days ago was just standing outside your house?

Get a grip, Kylan, you're going way over the top.

Drawing deep breaths to calm her nerves, she cautiously made her way over to the kitchen window. There was definitely no sign of the man. Whoever he was had gone. She knew that there had to be a reasonable explanation though for why she'd seen him. Maybe he lived locally and the route to his house took him down this road.

So how come you've never seen him out there before?

Perhaps he'd recently moved to the area.

You know everyone in this neighbourhood. If he'd moved in, you'd know about it. And instead of being so rational, just remember things don't always turn out okay.

Kylan pushed the thought from her mind and concentrated on making coffee. She reached into the cupboard and pulled out a mug with a quote written on the side in large black letters. It was one of a set of six that Tania had bought her and Lawrie when they first moved in, each bearing a different message.

To have a true sense of humour you have to laugh at yourself occasionally.

Kylan poured the coffee, still too shaken to realise the irony of the comment on the mug that she had selected.

The man had gone, Lawrie wasn't here, and she shouldn't

worry the police. For the time being, if she could just stop shaking, everything was okay. Best to get through the day and maybe she could try and talk to Lawrie about what had happened later.

She remembered how the receptionist had told her that there was no one in the English Department. So where was he?

Stop being so suspicious. You have no need to worry, he had probably just gone for lunch.

Kylan guessed she was overreacting. It was nearly one thirty. Very likely that he'd popped out for a sandwich. Either that or he was so engrossed in his work he hadn't heard the phone ringing. Lawrie was fine, she was fine, and tonight she would tell him about the guy from the grocery store, the same guy who had stood staring at her through the kitchen window.

He would probably laugh at her and tell her she was being paranoid, but at least she would have told him.

Lawrie knew her better than anyone. She had to share her problems with him. After all, who else was there?

She thought of Vic. Maybe she could mention the incident to him when she saw him later for dinner. He was a cop and, whilst he probably couldn't do anything to the guy for staring through her window, he might be able to give her some advice or perhaps offer to monitor the situation. Feeling more relaxed, Kylan finished her coffee then spent her afternoon clearing through the junk in the spare bedroom. It had been piling up for a while and she had no idea what she might find, or where exactly she planned to put it. It was a job that needed doing, though, and it would help focus her thoughts. Pouring a second cup of coffee, she took a final glance out of the kitchen window before making her way upstairs, ready to conquer the task at hand.

By the middle of the afternoon she had almost forgotten about the man at her window and, when he did briefly re-enter her thoughts, she realised that she had probably overreacted.

* * *

Lawrie returned to the house just after five, and pale eyes watched him from the shadows as he locked the door of the Volkswagen and climbed the porch steps to the front door.

The shadows. That was where the man had remained for the rest of the afternoon, hoping that Kylan would leave the house and he would have the opportunity to follow her. She hadn't, though, instead disappearing upstairs and out of his view for the rest of the afternoon.

He should have left then. There was other work to do, and he wasn't going to accomplish anything by hanging around the house. He was wasting time and not being professional, getting too attached to one subject, when there were others.

Already had been others.

And soon there would be more.

Tearing himself away, he headed down to his Buick, discreetly parked in the next street. He knew he had to push all thoughts of Kylan Parker from his mind and concentrate on the next victim.

Climbing into the Buick, he started the engine, shifted into drive, applied pressure to the gas and slid the car out of the parking spot. At the junction he signalled left and pulled out on the main road, heading in the direction of the college.

Time to look for the new victim.

When he was given the sign of who it was to be, it would be time to make his move.

Although it was Saturday night and since she had been in Juniper, Rebecca had been making an effort to go out and meet new people, this evening she wasn't sure that she could be bothered to get dressed up.

She had noticed on her way home that the old theatre on the corner of her block was doing an all-night screening of the *Friday the 13th* movies and decided that, instead of hitting the bars, she would head over there later to watch a couple of them.

On her first weekend in the city she had tagged along to The Coven with Heather, one of the other female officers who worked her shift. The nightclub wasn't really her scene though. Quite a few of the people in there appeared to be students and Rebecca would have preferred to have been somewhere with a slightly older crowd and a bar that didn't serve watered-down beer and spirits.

That said, she did have fun, and she made a few new friends, including one guy called David who was a lawyer with a city firm and seemed worth getting to know better. At least that was what she thought, until Heather pulled her to one side and warned her that he was a well-known married flirt. Disgusted, Rebecca had torn up the telephone number he had given her and successfully managed to stay out of his way for the rest of the evening.

She somehow always managed to luck out in the love department in one way or another. Back in Swallow Falls she'd had several boyfriends, none of whom had lasted very long. Two she'd caught cheating on her; another had dumped her for the football team. Then there had been the baseball incident, where, following a huge row with boyfriend number four, a jock called Rick Shapiro, she had thrown the ball at him, smashing him in the face and breaking his nose. Needless to say, she had never seen him again.

While Uncle Lou thought she was doing great, her mother told her that she was too feisty.

'You'll never get married, Rebecca, if you keep scaring your suitors away.'

As usual, Rebecca hadn't cared and hadn't agreed.

She wasn't in a big rush to get married and didn't believe there were many guys in Swallow Falls who had the balls to take her on anyway.

'They probably don't expect such behaviour from the Minister's daughter,' her mother had argued. *'Can't you try to be a little more refined, like Wendy?'*

Like middle sister, Wendy? That was a laugh. Stay at home, bake cakes and have babies. No, thank you. If anything, Rebecca aspired to be the complete opposite to Wendy.

It was soon after that fight that she'd applied to join the academy. And now here she was, a cop in the city, already involved in a murder investigation.

Hickok and Sutton had been over at the college for most of

the day, conducting further interviews, and when they'd returned neither of them had been particularly forthcoming about how well things had gone. Rebecca hadn't asked. She wasn't going to give Joel Hickok the satisfaction of knowing that she wanted to know. She had already had a pretty shitty day and the less time she spent in his company the better.

At various times during the week, she had tried to figure out what he was all about. At first, she'd just assumed that he was a chauvinist and liked to belittle women. From the way he treated Vic, though, it had quickly become apparent that he spoke down to most people, regardless of sex or rank – especially cops.

She loathed him for it, believing that no one was above good manners, but she had also worked with him closely enough to see that he was good at his job. He was thorough and dedicated, which she guessed was probably why he got away with acting like such a jumped-up jerk most of the time.

Her own day had been spent out on patrol with Vic. Although the shift itself had been pretty much uneventful, she'd really had about as much of Vic as she could handle. Vic and his continual rambling about how he was a big hero because he'd found the second body in the sewer. In the end he'd made a day spent with Hickok seem almost appealing.

Rebecca hoped sincerely that the two Feds would want them working on the murder case again on Monday, because she wasn't too sure she could handle another shift quite like today.

Right now, she was just glad to be away from it all.

The apartment that she rented wasn't the kind of place you wanted to spend too much time in. It was very basic, with one bedroom, a bathroom and a very small open-plan living room and kitchen. The walls were magnolia and, not having had time to do any kind of decorating, Rebecca had stuck a few cheap prints up that she had bought from a nearby market stall, in an attempt to cheer the place up.

At the moment, this apartment was all she could afford. On her first day in the city she had opened up a second bank account and planned on paying money into it every month until eventually there was enough for her to move. She didn't want anything lavish, just somewhere with a larger living room, thicker walls – she had noisy neighbours – and in a quieter location that would be safer for Sabrina.

Sabrina, named after her favourite Charlie's Angel, was the black kitten that she had adopted from the local animal shelter; right now she was hungry and purring around Rebecca's legs as she changed out of her uniform. Once dressed in comfortable jeans and her favourite black T-shirt, Rebecca took her through to the kitchen and opened a new can of cat food. Then she played back messages on her machine: two, both from her mother checking she was eating okay, and sat down to have a quick read of the paper she had picked up on her way home.

There wasn't much that she didn't already know about. Most were follow-up stories. There was a couple of new shootings and muggings, nothing really positive. Wondering why she had bothered to read it in the first place, she put down the paper and hit the remote for the TV, flicking until she came across an episode of *ER*. The news was always the same: brutal crimes and greedy politicians, just different names and different places.

The Feds were still trying to keep the murders under wraps and the paper just had a brief story on Rufus Lind, the second victim, saying that investigations were continuing. Max Sutton had insisted that everyone involved keep quiet until they'd established there was a definite connection to the Alphabet Killings, and Rebecca felt sure that she would be able to do a better job of keeping quiet than Vic would.

Already she'd had to stop him twice today from shooting his mouth off, first to the hot dog vendor and then a guy they'd stopped for running a red light. Discretion, she'd quickly come to realise, was not Vic's strongest quality and if the press got wind of what was going on, she would bet a month's salary it would be down to him.

She wondered how he was getting on out on his date with Jill and Kylan and her husband. He had talked constantly about it all day. Seemed to think he might get lucky with Jill tonight.

Poor girl.

Rebecca laughed to herself. Jill probably had no idea what she was letting herself in for.

Leaving the TV playing, she went into her kitchen and started rummaging through the various packet meals in the refrigerator for something to have for dinner. Her mother would have a fit if she saw the type of food Rebecca had been eating since she'd moved to Juniper.

Rebecca was the only one of her daughters who couldn't cook and, if it hadn't been for the invention of the microwave oven, she suspected that she would probably be spending most of her evenings either eating out or buying takeaway food.

At least she had plenty of the packet meals to keep her going for a while. During her visit to the grocery store with Vic, Rebecca had taken the opportunity to load her basket as full as possible. Of course, he had complained bitterly when the time came to pay, but Rebecca had threatened to go tell his friend, Kylan, who stood in the queue next to them, all about his little adventure in the sewer. It had worked, she guessed, because he didn't want word to get back to Kylan's sister, and he paid up without another word. As far as she was concerned, they were even, but she got the distinct impression that Vic felt she was one up on him and she had been watching her back for the last couple of days, not sure what to expect. Maybe she would get lucky, and he'd elope with Jill tonight. Then she wouldn't have to worry any more.

Her thoughts were interrupted by a loud knocking on her door.

Replacing her ready meal dinner back on the refrigerator shelf, she straightened, wondering who was there.

The knocking came again, sharp and persistent.

'Okay, I'm coming,' Rebecca yelled, irritated at the caller's impatience. Not bothering to enquire who it was, she pulled the door wide open.

She wished she hadn't when she saw Joel Hickok standing on her doorstep looking completely different out of his suit, dressed in jeans and T-shirt, but still wearing a cocky look on his face. She screwed up her nose, making no attempt to hide her disdain.

'Oh, it's you.'

Hickok gave her a crooked grin. 'That's a nice greeting, Angell.'

Not waiting for an invitation, he pushed his way into her apartment and glanced around, nodding. 'Nice pad, so long as you're not planning on swinging any cats.'

Rebecca gave an irritated sigh, not in the mood for his sarcastic attempt at humour. She had hoped not to see his face until after the weekend. 'What do you want, Hickok?' she snapped, feeling agitated.

'What do I want? That's nice. Get straight to the point.' He cocked an eyebrow. 'Shouldn't you offer to make me a coffee or something? I have just driven all the way over here.'

'To insult my apartment?'

'No, actually we're going out.'

'Out?'

'Yeah, we're gonna go do a little moonlighting.'

'Moonlighting?' Rebecca repeated, not liking the sound of the idea.

'Yeah, moonlighting. There are a couple of things I think we should check out over at the college.'

'But it's Saturday night.'

Hickok glanced briefly at the TV set. 'Well, you don't look like you have anything better to do.'

Rebecca couldn't believe his nerve.

'You can't do this,' she argued, shaking her head. 'You can't just barge in here and tell me we're going exploring over at the college on a Saturday night.'

'Sure I can.' Hickok slumped down on the couch. 'You see, Max's wife Rita is in town and they're out to dinner, so I need a temporary partner.'

'Who I figure is me.'

'Look, don't flatter yourself. It was between you and Boaz, okay?' His eyes skimmed over her body, coming to rest on her face. 'You're easier to look at.'

'Seriously?' Rebecca pulled a face, colour rushing to her cheeks. 'You're unbelievable,' she muttered, more to herself than to Hickok.

He grinned at her and raised his eyebrows questioningly. 'So, what do you say?'

How about 'Get lost, Hickok, and let me have Saturday night to myself'?

Keeping her thoughts to herself, knowing she should kick him out, but also curious about what he wanted to check out at the college, she smiled sweetly at him. 'Can't this wait until after the weekend?'

'No, it can't.'

'So, you have more information?'

'Not exactly. I just want to go over a few things.'

Oh great! He just wants to go over things.

'This is crazy. Give me one good reason why I should say yes.'

Hickok glanced at *ER* playing on the TV. 'What? You'd rather stay here and have a night in with Doctor Ross?'

Rebecca glowered at him. 'No. I had planned to go to the movies.'

'What, alone?'

'Is there anything wrong with that?'

Hickok shook his head looking amused. 'I guess not. Look, come on, just humour me, okay? We either find what I'm looking for, or I'm wrong and I end up looking like an idiot. Either way, I'll buy you pizza on the way home.'

'You think I want to eat with you?'

Hickok grinned. 'Don't be so picky, Angell. I don't think you're gonna get any other guys showing up on your doorstep tonight, do you?'

Rebecca scowled, wishing she had a baseball handy.

For once, realising that he'd overstepped the mark, he apologised. 'Look, help me out here and I'll put in a good word for you with Krigg, okay?'

'You promise?'

'I promise.'

She nodded, not quite sure what she was letting herself in for. 'Okay, wait here while I go get my jacket.'

* * *

Twenty minutes later they arrived at the college. Hickok drove again and, although Rebecca didn't bother to argue about the speed limit, she scowled disapprovingly at the speedometer.

Getting into the main building proved easy. Although they found the doors locked, Hickok soon located a night caretaker who asked no questions once the Fed had flashed his badge, and willingly provided them with a set of keys.

Still unsure exactly what they were doing there, Rebecca followed Hickok along the empty, dimly lit corridors, some of which she recognised from their previous visit, trying to remember the name of the horror flick she'd seen years earlier where in a similar setting a maniac with a knife had sliced up a bunch of kids attending a student dance.

Eventually they stopped outside a classroom.

'This is the one,' Hickok told her, unlocking the door and pushing it open.

'This is the one what?' Rebecca asked, following him inside.

He didn't answer her question. 'Close the door behind you. I don't want anyone finding us in here.'

'Why? The night caretaker already knows we're here.'

'Yeah, but I don't want anyone else to know we are.' Hickok looked up and met her eyes. For once he looked serious. 'So just close the door, okay?'

Rebecca did as she was told, not sure that she felt very comfortable being alone in a dark classroom with Hickok. She was about to flick the light switch on when she saw him pull a miniature flashlight from his pocket. Switching it on, he headed over to the desk at the front of the room. Rebecca glanced around the classroom at the empty desks, thinking how creepy the room looked without the usual chatter of students. Still unsure about being there, she joined Hickok over by the main desk, where he was already trying to get the drawers open.

Finding them locked, he pulled another bunch of keys from his pocket and proceeded to test each one in the lock.

Rebecca felt her heartbeat quicken. 'Hey, where did you get those?'

Hickok answered her, not even bothering to look up. 'They're friends of mine. Never know when you might need them.'

'Are they legal?'

'Legal, illegal, it's a fuzzy line, Angell.'

Giving up with the key he was trying, he moved on to the next one on the ring.

Rebecca glanced round at the door, half expecting someone to walk through and catch them at any moment. She could just imagine Hickok causing her to lose her job. Had she realised what exactly he'd meant when he said he was going exploring over at the college, she would have refused. He looked up at her, apparently sensing her unease.

'Look, relax, Angell. It's not a felony, okay?'

'Yeah, sure.' Pulling up a chair in the front row of the class, she sat down. 'So, seeing as you dragged me down here, I think you at least owe me the courtesy of telling me why exactly we are here.'

Hickok tried another key. 'You remember the professor I talked to on Wednesday, Lawrence Parker?'

'Yes.'

'This is his classroom. I just want to have a snoop around in his things.'

Rebecca raised an eyebrow. 'Well, why didn't you just look in his desk when you were last here? I'm sure he would have shown you.'

'Because I didn't have a search warrant, and I wasn't going be able to get one because he hadn't done anything wrong.'

'So, if he hasn't done anything wrong, why pick on the poor guy?'

'Because I've got a hunch, okay?' Hickok tried another key in the lock. This one turned and the drawer pulled open. At the click of the lock, he glanced up and grinned. Rebecca went to join him, perching herself on the edge of the desk.

'So what's this hunch, then?'

'Jeez you ask a lot of questions.'

'Then maybe you shouldn't have brought me.'

Hickok looked at her and gave a frustrated sigh. 'Look, the guy just didn't seem to be acting right. He was too calm, too prepared. And he definitely knew more than he was letting on about Emma Keeley.'

'We don't know for sure that Emma Keeley is dead,' Rebecca argued.

Hickok let out a sour laugh. 'She's dead. Don't doubt it.' He returned his attention to Parker's desk and began rummaging through the various papers in the top drawer. 'Jeez! How much crap does the guy keep in here?'

Rebecca shook her head. 'Do you really think that if this Parker guy *is* a murderer, he'd be likely to keep evidence that could be used against him in the drawer of his classroom desk?'

'Well, we have to start somewhere. We can hardly go breaking into his house.'

'Really? I'm glad to see you have some morals.'

Hickok grinned at her. 'Hey, I'm a nice guy, Angell. You just haven't given me a chance.' Closing the top drawer, he opened the bottom one. He pulled out a picture. A snapshot of a young woman. 'Hey, nice-looking lady,' he muttered in approval.

Rebecca recognised the face.

'Here, let me see that.' She took the picture from him and studied the young blonde-haired woman closely. 'I know her; this is Kylan.'

'Kylan?'

'Yeah, she's a friend of Vic's.'

Hickok pulled a face. 'Why would someone who looks like that want to hang around with someone like Boaz?'

Rebecca grinned. 'She's the sister of one of his ex-girlfriends. We ran into her a couple of days ago.'

'So this Kylan knows Parker?'

'Yeah... she's his wife,' Rebecca told him, casting her mind back to the conversation in the grocery store.

'His wife? Hey, small world.'

Rebecca shook her head.

'I can't believe I didn't make the connection before.'

'Well don't beat yourself up, Angell. You're just a cop. It's us guys in the suits that get paid to figure out the clever stuff.'

She glared at him. 'You know what? I think I'd like you a lot more if you didn't speak.'

Hickok glanced up and met her eyes. He gave a wry smile. 'No, I don't think so, Angell. I think you like me fine just the way I am.'

Rebecca felt herself redden. She broke away from his stare, wondering why it was that she got so easily embarrassed by his teasing comments. It wasn't as though what he said was true. *Was it?*

She watched as he slowly emptied the contents of the bottom drawer onto the desktop, half hoping that he wouldn't find what he was looking for, if only to see him proved wrong. That wasn't the only reason. Whilst she had every sympathy for the victims and wanted their killer to be apprehended, it just didn't seem right to violate this Parker guy's rights when they had not a shred of evidence against him, except Hickok's hunch.

A small pastel-pink envelope came out of the drawer. *Lawrie* was typed in black ink on the front. Hickok started to remove the letter inside. Rebecca widened her eyes, not believing what he was doing.

'Hey, you can't open that,' she protested.

Hickok glanced up. 'Sure I can.'

'It's private.'

'And when I'm done, I'll put it back and no one will be the wiser.'

'My God, is nothing sacred to you?' Rebecca shook her head. 'I'll bet you were the kid who read his sister's diary, weren't you?'

'Brothers.'

'What?'

He looked up at her with a grin.

'I don't have a sister, Angell. I have brothers.'

'Like I care,' Rebecca mumbled under her breath.

There was just one plain sheet of notepaper inside, the same shade of pink as the envelope. Hickok read the content of the letter to himself and nodded.

'I thought so.'

'What?' Rebecca asked, curious to know what he had found. He glanced at her, a mischievous glint in his eyes. 'I thought you weren't a snoop, Angell?'

'I'm not a snoop, but if it's important to the case I think I should see what the letter says.'

'Really?' Hickok teased.

She reached for the letter. 'Yes, really.'

He pulled it away so that she missed. 'Just admit it, Angell, you're a snoop.'

Rebecca made a second grab for the letter, this time getting hold of it. 'I am not a snoop, you stupid jerk,' she said, tearing it from his fingers.

She read the words on the paper, written in the same type as on the envelope.

I have to see you tonight. Meet me at The Coven, Emma

She glanced up at Hickok, irritated by the smug grin on his face. 'Okay, so you found a letter. So what? That doesn't prove Lawrence Parker is a killer.'

Hickok grinned. 'Nope, it doesn't, but I have a hunch that he is, and you have just had proof, Angell, that my hunches are always right.'

13

Kylan was glad that she'd decided to have a go at clearing out the spare room. There were a lot of things that needed sorting out and it was a job that she had been putting off. With Lawrie out of the house all day, it was the perfect opportunity, and she had no excuse to avoid it any longer.

Most things were piled into boxes and old bin liners. There was a lot of old junk: spare bed linen, clothes and unwanted wedding gifts. Things they'd brought with them when they'd moved and had never got around to finding a place for. As neither of them tended to use the room it had turned into a general dumping ground with all sorts of things finding a home among the bags.

Although she had worked hard for most of the afternoon, Kylan knew that the job was nowhere near finished. The contents of many of the boxes were still strewn across the floor and, with the exception of a few books and ornaments that had been taken downstairs, only the clothes in the bin liners had been sorted and packed away neatly in a case beneath the pine bed. At least she had made a start, which meant she would be more inclined to make sure the job got finished.

Lawrie, on arriving home, had been surprised she'd bothered. He seemed happy enough it was being taken care of, though, and left her to it. Kylan got completely distracted by the chaos that had been created and, when she eventually looked at her wrist-watch, she was shocked to find it was almost seven thirty.

Shit! Thirty minutes before Vic and Jill get here.

Cursing at Lawrie for not reminding her of the time, she left the room in a state of disarray and headed to the bathroom for a shower. When the doorbell rang thirty-five minutes later, she was wrapped in a towel, standing in her closet and deciding what to wear.

Lawrie was dispatched downstairs to pour their guests a drink while she finished getting ready and she had settled for a cream shift dress that accentuated her curves and showed off her tan. Quickly she ran a brush through her hair, applied a little make-up and dabbed her favourite perfume. With a final glance in the mirror, she left the room.

The reservation at Angelo's was for eight thirty. The four of them arrived fifteen minutes late. As they entered the restaurant Kylan heard Lawrie apologising to Vic, muttering something about women and timekeeping. She gave him a sharp poke in the ribs, and he turned and smiled at her.

'Watch it, Mr Parker,' she warned, a teasing glint in her eye.

Lawrie put an arm across her shoulder and pulled her close. 'Whatever you say, Mrs Parker.'

Vic snorted and raised his eyebrows at Jill.

'Young love, eh? I give all this mushy stuff another year, tops.'

'Cynic,' Kylan told him and the four of them laughed.

Jill Boleyn, Vic's date, seemed nice. A similar age to Kylan, she had a bubbly personality and didn't seem to take Vic too seriously, which was probably for the best. She was pretty and very much his type, with tawny brown hair that hung in ringlets around her face and deep blue eyes. She was tall too, probably not far off six foot, and had a wide grin that surfaced every few seconds.

Kylan was surprised to discover she was a doctor at the local hospital. With the exception of Tania, all of Vic's previous wives and girlfriends had seemed somewhat intellectually challenged. Maybe he was setting his sights a little higher these days.

The evening went smoothly. Vic and Lawrie, although chalk and cheese, got on well, and after dinner they went to a nearby bar, one which Vic frequented so knew a lot of people there. The whole time they were there, a stream of people, mainly fellow cops, kept stopping by to slap him on the back. Kylan had always known Vic was popular with women but was surprised to find out he was popular with guys too. Maybe they saw him as some kind of stud. At thirty-four he was living the high life whilst most of his colleagues were married off with kids and mortgages. Maybe they envied his lifestyle.

Did Lawrie envy his single life?

Although he never gave any hint that he was unhappy being married, Kylan knew only too well that overall appearances could be deceiving. Deceiving, misleading and ultimately dangerous.

'You still with us, Kylan?' Vic's deep voice broke through her thoughts.

She smiled at him and took the glass of white wine that he offered. 'I'm here, just my mind wandering.'

'I see. Our company not interesting enough for you?' Vic teased, giving Jill a knowing wink.

Kylan laughed. 'Vic, you lead the most colourful life I know. How could I possibly not find you interesting?'

Her comment brought smiles to the faces of Lawrie and Jill.

Vic also looked pleased, evidently taking her words as a compliment. 'You know, you guys will have to come ride with me and my partner, Angell, when we're out on patrol one day. See what it's like to be a cop.'

Kylan glanced at Lawrie and pulled a face. Apparently, she was wrong, and he had misconstrued her comment, applying it to his professional rather than personal life. The idea of riding around the city all day with Vic wasn't really her idea of fun and she struggled for a polite way to refuse his invite, glad when Lawrie stepped in with an excuse.

'It sounds fun, Vic. We'll have to take a rain check though. We're both pretty busy with work at the moment.'

Vic nodded. 'No problem. You just give me a call when you have some free time.'

'We'll do that.'

'Of course, I'll probably run into you on campus a few times over the next couple of weeks anyway.'

Kylan raised a brow. 'You will?'

Jill also looked interested. 'Thinking about furthering your education, Vic?'

Vic snorted. 'Hardly! We have got that dead student thing, though.'

His eyes met Kylan's as he spoke, and she glanced uneasily down at her napkin. She hoped the subject would be dropped as quickly as it was raised.

Jill seemed keen for more details. 'Yeah, I read about that in the paper. Some football player was killed, right?'

'Scott Jagger,' Vic told her. 'You know it was me and Angell who found his body.'

'You're kidding.'

'No, the guy was toes up in the sewer. I found the second guy as well.'

The second guy?

As far as Kylan was aware, Scott Jagger had been the only one found. A sick feeling welled in the pit of her stomach. She glanced at Lawrie who, like her, had bowed out of the conversation. He appeared to be listening intently to what Vic had to say while absent-mindedly swirling the ice around in his vodka glass.

Jill shook her head. 'There was a second guy?'

'Yeah, Rufus Lind,' Vic explained, only too eager to share the information.

'Jeez! Two murders. That's kind of a spooky coincidence after everything that happened at the college before. Do you think it's the same guy?'

Vic shrugged. 'It's doubtful. More likely we have a copycat. They're not the only victims either. There's a girl as well.'

'A girl?'

'Yeah, some pianist called Emma Keeley.'

'You've found her body?' Lawrie spoke suddenly.

Kylan noticed his voice sounded strained.

Vic nodded. 'Well, we haven't actually found her body yet, but the Feds are pretty sure she's dead.'

Kylan swallowed hard, starting to feel nauseous. She looked to Lawrie for reassurance as the conversation between Jill and Vic became a blur. His attention, though, had returned to the glass in his hand and he looked a million miles away. Trying to block out what Vic was saying, she focused on her husband's face, curious about his reaction to the news that Emma Keeley was missing. Right now, she needed him, and he didn't seem to be there for her.

You've found her body?

The way Lawrie had asked Vic, it was as though he already knew Emma was missing. If that was the case, how come he hadn't said anything to her? The thought struck her that maybe

Lawrie knew more about what had happened to Emma Keeley than he was letting on. She could think of no other reason why he would intentionally keep the news from her. So much for sharing. That was what a marriage was supposed to be about, wasn't it? Sharing and honesty and remaining faithful to one another.

Emma Keeley had been a big temptation. There had never been any doubt about that.

Beautiful, clever, popular and graceful, she was by far the most stunning girl on the campus, and it was down to that fact alone that every single student knew her name. She was the perfect catch for any guy.

Quit beating yourself up and being so suspicious. Lawrie doesn't know anything and the only reason he hasn't told you that Emma Keeley had disappeared is because he doesn't want to worry you.

Her attempt to reassure herself wasn't really working, and Kylan found herself watching Lawrie, studying his dark eyes and expressionless face and wondering just how much she could trust the man she had married.

* * *

The house wasn't difficult to find.

Aside from looking up the address at college, Justine had followed Lawrie home the previous night. Not having a car of her own, she had had to take a cab and a small surge of excitement welled in her stomach as she remembered climbing in the back seat and instructing the driver to follow the car in front. Just like in the movies: close enough to ensure they didn't lose him but keeping enough distance between them to make sure they weren't seen.

The driver hadn't asked any questions. That had surprised her a little. Maybe he was used to strange requests. That, or perhaps he just wanted his money. When he had dropped her off at the end of the road, he'd offered to wait for her, but Lawrie didn't live too far away from the college and Justine decided that walking was better than paying the return fare. Besides, she wanted to check out where Lawrie lived, and she wouldn't be able to do that very well with some cab driver hanging around.

Justine had cautiously made her way down the road she'd seen his car turn into, hoping that he wasn't still outside. After all, she didn't want to risk running into him. Fortunately, the road had been empty and Lawrie's house easy to find, standing right at the end of the row. The front porch light was on, and two windows had light coming from them.

So, this was where he lived.

Justine had ended up hanging around the house for close to an hour. Desperate to get closer, but too scared of being seen. It was then she'd decided she would come back when the place was empty. She'd already overheard Lawrie discussing a dinner date that he and Kylan had planned with friends for Saturday night and figured that it would be as good a time as any to pay a visit. Now she was here though, she wasn't so sure.

There were two lights on inside the house. One that came from the hall, the other from what was probably the living room. The same two lights that had been on the previous night. Maybe they were still there or perhaps the date had been cancelled. A lot of people left lights on when they went out, though, to deter people from breaking in.

To deter people like you.

Justine pushed the thought from her mind. It wasn't as though she was planning to steal anything. She only wanted to look around. She returned her attention to the house. Aside from the two lights, there was nothing else to indicate anyone was home.

On the other hand, there's nothing to indicate anyone isn't.

A chance she was going to have to take. Now she had paid another cab fare to get here there was no way she was turning around and going back. Slowly she began to edge towards the driveway, her eyes cautiously checking the houses either side. Although they were separated by bushes, there was no way of telling if someone was watching her through a crack in the curtains. Maybe even calling the police.

Maybe. Maybe not. If she walked away now, she knew she would later regret it.

What if I get caught?

The thought was scary. If Lawrie found out what she was doing, she would die of embarrassment.

She weighed it up against how badly she wanted to see the inside of his house, to see the bathroom where he showered, the wardrobe full of his clothes, the bed where he slept.

You won't get caught. Not if you're careful.

Convincing herself she was right, Justine opened the gate and stepped into the garden, oblivious to the pair of eyes watching her from across the street.

14

Entry into the house was easy.

Had she had to break a window to get in, Justine would have turned around and gone back to campus. She wasn't a criminal or a vandal and, however much she wanted to see the inside of Lawrie's house, she wouldn't cause any damage.

Her initial plan had been to check for unlocked doors or windows. She knew that back in the small town where she had grown up, people were constantly forgetting to shut windows before they went out. Hopefully Kylan and Lawrie had the same bad habit.

She tried every door and window on the ground floor, taking extra caution when she was round the front of the house not to be seen by any neighbours. All were locked securely. Finally realising that she wasn't going to get in that way, Justine admitted defeat and moved to her second – and less likely to be successful – plan of checking for hidden keys.

She checked the top of the back door, underneath a row of flowerpots that stood on the backyard patio and tried to get into the shed, without success. Then she tried the two flowerpots that sat either side of the small fishpond next to the shed. Her heart skipped a beat as she saw the small silver key hidden beneath where the second flowerpot had been sitting.

She'd found it.

Thinking how easy it had been, she took the key and replaced the flowerpot, then made her way back up to the house. She headed for the back door, hoping that the key would fit so she wouldn't have to go around the front and risk being seen by anyone who might happen to be passing by.

As she slipped the key into the lock it crossed her mind for a fleeting second that it might not be a house key. The shed had been locked and was right next to the pond. Maybe she wasn't going to be as lucky as she'd initially thought.

You might only get to see the inside of Lawrie's shed instead.

The key seemed to fit. Holding her breath, she turned it in the lock. It moved easily and she was relieved to hear the click as the door unlocked. Tentatively she pushed down on the handle and eased the door open.

She found herself looking into what appeared to be a small cloakroom. The light wasn't on, but the moon shining through the window covered everything with a pale hue. Justine stepped inside, carefully closing the door behind her, and glanced around.

A rack on the opposite wall was filled with various coats and jackets. Looking closer, she recognised a cream-coloured suede jacket that she had seen Kylan wearing around campus before. The walls either side were filled with wooden shelves. To Justine's left the shelves contained a mixture of video cassettes, all originally boxed, and books, both fiction and non-fiction. The shelves to the right were mainly filled with plants and ornaments.

There was no door to the cloakroom; instead, an archway

which separated the room from the rest of the house. Deciding she'd seen enough of the cloakroom, Justine headed through the archway and into a hallway that ran the full length of the house. The floor of the hall was polished wood and as she stepped on it her shoes made a loud, echoing clack. Even though she was certain there was no one home, she still felt uncomfortable making any kind of noise, so raised her feet onto tiptoe before continuing.

She conducted a quick tour of the downstairs of the house.

The peach-coloured living room with two beige couches and an elegant-looking sideboard that was partly lit by a table lamp; the kitchen, a room she avoided going into as it looked directly over the main street; and a room that seemed as though it was used as some kind of study. She wondered if this was Lawrie's secret room. A room where he could come to be alone, away from Kylan; a room where he spent a lot of time and had his deepest thoughts.

Then she saw the framed picture on the desk: Kylan and Lawrie, their arms around each other, smiling for the camera.

Feeling sick she turned away.

As she climbed the plush carpeted stairs to the bedrooms, she felt a mixture of nerves and excitement. She was almost there. Almost to the place she most wanted to see. Although it wasn't cold, she had goosebumps on her arms.

At the top of the stairs she found herself on a small landing with three white doors leading off, all of them shut. Justine opened the one closest to her. Through the darkness she could make out a bedroom. She doubted it was Lawrie's bedroom though, as the large pine bed was bare of linen, and it was scantly furnished. The room wasn't empty, however; it was littered with boxes, some full, others with their contents strewn across the floor. Justine could see photo albums, ornaments, lamps and books amongst the clutter. This was obviously just a spare room used for storing junk.

She was tempted to root through the photo albums, see if she could find some pictures of Lawrie when he was younger. Remembering the picture in the study stopped her. She didn't want to risk seeing any more pictures of him with Kylan and chances were that if she did look, she might find some wedding photographs. Something she definitely didn't want to see.

She closed the door to the spare room and tried the next door. This one led into the bathroom. Knowing she was at the back of the house and unlikely to alert suspicion, Justine pulled at the light switch cord. Light fell onto the room and the extractor fan started to whirl, making her jump. The bathroom suite was deep forest green with gold-coloured fixtures, and the room had been decorated with a coastal theme. Decorative white and gold starfish and sea horses hung by hooks from the wall forming a border around the bathtub; the toilet and toothbrush holders were in the shapes of crabs; and several large white shells sat on the vanity unit containing soaps and bath oils.

Above the vanity unit was a mirrored medicine cabinet. Justine pulled the door open and glanced inside at the shelves crammed with bottles and tubes. Spotting a packet of condoms jutting out from behind a bottle of sleeping pills, she quickly closed the mirrored door.

A towel rack stood next to the bathtub, and two large cream towels were draped over it. The top one still looked damp.

Was this Lawrie's towel? Had he used it to dry himself after his shower, before he went out this evening? She picked up the towel and held it to her nose. It smelt of musky soap.

Glancing at the shelves again, she noticed that one of the soaps sat in a shallow pool of water. She imagined Lawrie in the shower using the soap to cleanse his skin before stepping out of the water and into the towel. She rubbed the towel against her cheek. It felt soft and fluffy and slightly damp from where it had been used.

This was the closest she had come to Lawrie, and she planned to savour every moment. Stepping over to the vanity unit, she turned on the hot water faucet, picked up the bar of soap, held it under the warm running water then caressed it against her cheek. She rubbed it against her skin, building up a lather, before replacing the soap and rinsing her face under the faucet. She returned to the towel and buried her face in it, thinking about how she was using Lawrie's towel and Lawrie's soap.

When her face was dry she took his toothbrush from the crab holder. It was easy to tell which of the two brushes belonged to him. One was pink and one was green; Lawrie's had to be the green one. Squeezing minty toothpaste onto the bristles, she began to brush her teeth. She watched herself in the large mirror on the wall, feeling now that she was really part of Lawrie. What would he say if he could see her standing here in his bathroom, using his things as if they were her own? What would her classmates back at college think if they knew she was here in his house?

For a moment she felt proud, privileged. Then she started to feel slightly ridiculous.

Jeez! Look at you, Justine. You've broken into someone's house and you're using their soap and toothbrush.

What kind of freak are you?

Feeling colour rush to her cheeks, Justine removed the toothbrush from her mouth and spat the paste out into the washbasin. She quickly wiped her mouth dry with the back of her hand and rinsed the toothbrush clean before replacing it in the holder. Checking everything was how she had found it, she tugged the light switch off and left the bathroom.

Given how irrationally she had just behaved, she wondered whether or not she should continue her search. Maybe it would be for the best if she left and forgot the whole thing.

Besides, she didn't want to risk Lawrie and Kylan coming home and finding her. If they arrived home and she was still upstairs, she'd never be able to get out without them seeing her.

Feeling a twinge of disappointment, but knowing she was making the right decision, she headed for the stairs. She glanced back briefly over her shoulder at the one door she hadn't tried: the door to Lawrie's bedroom.

She wondered what it was like, what colour his sheets were, what personal objects he had in there.

A quick look won't hurt.

She had to go. She had to go before they came home.

Just one quick look. You'll only be ten seconds.

If they came back and caught her.

They won't catch you, Justine. You're already here, just moments away from what you really want to see.

Drawing in a shaky breath, Justine turned and climbed back up to the landing. She went straight to the last door and clasped her hand on the knob. Before entering she hesitated, questioning again whether she was doing the right thing.

Go on. This is what you've been waiting for, isn't it?

Slowly she twisted the knob, eased the door open and stepped inside.

The room was larger than she had imagined, pale and shadowy from the light of the moon. The bed was on the opposite wall to the door, in the centre of the room, and was large and brass and kind of old-fashioned looking. Justine wondered if maybe it was one that had been passed down in the family. The sheets on the bed were plain and pale, blue she thought, though it was difficult to tell in the darkness, and on both sides of the bed were small white cabinets, each holding a brass lamp. The closets in the room ran the full length of the left wall. They were white and louvered with gold-coloured handles. There were four doors, one of them partially opened. Unable to help herself, Justine headed for the open door.

Was this the closet that contained Lawrie's clothes, the blue jeans and black sweater that he so often wore in class? She pulled the door fully open. The closet was walk-in and contained several dresses and blouses. On the floor were shoes, some heeled, some flat.

Kylan's closet.

Undeterred, Justine moved on to the second closet. Opening the door, she found what she was looking for. Jeans, shirts, sweaters, sneakers. She stepped inside Lawrie's closet and went through the entire rack of clothes, touching everything, before taking a shirt off the hanger and slipping it over her own sleeve-less blouse. She liked the way it felt against her bare arms, so soft and silky smooth, and the way it smelt of his cologne. Standing in the closet, wearing Lawrie's shirt, Justine imagined a scenario where Kylan was out of town and she had accompanied Lawrie back to the house. Back to the house where they had spent the night making passionate love. She glanced over her shoulder at the brass bed, visualising the crumpled pastel sheets where their bodies had lain entwined. The next morning, she had dressed in one of Lawrie's shirts and wandered around the house in front of him, teasing him with the knowledge that she was completely naked underneath.

The fantasy was good. Slipping off the shirt she returned it to the hanger and looked for other clothes she could try on. Folded on a shelf within the closet, she found a collection of ties. Justine had never seen Lawrie in a tie before. For college he favoured sweaters and T-shirts; she imagined he looked pretty sexy all dressed up in a suit and tie. Removing a black-and-green checked tie from the shelf, she unfolded it and slipped it round her neck.

She lifted the collar of her blouse and fed the tie underneath, then fastened it into place. She glanced at her reflection in the closet mirror that hung on the inside of the door, thinking about how she was wearing a tie against her neck that had at some point been against Lawrie's neck.

The tie still on, she walked out of the closet wondering what else she would find in the bedroom that belonged to him. An old-fashioned white dressing table stood on elegant carved legs in the corner of the room, next to a freestanding full-length mirror. The dressing table seemed to mostly contain Kylan's things: perfume, moisturising creams, delicate chains and earrings in a little crystal trinket bowl, a pine brush and mirror set.

Nothing of Lawrie's. Nothing of any interest to Justine.

She moved on to the white units that ran along the wall next to the dressing table. Filled with glass vases, some containing flowers, some empty, brass patterned picture frames containing photographs that she swiftly skipped, candle holders, the wax of the candles nearly burnt away, and little wooden bowls containing potpourri.

On the end of the unit sat a CD player, and on a shelf directly above was a collection of discs. Justine glanced briefly through the titles: mostly a mixture of soul and classical. Different genres, but very romantic.

Did Lawrie and Kylan make love to this music? Maybe with candles burning in the background to create a romantic setting? Justine pushed the thought from her mind. The idea of them making love made her feel ill. The idea that they even slept together in that brass bed made her feel ill.

She looked at the bed and wondered which side Lawrie slept on, before realising there was an easy way to tell: the two bedside tables. Each had a drawer which was bound to contain personal items. It should be easy to tell which one belonged to Lawrie. Excited, Justine made her way across to the left-hand side of the bed and, sitting down on the edge of the firm mattress, pulled the drawer of the table open. It contained cufflinks, menthol sweets and a couple of well-worn paperbacks. Knowing that she was on the right side of the bed, Justine closed the drawer and laid her head down on the pastel pillow. She closed her eyes and buried her face in the soft cotton. It smelt as though it had been freshly laundered and had the scent of warm and musky fabric conditioner. It smelt of Lawrie.

She was here, where she wanted to be, and never wanted to leave. Perhaps if she went to sleep, when she awoke, she would find him in bed beside her. She inhaled deeply and hugged the pillow tighter. Now she had laid her head down, Justine realised just how tired she was. If she could sleep for just a little while, no one would be any the wiser.

Would they?

The sound of a car engine startled her from her fantasy. Her eyes sprang wide open and she sat up fast.

Shit! Lawrie and Kylan.

Knowing that time was of the essence and that she couldn't risk being caught, she moved quickly, closing the closet doors and straightening the sheets where she had been lying. She left the room and quietly but quickly made her way down the stairs, praying that she wasn't too late.

15

The Blue Moose Tavern was one of several bars situated in Juniper, but, unlike its rivals, many of whom sold poorly measured drinks at inflated prices, it had a reputation for good hard liquor and cheap beer.

On weeknights, the old jukebox at the back of the tavern pumped out John Lee Hooker, Muddy Waters and B.B. King, creating an atmosphere of smoke and blues. Saturdays and Sundays attracted local bands who kept the clientele of bikers and more earthy locals entertained with a fusion of rock, jazz and soul.

The band playing as Rebecca and Hickok entered was knocking out a loud but enthusiastic cover of 'Knock on Wood'. Rebecca had seen them play the bar before and was glad that she'd chosen the Blue Moose above the movie theatre, even though it did mean being stuck in Hickok's company. In fairness to him, after leaving the college he had kept to his word and offered to buy pizza, but Rebecca's adrenalin was still rushing from their illegal adventure, and she had suggested a drink instead.

He had looked a little surprised when she'd instructed him to pull into the tavern's parking lot, and she guessed that he probably didn't have her pegged as the kind of girl who liked to frequent blue-collar bars. The truth was that the Blue Moose reminded her of the bars back home and, while she was eager to experience city life to the full, it was comforting sometimes to go somewhere that felt familiar.

The place was rammed, and Rebecca picked her way through the crowd to get a space at the bar. She waved to Ed, spotting him pouring whiskey for customers at the far end of the counter, and he nodded to her, mouthing that he would be over in a minute.

'So, Angell, this is where you like to hang out?' Hickok leant back against the bar, observing the crowded room. Rebecca waited for a sarcastic comment, but instead he nodded his approval. 'I'm impressed.'

'You are?' she asked, studying his profile, a little taken aback.

He turned to look at her and gave a crooked smile. 'You look surprised.'

'I am, I guess.' Rebecca shrugged. 'I wasn't sure this would be your scene.'

'Really? And what did you think was my scene?'

'I don't know. You're from New York, right?'

'Born and bred.' Hickok grinned. 'You know, Angell, there are plenty of good blues clubs in Greenwich. I grew up in places like this.'

'I see,' Rebecca said, nodding, not sure that she liked having anything in common with Joel Hickok. She was tempted to ask him how come he'd grown up to be such a jerk, but seeing as they were getting on reasonably well, she decided it was best to leave it. She was fed up with fighting all the time. If it wasn't with Hickok, it was with Vic. She might as well make the most of Hickok's good mood while it lasted.

Ed finished serving his customers and came over to them. He grinned at Rebecca.

'Hello, stranger, haven't seen you in a while. Gotta be a whole three days?' He winked at her. 'That's some kind of record, I believe.'

'Come on, Ed. You'll be giving people the impression I'm some kind of lush.'

'Now, there's a thought,' Hickok commented, smirking when Ed glanced in his direction.

'I don't believe you've had the pleasure of meeting my drinking buddy, Joel Hickok,' Rebecca said dryly, waving a hand in Hickok's direction.

'Hey,' Ed grinned. 'So, are you guys dating?'

His question brought a snort from Hickok and a blush to Rebecca's cheeks.

'When hell freezes over,' she muttered, wondering why she felt embarrassed. She smiled sweetly at Ed, ignoring the smug look on Hickok's face. 'Actually, we're working together.'

Ed nodded in understanding. 'I see. You're a cop too?'

Hickok gave a derisive laugh. 'Hardly.'

Rebecca fixed him with an icy glare. 'He works for the FBI,' she explained, thinking that Hickok should return home to his mother and learn some manners. Determined not to let him rattle her, she changed the subject. 'So, Ed, have you anything nice waiting behind the bar for me?' she asked.

He laughed and nodded. 'You'll be wanting the usual, right, Rebecca?'

Hickok watched him produce a glass and a bottle of Bourbon and arched a brow.

'The usual, eh? I had you pegged as a white wine spritzer type of girl.'

'Seriously?'

She downed the shot of Bourbon Ed had poured for her. 'Another?' he asked.

She glanced at Hickok briefly before nodding at the bartender. 'Definitely.'

* * *

Joel watched Angell knock back another shot of Bourbon while nursing his second beer and thinking what a bag of contradictions she was. He had initially thought she was going to be girlish and naive, coming from a small backwoods town like Swallow Falls, but she had proved on more than one occasion that she could take care of herself. She had also proven that she was a stickler for rules, lecturing him on speeding and worrying about breaking into Lawrie Parker's classroom, which suggested that she was too strait-laced to have any vices. Yet here she was looking right at home in a rough and ready blues tavern, knocking back shots of Bourbon as if it were lemonade. He was curious to know which persona was the real Rebecca Angell.

He watched her lick the taste of Bourbon from her lips and wondered what it was that he found so appealing about her. There weren't many women in the place and, of those there were, Angell was the most underdressed in her faded jeans and black T-shirt. Unlike for work, she wore her hair loose and it fell down her back, long and straight, shining blue black in the dimmed lights.

There was something about her. Something in the way she looked and something in her attitude. She seemed streetwise yet vulnerable, and although she was sexy, she never quite managed to shrug off that image of the girl next door.

On the whole, Joel didn't have a lot of time for women. The youngest of five sons, his mother had left home when he'd still been a kid and, of his brothers, three of them were now divorced. He had formed the opinion a long time ago that marriage and relationships were too much trouble, which was why he was never prepared to involve himself with any girl who looked like she might want commitment.

With Angell it would be so easy to go to bed with her, no strings attached. Of course, he knew he couldn't. He had to keep his personal life separate from his professional life. That was what he kept telling himself each time he saw her and why he was trying so damn hard to antagonise her into hating him. Aside from loving the way she looked when she got mad, he knew that if she hated him enough, she would never sleep with him, and then he wouldn't have to worry about getting into any awkward situations with her.

Right now, it seemed as though he was doing a pretty good job. Never quite sure how she should take him, she was currently giving him the cold shoulder, her attention focused on the band in the corner of the room, who were performing a rousing rendition of 'Try a Little Tenderness'.

The music had drawn a large crowd and a handful of people had cleared a space to use as a dance floor. One couple, a fat guy with a cigar clenched between his teeth, and his partner, an ugly woman in a yellow dress, seemed oblivious to the number of people standing around them and were taking up more room than was necessary, knocking into the crowd at regular intervals, in particular a group of bikers who were seated at a table not far from them.

Joel could sense the trouble brewing before it actually happened. One of the bikers, a muscular guy with greasy blond hair and a black eye patch that made him look a little like a pirate, was looking increasingly fed up with being jostled. He managed to keep his cool until the cigar guy pushed his partner too hard and she crashed into him spilling his beer.

Jumping to his feet he shook his fist at the cigar guy.

Joel couldn't hear what was said above the music, but the threat seemed lost on the cigar guy who didn't even bother to stop dancing. As he swung the woman in the yellow dress around, Pirate took a step forward and grabbed hold of his shoulder, pulling him to a halt. The cigar guy turned on him indignantly and there was a further exchange of angry words, before he foolishly stuck out both hands and pushed Pirate away.

Seconds later, both men were wrestling on the floor with the crowd closing like a barrier around them as they cheered them on. The band, unconcerned with the furore, continued to play and Joel guessed this wasn't the first fight they had witnessed in the tavern. He turned to Angell to make a comment and found her bar stool was empty. Looking back toward the brawl, he caught sight of her dark hair as she disappeared into the crowd.

'Shit!' he muttered, taking a swig of beer and putting his bottle down on the counter. Following her, he wondered just what he was about to get himself involved in.

Any hopes that Angell had gone merely to watch were dashed the moment he heard her yelling, her voice barely audible above the music.

'Stop! Police!'

Idiot woman.

As he pushed his way to the front of the crowd, he saw her grab hold of the cigar guy, trying to drag him off Pirate who lay trapped beneath him on the floor. Briefly releasing his grip on Pirate, cigar guy lashed out with his elbow, knocking Angell flying back into the crowd. There was laughter, a loud cheer and a couple of people started clapping.

One guy yelled out loudly, 'You go get him, sweetheart!'

Looking a little disgruntled, Angell climbed to her feet, dusting down her jeans. Joel shook his head, swearing under his breath as he watched her move in for a second attempt. Damn Rebecca Angell.

Pirate had seized the opportunity she had given him to get out from beneath cigar guy and both men were now on their feet, arms wrapped tightly around each other, performing some kind of bizarre dance. Without warning, Angell launched herself at cigar guy, this time successfully catching hold of his left arm and twisting it behind his back.

Cursing loudly, Joel pushed his way in behind Pirate, trapping him easily in a headlock, and between the two of them they managed to pull both men apart. Although Pirate relented, seeming almost relieved to be pulled out of the fight, cigar guy wasn't so forgiving, and Joel watched him fight furiously against Angell as she struggled to catch a hold of his right arm. Without warning, he lurched forward, sending her flying over his head. As she landed in an ungraceful heap on the floor, he glanced up, locking his sights again on Pirate. Seeing cigar guy's raised fist heading towards him, Pirate jerked in Joel's grip. He managed to duck at the last moment, and Joel felt the smack of the fist as it landed on his jaw. Dazed, he staggered back a couple of steps, fighting to keep hold of Pirate and the two of them tumbled to the floor. As he pushed the biker off him, the cavalry finally arrived in the shape of Ed and two other guys, and between them they caught hold of cigar guy.

Angell, still on the floor, glanced around. As she caught sight of Joel, her eyes widened.

'Shit!' she muttered, crawling across to where he was sitting. 'Are you okay?'

He glared at her. 'I just got thumped in the face, Angell. Do I look okay?'

She stared at him for a long moment, seeming more amused than sorry.

Joel shook his head incredulously. 'Jeez, Angell! Aren't you even going to apologise?'

'Apologise for what?'

'For this! I just got hit because of you.'

'Because of me?' This time it was Angell's turn to look shocked. 'If I remember correctly, Hickok, I never asked you to get involved. I was doing fine all by myself.'

Joel snorted in contempt. 'Yes, of course you were, Angell. You were doing a great job of getting thrown over his shoulder.'

He watched her shake her head in disgust. 'I can't believe what an arrogant, bull-headed pig you are. Every time you do something nice, you have to go and follow it up by being a jerk.' She got to her feet, staring down at him with her hands on her hips, her green eyes flashing angrily. 'Look, Hickok, I'm sorry that *I* got you involved in this brawl, and I'm sorry if you think I was rude for not apologising to you, but you know what? I'm not sorry that you got smacked in the face and I hope it hurts like hell tomorrow.'

Her little speech finished she turned defiantly on her heel and, holding her head up high, stormed through the crowd and out of the bar.

Joel watched her go, hating himself for being such a jerk to her and annoyed that he was even more attracted to her than before. He did not have time for a stupid crush. There was a killer out there who needed to be caught, a killer who they had barely any leads on, who could be ready to strike again at any time, meanwhile here he was sniffing around after a rookie police officer. Muttering to himself that he should learn to get his priorities right, he climbed to his feet and followed Angell out of the door.

16

Vic dropped Kylan and Lawrie off just before eleven.

They had left the bar early, Kylan had feigned a headache so she could get home, and she was pleased when they declined to come in for coffee; Jill saying she had to work the next day; and Vic claiming to have an early morning game of racquet ball arranged with one of his work buddies.

It wasn't that she hadn't enjoyed their company. In fact, the evening had gone well. She just felt a little uncomfortable about the conversation that had taken place about the murders and longed to be in the more familiar surroundings of her own home.

Lawrie had also seemed pleased to be home early. He looked tired after spending the whole day at college and Kylan guessed he couldn't wait to get to bed. He went up first while she stayed down to lock up and make coffee. She took him up a cup and he sat in bed drinking it while she went into the bathroom to wash the make-up from her face and brush her teeth.

When she returned to the bedroom, she slipped out of the dress that had received such approving looks from both Lawrie and Vic, hung it back up in her closet and changed into the silky pink chemise that Lawrie had bought her for her birthday. She climbed into bed beside him and planted a kiss on his cheek, then settled back against her pillow to read more of her book. Now that she didn't have to worry about dinner plans and strange men at the window, she figured it would be easier to concentrate. That, and knowing that Lawrie was in the house with her. Despite her hopes, her mind continued to wander, replaying snippets of the conversation that had taken place earlier that evening. Every time she tried to concentrate on a page, her mind kept flashing colourful visions of Emma Keeley, Scott Jagger and Rufus Lind. She tried to relax by breathing deeply, listening all the time to the perpetual sound of Lawrie's soft breathing as he drifted into a deep sleep.

Eventually she gave up on reading. Slipping her bookmark into the page, she set down the book on the nightstand and told herself for the hundredth time that she had nothing to worry about. Everything was going to be fine.

* * *

Catherine Maloney hadn't been looking for a boyfriend, hadn't even wanted a boyfriend. She had conjured up quite a reputation as a flirt during her three years on campus, and enjoyed her popularity with the male students, always happy to play the field. However, the first time she laid eyes on Aidan Reilly she was forced to change her mind.

She had met him in The Coven, where he'd been trying to catch her eye, trying to charm her with a devilish smile. She had in turn played games for a while, one minute looking back, the next flinging her arms around various male friends. Finally, fed up with waiting for him to make a move, she had thrown caution to the wind and gone across to introduce herself.

They had soon got talking. Catherine learned that he was twenty-five, new to the area and had recently gotten a job as an intern at the local hospital. He had bought her a drink and the two of them had spent the evening flirting with each other. At the end of the night as he got up to leave, he had suddenly leaned forward and kissed her full on the lips. It had been a warm and passionate kiss, a lover's kiss, not one shared between two strangers in a bar, and she had watched him leave with her mind in a spin.

He hadn't told her he would call, but Catherine knew he would be in touch again and for the next few days she was walking on air, talking non-stop about him to all of her close friends. It had been on Friday morning that she'd received his note. It had been left wedged into the side of her locker in a plain white envelope, her name written in bold type across the front. Inside the envelope was a joker playing card and a plain sheet of notepaper containing a typed message.

Catherine,
Meet me Saturday midnight at the old bridge. Love, Aidan xxx

She had reread the note several times, unsure of the significance of the joker and thinking that the guy had to be crazy to believe that she would meet him in a dark and deserted place in the middle of the night. What was even crazier though was that she knew she would go. Catherine Maloney had never been one to back away from a little excitement and danger and she was desperate to see Aidan again. If it meant taking a few chances, then so be it.

As she was getting ready to go out Saturday night, it crossed her mind that she was making a foolish decision. She thought of

Scott Jagger and Rufus Lind. Both students had been found murdered only recently and she'd heard the rumours that they were victims of Professor Boone, who had returned to his old hunting ground.

The cops and the college faculty were, of course, trying to play down any chance of a connection to the infamous Alphabet Killings and, with Boone probably dead, it looked likely that there might be a copycat killer on the loose. If that were true, what proof did she have that it wasn't Aidan Reilly?

Telling herself that she was being paranoid, she pushed the notion to the back of her mind. Conveniently choosing to forget that Emma Keeley had now been missing for over a week, she concentrated on the fact that so far, the killer's victims had been male – a category that she thankfully didn't fall into.

She had decided when she had first read the note that she wouldn't tell anyone where she was going, not even Beth, her roommate, who she knew would try to talk her out of it. If any of her friends found out that she was going to the old bridge alone, they would probably insist on tagging along. Catherine didn't want anyone with her. No one was going to ruin her night with Aidan.

For once in her life, she made the effort to dress up, borrowing from Beth a short black dress that was cut too low at the front and clung dangerously to her curves and wearing it with her one pair of spike-heeled shoes. She told her roommate she had run into Aidan on Friday and that he was taking her out for a meal, and as she watched her swallow the story hook, line and sinker, she added with a smile that she shouldn't bother waiting up because if she got lucky, she probably wouldn't see her for the rest of the weekend.

Like most of the others, Beth had decided to stay in. Usually, they all went to The Coven on a Saturday night, but the murders had pretty much killed off any enthusiasm for clubbing. Instead, a group of them had arranged to meet in one of the rooms for an evening of beer and board games. Catherine thought they were being a little extreme. No place was particularly safe these days, but it was ridiculous to let a couple of murders ruin their fun. She kept her opinion to herself, though, and left her roommate, telling her to have a good time.

As she wasn't meeting Aidan until midnight, she spent the evening in the movie theatre, wisely choosing a Stallone double bill over the *Friday the 13th* evening, not wanting to give herself the jitters.

The second movie finished at just gone eleven thirty and, after wasting fifteen minutes in the ladies' room retouching her make-up, Catherine went outside to flag down a cab. She knew the old bridge, having been there once or twice with other boyfriends. It was downtown and backed on to a park, and despite its reputation for drunks and vagrants, it had always proved to be popular with couples. Somehow, Catherine didn't think there were likely to be many of them out there tonight; not fancying the idea of being there alone, she hoped Aidan would show on time.

As the cab headed away from the crowds and the bright lights and into the quieter, darker streets, she felt for the first time a small knot of apprehension forming in the pit of her stomach. She wasn't sure whether it was the excitement of knowing she was going to see Aidan or unease, just in case he didn't show, and she was left standing all alone down by the old bridge. She considered asking the cab driver to hang around if she was first to arrive but figured it would get too expensive. It was silly to worry. Realistically, she was more likely to run into danger back in the direction of the campus.

The cab followed the dimly lit road that led around the side of the park and Catherine saw the warehouses on the opposite bank of the river come into sight. It had been months since she'd been near the old bridge, and she wasn't surprised to see nothing had changed.

'Where do you want to be dropped, sweetheart?' the driver asked.

'Here will be fine.' She saw his disapproving look in the rearview mirror and added quickly, 'I'm meeting a friend.'

'Well... if you're sure.' He pulled the cab to a halt, and she climbed out. 'That will be twelve dollars.'

Catherine reached in her purse and paid the fare.

'You sure you don't want me to wait?' he asked again.

She smiled her most confident smile. 'I'll be fine, thanks.'

Nodding at her, still seeming unsure, he pulled away. Catherine watched him go, his headlights becoming fainter, eventually disappearing amongst the blur of trees in the park. For a moment she could still hear the distant drone of his engine, but when that was gone, she was alone, in silence.

Silence, except for the occasional lapping of water against the riverbank and the low whistling of the wind. She pulled her cotton jacket tighter, wondering if perhaps she should have dressed more sensibly.

Never mind, Catherine. Hopefully you'll have someone to keep you nice and warm soon.

She glanced over her shoulder at the bridge. No sign of Aidan. She hoped he was definitely coming. She turned and started to walk towards the arranged meeting place, thinking about how it was supposed to be a girl's prerogative to be late, not the guy's. Arriving at the bridge, she looked at the rickety old planks and the rusty railings and wondered if she dare step on it. The old ruin was a danger and should have been pulled down years ago. Danger was fun, she reminded herself. Danger and mystery.

Taking a chance, she took a tentative step onto the bridge and attempted to steady herself by grasping at the railing.

Shit. I'll probably fall in and drown before he gets here.

There was a possibility of it happening if she lost her footing.

Maybe he'll get here just in time to save me.

Nice fantasy, but she knew it wasn't realistic. Hearing footsteps behind her, Catherine turned to look over her shoulder, the corners of her mouth turning up into a broad smile ready to greet Aidan. The face looking back at her wasn't Aidan's.

Her mouth dropped open in surprise and the question formed in her mind.

What are you doing here?

Before she had a chance to say the words aloud, a heavy metal bar swung toward her, knocking her hard on the forehead. Letting go of the railing, Catherine stumbled forward, into darkness and into the arms of her killer.

17

MONDAY 28 APRIL 1997

Monday morning was all paperwork.

Although Rebecca was enjoying being a cop, she had already grown to dislike the parts of the job that kept her tied to her desk, and she especially hated it when the only company she had was Vic Boaz. Her worst suspicions had been confirmed when she had arrived on shift and found the files piled high on her desk. Although they had already been through all of the available evidence and information, Sutton was convinced they must have missed something important along the way. Hence it was Rebecca and Vic who got to do the dog work.

Rebecca had already made a start when Vic rolled in twenty minutes late. Surprisingly, he seemed to be in a pretty good mood, whistling and grinning broadly. She just hoped it wasn't the kind of mood that was going to irritate her. She watched as he hung up his jacket and joined her at the double desk, a paper bag filled with doughnuts in his hand.

'Want one?' he asked, waving the bag in her face. 'They're nice and fresh. I only just picked them up.'

The smell of the doughnuts wafted in the direction of Rebecca's nose, making her stomach rumble. She'd only had a couple of cups of coffee before leaving her apartment and now wished she'd had something more substantial. Although she was trying to keep her weekdays free of junk food so she didn't have quite so many calories to burn off when she went running, she didn't see why the hell she should have to keep sitting and watching Vic stuff his face.

'Sure, why not?'

Digging her hand into the bag she pulled out one of the sugared rings. It was still warm and burnt her fingers. She quickly grabbed a tissue from the box on her desk and dropped the doughnut onto it. Vic, meanwhile, took out a doughnut for himself and proceeded to stuff it in his mouth, apparently not bothered by how hot they were. He glanced down at the files on the desk and grinned.

'Hey, paperwork. My favourite.'

Rebecca raised her eyebrows, a little sceptical. 'Really?'

She wasn't used to seeing him in a good mood. Usually, he spent the day bitching and coming on to her. To have him smiling and being nice was a little unnerving and made her wonder what he was up to.

'Well, get stuck in, buddy,' she muttered, 'because there's plenty of it to do.'

'Hickok?' he questioned.

'No, Sutton.'

'Really?' Vic looked mildly surprised. 'I thought he was the better one of the two.'

Rebecca shook her head.

'He thinks we must have missed something and wants us to go through it all again.'

'And while we do that, they are where?'

'Hickok thinks he has a lead on one of the professors at the college.'

Rebecca felt a little guilty as she remembered her aiding and abetting adventure over at the college on Saturday night. She hoped that Hickok would keep to his word and not tell anyone what they had done. Remembering the terms on which they had parted, she didn't fancy her chances.

She had only seen him briefly that morning, during which time he couldn't have uttered more than five words to her, and she figured that he was probably still mad at her about the fight at the bar. Although it would have been easy to apologise and clear the air between them, Rebecca had no intention of doing so. The idea of grovelling to Hickok was enough to make her want to throw up and she knew that she would rather take her chances, even if it did mean stepping on eggshells every time she was around him.

She had been pleased to see that his jaw had swollen up nicely and that he had been sporting a large purple bruise. Although she had resisted commenting on it, she was curious to know what he had told Sutton. The older agent hadn't mentioned anything to her, so she guessed whatever he had said hadn't been the truth.

Finishing his doughnut, Vic reached inside the bag for another.

'One of the professors, hey? Well, let's hope he's right and they get the guy then.' He grinned broadly. 'Might save us both a lot of reading.'

'Let's hope so.' With a half-smile, Rebecca turned back to the report she had been reading.

Vic, meanwhile, started to sift through the top file on his own desk. He started to whistle again as he worked and she was aware of him looking up in her direction every now and then, as though his mind was somewhat preoccupied. Eventually, she glanced up herself, only to see him watching her, a big grin spread across his face.

'What?' she asked, feeling a little agitated.

Vic shrugged his shoulders innocently. 'What *what*?'

'Quit staring at me, will you?'

'I'm not staring at you.'

Self-consciously, Rebecca reached her hand to her cheek. 'Yes, you are. What is it? Have I got something on my face?'

'Nothing's wrong, for chrissakes. I'm just in a good mood, okay?'

Rebecca stifled a laugh. 'I didn't know you had good moods.'

'Yeah?' Vic narrowed his eyes slightly. 'Well, now you know I do.'

'So why are you in a good mood then?'

'Why would I tell you?'

Rebecca threw her pen down on the desk, shaking her head in disbelief. The guy was dying for her to ask him, and now he was planning on making her beg? 'Come on, Vic, you've been acting like the cat that got the cream ever since you got here. You obviously want to tell me something. Well, go ahead and tell me. I'm listening.'

'So I see.'

'Did you win the lottery or something?'

Vic pulled a face. 'You really think I'd be here right now if I had?'

Rebecca didn't even have to think about the answer. 'So what's happened that's so great?' she pushed.

'Well, I guess I did have a pretty good weekend.'

'Define good.'

Vic grinned. 'I got laid.'

'Oh,' Rebecca said, suddenly wishing she hadn't asked.

'Yeah, sorry, sweetheart.' He winked at her. 'Looks like you missed your chance.'

'I'm crushed.'

'I can imagine.'

'So who was it then? Jill?'

Vic nodded and grinned.

'Yeah, we were going at it hot and heavy for most of the weekend.'

Rebecca gave a sardonic smile. 'Lucky girl.'

The grin disappeared as quickly as it had surfaced. 'Hey, quit it with the smart comments, okay?'

'Yes, sir.'

'I mean it, Angell,' he threatened, a scowl breaking out across his face. 'I'm getting a little sick and tired of your big mouth. You think you know everything, don't you?'

Ignoring his outburst, Rebecca grinned at him across the desk. 'Well, it's nice to see your good mood lasted a long time.'

Vic glowered at her, his face reddening.

Aware that he had a short fuse and not wanting to push him too far, she backed down. Although the guy could be a jerk, he had for once come into work in a good mood. She didn't want to be the one to go and ruin it. Keeping her tongue in check, she smiled sweetly at him.

'So, you and Jill are a steady item now?' she asked, trying her best to sound genuinely interested.

Vic gave her a dubious look before answering. 'Hardly. You think I want to be tied down to one woman?' He raised his eyebrows suggestively. 'Still, I am meeting her for lunch today, so who knows what we might end up doing.'

Rebecca screwed up her nose, feeling disgusted at the thought. She glanced down at the half empty bag of doughnuts sitting on the desk between them.

'Well, you'd better cut those sugared rings out, pal, or you won't have an appetite.'

Vic's grin returned to his face as he rubbed his belly. 'Sure I will,' he said, reaching for another doughnut and cramming half of it into his mouth. 'Good sex is enough to give any guy an appetite,' he mumbled through his mouthful.

Rebecca screwed up her nose. 'You know what?' she muttered, half under her breath, 'I really didn't need to know that.' Rolling her eyes, she turned back to her paperwork.

* * *

They broke for lunch at one.

Vic disappeared to meet Jill and Rebecca went window shopping before stopping at one of her favourite coffee houses for a cappuccino. As she sipped her drink she wondered how come it was so easy for Vic to meet someone and so difficult for her. After all, she'd been in the city now for over a month and, aside from her brief liaison with the philandering David, the closest she'd been to a date was on Saturday night when she had gone to the Blue Moose with Hickok.

Not that she would ever count that as a date. Beer and Bourbon with her favourite FBI Agent was not an experience she wished to repeat.

You could do worse.

And you could do better.

Special Agent Joel Hickok, with his dishevelled dark hair and taunting eyes, wasn't a bad-looking guy. He was a couple of inches taller than Rebecca, who stood at five-nine in her bare feet, and he was in good physical shape. That didn't change the fact though that he was rude and arrogant and had a boorish attitude, and that he made her so mad at times she just wanted to punch him.

Punch him or kiss him?

Remembering the feelings that had surfaced immediately after their fight on Saturday night made her uncomfortable and she immediately scolded herself.

You do not have feelings for Joel Hickok.

You hate the very ground he walks on.

He is a stupid, ill-mannered jerk and it would suit you fine if you never laid eyes on him again.

Done with her pep talk, Rebecca tried to focus her attention on the case. She went over the reports she had read that morning, trying to think if there was anything that she could have missed. The one thing that still didn't add up was why the killer hadn't restarted the alphabet from the letter I. Despite Hickok's theory that the victim was already accounted for, Rebecca wasn't so sure he was right. Surely the main intention of the Alphabet Killer was to kill twenty-six students. If the copycat killer didn't start from where Rodney Boone had left off, then there would only ever be twenty-five deaths accounted for.

Maybe the answers they needed weren't in the files on the current murders. Perhaps instead they should be rereading the files on the original crimes that had been committed by Boone himself.

Rebecca knew that the files were back at the police precinct, where Hickok and Sutton had gone through them all themselves. Not believing Boone to be responsible for the current murders, they had only taken the necessary background information. Maybe they had missed something.

Finishing her drink, she hurried back to the precinct, eager to pull the files on Boone. When Vic returned five minutes after her, smelling strongly of Jill's flowery perfume, she had already retrieved the files from records and had them sitting in a pile on the desk.

Vic looked at her questioningly. 'What's all this?'

'Files on the Alphabet Killings,' Rebecca told him, not bothering to look up.

Vic hung up his jacket and came over to the desk. 'There were only a couple of files here when we went to lunch. Now there's more than double that. What's going on, Angell?'

'I pulled out the files on Boone and the original victims.'

Vic narrowed his eyes. 'Why?'

'Come on, Vic. You know as well as I do that we've been through all of the evidence with a fine-tooth comb. Maybe we need to go back over the original files.'

'I thought our FBI buddies had already done that.'

'They did, but only briefly. They might have missed something.' Vic nodded. Rebecca watched him deliberating, hoping he would agree with her decision.

'Well... I guess it wouldn't hurt,' he said eventually.

She smiled, relieved. 'My thoughts exactly.'

'This is your idea, though,' he warned. 'So you get to do most of the reading, okay?'

'Okay, that's fine.'

Rebecca passed him a couple of the files before turning back to the one she had in front of her. Opening the top page, she started to read the murder report on Boone's first victim, Danielle Adams.

18

WYEFIELD, CALIFORNIA. FEBRUARY 1968

Helen White had tried to kill herself on a Tuesday.

It was easy to remember the date, because the particular Tuesday she had chosen had been Rodney's twelfth birthday; he often wondered if she had picked it for that reason or whether it had just been a bizarre coincidence.

Being a Tuesday, he and Clifford had been at school and, despite it being his birthday, the day hadn't been unlike any other. His mother, as usual, had spent the day at home with his youngest brother, entertaining her various men friends.

Rodney had wised up enough over the last year and a half to know what went on behind her closed bedroom door and, although he didn't like it, he knew better than to say anything. As long as he did his chores, his mother tended to ignore him, and he had grown to understand that it was better to be ignored than to endure more of the physical abuse he had suffered in the months that had followed his father's death.

He remembered clearly how he and Clifford had walked home from school and how he had been quaking in his shoes because his teacher had given him a report card with a succession of Fs. The marks had come as a huge disappointment to him. He had worked so hard, both in class and at home, having decided that he wanted to go to college after school and train to become a professor like his daddy had been.

His disappointment was nothing compared to the fear he felt as he neared the house. He had promised his mother that he would improve his grades and dreaded what she would do when she saw the report card.

Of course, he was worrying unnecessarily, for his mother never got to see the report card. When they entered the house, they found her slumped face down on the bedroom carpet, her cut wrists creating puddles of red on the dull grey carpet, and a blood-covered kitchen knife at her feet.

Clifford had started screaming and, in a daze, Rodney ran to the phone to call for an ambulance. He could hear the sound of crying in the background as his shaking fingers dialled the number and he tried to calm Clifford, telling him to go and check that their brother was okay.

The ambulance came, followed by two police cars, and the officers remained long after Helen White had been taken to hospital, asking a hundred questions and confusing Rodney, who was feeling alone and scared, worrying about what was happening to his mother and what was going to happen to him and his brothers.

It was hard to believe that night had been almost two years ago, but just like the night when his daddy had been killed, it would always be with him in clear and colourful detail.

His mother had survived her suicide attempt, but never returned home. The doctors declared her mentally unstable, and she was allowed to see the three of them one more time before she was taken to the nursing institution where, it was claimed, she would be made well again. But in truth she still resided there to this very day.

As they had no other family and were too young to fend for themselves, Rodney and his brothers had been brought to Wyefield, the nearest city to San Palimo, and placed in the Wyefield Children's Home to await adoption. Rodney recalled the day they had arrived and how after settling in they had spoken to social workers, who promised that the three of them would remain together.

He had clung to that promise every time the prospective parents had come to visit, looking for a child to make their family complete, always drawn to the youngest brother, often prepared to make room for eight-year-old Clifford, but never wanting to take on the responsibility of a thirteen-year-old boy.

Eventually the day came when the home gave up trying to place the three of them together and it was decided that they would have to go separately.

Although nobody actually ever spoke the words aloud, Rodney could read the vibes well enough to know that he would likely spend the rest of his childhood in the home.

As everyone expected, the youngest was the first to go, taken on by the doting parents of three girls who wanted a boy to make their family complete, and it was less than a month after he had gone that the news came that Rodney had been dreading.

A home had also been found for Clifford.

Although he had already lost his mother, his daddy and one brother, Rodney found the idea of losing Clifford almost unbearable. His brother had been his one ally since his daddy had died and together, they had looked after each other. Without Clifford, Rodney wasn't sure he could go on.

Of course, he somehow managed to, forcing himself to face each day, knowing that nobody wanted him and living for the promise that his brother had made him during their last conversation before they had said goodbye, that no matter where he was or what happened in the future, he would one day come back to find him.

Sitting on the large window ledge in his room at the home, watching the traffic passing by on the busy road two floors below, Rodney remembered Clifford's promise and knew that he could trust him to keep it. Almost a year had passed since the two of them had seen each other, but not a day went by when he didn't think of his brother, wondering what he was up to and wanting to know how he was getting on with his new family.

He stared thoughtfully at the worn brown suitcase sitting on the floor, packed with his meagre possessions. Being alone had changed him in many ways. It had made him grow up and realise that if he was going to get on in life, he would have to become a survivor. He had learned to channel the emotions running free inside him, quashing down any feelings of love and joy he experienced, and releasing them instead through acts of fear and pain. He wondered if it was because of these necessary changes that the Boones had picked him.

As they sat and studied him intently during their first meeting, Cedric and Phillipa Boone must have sensed his new inner strength and known he would grow into a son they could be proud of.

Seeing their car pulling up outside the main door, ready to collect him and take him away to his new home, Rodney climbed down from the ledge and collected his case, determined that he would not let them down.

19

JUNIPER, OREGON. TUESDAY 29 APRIL 1997

Emma Keeley had been found.

The body of the beautiful, raven-haired pianist had washed up on the banks of the river down by the old bridge and had been discovered early Tuesday morning by two joggers.

Like the others, she was naked, and the back of her neck had been carved.

Joel Hickok and Max Sutton, together with the local pathologist and a team of officers, hurried to the scene, and the whole section of river was immediately sealed off.

The pathologist, Greg Withers, a burly man in his fifties who, like fine wine, had aged well with few wrinkles and just a hint of silver in his thick red hair, was already known to both agents, having been responsible for the reports on Scott Jagger and Rufus Lind. As he worked, the three of them discussed different aspects of the case, in particular the area in which Emma's body had been found.

So far, the killer had copied Boone, dumping his victims in the sewer each time. Was there a reason he had now decided to change location?

As they talked, a small crowd of morbid sightseers began to gather behind the police tape, along with the photographers and reporters who had been first on the scene. Max rolled his eyes when he saw them.

'Sick fucks. I can't believe that people get off on seeing this shit.'

Joel gave a twisted smile. 'Who wants to pay for TV when you get the real deal for free?'

'You know what this means, don't you?'

'We get to be celebrities?'

'You wish, pal.' Max let out a sour laugh. 'We get to do a press conference and let everyone know what's going on here.'

Joel shrugged. 'And you're cut up about that? It was inevitable that people were gonna find out sooner or later.'

'Yeah, well I'd kind of hoped for later. Once the press start blowing things out of proportion there's gonna be a whole lot of pressure on us from head office to get things wrapped up, and that's not good seeing as we currently have jack shit.'

Joel nodded thoughtfully. 'You know, we don't have to tell them everything.'

Max looked at his partner. 'You want to hold something back?'

'It wouldn't hurt. We could always play it like a one-off homicide and that way, hopefully, there won't be too much suspicion.'

'What about the other two, Jagger and Lind?'

'What about them?'

'It doesn't take a genius to connect them to Emma Keeley.'

Joel pulled a face. 'So? If people find out, they find out. We can deal with it when it happens. No need to go handing the press everything on a plate now, is there?'

'I guess not.' Max glanced at the crowd, drawn to the flashing bulbs. While he liked Joel's way of thinking, he didn't see it working. The original Alphabet Killings had been big news in Juniper.

When people found out that three students had been killed, they would have to be pretty stupid not to put two and two together.

'I don't know,' he said shrugging. 'We'll play it by ear.'

* * *

Angell and Boaz were still at work on the Alphabet files when Joel and Max arrived back at the precinct. It had been Angell's idea to go over the files on the original murders again and, although it was a good idea, Joel wondered if maybe it was one she was beginning to regret.

When the call had come in that a body had been found down by the river, Max had insisted that she and Boaz stay behind; while Angell had accepted his decision, she had looked disappointed, and judging from the moans coming from Boaz before they had left, Joel guessed that he had probably given her a hard time as well.

Angell looked up as they walked in the room and met his eyes. 'Was it her?'

Joel knew she meant Emma Keeley. Nothing had been said about who the girl might be before they had left, but he knew the others were as certain as he was who they would find.

'Yeah, it was her.'

'Oh.' Angell shrugged and tried to look like she wasn't bothered. She turned back to the file she was reading.

Joel knew that Emma's death would affect her more than the others. She had never been involved in a homicide before and, although she tried to make out she was tough, being in Emma's room, touching her things and talking to her friends, she'd let herself get a little attached. Given time and experience she would eventually learn to distance herself and not let her emotions get in the way.

Pausing by her desk and dropping down to her level, he spoke in a low voice. 'You know, Rebecca, it was inevitable that we were gonna find her. If it makes it any easier, the pathologist said she was dead before he started cutting her up. He killed her with a blow to the head, so she wouldn't have known anything.'

Angell glanced up at him, a look of surprise on her face, and he immediately narrowed his eyes defensively. 'What?'

'You were being nice,' she said, a smile playing on her lips. 'I'm sorry, Hickok, it's just I've never seen you be nice before. That's all.'

Shaking her head and still looking faintly amused, she turned back to her work.

'What? Of course I was being nice. I'm a nice guy. Jeez!'

Pulling a face at the back of her head, Joel got up. He saw Boaz grinning across the desk at him.

'And what the hell are you smirking at?'

'Nothing.' Boaz's grin widened. 'I guess I'm not used to seeing your nice side either.'

Joel scowled at him, not appreciating being mocked by someone like Boaz. 'Yeah? Well don't get too used to it.' He gave an irritated sigh. 'I'm gonna go get some coffee. Why don't you two hurry up and finish reading those files. It might be nice if we can get some kind of lead on this killer before the year is out.'

Boaz saluted him and Joel couldn't be bothered to retort. Instead, he just shook his head and walked away, wondering why he had been fool enough to make an effort in the first place. Max followed him over to the vending machine, a sly look on his face. He nudged Joel.

'So, buddy. What was all that about?'

'What was all *what* about?'

'You and Angell?' Max gave a toothy grin. 'Is there something going on between you two that I should know about?'

Joel narrowed his eyes. 'No,' he answered sharply.

'No there isn't or no you don't want me to know?'

'Both.'

Max nodded, his grin spreading. 'Well, I had to ask. First, you're being all secretive about how you got that bruise and now you're checking up on her to make sure she's okay. Let me guess. You came on to her and she socked you one?'

'What? Don't be an idiot.'

'Okay.' Max nudged him again. 'But you like her, right?'

'No, I don't like her,' Joel snapped, wishing the subject would drop. 'I was just trying to be nice. Jesus! Why does everybody have such a problem with that?'

Max shook his head innocently, though his grin remained intact. 'Who said anything about a problem? I don't have a problem. No problem at all.'

* * *

Rebecca watched Hickok and Sutton talking and wondered what it was that shocked her the most: Emma Keeley's body being found or Joel Hickok being nice to her? He had even called her by her Christian name. Maybe he'd gone out and gotten himself a personality transplant since she'd last seen him. Either that or he'd been taken over by some alien life form. Thinking of the film *Invasion of the Body Snatchers*, she smiled. Then immediately felt guilty. Emma Keeley had been found mutilated and dead and here she was, thinking up jokes. Vic's voice interrupted her thoughts.

'What's up with you?' he questioned, eyes narrowed and studying her carefully.

'Nothing.' Rebecca pulled a face. 'I was just thinking about Emma Keeley and what happened to her. Stupid, huh?'

Vic shrugged his shoulders. 'No. You're a woman. No one is expecting you to handle it well.'

'Excuse me?' Rebecca snapped angrily, not sure if she had heard the Neanderthal right. 'This has nothing to do with being a woman. I'm being human, for God's sake. What the hell is up with you, Vic? Don't you have any feelings?'

'Of course I do,' Vic snapped, his face reddening with anger.

'Then how come this doesn't seem to bother you? How come you and Hickok and Sutton can all just carry on as though nothing has happened?'

'You get used to it.'

'Really? You get used to it, do you?' Rebecca scorned. 'Well, you know what, Vic. I don't know if I want to get used to it, seeing people die.'

Vic leaned across the desk, his thick brows knitting together in a scowl. 'Yeah? Well get over it, sweetheart,' he said in a low gruff voice. 'You're gonna see some real bad shit out there, so you'd better learn to deal with it. I need a partner I can count on, and right now I'm not sure if you're up to the job. Cut your emotional ties now or pack your bags and get the hell back to Swallow River.'

'Swallow Falls,' Rebecca corrected, biting down on the surge of anger she could feel rising inside of her. How dare Vic Boaz lecture her about how she should feel and what kind of cop she should be?

Nobody got away with speaking to her the way he just had and if she hadn't wanted to hold on to her job so badly, she would have punched him right now, regardless of the fact he had about six inches on her and probably outweighed her by close to seventy pounds.

'Swallow Falls,' Vic repeated with a grin. 'Whatever. One hick town is the same as any other.' He leaned back in his chair and crossing his arms looked her square in the face. 'So what's it gonna be then, hick girl? You gonna bail on us?'

Rebecca gave him a thunderous look. Beneath the desk she clenched her fists together, wishing more than anything she could wipe the smirk off his face.

'No, I'm not gonna bail,' she said tightly, forcing her own sarcastic smile. 'In case you've forgotten, we've still got a killer to catch.'

20

THURSDAY 1 MAY 1997

Sitting in one of two hard-back chairs in the interview room, Lawrence Parker shifted to a comfortable position and stared icily across the table at Joel Hickok. Joel returned the stare, glaring into Parker's black eyes. Devil Eyes.

'I hope this is important. I'm missing classes.'

'It's important.'

'Am I under arrest?'

'No. Don't think about leaving until I'm done though. I can easily get a warrant to bring you back. We'll also want to take your prints before you leave.'

'Really? So you think I've committed a crime?'

'Have you?'

'Not that I was aware of. Though, come to think of it, there was that red light I ran a couple of weeks back.'

'You're not here because of a red light, we both know that.'

'I'm intrigued then. Tell me more.'

'How well did you know Emma Keeley?'

'As well as I know any of my students.'

'And how well is that?'

'I tutor them in English, Agent Hickok. You may be familiar with the subject?'

'Is that the only subject you tutor them in?'

'Yes.'

'Any of your students ever need extra classes?'

'No.'

'So Emma Keeley didn't need extra classes?'

'Emma was top of her class. She had a bright future ahead of her.'

'Not any more.'

'No, not any more.'

'How about socialising? You ever socialise with your students, Lawrence? You mind if I call you Lawrence? Mr Parker seems a little formal.'

'It's Lawrie, and no, I don't socialise with my students.'

'Why's that then, Lawrie? Have you got a hang-up on the old student–teacher thing?'

'Hardly... I'm married.'

'Oh, that's right, you're married. Your wife's a student, isn't she? Guess you're not bothered by the student–teacher thing after all.'

'I don't tutor Kylan; she has other classes.'

'You tutored Emma Keeley, though, didn't you?'

'Twice a week.'

'What did you think of Emma? Did you think she was pretty?'

'What's your point, Agent Hickok?'

'My point is trying to establish who killed Emma Keeley.'

'You think I killed her?'

'Did you?'

'Don't be ridiculous. Of course I didn't.'

'So you didn't kill her, didn't have intimate relations with her, in fact, you didn't do anything except tutor her in English twice a week?'

'That's correct.'

'Why do I have a problem believing that?'

'I wouldn't know, Agent Hickok. It seems to me that you have quite a few problems.'

'What, are you a psychologist now as well as an English professor?'

'No... just a guy trying to do his job. A job, incidentally, that you're keeping me from doing.'

'Well, I'm afraid you're going to have to bear with me because we still have a lot of ground to cover.'

'Such as?'

'Such as, if you weren't having an intimate relationship with Emma Keeley, why was she sending you notes?'

'What?'

'You heard me. Notes, letters... saying she had to see you.'

Silence.

'You do know the notes I'm talking about, don't you, Lawrie?'

'How do you know?'

'I work for the government. I know everything, and anything I don't, I make it my business to find out.'

'You've been snooping through my things?'

'I wouldn't say that. You're a difficult man to get to know, Lawrie. You have too many secrets. I had to be resourceful.'

'You didn't have a warrant. You broke the law, Agent Hickok.'

'Cut the crap, Lawrie. Emma Keeley is dead, and you know more about what happened to her than you're letting on.'

'I don't know anything about her death. I told you that already and I promise you I was telling the truth.'

'You were seeing her.'

'I'm married.'

'So? You think married men don't screw around?'

'I love my wife.'

'That's what they all say.'

'I'm telling you... nothing happened between me and Emma Keeley.'

'So why was she sending you notes? Crush on the teacher?'

'Emma had problems. I was just trying to help her sort them out.'

'What kind of problems?'

'She'd been seeing a guy who worked in the city. An older guy.'

'And?'

'And things turned sour.'

'Go on.'

'He was a lawyer, rich and...'

'And he was married.'

'How did you know?'

'They always are.'

'Emma broke off the relationship, but the guy kept calling her, asking to see her.'

'So what, she turned to you?'

'She needed someone to talk to.'

'I see... and you were her knight in shining armour?'

'It wasn't like that.'

'Sure.'

'Like I said, she just needed someone to talk to.'

'Did your wife know about her?'

'There was nothing to know.'

'I take it that means no?'

'My relationship with Emma was purely platonic.'

'And what about Emma's relationship with you?'

'What are you suggesting?'

'Did Emma view you strictly as a friend?'

'She was going through a difficult time.'

'A difficult time where she was perhaps becoming confused about her friendship with you?'

'Nothing happened.'

'But she would have liked it to?'

'She just wasn't thinking straight at the time.'

'She made a play for you?'

'I told her I wasn't interested. Nothing happened.'

'Was that why she was sending you notes?'

'She wanted to meet up.'

'And did you meet up?'

'No, I never saw her again.'

Joel Hickok tried to read into the black eyes. Was he telling the truth?

He flipped the page of his notepad over, glanced briefly at what he had written down then he locked eyes with Lawrie Parker again and asked, 'How well did you know Rufus Lind?'

* * *

Rebecca didn't leave work until late Thursday night, staying until all of the files on the original victims had been thoroughly reread. She had spent the latter part of her afternoon trudging around in the sewer with Vic, Sutton and a few of the other officers after a call had come in from the college reporting a female student missing since Saturday night. Within an hour they had recovered two bodies, both within a hundred feet of one another, both naked and carved, and both serving as a stark reminder that the killer was starting to strike with increasing regularity. If they didn't catch him soon it was inevitable that several more students were likely to lose their lives.

Vic hadn't shared her enthusiasm for working late and had long gone, claiming to have arranged a date with Jill, and although Hickok and Sutton were both still there, they had spent much of the evening in the office that Krigg had provided for them, locked in discussions and talking on the phone.

There were now only the files on Boone himself left to be reread and those she and Vic had on their desks ready to tackle the following morning. Although they hadn't found any leads in the files on the victims so far, Rebecca was convinced they were missing something.

As she drove home, she mulled over what she had read:

Danielle Adams: Popular student. Strangled.

Patrick Bell: Surfer. Strangled.

Lydia Chapman: Grade A student. Suffocated.

Jonah Devlin: Popular student. Strangled.

Erika Estes: Cheerleader. Strangled.

Willard Frey: Footballer. Strangled.

Pamela Gilcrest: On the Student Committee. Suffocated.

Marcus Hyde: Editor of the college paper. Strangled.

They had all been popular or prominent figures around the campus and they had all been killed by methods of asphyxia and in alphabetical order.

There had to be something that they had missed.

Marcus Hyde had been Boone's last victim before he had disappeared. At least, the last victim who had died.

Maybe that was it. Perhaps it wasn't the eight dead victims they should be looking at, but instead the one survivor.

Victim I.

21

JUNIPER, OREGON. SEPTEMBER 1988 – JULY 1989

The first semester of college had turned out to be a much more pleasant experience than she had dared hope.

That last week of summer, the one week she had never wanted to end, had finished all too quickly, and then she had been left with only a handful of good memories and a sickly feeling of fear about the future. Fear about leaving home for the first time, fear about whether or not the long-distance relationship with her boyfriend, Michael, would work, and fear about fitting into her new life.

Those fears had been mostly unfounded.

Leaving home had at first been difficult. Those first few days had been strange, waking up in a strange bed in an unfamiliar room, knowing that she would be eating breakfast with a group of strangers, sitting on plastic chairs around a plastic table in a large echoing cafeteria, instead of with her family in the comfortable surroundings of her own home.

Her roomie, an energetic blonde named Miranda Ingram, proved to be a lot of fun and was also very popular with the other students, which meant Jennifer had no problem making new friends. Miranda also seemed to know all of the best places to go in town and was constantly finding new things for them to do, which didn't leave much time for being homesick.

The only thing that hadn't worked out was Michael.

At first, she had tried to keep the relationship going, mainly wanting to keep a part of the past with her, but he hadn't been good at writing and, in time, she had come to realise that he wasn't that important to her. He had, like many other things, become a memory. A nice memory, but nothing more.

There were other guys on campus that held her attention now and, whilst she had no intention of playing the field, it was fun to copy Miranda and flirt a little.

In fact, she had copied Miranda in more ways than one, all at her roommate's request. Hip clothes, more make-up, her long brown hair cut into a shorter, more fashionable style. Miranda smoked and drank and partied all night, and her influence didn't take long to rub off. Soon the old Jennifer Isaac, with her plain looks and demure personality, had gone, and a new, more confident, brash and flippant model had appeared in her place.

When she had returned home for Thanksgiving, her family had all noticed the change. Her father didn't approve. He didn't say anything, but she could tell from the way he kept looking at her clothes and from the odd comments that he made. Her mother, on the other hand, just seemed pleased that her little Jennifer had fitted in so well.

She saw Michael once before she returned, and it had been then that things had officially ended. He was already seeing someone else, her old school friend Vickie, and when she told him it didn't bother her, she was telling the truth. Nothing seemed to bother her much these days.

Thanksgiving ended and she returned to college. Life carried on in much the same way. Both she and Miranda continued to burn the candle at both ends, studying during the day and partying during the night. Due to lack of sleep, they began to skip the odd classes and eventually their grades started to slip.

It was around that time that the whole business had started.

Danielle Adams, a loud-mouthed senior with peroxide hair and a reputation for being an easy lay, had disappeared a couple of weeks before the Christmas break. No one knew where she had gone or what had happened to her. The police investigated, but drew only blanks, and it was rumoured that she had skipped town. After Christmas, when she still failed to materialise, the stories stopped circulating and eventually, interest in what had happened to her died completely.

The next one was Patrick Bell, a freshman like Jennifer, whom she knew only enough to say hello to. His attendance record was already pretty bad due to his fondness for taking extended weekend breaks to go surfing with his beach buddies. Therefore, not many eyebrows were raised when he failed to show up one Monday morning, and no one thought any more of it when he still hadn't appeared by the end of the week.

It was Lydia Chapman's disappearance that caused the main stir. Like Danielle, Lydia was a senior, though that was where the similarities ended. Unlike Danielle, Lydia was clever, sophisticated and came from a secure family background. She didn't drink, didn't smoke and didn't like to party. Despite this, she was still a very popular figure around the campus and had been dating the college star quarterback, Billy Vale, since her freshman year.

She vanished while on her way to meet Billy one Tuesday evening. It had been their two-year anniversary and the two of them had planned to have a romantic dinner to celebrate. Billy had a big game beforehand and had offered to come back to the campus to pick Lydia up. She had refused, arranging instead to meet him at the restaurant. Three hours later, when she hadn't shown up, Billy had gone back to the college and found her Volkswagen still parked in the parking lot.

Lydia wasn't anywhere to be seen.

The police launched a big search for Lydia Chapman. Her father, Drake, worked for the governor's office and demanded all the manpower possible to help find his daughter. A week after she disappeared, a local bum was arrested on flimsy evidence and later released. Three days after his release, Lydia Chapman's body turned up. She was discovered by sewage workers floating in one of three plastic sacks beneath the city streets. The other two sacks contained the bodies of the now forgotten Danielle Adams and the never missed Patrick Bell.

The whole campus was buzzing with gossip. Cops seemed to be everywhere, and the local police chief came down to talk to the students, to warn them to take precautions, but also to reassure them that they were safe and to quash the rumours that there was a psychotic killer on the loose, hungry for more victims.

No one believed him. Three students were dead, and Jennifer had heard details of what had happened to them all. Libby Trehearn, a friend from her English class whose brother-in-law was a cop, knew all the gory details and was only too willing to share them with anyone who wanted to listen. All three of the victims had been taken somewhere deserted and either strangled or suffocated. The killer had then carved their bodies up using some kind of sharp instrument. Libby had been quick to point out that it was possible the students may have just been unconscious, not dead, when they were cut. When the killer had finished mutilating them, she told them, he wrapped their naked bodies in plastic sacks and dumped them in the sewer.

The stories unnerved Jennifer a little. Miranda assured her they would be safe, just so long as they stayed together, and by the time the killings had made the national news and her worried parents had called wanting her to come home, she had decided she would stay, believing that both she and Miranda were invincible as far as the killer was concerned.

Her attitude didn't change, even when her classmate, Jonah Devlin, became victim number four. Miranda and Jonah had gone out a couple of times before Christmas and, as her roommate seemed unaffected by his death, Jennifer decided she wouldn't let it bother her either.

They seemed to be the only two on campus who were carrying on with life as normal, though at the time Jennifer was too caught up in her own little world to notice.

The clubs and bars had pretty much died a death as a result of the murders and on Friday and Saturday nights the streets that had at one time been filled with partying students now bore more of a resemblance to those of a ghost town.

After Jonah's death things did seem to quieten down a little.

There were no more murders and, while the police still seemed no closer to catching the killer, a sense of normality gradually returned to Juniper College. Easter came and went, the weather started to warm up, and Jennifer found herself preoccupied by a senior student.

They hadn't actually spoken. In fact, she'd only seen him on campus for the first time just after she returned from Easter break, and didn't even know his name. All she did know was that he had sexy dark eyes and that, on the couple of occasions he had noticed her, her legs had gone weak at the knees. She couldn't help but wonder how come she hadn't seen him around before.

This was the first secret she had kept from Miranda. So far, she had shared everything with her roommate, from details of her split with Michael to more recent worries about her plunging grades.

Jennifer hadn't had any serious crushes on guys at college. Sure, she had dated a few students: Nick the footballer had been a laugh; Marcus the editor of the college paper had been more problematic. He had been cute, and she'd liked him as a friend, but Marcus had wanted commitment that she wasn't prepared to give, and things had ended badly. Both of these brief relationships had been the topic of many late-night discussions with Miranda, with her more streetwise friend offering, often quite forcefully, her opinions.

This time, if there was to be a *this* time, things were going to be different. Although they hadn't yet spoken, Jennifer liked this guy and was determined to play things her way, not Miranda's, which meant not throwing herself at him, for one thing. So she kept her crush to herself and looked forward to every Friday afternoon when she was guaranteed a chance of seeing him as she awaited her late-afternoon English class.

He had the class before her, and she always made sure that she was there early for when he left the room. Occasionally he didn't see her; often, though, he would notice her waiting and smile.

Jennifer wasn't sure if he realised she fancied him. If he did know, he never let on, and he never ever reciprocated.

Gradually she grew more and more frustrated. She began to wonder if maybe he had heard bad things about her. Miranda, she knew, was notorious around campus. Maybe he thought that she wasn't serious enough for a proper relationship. Conscious of this thought, Jennifer slowly but subconsciously began to change. She wore less make-up, cut down on the smoking and drinking, and began to distance herself from the crowd that she hung around with. The change was so gradual that no one really made any comments. Except Miranda, of course, who occasionally remarked that her best friend was becoming a bit of a killjoy.

It was during this period that the murders started up again.

This time the first victim was a second-year student named Erika Estes. Both Jennifer and Miranda knew Erika quite well, though neither was aware that she was actually missing until reports that her body had been found started pouring in. Almost as though to prove he was back, the killer struck again almost immediately, claiming another two victims in the space of forty-eight hours, the bodies of Willard Frey and Pamela Gilcrest, bringing his grisly total to seven.

This time, the murders shook Jennifer enough from her daydreams to make her miss her Friday afternoon rendezvous and, for the first time since Danielle Adams had gone missing, she actually started to seriously contemplate the events that were taking place around her. The one thing that shook her more than anything was the conversation that she had with Miranda in their room late on the Saturday night following the discovery of Pamela Gilcrest's body.

Neither of them had talked much about the college murders. It was as though they both felt that by blocking everything out, they didn't have to accept the harsh reality of what was really happening. Aside from the pep talks they regularly gave each other about sticking together and everything being fine, this was the first time they had actually discussed what was going on.

Miranda had initiated the conversation. She had been sitting by the window, her long fingers curled around a cigarette as she gazed thoughtfully out across the playing field.

'I wonder why he does it,' she had pondered aloud.

Jennifer hadn't answered. Although she knew immediately who Miranda was talking about, the question had taken her by surprise. She also wasn't quite sure how to answer.

'I guess it must be some kind of sex thing,' Miranda continued. 'I bet he gets off on the killing.'

Jennifer joined her friend by the window.

'I don't care why he does it,' she said, trying hard to swallow down the ball of tension that had formed in her throat. 'I just think he's sick, and I hope the cops catch him soon.'

'You bet we do,' Miranda agreed, turning to look at her. Jennifer wasn't sure what she was getting at.

'What do you mean?' she asked, a little unnerved by the slightly twisted smile on her roommate's face.

Miranda stubbed her cigarette out on the window ledge.

'Come on, Jen, don't tell me you haven't thought about it.'

'Thought about what?'

'Danielle Adams, Pat Bell, Lydia Chapman, Jonah Devlin, Erika Estes, Willard Frey, Pam Gilcrest.' Miranda counted on her fingers as she spoke.

'What are you getting at?' Jennifer asked, not at all sure what point Miranda was trying to make.

'Adams, Bell, Chapman, Devlin, Estes, Frey, Gilcrest. A, B, C, D, E, F, G.'

'So?'

'So think about it. Think about the alphabet. A, B, C, D, E, F, G. The next letter is H, and what comes after H, Jen?'

'I.' Jennifer swallowed hard.

Miranda nodded at her friend, raising her eyebrows questioningly.

'So who do you reckon it's going to be? Who do you reckon he will go for?' she asked. 'Will it be Miranda Ingram or Jennifer Isaac?'

22

JUNIPER, OREGON. FRIDAY 2 MAY 1997

It was Joel's idea to go public. Although he had initially been against any kind of publicity that might attract the press, knowing that any news stories would only result in widespread panic, the whole thing was now too big to contain.

Although the latest victims had yet to be positively identified, it was very likely that the female victim would turn out to be Catherine Maloney and suspicions were running high that the male victim would eventually be identified as Kevin North, another student who hadn't been seen over the past couple of days.

The killer had now claimed five victims, and it was assumed that he was already thinking of striking again.

Messages were put out over the college mic system throughout Friday morning and at twelve thirty, one hundred and fourteen students gathered in one of the larger committee halls on campus, most of them talking or whispering, a few of them laughing and cracking jokes. All of them were curious to know what was going on, and several already had their suspicions.

All of them had a surname that began with the letter O.

Once he was sure that all the relevant students were present, Max stood up and asked for quiet. Then he addressed them.

'Thank you for all making the effort to come here in your own time. I'll try to keep things as brief as possible. My name is Special Agent Max Sutton and I work for the Federal Bureau of Investigation. This is my colleague, Special Agent Hickok.' He waved a hand in Joel's direction. 'We came to Juniper a couple of weeks ago to investigate the death of a student named Scott Jagger. I'm sure that some of you probably knew him and may have even shared classes with him.' He paused, letting the name sink in. 'There has been a lot of gossip passed around following Mr Jagger's death. I guess you're all aware of the eight students who were killed in Juniper eight summers ago and most of you have probably heard at least one of several stories concerning Mr Jagger, some of which are true and some of which are false.

'The one thing I can confirm to you now is that Scott Jagger was murdered.' Max paused and glanced at the crowd. A few murmurs rose before they waited for him to go on.

He coughed, clearing his throat before he continued.

'Since we have been in Juniper, four more students have been found dead. I can confirm that two of them are Rufus Lind and Emma Keeley. The identity of the other two victims, however, will have to remain confidential until their families have been notified. I'm afraid, people, that we appear to have another serial killer on our hands, and the reason you have been gathered here today is because you all fit the profile of the killer's next victim.'

Joel watched carefully, half expecting to see the entire room erupt in panic. Instead, there were just further murmurs. He guessed that most of the students already had a pretty good idea about what was going on.

As Max was about to continue speaking, a tall skinny guy with lank hair stood up and poked a finger at him.

'You're bullshitting! This is all just a joke, right? Just some sick joke.'

Max shook his head. 'I'm not joking, buddy. Believe me, I wish I was.'

'Bullshit!' The student repeated, looked disbelieving.

Dean Edwards, who was sitting beside Joel, stood up and fixed the student with angry eyes.

'Sit down please, Mr Ottinger, and let Special Agent Sutton continue,' he said in a tone that managed to be polite, calm and authoritative all at the same time.

Ottinger looked a little uncertainly at the Dean for a moment then, with a glare in Max's direction, he sank back into the crowd. Max cleared his throat again and continued.

'The reason you've all been called here today is not to scare you, but hopefully to prevent anyone else from being killed. If our man continues to follow his pattern, his next intended victim will be female so, ladies, we need you to be extra vigilant. That doesn't mean that you gentlemen can rest easy. He might not necessarily stick to the pattern. We've already doubled campus security, and there will also be police officers patrolling the grounds both day and night, so someone will be on hand should any of you find yourselves in trouble.

'I'm sure that some of you will want to perhaps go home for a while until this is all over, and that's fine. However, for those of you who stay, we've decided to impose a curfew. We don't want anyone out alone after eight o'clock. Stay in your dorms and stay in groups. This guy won't attack you unless you're alone. Play safe for the next couple of weeks and hopefully we'll have him caught by then.'

Joel studied the faces in the crowd. Some looked frightened, some looked annoyed, others looked amused. Evidently, they, like Ottinger, found the whole thing a joke. He wished it was a joke. It wasn't, though, and if they didn't find Rodney Boone's successor soon, one of the students in this room was likely to lose their life.

* * *

The call was made from a payphone booth on the east side of town, just after midday. It took some time for him to be connected and while he waited, watching the busy street around him, he whistled a tune, 'Waltz of the Flowers' by Tchaikovsky.

He smiled, realising how inappropriate it was, and stopped. Eventually he heard the phone click and the now familiar voice answer.

'Hello?'

'It's me,' he said, identifying himself. That had been the deal from the start. No names, at least not on the phone. You could never be too sure who might be listening in, even on a public phone. 'I have some news for you.'

'You do?' The voice sounded hopeful. 'Good news?'

'I think so.'

'Do tell.'

He thought of Kylan Parker.

'I was right. She is the one.'

'You're sure about that?'

'I've checked her out very carefully. It's definitely her.'

'Good.' There was a pause. 'She has to be a victim. I know her initial doesn't fit into the pattern, but then I guess she is an exceptional case, isn't she?'

'Yes, she is,' he said, nodding his agreement down the phone, even though he knew he couldn't be seen.

'Make sure you keep an eye on her. We can't afford to let her slip through our fingers.'

He let out a small laugh.

'Don't worry about that. I'm watching her very carefully.'

'Good. Don't forget that we have to find one more victim first.'

'I haven't. That's what I'm working on now.'

'Do you know who it's going to be?' the voice questioned.

'Not yet.'

'You haven't forgotten about the joker, have you? Remember what I said about each victim receiving—'

'I know about the joker,' he interrupted, a little too abruptly. 'We've been over this before, remember?' He softened his voice before continuing. 'You don't have to worry about anything. I promise you that I have the situation under control.'

There was a long pause before the voice answered, this time in an almost pleading tone.

'I know you do and please don't think that I don't trust you. I do. It's just very important to me that the job is completed. Do you understand?'

'I understand.'

He had understood from the beginning the importance of the situation. Murder was not something to be treated lightly.

'Good.' The voice seemed reassured. 'I guess I'll leave the matter in your capable hands.'

'I won't let you down.'

'I know you won't.' There was another pause. 'Well, I guess I should leave you to get on. You'll call me as soon as you have any further developments?'

'Of course.'

'Okay. Well good luck and happy hunting.'

The line went dead.

'Happy hunting,' he repeated to himself as he replaced the receiver, the faces of potential victims coming to mind.

* * *

'I think it went well.'

'Sure it went well. Did you see the looks on their faces?'

Max shook his head and laughed. 'Trust me, it went well. Before we went in there, I had visions of everyone trampling in a mad stampede to get off campus.'

The idea made Joel smile. 'Come on, we told them there was a killer on the loose, not a pack of brain sucking zombies.'

'Yeah, I guess so.' Max swung the car into the parking space behind the police precinct and switched off the engine. 'Maybe I was the one who was overreacting.'

'Let's hope so.' Joel clicked off his seat belt and opened the door. 'We have enough to deal with without having to worry about hysterical students.'

'Tell me about it.'

* * *

When he returned to the campus, he reflected on the conference that had taken place earlier; the two Federal Agents having decided it was time to warn the students that a killer was on the loose.

Of course, several people already suspected that was the case, but this made it official.

The Feds decision to come clean had caused him, as far as he could see, two problems. His first thought was of Kylan. Sitting in the cafeteria sipping the acidic coffee, he wondered where she was. Did she know yet about what had gone on? And if so, what did she make of it all?

Although the only students who had been brought in to see the Feds were those who had the initial O, news of the murders was now sure to spread like wildfire. It was highly unlikely that, by the end of the night, there would be a single student left who didn't know about what was going on.

What would Kylan do when she put two and two together?

She'd seen him twice now. Firstly, in the grocery store, then last Saturday at her house, and, on both occasions, she had been understandably spooked. Chances were that once she heard about the murders, if she hadn't already heard the rumours, she would either bolt or go to the police about him.

He couldn't afford to let her do either and he realised that he would have to watch her extra carefully.

His second problem was more imminent. Although the Feds hadn't been specific about why those gathered for the conference were the most likely victims, people weren't stupid, and it was obvious that every student who had been in the room had the same surname initial. The original Alphabet Murders had been notorious, and everyone was going to know it was the same pattern with the current victims. Once he had found victim O, it was going to be difficult to get her alone. Everyone was likely to be taking extra precautions, probably hanging round in large groups watching each other's backs. And then, of course, there were those who would probably leave town, hoping to get away until it was all over.

He gave it some thought, his mind working overtime on how it would be possible to get the next victim and wondered if he was worrying unnecessarily. It might be a lot easier than he thought. Not everyone was as highly strung as Kylan Parker and most of them would probably let their guard slip at some point.

That was the problem with people these days, they all seemed to have the attitude that it couldn't happen to them. Sipping his coffee, he smiled, thinking how very wrong they were.

* * *

As they walked into the precinct, Joel saw Rebecca Angell glance up from her desk. As soon as she realised it was him, she scowled. Grinning broadly, he waved in her direction, expecting to get a snide comment. She didn't bite though and, glowering silently instead, turned back to her work.

He guessed that he deserved it. Ever since their conversation following the discovery of Emma Keeley's body, he'd felt a little uncomfortable around her and, in the end, had decided it was easier just to go back to giving her a hard time.

He was being a jerk and he knew it, but he carried on regardless, reminding himself that it was the best course of action in the long run. He didn't need the trouble of falling for someone like Rebecca Angell. Most women were trouble enough, but this one was too smart and sassy for her own good.

Strolling past her desk, he pulled open the second drawer of the filing cabinet where they had been keeping all the information on the murders committed by Boone and started flicking through the files.

Angell watched him suspiciously.

'You know we've been through that entire cabinet already.'

'I know, I know.' Finding what he was looking for, Joel pulled out the file and closed the drawer. As he walked past her, he dropped the file on her desk.

'Victim I?' she said, studying the front page and glancing up at him, her eyebrows raised questioningly.

She had made the suggestion to him that they try to contact

Boone's one surviving victim, when she'd seen him out in the parking lot first thing that morning. At the time, Joel hadn't really paid attention. He'd been in a foul mood since learning that Lawrie Parker's prints didn't match those on the vodka bottle. That, and knowing they now had another two unsolved murders, was enough to make him unnecessarily irritable. He recalled how he had snapped at her, telling her to quit wasting his time with stupid ideas, and how she had responded with a barrage of abuse, before storming off ahead of him into the office, letting the door slam in his face.

He had watched her go, loving how sexy she looked when she got mad and hating the fact that he noticed. It was almost worth pissing her off just to watch her cheeks flush and her green eyes flash angrily.

Throughout the morning he had thought about her suggestion more and more, realising that it wasn't really such a bad one and, although he wasn't sure they would gain anything from talking to Boone's one surviving victim, at this stage it seemed they had nothing to lose. Except of course his pride, which he now had to swallow in front of Angell by admitting she was right.

'I was thinking maybe we should call her after all,' he grudgingly conceded, not prepared to stoop to a full apology. 'See if she's living locally and, if she is, then maybe we'll bring her in for a chat.'

Angell nodded, though chose not to say anything. She didn't have to. The gloating smile on her face was enough to let him know that she had won.

He watched as she opened the file, knew there wasn't much information on Boone's one surviving victim, just a police report on the attack and a copy text of the witness interview. Picking up the telephone, she began to punch in the number at the top of page.

23

JUNIPER, OREGON. SATURDAY 11 JULY 1989

When she heard that the police had found the body of Marcus Hyde, Jennifer went up to her room and started to pack.

Things were getting a little too close for comfort and she was more than a little scared. Ever since the conversation she'd had with Miranda a week earlier, she'd been on edge. Marcus's death had just pushed her over. At first, she had told herself she was being paranoid. Miranda's theory that the killer was working through the alphabet was crazy and it was no more than pure coincidence that the surnames of the seven victims matched the first seven letters of the alphabet. The more she thought about it, though, the more she couldn't help but wonder if maybe it might be true. Marcus Hyde, her ex-boyfriend and the eighth victim, had just about confirmed her fears and now she was worrying herself silly about who the next intended victim was.

Miranda Ingram or Jennifer Isaac.

Of course, there were probably close to a hundred students at the college whose surname had the initial I, but with twenty-five letters taken out of the alphabet, things had been narrowed down just a little too much for her liking. If she went home for a while, waited until it was all over, everything would be okay, and she could return safe in the knowledge that her life was not in danger.

She had just about finished packing when Miranda walked into the room. Until now, Jennifer had kept her plans to leave a secret, knowing that her friend would try to stop her, and she was right. Miranda eyed the case suspiciously.

'What's that for?' she asked, sitting down on the edge of her bed. Jennifer avoided looking at her.

'I think I'm gonna go visit my folks.'

'In the middle of the week?'

'Yeah, I figured I'd leave today.'

There was silence for a moment. Jennifer could feel Miranda's eyes watching her. Eventually she asked, 'Why?'

'My mom's not feeling too good,' Jennifer lied. 'I said I'd go home and help out until she's back up on her feet.'

Another silence followed.

'I don't believe you. You're going home because of the murders. You think you're going to be the next victim, don't you?'

Jennifer turned to face her friend. 'So what if I am going home because of the murders? Don't I have a right to be scared? Or do you think I'm just crazy?'

Miranda shook her head. 'No, you're not crazy. I do think you're overreacting though.'

'How am I possibly overreacting? If you're right about this alphabet thing, then the next victim is going to have the surname initial I. That's you and that's me.'

'And God knows how many other students on campus.'

Jennifer shook her head. 'You just don't get it, do you? Jonah's dead, Erika's dead, Marcus is dead. They were our friends, Miranda. If he can get them, he can get us.'

Miranda rolled her eyes, already looking bored with the conversation.

'I told you on day one, Jen, if we stick together, we'll be fine. He only kills one at a time. He's not going to go for us so long as we stick together. If we're careful we'll be okay.'

'Marcus was careful. Look what happened to him.'

'Well Marcus couldn't have been that careful, because he's dead,' Miranda said sharply. Her expression softened, and she gave Jennifer her most pleading look. 'Come on, Jen, don't let this sicko rule your life. If you stay, I promise we'll watch each other like hawks.'

Jennifer hesitated. Home was safe. 'I don't know. I really don't want to be here right now.'

'And what about me when you go? What if I'm his intended victim? Who's going to look out for me when you're gone?'

'Well, you could go home for a while as well.'

Miranda shook her head. 'No way,' she gave a derisive laugh. 'I'm staying here. I'm not going to let some dumb killer scare me off.' She raised her eyebrows questioningly at Jennifer. 'I guess if he wants me, I'll be pretty easy prey once you're gone, won't I?'

'Don't do this to me, Miranda.'

Miranda ran her fingers through her thick blonde hair.

'Do what? You're going home. I'm not going to stop you.'

Jennifer turned away, back to her packing, and started to fold the sweaters that she had laid out on the bed. She didn't want to look at Miranda, didn't want to see the accusation in her eyes.

'I hear he likes to either strangle his victims or suffocate them,' Miranda said in a casual voice. 'What do you reckon he'll do to me, Jen?'

Jennifer ignored her, knowing that Miranda was just trying to make her feel guilty about leaving. Right now, she was doing a pretty good job. Eventually she heard her friend get up and walk across to the door. She thought she'd already left the room when she called back to her.

'Hey, Jen?'

Jennifer glanced up. Miranda stood in the doorway holding the black leather belt Jennifer hadn't yet packed.

'What?'

'Remember to pack this, okay? I don't fancy waking up tonight to find it wrapped around my neck.'

Smiling dryly, Miranda threw the belt at her and left the room.

Jennifer watched her go. She sighed loudly and cursed under her breath, hating Miranda for making her feel so damn guilty and annoyed with herself for giving in. As she bent to pick the belt up, she noticed a playing card lying on the floor, just under her roommate's bed.

The joker.

Frowning, she picked it up, wondering when Miranda had developed an interest in cards, then dropped it on the desk at the end of her friend's bed. Turning to her case, she began to unpack her clothes.

* * *

She didn't see Miranda again until dinner, having taken precautions to avoid her. She didn't want to give her the satisfaction of knowing she had won.

As she suspected, when she entered the cafeteria and her friend saw her, a broad grin spread across her face. The earlier conversation and all talk of Jennifer leaving had been wiped from the slate and everything was back to normal.

Normal, except for a serial killer running amok on the campus.

It had crossed Jennifer's mind on several occasions that the killer might be someone she knew. Maybe a fellow student or professor. The thought was scary; more so than if he was a complete stranger. In all of her lectures, in the cafeteria at meal-times, the clubs at night, it was possible that she may have conversed with a murderer.

During dinner, Miranda made plans to go over to the student bar on the other side of the campus. Jennifer didn't want to go. Like most of the other students, she had come to realise that she was safer if she stayed in her room after dark. Miranda was being bull-headed though and said she would go even if it was by herself. Remembering that they were supposed to be watching out for each other, Jennifer reluctantly agreed to go with her.

As the two of them got ready in their room, she kept wondering if she had made the right decision in staying. After all, why should she be made to feel guilty about Miranda? She should have gone home if she wanted to. As usual, Jennifer had been weak-willed enough to give in. She made a decision there and then that she would have to try to be more assertive in the future. That was if she was going to have a future after being dumb enough to stay.

* * *

The student bar, like most of the bars in town, was dead and Jennifer would have been surprised to find it any other way. Only half a dozen of the tables were occupied, and she didn't recognise any faces from her own dorm. She guessed that most of the students there came from the dorms situated close by the bar. Nobody else would be foolish enough to wander further given the circumstances.

That was with the exception of her and Miranda, of course.

Although Jennifer didn't recognise anyone, Miranda spotted a couple of guys that she knew over at one of the tables in the corner, and she dragged Jennifer across, introducing them as Mike and Jason. Both were second-year students and seemed good fun. Mike appeared to be entranced with Miranda and flirted with her continually, while Jason, who made clear that he had a girlfriend and wasn't coming on to Jennifer, turned out to be a master of one-liners and kept her amused with witty anecdotes and jokes. The four of them were on their second round of drinks when Jennifer looked up and saw him: the senior from Friday afternoons.

Lawrie.

She knew his name now, having overheard a conversation he'd been having with a friend one afternoon, and she watched him for a few minutes, only half paying attention to the story that Jason was recounting, as she tried to figure out if he was with anyone.

Lawrie sat on a bar stool, dressed in a black shirt and black jeans, chatting to one of the guys serving behind the bar, but he appeared to be pretty much alone. Needing to pee and knowing that to get to the bathroom she had to walk past the bar, Jennifer made her excuses and squeezed past Jason. She wasn't too sure what exactly she planned on doing when she got to the bar, considering that in the last couple of months she hadn't actually managed to pluck up the courage to speak to the guy, but she hadn't seen him there before and, with her courage fuelled by the alcohol, wasn't about to waste an opportunity.

Instead of approaching him straightaway, she squeezed past him unnoticed to the bathroom first, wanting to pee and check her appearance before she made her move. Judging by the full bottle of beer he was holding, she felt pretty confident that Lawrie wasn't going anywhere just yet.

The bathroom was empty. Jennifer used the only one of the three stalls that didn't have a broken door, washed her hands, ran a comb through her hair and touched up her lipstick. She smiled at herself in the mirror, trying to build up her confidence.

'Go out there and knock him dead,' she told her reflection in a low voice.

The couple of drinks she'd had were already making her feel a little lightheaded and she was feeling pretty good about herself. Pushing open the bathroom door, she headed straight for the bar, still not having a clue about what she was going to say.

Lawrie's bar stool was empty.

Disappointed, Jennifer looked around to see where he'd gone and crashed straight into Professor Boone.

'Oh my God!' she yelled, almost jumping out of her skin. 'Jeez! Sorry, Professor, you startled me.'

Professor Boone smiled at her and put a hand on her shoulder. 'No harm done, Jennifer. Accidents happen.'

'Yes, I guess so.'

She watched him walk away thinking how strange it was that Professor Boone was in the student bar. Sure, there were plenty of professors who frequented the place, but it didn't seem to be Boone's scene, and he kind of looked out of place.

Unable to see Lawrie anywhere, she headed back to her friends. At the table, she noticed one of them was missing.

'Where's Miranda?' she asked.

Jason pointed to the door.

'You've just missed her, she left two minutes ago.'

Jennifer looked at the door, wondering what had happened to Miranda's plan for them not to split up. She checked her watch and saw that it was ten forty. Chewing her bottom lip, she deliberated over what to do. The bar would be closing in twenty minutes, and she didn't feel that she knew Mike and Jason well enough to ask them to walk her back to her dorm. If Miranda didn't return soon, it looked like she was going to have to do the walk by herself.

24

When Jennifer stepped out of the door of the student bar, she spent a moment glancing around at the stone-grey buildings that flanked her, in the hope that she might see Miranda. The bar, which opened onto a square, was on the older part of the campus and stood facing the library, while two buildings either side had both been converted into dorms. It was possible that Miranda had gone to pay a friend a visit. If she had though, Jennifer had absolutely no idea which of the dorms she might have gone into and wasn't about to waste her time looking.

Personally, she didn't like this part of the campus. Although the old buildings had more character than the purpose-built modern blocks that she and Miranda lived in, they were also far creepier. The stairs creaked and the rooms echoed, and it often seemed as though there was a ghostly presence stalking the hall-ways. Of course, it was probably just her imagination, but with the knowledge that a killer was running loose on the campus, she didn't need anything else to add to her jitters.

As she started to make her way across the square to the archway that led past the library, she looked up at the hundreds of windows that looked down on her. Many of the lights were turned off; a few were on, but of those, most had the blinds drawn. Jennifer realised that anyone could be watching her from one of the darkened rooms. Maybe someone she knew from class or someone who had been in the bar. Possibly even Miranda.

Or perhaps the killer.

Swallowing hard, she picked up her pace, the clatter of her heels creating a loud echo as they hit the stone path. She reached the other side of the square and found herself swallowed by dark shadows for a brief moment as she passed through the archway. Emerging the other side, she was relieved to see the familiar beam of the first of the many street lamps that illuminated the main campus path.

How could Miranda ditch her like this? So much for watching each other like hawks.

Jennifer cursed herself for being fool enough to listen to her so-called friend. The campus grounds were empty for a good reason. People were scared, and she and Miranda had more reason to be scared than most. After all, they fit the profile of the killer's next intended victim. Right now, they should both be back in their room, with the door locked, surrounded by friends and safe from harm.

But instead, where are you? Alone in the dark and a ten-minute walk from your dorm. Just like a sitting duck.

God! How could she be so stupid?

In an attempt to take the edge off her fear, she tried to think of more pleasant subjects. Her family back home, the letter she had received from her sister, summer vacation, now only a few weeks away, Lawrie...

There's a killer on the loose. A sick sadistic killer and you fit the profile of his next victim!

Her grades were getting better. The last couple of months

they'd been steadily improving. She'd even managed to get a couple of As.

He likes to mutilate his victims...

Subconsciously, Jennifer began to pick up her pace. In the distance she could see the towering block in which her room was situated. Another five minutes and she would be back on familiar territory.

The evening was warm and, aside from the sounds of her shoes clipping the concrete, very silent. Her heart started to beat faster, and she could count the beats in between her feet hitting the pavement.

Beat beat, click! Beat beat, click!

She was very aware that she was all alone, the only person outside making any noise; the only idiot foolish enough to be wandering across the campus at night.

Beat beat, click! Beat beat, click! Beat beat, thump! Click! Beat beat, thump! Click!

Hearing the unfamiliar thump, Jennifer realised with a sudden wave of panic that maybe she wasn't alone after all. She increased her pace until she was almost breaking into a slow run.

Beat, click! Beat, click! Thump! Beat, click! Beat, click! Thump!

She tried to tell herself it was no one to worry about. It was probably just another student. Probably even someone that she knew from her own dorm.

If you're so sure, just look over your shoulder. Put your mind at ease.

Jennifer wanted to look. She couldn't bring herself to turn her head though, scared of what she might see. There was a killer on the loose. How could she possibly kid herself that it was all right?

What if he was in the student bar watching you? What if when you left, he followed you?

God! Why the hell hadn't she asked Mike or Jason to walk her back to the dorm? It didn't matter that she barely knew them. They would have understood, given the circumstances, wouldn't they? She could feel her insides knotting with fear. Her legs started to tremble.

A slight breeze rustled through the leaves of the giant trees overhead. To her left were the campus tennis courts; the bars of the surrounding metal fence clinked together as they were battered by the light breeze. The football pitch was over to the right. A large black mass of ground that looked completely different at night when there were no jocks running the field.

She was all alone. If she was attacked now, no one would be there to rush to her aid. No one would hear her screams.

Unable to stand the torment any longer, Jennifer turned and glanced over her shoulder.

She breathed in a huge sigh of relief as she recognised the familiar features of Bryan Waller, the tall, lithe, basketball player who shared her Monday afternoon lectures, jogging towards her.

'Bryan! Jeez!' She put a hand to her chest, feeling the racing beat of her heart start to slow. 'You scared the crap out of me.'

Bryan flashed her a lopsided grin. 'I'm not surprised, out here all by yourself.' He looked her over, and Jennifer saw his eyes narrow slightly with concern as he realised just how much he'd scared her. 'What are you doing out here anyway?'

'Don't even ask.'

'You know, it's not a very sensible idea, Jen, going for late-night walks by yourself,' he scolded. 'Not when you know there's a killer on the loose.'

Jennifer raised a questioning brow.

'You're out here.'

'Yeah, but I have to run. Besides, I don't think I'm in any imminent danger.' He stared at the floor, avoiding looking at her face. Jennifer didn't need him to spell out what he was thinking. Bryan

Waller didn't have anything to worry about for the time being because he fell further down on the wanted list.

She managed a weak smile. 'I'm not out here by choice, you know. I kind of got ditched.'

Bryan glanced up at her. 'Miranda?'

'How did you guess?'

Shaking his head, he sighed and gave her a knowing look. 'Come on, Jennifer,' he said, hooking his arm through hers. 'I'll walk you back to your dorm.'

* * *

Jennifer had half hoped to find Miranda back in the safety of their room, but her friend was obviously planning a late night with whoever it was she had gone to see.

She had better not be gone too long. Aside from wanting to sound off at her for the way she'd been ditched, the idea of spending the night alone in the room kind of spooked Jennifer. Despite the warmth of the night, she pushed the window shut and bolted it, remembering how a couple of the dead students had actually been attacked in their rooms. She didn't plan on leaving the killer an easy opportunity to get in. Before undressing, she also checked under both beds and in the closet, knowing that although she was probably being stupid, she wouldn't be able to sleep unless she did. Finally satisfied that the room was secure, she collected her nightshirt, towel and toiletries bag and, stopping to lock the door behind her, headed down to the communal washrooms.

They were empty. Jennifer hadn't expected to find them any other way. Most of the students in her block were probably already in bed. She placed her things down on the shelf unit beside one of the shower cubicles, slipped out of her jeans and T-shirt and hung them on one of the empty hooks. Unzipping her floral-patterned cosmetic bag, she took out her soap, shampoo and a hair clip, and, noticing her room key sitting exposed on the shelf, she slipped it inside the bag before zipping it back up.

After taking a quick glance around the washroom to make sure she was definitely alone, Jennifer stepped into the shower. She placed her soap and shampoo down on the shelf inside the cubicle and turned on the faucet. As she waited for the water to heat up, she smoothed her hair back with her hands, folded it into a knot and clipped it on top of her head, then testing the temperature with the back of her hand she stepped into the warm spray.

While she showered, the thought occurred to her that anyone could enter the washroom, and she probably wouldn't hear them. The hot powerful spray felt good against her skin and the thought was only brief as her body started to unwind and relax. She soaped herself down, pulled off her hair clip and washed her hair. When she was finished, she reached for her towel, wrapping it around her body.

She stepped from the cubicle. The whole room was warm now, and condensation from the heat of the water had steamed up the mirror on the opposite wall. Knowing she was alone, Jennifer pulled the towel free, leant forward and began to squeeze the water from her hair.

A sudden clicking noise behind her made her jump.

Clutching the towel to her breasts she swung round, trepidation sweeping through her body.

Nobody was there.

Although she was certain that she had heard the noise, she knew there was no way it could have come from inside the washroom. The place was empty. From where she stood, all five of the shower cubicles, including the one she had just used, had the curtains pulled back and were exposed enough for her to see that there was no one hiding in any of them.

The noise had made her feel uneasy, though. Quickly she pulled her hair back into the clip then, standing with her back to the wall, she slipped on her nightshirt. It was an old one, but it was her favourite. Short, white and made of soft cool cotton that felt good against her skin. But now, wearing it made her feel exposed, standing here in the washroom, worried about who might be lurking out in the hallway.

Biding her time before she had to leave the safety of the room, she slowly packed away her soap and shampoo and checked that her room key was still in place.

It was; Jennifer let out a sigh of relief.

She took her toothbrush and paste from the bag. As she brushed her teeth she wondered if perhaps she should go wake up Alex and Karla who shared the room next door to her and Miranda. She knew they wouldn't object to her crashing on their floor. At least that way she knew for certain that she would be safe. Liking the idea, she spat and rinsed under the faucet.

As she brought her head back up, her eyes came into line with the mirror. The condensation on the glass was slowly beginning to clear. In the reflection, she saw her face.

Behind it, she saw another face. An older, male face that she instantly recognised.

Her first reaction of surprise quickly turned to fear as the eyes bore into hers and a cold smile formed on his lips. As Jennifer started to turn, a scream stuck in her throat. He was too quick for her though, and a sharp kick to the back of her knees sent her flying forward. Her chin smashed against the edge of the wash-basin, sending her teeth crashing into her upper lip. She tasted blood, felt sharp pain blast through her face and dropped to the floor.

Her head was whirling, fast, too fast to think, and she rolled to her side ready to throw up. Before she made it, her eyes blacked and she passed out.

* * *

She awoke to find herself on a hard floor.

At first, she thought there was something wrong with her vision.

Everything seemed distorted and fuzzy, and hot. There was no air. Something was covering her face. Something plastic.

I've got a plastic bag over my goddamn face!

Everything that had happened came flooding back to her. The washroom, the face in the mirror, hitting the floor, the taste of blood. And then the sudden realisation that she couldn't actually breathe.

I hear he likes to either strangle his victims or suffocate them.

Miranda's words rang through her head. *Who do you reckon he's gonna go for? Miranda Ingram or Jennifer Isaac?*

Miranda Ingram or Jennifer Isaac? Miranda Ingram or Jennifer Isaac?

Frantically, Jennifer clawed at the plastic. It was held tightly in place by something that was fastened round her neck. Hot breath from her mouth coated the plastic, steaming it with condensation.

In the distance she heard laughter and she became aware of a blurred shape a few feet away. Sitting, watching.

It was him. He was getting a kick out of watching her suffocating. His laughter grew louder. It hurt her ears.

Got to get the bag off. Got to get it off before I die.

Beads of sweat rolled into the corners of her eyes. Each drop stung and she longed desperately to wipe them clear. The plastic grew cloudier, her breathing was getting louder and raspier.

Eventually, the noise she was making as she gasped for air drowned out the sound of the laughter.

Then she passed out again.

* * *

This time she thought she had actually died.

This was the afterlife, and she was on her way to Heaven, or wherever it was that people went. She was glad they had music there. It was kind of tinny, but familiar. Tchaikovsky, she thought.

Her mind struggled briefly with the issue of whether or not she'd been good enough to go on to Heaven, should such a place exist. She was aware of feeling cold, and there was something hard pressed against her face, her chest, and her legs.

Weren't you supposed to float when you died?

Then she was aware of the pain. The pain in her lip, the pain in her chin, the pain in her chest each time she breathed, and she knew that she wasn't dead.

So, where was she?

Her head was fuzzy, her throat tight. Sore from whatever had been wrapped around it. She remembered the plastic bag. She remembered how he'd been sitting there laughing and she wondered where he was.

Slowly she tried to lift her head.

The room was dark with shadows, the only light coming from two candles. She was in some kind of tool shop. A workshop, perhaps. Various hammers and drills hung from hooks on the walls and there were several planks of wood stacked up in one corner. The room was small. She could see there was a door, though it was shut and, she guessed from the keyhole, probably locked; there appeared to be no window, so it was possible that she was in a basement or cellar.

She had no idea where she was. Maybe she was still on campus somewhere or perhaps he had taken her to his house. At the moment, all she knew was that she was in a workshop listening to Tchaikovsky.

Looking down, she could see that she was lying on some kind of wooden table, probably a workbench and, to her horror, she realised that aside from a white sheet that had been draped over her body, covering her from the bottom of her spine down to her ankles, she was completely naked.

She didn't know where her nightshirt had gone or when he had taken it off, but the thought that he had undressed her and touched her made her skin crawl.

This must be where he brings his victims to carve them up.

The thought struck fear into her, but she tried to remain calm, rational. He'd left her down here alone, so maybe he thought that she was already dead. Thinking of the plastic bag and how tightly it had been wrapped around her face, it occurred to Jennifer that she should be dead. But she wasn't, and that meant only one thing to her. If she was alive, she had a chance.

As thoughts of escape rushed through her mind, the stomp of footsteps on stairs, growing closer and closer, shook her to her senses. Quickly she glanced around. There were plenty of weapons on the various shelves. Axes, blades and saws. No time to get to them, though.

The only thing within her reach was a screwdriver lying on a surface close to the bench. It was small and probably blunt, and if she was going to use it, she would have to jam it really hard. Quickly she grabbed the small weapon and hid it in her hand under her belly. Then she lay as still as possible, her eyes closed, waiting for a chance to make her move.

She heard a key turn in the lock and the sound of the creaking door as it swung open. He came into the room, closing the door behind him and crossed to where she lay.

She was aware of his presence as he stood above her, then the touch of his hands as he lifted her hair, draping it to the side of her head. Fingers that were soft and smooth began to caress her neck. He leant closer blowing warm breath on to the back of her ear. Jennifer tried to remain as still and calm as possible, not wanting to let him know that she was still alive. Any moment now she would turn and plunge the screwdriver into him.

Any moment now.

She just had to pluck up the courage first.

The fingers went away. He went away. She could hear him over at one of the shelves; he sounded as though he was picking up something heavy. An axe or a saw.

Shit! He's gonna cut me up. Should have spiked him when I got the chance.

He returned to the table. Jennifer could feel her heart beating fast, much too fast, and she hoped that he couldn't hear it.

What are you waiting for, Jen? Do it now!

She couldn't will herself to move.

Now! Do it now!

Something sharp pierced the back of her neck, tearing into the skin.

This time there was no chance of playing dead. Screaming loudly, she rolled onto her side slamming the screwdriver into the air. She missed the first time but, catching him off guard, was granted a second chance. She plunged the screwdriver into his belly, ramming it as hard as she could.

A look of surprise passed over his face. Surprise that she was alive and then shock as he realised what she had done to him. He looked at her with accusing eyes. Eyes that were stone cold, but also made her feel as though she had in some way betrayed him. As though it was his God-given right to take her life, and she shouldn't attempt to stop him.

Jennifer swallowed hard. Her whole body frozen to the table.

Those eyes.

Stone eyes. Dead eyes. Eyes of pure evil.

He broke away, glancing down at the handle of the screwdriver, the cold steel embedded deep inside him. Blood was already pumping from where his skin had been pierced, soaking through his shirt. Deep red, almost black.

He bleeds black blood! He's the goddamn Devil.

Jennifer willed herself to move, knowing that she had to get out of this hellhole. A strangled cry escaped his lips and, dropping the knife that was clenched in his hand, he stumbled backwards, crashing into the planks of wood.

Forcing herself to seize the chance, she threw herself off the table, the sheet still clutched around her, and ran for the door. Her head felt heavy, her limbs achy and weak.

Gotta get out of here. Gotta get out of here.

She reached for the handle of the door, clenching it tightly in her fist, and willed it to turn.

As the door started to creak open a strong arm banded around her waist, lifting her from the floor and carrying her back into the room.

'No! No! Put me down! Get off me!' she screamed loudly, kicking and struggling against his grip.

Reaching her arms over her head, she grabbed fistfuls of his hair and tugged as hard as she could. Although he didn't let go of her, he released one arm and, grunting loudly, tried to wrestle himself free. Keeping hold of his head, Jennifer worked the fingers of one hand down onto his face. She felt the broad plain of his forehead, the thick hair of his brows, and the softer flesh of his eyelids. Using her thumb and forefinger, she stabbed him hard in the eyes. Screaming loudly, he released his grip, dropping her to the floor.

Jennifer landed uncomfortably on her knees. Ignoring the pain, she rolled over to face him, clutching the sheet across her chest, ready for another attack.

His back was still to her, and he was yelling and screaming as he stumbled around like a blind man, holding his hands over his eyes.

She knew that she should run. This was her chance, her one chance of escape. Of course, she still had no idea where she was, and it was possible that when she reached the top of the stairs, she might find herself locked in.

She hadn't hurt him enough to stop him from coming after her, and she didn't doubt that when he did, he would be mad as hell. Glancing down at the floor, she saw the knife that he had dropped. The same knife he had planned to cut her with.

She reached forward and, grabbing hold of the handle, pulled the weapon towards her. It was heavy and at least twelve inches long with a sharp-edged blade that was already smeared with a few drops of her own blood.

The bastard was going to cut me with this.

Spurred on by a mixture of fear and anger, Jennifer picked herself up from the floor and lunged herself forward, ramming the knife hard into his back.

As the blade sunk in, an anguished cry tore from his lips and he stumbled forward into the workbench, knocking the two candles to the floor.

Jennifer stared at him through a sheen of tears as the flames started to rise, barely able to believe what she had just done. She wiped at her eyes with a shaking hand, watching him sink to the floor, and drew a raspy breath.

Oh my God! He's dead. I've killed him.

Suddenly finding the energy to move, she turned and ran for the door. She passed through it without looking back, then once outside turned and slammed it shut.

There was no key in the lock and she guessed that it was probably in one of his pockets. She told herself though that it wasn't really necessary to lock the door. If he wasn't already dead from the stab wound she had inflicted, the flames would soon take care of him. There was no way that he could come after her now because either way, he was dead, and no matter which way she looked at it, she had been the one who had killed him.

* * *

It was over an hour later before the police were called.

Back in the house, Jennifer hadn't wasted time looking for a phone, knowing that by the time she found one, the whole house would be engulfed in flames, and it wasn't until she finally stepped outside that she had realised just how isolated the property was.

There was one car parked out front, a silver Plymouth. After trying the doors, only to find them all locked, she had hiked along the quiet backwoods road at the end of the driveway for more than a mile, her pace slowed by her injuries, before she eventually stumbled upon a farmhouse.

The front door was opened by a thin-faced, elderly woman dressed completely in black, and her jaw had dropped open as she took in the sight of the girl standing on her doorstep dressed only in a sheet.

Jennifer bit her bottom lip nervously.

'Can you help me, please?' she asked in a shaky voice. 'It's my English professor. He just tried to kill me.'

25

JUNIPER, OREGON. SATURDAY 3 MAY 1997

He had shown up just when things seemed as though they'd hit an all-time low.

Her grades were gradually slipping, Lawrie Parker barely knew that she existed and now, to top it all off, a serial killer with a penchant for college students was on the loose and hungry for his next victim. A victim whose profile she apparently matched.

When he had approached her, the conversation that had taken place hadn't been at all what she'd expected, but after just five minutes of chatting with the guy, she soon discovered that nothing about him was predictable and nothing was quite as it seemed. She wasn't attracted to him, didn't know him and, under current circumstances, knew that she shouldn't really trust him. After all, she knew nothing about him and there was every possibility that he might be the man responsible for the five murdered students. She had been curious, though, curious to find out what he had to say and also interested in finding out just how come he knew her so well.

The first time she had seen him had been late on Friday afternoon. She had been depositing the books from her last class into her locker and curiously studying the plain white envelope that had been wedged in the door, bearing her name in bold black print. She had noticed him watching her from across the hallway, leaning against the wall next to a fire hydrant, and wondered for a brief second who he was. As far as she was aware, he wasn't a student, and she was pretty certain that she'd never seen him before. Not appreciating his scrutiny, she had turned her back to him while she opened the envelope, eager to know what it contained.

There was no letter inside, instead, just a playing card of a joker.

Justine stared at it curiously, wondering who had sent it to her and what it was supposed to mean. She glanced around the busy hallway. Most of the other students were either engaged in conversation or hurrying back to their dorms. Nobody was paying any attention to her. Nobody, except for the guy standing next to the fire hydrant.

She glanced up at him with a surge of anger as she realised that she was still being watched. Before she had the chance to tell him to quit staring at her, he had pushed himself away from the wall and disappeared into the crowd.

* * *

The second time she had seen him had been in town late on Saturday afternoon and this time he had actually come across and spoken to her. Luke had gone home for the weekend and, at a loss for what to do, she had gone shopping. After three hours spent trailing around various clothes stores, she had decided to treat herself to a cup of coffee and a chocolate fudge sundae in one of the many diners in town.

To be truthful, she was putting off returning to the college campus. Although she had known about the murdered students before the FBI visit, it had scared the hell out of her to find out that she fitted the profile of the killer's next victim. She had spent most of Friday afternoon toying with the idea of going home. Her parents, though, were out of town until Sunday night and she didn't have enough money in her account to pay for the bus fare home. In the end she had decided to wait until they returned, then give them a call to discuss it.

As she sipped her coffee, she tried to distract herself with thoughts of Lawrie. She found it difficult to believe that it had been a whole week ago that she'd paid him a visit. Her heartbeat quickened slightly as she remembered how she'd been inside his house, inside his bedroom and how she had worn his shirt and his tie. She wondered if either he or Kylan had noticed the tie missing, and then realised she didn't really care. Although she had taken it by accident, she would hold on to it as a little keepsake to remind herself of that night. A souvenir. Her own little part of Lawrie.

Lost in her thoughts, she didn't at first notice the man sitting at the counter watching her and, when she did finally notice him, it appeared that he was trying to catch her attention and get himself an invitation to join her. Although he didn't receive one, he climbed down from his stool and made his way across to her table anyway.

Justine had planned on ignoring him or, if he was persistent, telling him to get lost. But he took her by surprise.

'Hello, Justine.'

She gawped at him, wondering how come he knew her name when she'd never laid eyes on him before.

'Who are you?' she blurted, forgetting that she had planned on ignoring him.

Instead of sitting in one of the empty chairs opposite her, he took a seat at the table beside her. Evidently, he didn't want to crash on her space. Smart move, she thought, and repeated her question.

'Who are you?'

He offered his hand. 'Let's just say I'm a friend.'

His grip was strong, almost crushing, and she pulled her hand away.

'Okay, friend. So how the hell do you know who I am?'

'I've been watching you, Justine.' He smiled and the lines around his eyes crinkled. 'I think we should talk. Can I perhaps meet you somewhere later?'

Justine rolled her eyes. Here it was: the pick-up line. He must have seen her around campus and asked one of her friends what her name was.

'We don't need to talk and no, I'm not meeting you anywhere.'

'It's very important we talk, Justine. I really think you should reconsider.'

She laughed scornfully.

'I'm not meeting you. No way! In fact, I think you'd better leave. And just so you know, I already have a boyfriend.'

The man's smile grew wider. 'It's not Lawrie Parker though, is it?'

Justine's jaw dropped open. She felt as though a knife had been plunged into her chest.

'What do you mean?' she asked, her voice coming out in a high-pitched squeak.

'I think you know what I mean.'

'I don't. Tell me.'

'I think Justine has a little crush on her professor.' His tone was teasing and singsong as he looked at her expectantly. 'You do, don't you?'

Justine squirmed uncomfortably in her seat, heat rushing to her face. 'I want you to leave now.'

'No, you don't. I can help you, Justine, and I think you'll be very interested in hearing what I have to say.'

Justine glanced around the crowded room, checking that no one was looking in their direction. It crossed her mind that maybe the guy had been sent to play a practical joke. If he had though, how the hell did he know about her liking Lawrie? How the hell did anyone know about Lawrie?

Had she really been that obvious?

She glared at him. 'I don't want your help. In fact, I don't want anything to do with you at all, so why don't you just fuck off.'

The man didn't move. Instead, he smiled at her.

Justine repeated her request, this time hissing the words. 'I said fuck off!'

Again, he didn't move, only glanced around to see if anyone was in earshot of their conversation. The diner was busy though, and no one seemed to be paying any attention to the two of them. He turned his focus back to her.

'So, tell me, Justine, did you have a nice time playing in Lawrie's house last Saturday night?'

Justine stared at him, not believing what she was hearing. She swallowed hard. 'What did you say?'

'You heard what I said. Still want me to "fuck off"?'

She didn't answer, couldn't answer. She was completely lost for words. How did he know? She found herself in a dangerous situation. So far, she hadn't admitted to anything. Not that it mattered, as this guy seemed to know everything there was to know about her. Perhaps he was planning to blackmail her. Maybe threaten to go to Lawrie and tell him everything.

He can't prove anything, though. It would be my word against his.

In her mind, she tried to retrace her steps through Lawrie's house. Had she left any incriminating evidence that this guy could use against her? He must have something. Had he watched her in the house, maybe taken photos? Not sure how to play the situation, Justine waited for him to continue.

He smiled at her. 'You're going to let me stay, then? That's good. Of course, I don't know really why I should help you. After all, it seems to me that you've got a bit of an attitude problem.' He leaned back comfortably in his chair, though his eyes remained lingering on her face. 'So, tell me, then, why you did it, Justine. Was it for the excitement of breaking into someone else's house? Or perhaps you just wanted to check out the competition. Kylan Parker is very pretty, isn't she?' He paused, looking thoughtful for a moment. 'If I had to hazard a guess, I would say that you did it for kicks. Did you go into the marital bedroom while you were there? Perhaps have a look through the closets or try out the bed?'

As he spoke, Justine's cheeks burned and she had trouble breathing.

'A regular little Goldilocks, aren't you? Of course, you don't have a chance in hell of getting Lawrie away from Kylan, but then you probably already know that. I mean, look at you. Your hair is too dull, and you don't have her beautiful doe eyes. Still,' he smiled cheerfully, 'I guess there's nothing there that can't be fixed with a bottle of bleach and some tinted contact lenses.' His eyes dropped to her breasts. 'I don't really know what you can do about the rest of you, though. To say you're flat-chested would be an understatement. I guess you'd better hope that Lawrie likes the pancake look.'

Anger overcoming her embarrassment, Justine raised her hand to slap him. He caught her wrist and squeezed it tightly. Narrowing his eyes, he spoke with a harsh tone.

'Think before you act, sweetheart. I know everything there is to know about you, don't ever forget that, and don't forget how easily I can bring you down if I have to.' His tone became gentler and he smiled at her. 'I say "have to", but that doesn't mean I want to. I need you, Justine, and you need me. If we work together then nobody else will ever have to know your dark and guilty secret, I promise you that.'

Justine studied his face, not sure whether she could trust him. Thinking about it realistically, she knew that she didn't really have much of a choice. Fighting the urge to get up and run, she instead shifted her chair closer to him.

'Go on, then. Let's hear it. What do you have to say?'

He smiled again, and his eyes crinkled.

'Like I said, Justine, we have a lot in common, the two of us. We both want something which is at the moment unobtainable to us. But I think that if we work together, we might be able to change that situation.'

'I don't get what you mean,' Justine said, beginning to understand exactly what he meant. She felt her heart skip a beat. 'You want Kylan, don't you?'

He didn't answer, instead giving her a faint smile that led her to believe she had guessed correctly. She chewed her bottom lip, realising that maybe the situation wasn't quite as bleak as it had initially looked. If she worked with him, then maybe she really would have a shot at getting Lawrie.

'Okay, you've got me interested. A little bit interested.'

'Good. I knew I could count on you, Justine.'

Justine nodded, still feeling a little uneasy. 'So, what's your plan then?'

He glanced around the diner again before shifting his chair a little closer.

'I want you to meet me tonight. I'll pick you up outside this diner, and then I'll tell you the plan.'

Justine stared at him, aware the colour was draining from her face. 'You want me to go off alone with you?' she asked, not liking the idea at all.

'Why not?'

'I can't. We have a curfew.'

'A curfew? Really?' He looked at her and smiled. 'Don't worry, Justine, I'll look after you.'

Justine shrugged. 'I don't know. I'm not sure it's a good idea.'

'Why not? You do want to do this, don't you?' His tone was baiting.

'Do I have a choice?' she mumbled, more so to herself, as she remembered what he had said about Lawrie.

'No, I guess you don't.'

'I didn't think so.' Justine gazed uncomfortably at her lap.

'You've got to learn to trust me, Justine.'

'Trust you? You're blackmailing me, for Christ's sake!'

The man rolled his eyes. He leant forward, a slight look of irritation on his face. 'Look, don't be so melodramatic. I'm not forcing you to meet me tonight. If you want, get up and go and pretend we never met.' He paused, grinning at her. 'Of course, I won't be able to offer you any guarantees that Lawrie won't find out about his late-night visitor.' He studied her face carefully. 'It's up to you, Justine; the decision's all yours. You want to walk away? You want to call my bluff? Then go.'

Justine shuffled uneasily in her seat. She glanced at the door of the diner, knowing that if she got up and walked through it now, she would never be able to face Lawrie Parker again. Not sure she was doing the right thing, she stayed where she was, her gaze focused on her lap.

She heard the man's voice, this time less forceful.

'Good girl, Justine. I knew you'd do the right thing.'

She looked up at him, forcing a smile, and hoped that she was.

26

Rebecca pulled open the front door and rolled her eyes when she saw Joel Hickok standing in the hallway.

'Let me guess, you want to go exploring again?'

Hickok grinned and held up a pizza box. 'Pepperoni and mushroom okay?' he asked, ignoring her question and pushing his way past her into the living room.

'Come in, why don't you?' Rebecca muttered under her breath, not making any effort to stop him, and swung the door shut. She was a little surprised to be getting a visit from Hickok, who had been blowing hot and cold towards her all week. One minute he was being Mr Nice Guy and acting all concerned about how she was handling things then, before she had a chance to wonder if perhaps she had him pegged wrong, he'd do something that proved him to be an even bigger jerk than she already thought him to be. Like on Friday morning, he had bitten her head off in the parking lot for suggesting they contact Jennifer Isaac, but then later on that day, having thought it over and decided it was in fact a good idea, not even having the decency to apologise. Maybe that was why he was here now. Perhaps he had come to tell her he was sorry.

Possible, but unlikely. Although she had only known him for a couple of weeks, Rebecca had quickly come to the conclusion that Joel Hickok got a real kick out of irritating her. She knew that she should try to rise above his puerile attitude and not let it bother her, but he was too good at making her bite.

She watched him set the pizza box down on the table, next to her open notebook, and cringed inwardly, hoping he wouldn't notice the notes she had made. Her attempts to get in contact with Jennifer Isaac had proved unsuccessful. Rodney Boone's one surviving victim had returned to her family home in New York, and she had only stayed there for a couple of months before the whole family uprooted and moved away.

There was no recent address or contact number on the Isaac family, but Rebecca didn't doubt that by making a few phone calls she would easily be able to locate them. Hickok had told her not to bother, claiming that it was a waste of time tracking her down unless she still lived locally as they couldn't afford the time or the manpower to go see her. Although Rebecca disagreed with him, she didn't push the matter as she was eager to concentrate on the files she'd been studying about Rodney Boone. The more that she read about the serial killer, the more she managed to convince herself that he was still alive and had something to do with the recent spate of murders.

It made perfect sense.

Boone's body had never been recovered from the fire, so it was probable that he was alive, but too injured to continue the killings alone. Therefore, it was plausible that he had found himself a disciple to finish the job for him. Her theory would explain why the murders had ceased for eight years, why there were slight differences in the way the victims were killed, and why the prints on the vodka bottle hadn't matched up to those of Rodney Boone's.

Unfortunately, neither Hickok nor Sutton shared her view, still believing that the two sets of murders were unrelated and suspecting that the recent killings were probably the work of someone at Juniper College. Hickok's theory on Lawrence Parker had been shot to pieces, and the two Feds had decided to try and get the prints of everyone in the college, in the hope that they would get a match to the print found on the vodka bottle. They had already spoken with Dean Edwards about their plans and he had given them his full support. On Monday morning they intended to set up a room in the main building of the college where the long and drawn out process of collecting the prints would begin.

Rebecca knew it was possible that they might net themselves a killer, but she was also aware that by the time everyone's prints had been collected, the series of murders would probably be complete. That was why she had decided to do a little after-hours snooping into Rodney Boone's background. She knew it was unlikely she would uncover anything new, but that wasn't about to stop her. Her mother had always complained about how she tried to take on the impossible, and she guessed it must be her stubborn streak again.

Of course, on most occasions her mother had turned out to be right, but that never stopped Rebecca, who was a firm believer that if you didn't try then you'd never know, from giving things her best shot. That thought in mind, she had spent much of her afternoon on the telephone talking firstly to Information then to Wyefield Children's Home and finally to the San Palimo Town Library.

While she had uncovered quite a bit of information on Rodney Boone's childhood, which she had planned to share with

Hickok and Sutton on Monday morning, she had hoped to come up with a good story first as to why she had gone behind their backs. Watching Hickok studying her notes, she realised that the story was no longer going to be necessary.

Finished looking at the page listed full of names and phone numbers, he glanced up at her and frowned. 'What's this?'

'Just a few notes I've been making,' Rebecca mumbled, feeling a bit like a child who'd just been caught doing something she shouldn't.

Hickok raised his eyebrows sceptically. 'So, have you actually been calling these people, or did you just decide to write their numbers down for fun?'

'That's none of your business!' Rebecca snapped, perhaps a little too abruptly, having decided that anger was her best defence. 'What I do in my free time is up to me.'

Instead of biting back at her like she expected, Hickok lowered himself onto the couch and gave her a sly smile. 'You know. You're way too uptight. Maybe you should try getting out more.'

Rebecca's mouth dropped open. She was a little surprised that he wasn't mad at her, but also amazed that he seemed to think he could continually insult her.

'Like you, you mean?' she retorted. 'I've noticed that your social life seems to revolve mainly around my doorstep these days.'

'I like you, Angell. Be flattered.' He grinned at her and pulled the lid off the pizza box. 'Pizza?' he asked, offering her the box.

Rebecca gave an exaggerated sigh, secretly relieved that he hadn't blown up at her for defying his orders. Taking a slice of pizza, she sat down on the floor in front of the table.

'So, you've been doing a little after-hours research on Boone, have you?' Hickok pushed.

'You know I have, so why bother asking?'

'I was trying to give you the benefit of the doubt, as I hoped you weren't really that stupid.'

'Hey! I am not stupid.' Rebecca glared at Hickok, angry with herself for allowing him to draw her into another fight. 'I thought that in order to investigate a crime properly you had to explore every possible angle.'

'Rodney Boone has got nothing to do with the recent murders.' Hickok shook his head, seeming both exasperated and amused. 'The man gets stabbed with a butcher's knife, locked in the cellar and caught up in a fire. Okay, I admit his body was never found, but you're trying to tell me that eight years after disappearing without a trace, after no one has heard a word from him, he suddenly comes back to the scene of his original crimes to start killing again?' He laughed sarcastically. 'Jeez, Angell! This is real life, not the fucking twilight zone.'

'What I'm suggesting is not as stupid as you're trying to make it sound,' Rebecca argued through gritted teeth, fighting to keep control of her temper. 'Sutton himself admitted that Boone could quite possibly still be alive.'

'Sure, it's possible. Remotely possible. If he is, though, the guy has to be looking like a piece of toast. You really think he's in any fit condition to start killing again?'

'You don't know what kind of condition he was in,' Rebecca argued. 'How can you say for sure that he didn't manage to get out of the house before the fire took hold?'

'Because he was trapped in the fucking cellar with the butcher's knife in his back.'

'Was the cellar door locked?'

'No! I don't know.'

'Then it's possible that he could have managed to crawl away.'

'Yeah, sure,' Hickok agreed in a patronising tone. 'He's some kind of superhero, right? He manages to escape from the house and then he flies away before the cops can get there to arrest him. Oh, and let me guess, the reason no one's been able to find him for the past eight years is because he can make himself invisible. Jesus, you idiot, would you listen to what you're saying?'

'It's not as ridiculous as it sounds,' Rebecca protested.

'Yes, it is. I know you have a crazy streak, Angell, but what you're suggesting is completely insane. You must watch way too much television.'

'I do not!' Rebecca said indignantly.

'Yeah? Well I'm surprised. I thought that maybe all those zombie flicks were starting to go to your head.'

'All I'm trying to say is that Boone is probably still alive. I never said that I thought he was our killer.'

'At last, you've managed to say something rational,' Hickok clapped his hands together. 'In case you've forgotten, we already know he's not our killer. The print on the vodka bottle already told us that.'

'Exactly. So maybe the print belongs to someone who is helping Boone.'

Hickok raised his eyebrows disbelievingly. 'You're kidding, right?'

Placing her slice of pizza down on the edge of the box, Rebecca reached for her notebook on the table and started to leaf through the pages.

'Just hear me out before you make any kind of judgement.'

Hickok gave an exaggerated sigh. 'Great! I get to listen to another one of your lunatic ideas,' he muttered, leaning back against the cushions and looking at her expectantly.

Rebecca studied him for a moment, briefly wondering why it was she had chosen to sit on the floor instead of next to him.

Sexual tension. You're putting up barriers.

She dismissed the idea immediately and turned back to her notes, ignoring the colour she could feel rising to her cheeks.

'I called the children's home in Wyefield where Cedric and Phillipa Boone adopted Rodney from when he was a kid,' she began. 'The home was moved to a new location about ten years ago and a lot of the adoption records were lost along the way. I spoke to one of the old caretakers though, who started around the time that Boone was there, and he was pretty certain that Boone had two younger brothers who were both adopted by different families a year or so earlier. He couldn't remember much else, so I decided to go back further and call the San Palimo Police Department – San Palimo is the town where Boone lived with his real mother, Helen White, before she tried to kill herself,' she elaborated, glancing up at Hickok. Hickok rolled his eyes. 'I know that. I'm not stupid.'

Choosing to ignore him, Rebecca continued. 'So anyway, they put me in touch with the town library where all of the records are kept and I spoke to a woman there, Karen Harris. She only has limited information. Apparently, they're not computerised yet and most of the files are stacked up out back. She told me that there had been some kind of family tragedy in which Boone's father was killed.'

Hickok frowned at her, his brow knitting together. 'So what are you trying to prove, Angell? That Boone has brothers? That his father died?'

'Quit interrupting me, will you? I haven't finished yet.'

'You mean there's more?' Hickok grinned. 'Great, go on, I'm all ears.'

Rebecca scowled at him, wondering why she was bothering. She continued anyway, determined to say her piece. 'Karen Harris told me that there's another librarian she thinks we should talk to. A woman called Agnes Barnes. Apparently, this Agnes lady is the eyes and ears of the town and knows just about everything that goes on.'

'Why would we want to talk to her, Angell?'

Rebecca bit her lip. 'Because she might be able to tell us more about Rodney Boone's two brothers.'

'Oh, I see. And we want to know more about Rodney Boone's brothers because...?'

'Because maybe they know where he is.'

'Of course!' Hickok laughed scornfully. He leaned forward and took another slice of pizza from the box. 'We're talking about three kids from a children's home, Angell,' he mumbled through his mouthful. 'They were all adopted by different families. I doubt that Boone's brothers even know who he is, so they're hardly gonna be harbouring him from the law!'

'It's possible.'

'No, it's not possible. It's stupid.'

Rebecca shrugged, telling herself that she should have expected this kind of reaction.

'I still think that someone should go down to California and talk to Agnes Barnes,' she persisted. 'Okay, so it might not lead anywhere, but it's got to be worth a shot.'

Hickok nodded. 'Maybe when this investigation is over, we'll follow up your lead. Right now, I think it's more important to catch our killer.'

'So, you still won't accept that Boone might be involved with the recent murders?' Rebecca pushed.

'Nope.'

She glared at him. 'You are such a narrow-minded jerk, it's unbelievable.'

Hickok shook his head. 'I'm not narrow-minded, Angell. I'm just being logical. You, on the other hand, are so nuts you should be institutionalised.' He gave her a teasing grin. 'I guess you're lucky I've got a soft spot for crazy women.'

Rebecca glared at him, infuriated at how stubborn he was being and even more infuriated that as he sat there watching her with taunting eyes, dark hair falling onto his forehead, she was finding herself undeniably attracted to him. To hide her feelings, she got to her feet and, grabbing hold of the empty pizza box, carried it through to the kitchen. She heard Hickok get up and start to follow her and for a moment she panicked, wondering if he knew what she was thinking. She didn't want to have to deal with what she was feeling. Not now. Not ever.

She turned and saw that he was standing in the archway that separated the kitchen from the living room. He studied her face for a moment, looking as though he was about to say something, and she caught her breath as she realised that they were both thinking the same thing.

For a moment a thick silence hung between them. Hickok had lost his cocky grin and there was a fervid, almost hungry look in his eyes. Rebecca watched him, a little unsure what to expect.

The shrill ring of the phone sounded beside her, making her jump and cutting through the tension like a knife. The moment lost, Hickok gave a nonchalant shrug and turned back to the couch. Rebecca watched him, feeling both relief and disappointment. She listened as her answer machine picked up the call, wondering why it was she was suddenly finding herself attracted to an arrogant, self-important jerk like Hickok.

Maybe he was right. Maybe she was nuts.

Her mother's voice echoed out of the answer machine. 'Rebecca? Rebecca, are you there? Rebecca, it's your mother...' Not wanting to have one of Sarah Angell's mother–daughter chats in front of Hickok, Rebecca chose to ignore her, letting the machine take her message. As she listened to her mother run on about nothing in particular, she shrugged apologetically at Hickok, who sat watching her with a bemused expression.

'That's my mother,' she told him, feeling the need to explain.

'Yeah, she said.'

'She just likes to check that I'm doing okay.'

'So I hear.'

'She's not really as bad as she sounds,' Rebecca said, screwing up her nose. 'Well, okay. Maybe she gets a bit carried away.'

Hickok nodded, the cocky grin returning to his face. 'Really? Well I guess now I can see where you get it from.'

27

Justine arrived at the diner first and stood waiting outside, nervously chewing on her nails.

She waited for fifteen minutes, until eventually a brown Buick pulled up and the man who she had met earlier stuck his head out of the open driver's window.

'Ready to go, Justine?' he asked, a grin lighting up his face.

Justine didn't want to get in the car. She didn't make a habit of riding with strangers and was even less eager at the prospect of riding with this one. Unfortunately, as he was blackmailing her, she didn't really have much choice. Reminding herself of what would happen if she didn't go with the man, she climbed into the passenger seat.

As they drove, Justine babbled nervously, and the man listened. At least she thought he was listening until she asked him a question and got no reply. She tried again, this time her voice louder and her tone sharper.

'I asked if you live locally?'

This time he looked at her and gave a half-smile.

Guessing that he didn't want to talk, Justine turned and

looked out of the window. She was uncomfortable being with him and her stomach was grinding nervously.

Maybe it was the not knowing where they were going or what they were going to do. Or perhaps it was because, until now, her lust for Lawrie Parker had been secret. Her own personal secret. Maybe it was knowing that someone else now knew that secret that was making her so nervous and excitable. Or perhaps it was the fact that since she'd climbed in the Buick, the guy had undergone a complete personality change.

While she talked, he drove in silence and it was almost as though she no longer existed to him or, as though, now he had her where he wanted her, there was no longer any need to keep up the charade. A shiver ran down Justine's spine as she recalled the warning they had been given at college just the day before.

You all fit the profile of the killer's next victim.

She wondered how come the cops seemed to know who the killer's next victim would be. There were thousands of students who attended the college. Thousands of potential victims.

Besides, this was different. This guy, he'd been watching her, he'd told her so. He needed her help. He'd told her that they were after the same thing. He knew everything about her.

And she realised she knew absolutely nothing about him.

It doesn't matter. He's blackmailing you. He's hardly going to kill you.

She tried to restart the conversation.

'You didn't tell me what you do for a living? Do you work at the college? Is that how you know Lawrie and Kylan?'

He glanced at her. 'You ask a lot of questions.'

'Well, I hadn't noticed you, that's all. If you worked at the college, I meant,' Justine pushed. 'So, do you?'

'At the moment... yes. The reason you haven't noticed me is because in my line of work I have to be very discreet.'

'Oh,' Justine mumbled, not really sure what he meant. 'So how do you know Lawrie and Kylan?' she asked, trying a different approach.

He gave a knowing smile that made her feel even more uncomfortable. 'Let's just say we go back a long way.'

'I see. Old friends, are you?' She giggled nervously. 'Dumb question. I guess you can't be that close friends if you're going to help me break them up. Of course, I'm sure you have your reasons.' As she continued rambling, her mind returned to the murders.

Scott Jagger, Emma Keeley. She remembered the cop who'd been talking to Mandy Tyson in the cafeteria that day, and how at the time she'd wondered what had been going on.

Now of course she knew.

Emma Keeley had been so beautiful alive, and Justine couldn't help but wonder how she looked dead. A cold, dead corpse. Justine had never seen a dead body before and, thinking about it now, she didn't ever want to. She tried to push the image of Emma Keeley from her mind and instead turned her thoughts to Rufus Lind, the college clown. His face was clear in her mind: the carrot-red hair, the wide blue eyes. Come to think of it, she could picture all of them clearly in her mind. Scott, Emma and Rufus. Three students, all very different, but all well known around campus. Why had the killer chosen them?

Her mind ventured further back. These weren't the only murders that had taken place at Juniper College. She vaguely remembered her father talking about the killings that had taken place on the campus a few years back. She hadn't believed him at the time, thinking that it was just some spook story that he'd made up to scare her. Since she'd been in Juniper, though, she'd realised his stories had been true. Most of her friends on campus knew details of what had happened.

How the Alphabet Killer had been a college professor who had stalked and murdered several of his students. How he had selected his victims from the register. Always in alphabetical order. How one of his victims had fought back and left him for dead in a burning house. How the police had never found his body.

Graffiti in the washrooms told of his name: Professor Boone.

And the classroom in the English block, where he had taught, stood empty because the current professors didn't wish to be tarred with the same brush, and the current students disliked the idea of having lectures in the place where the serial killer had selected his victims.

Justine thought it ironic that, only a few years later, the same college had become the hunting ground for another serial killer. Did he, like the Alphabet Killer, have some weird hang-up?

She thought about his victims again. Scott Jagger, Emma Keeley and Rufus Lind. Jagger, Keeley, Lind. J, K, L.

It was just a bizarre coincidence, wasn't it? Then she remembered that the police had found five victims, but two of them still hadn't been named. What if the unnamed victims had initials M and N? That meant that a person with the initial O was to be the next intended victim.

O for Orton. Justine Orton.

'You all fit the profile of the killer's next victim.'

She cast her mind back, trying to remember some of the other students who had been in the hall. Mary Osborne, Judy O'Brien, Keith Ottinger. They all matched the next victim's profile because they all had the same initial.

The initial O.

Justine had to bite down on the sickness that rose suddenly. A cold sweat broke out on her forehead. This wasn't possible, was it? She couldn't be the killer's next victim. And this man in the driver's seat beside her, he wasn't a killer. He needed her. He'd told her so.

He needed her to help him and in return he would help her to get Lawrie. Wouldn't he?

Thinking about it, he hadn't specifically told her that he was going to help her get Lawrie. Only that they both wanted something that was at the moment unobtainable to them. What if she had misread him? What if it wasn't Kylan Parker he wanted?

'Where are we going?' she asked, swallowing down hard on the bile rising in her throat.

He looked at her, acknowledged she'd spoken, but didn't answer.

Justine drew in a shaky breath; tried to calm her shaking nerves. 'Please! Where are we going?' she asked. 'You still haven't told me.'

The man gave an irritated sigh. 'Haven't you figured it out yet, Justine?'

'Figured what out?'

'You're the next one on the list.'

'What list?' she asked, disbelieving. 'What are you...?'

'I lied to you back in the diner,' he said, interrupting her. 'I had to get you by yourself, and I knew you wouldn't come willingly.' He looked at her again and this time seemed for the first time to really notice she was there.

Justine was aware of the Buick increasing speed and it passed through her mind that she wasn't wearing a seat belt. They might crash if he didn't return his attention to the road.

'You just don't get it, do you?' He shook his head angrily. 'I'm talking about the Alphabet Killer, Justine. You've heard of him, haven't you? You've got the playing card. You're going to be the next victim.'

Justine looked into his eyes and knew that he wasn't kidding.

She turned away, her mind in a spin as she tried to figure out what the hell she was going to do.

You'd better come up with something quick. He's planning on killing you.

A bend appeared in the road ahead, and the Buick began to brake sharply. With no time to think, she pushed down the handle of the door with shaking fingers and shoved it open.

Without looking back, she jumped.

* * *

After she'd jumped from his car, he'd pulled over to the side of the road and given chase, believing that he would catch her easily. Although the water-filled ditch where she'd landed had softened her fall, she had still appeared to be limping badly. But he was wrong. They were in thick woods and there were plenty of places for her to hide. Eventually he'd had to give up the hunt and return to his Buick alone.

He knew he should have panicked. She'd seen his face and would be able to give a good description of him to the cops. If they found him out now, he would never be able to complete the job. Somehow, though, he didn't think that Justine Orton would be picking up the phone and dialling 911. She knew that he knew things about her that no one else did. Maybe only little things, but things, nonetheless, that she wouldn't want to be spread around. If she told the cops what had happened, she would have to tell them what she was doing in the car with him in the first place, and then everyone would find out about Lawrie and her obsessive crush.

He suspected that Justine Orton would rather keep quiet than suffer any kind of embarrassment.

He had really lucked out that night, seeing her break into Lawrie and Kylan Parker's house.

Of course, he had gone there in the hope of seeing Kylan and, realising she was out, he had been on the verge of returning to the campus. Two minutes later and he would never have seen the skinny girl with the cropped hair sneaking into the backyard.

It hadn't taken him long to put two and two together.

She wasn't a thief. Any doubts he'd had on that front vanished when he watched her emerge from the house half an hour later, empty-handed. That had made him all the more curious to know what she was doing breaking in. After he had watched her open the envelope that contained the joker playing card the previous afternoon, he had paid a visit to her room, looking for leverage to use to get her alone. The doodles on the inside cover of one of her notebooks and the picture of Lawrie Parker cut from one of the student papers soon confirmed his suspicions that Justine Orton had a little crush on her English professor, and he realised that the best way to her would probably be to use a little blackmail.

His plan had worked well, and he'd successfully managed to get her alone. What he hadn't counted on was her throwing herself from his car, and he certainly hadn't counted on losing her. Whatever happened, he had to get her back.

Justine Orton had the card. She had to be the fifteenth victim.

Playing on a hunch that she would go straight back to the campus, he swung his Buick around and headed in the direction of Juniper College.

* * *

Justine Orton unlocked the door to her room just after midnight. With it being so dark, she didn't see the figure sitting, waiting patiently for her on the edge of her bed, not until she had actually stepped into the room and closed the door. She flicked the light switch on and gasped loudly.

'Hello, Justine.'

Justine drew a deep breath, feeling her heartbeat quicken, as her eyes darted to the black-and-green check tie pulled taut in the gloved hands. The tie she had stolen.

She took a step back and crashed into the door. Whirling round, she clenched the doorknob with both hands. Before she could pull it open, one of the gloved hands grabbed hold of her by the arm and wrenched her back into the room.

She stumbled to the floor, landing on her knees, and cried out loudly in pain.

Oh my God! This isn't happening. This can't be happening.

But as she saw the black and green tie drop down in front of her eyes, then felt it wrap tightly around her throat, Justine Orton realised that she was wrong.

28

MONDAY 5 MAY 1997

He watched them from the car. The three of them walking side by side, hips swaying, books under their arms, the slight breeze playing with their hair.

The brunette, the tallest of the three, was in the middle, the redhead to her right, the blonde to her left.

He watched them walk from the building where they'd just had their last class, heading for the cafeteria, probably to grab a quick drink before their next lecture began, and wondered if he dare chance going inside himself. Maybe buy a coffee, sit in the corner, try not to stand out, and watch.

He had watched all three of them now for the last couple of weeks. The brunette, Alison McClaine and the redhead, Donna Randall, had been a pleasant way to pass the time. Alison was tall and curvy, Donna, petite, but nicely packaged. Both wore their hair long and he liked how when they walked it bounced from side to side, just like they were in a shampoo commercial.

The blonde though was the reason for his watching them in the first place and, now that Justine Orton was dead, it was important that he keep track of her every movement. Alison and Donna were just extra perks of the job.

He watched them disappear inside the block that housed the cafeteria and debated. The way he figured it he had two choices. One, he could sit in his car and wait until they came out, probably only to watch them disappear into some other building; or two, he could go inside, but risk being seen. Definitely a risk, but a worthwhile one at that. He debated for a short moment then, snatching the keys from the ignition, he opened the car door and stepped out.

* * *

Kylan had the feeling that she was being watched.

Ever since the guy from the grocery store had appeared at her kitchen window, she had been spooked and, at regular intervals over the past week she had looked over her shoulder, half expecting to see him standing there watching her. He hadn't been there though, and she wondered how come this time she was so certain she was right.

Sixth sense maybe, but grocery store guy or not, someone was definitely watching her.

Feeling self-conscious, she flicked a strand of hair away from her eyes and glanced cautiously around the cafeteria. She saw a lot of students she recognised. A couple of professors were deep in discussion on the far side of the room. No one was looking at her and there was nothing that should have alerted her suspicion. Still, she felt uneasy.

'Hey, Kylan, what do you think?'

Interrupted from her thoughts, Kylan was aware of Ally waving a hand in front of her face.

'Huh, what?' she asked. 'What do I think about what?'

Ally glanced at Donna and gave a playful smile. 'Looks like someone's been on vacation.'

Donna nodded and then looked at Kylan, her brows knitting together in concern.

'Are you okay?'

'Yeah, sure, why wouldn't I be?'

'I dunno. You looked kind of out of it.'

'Did I?' Kylan screwed up her nose, deciding to come clean. 'I thought someone was watching me.'

'Who?' Ally and Donna both asked in unison, turning to look over their shoulders.

'Stop it!' Kylan hissed. 'I was wrong, okay? There's nobody there.'

She hoped she was right.

Ally looked back at her. 'You have been really jumpy recently. What makes you think someone is watching you?'

Kylan shrugged, feeling a little stupid. 'I don't know. I guess I must be getting paranoid.'

'Just a little.'

'Must be the stress of married life,' Ally teased, a wide grin spreading across her face.

Kylan played along. 'Yeah, I guess that's what it is.'

'I reckon you're probably on edge because of the murders,' Donna told her. 'Everyone's a little freaked by what's going on. It's only natural to get paranoid. Especially after what happened with Catherine.'

'You're probably right,' Kylan agreed, eager to drop the subject.

The murders were something that she really didn't feel comfortable discussing. All three of them had shared classes with Catherine Maloney and they'd often socialised with her on nights out. Kylan was surprised at how well Donna and Ally were taking the news of her death.

They had only found out late Friday afternoon when Donna had bumped into Catherine's roommate, Beth, as she was coming out of the Dean's office, tears streaming down her face. As soon as Donna learned the news, she had immediately called both Ally and Kylan. All of them knew that Catherine had met a guy called Aidan a couple of weeks back and Kylan had listened to the news, her heart pounding in her chest, as Donna told her how the last time Beth had seen her roommate, she was supposed to have been going on a date with him. It seemed that Catherine had told her not to expect her back in a hurry, but while Beth had thought she was off having a good time with Aidan, her friend's body was lying in the sewer.

Apparently, the police had already established that Aidan hadn't killed Catherine Maloney. The intern had been working a late shift and had dozens of witnesses who could verify his whereabouts. While at the moment nobody was sure what had happened, they all knew it was because of her rashness and ill-judgement that Catherine Maloney had ended up dead.

Kylan wondered what her friends would say if she told them about the grocery store guy. About how he'd showed up outside her house the week before last and stared through the window at her. A shiver ran down her spine as she thought about it.

Was he a killer?

What would Donna and Ally say after knowing what had happened to Catherine? Would they take her fears seriously?

Kylan knew she was being stupid. He was probably harmless. She had, after all, only seen him a couple of times. Besides, if she did tell her friends about him, they would probably make her tell Lawrie, and that was something she didn't want to do.

Over the past week, since she'd had time to adjust to what

had happened, she had decided it best that he didn't know about the guy. Firstly, she knew he was busy and didn't think it fair to burden him with something that was probably completely trivial. They had both experienced enough of her paranoia over the last few years. Lawrie had just settled into his job and there was no way she was going to give him the additional worry that she thought she might be losing her mind.

Aside from that, she was also scared of how he would react. Although much of the time he was calm and placid, Kylan knew that when really provoked Lawrie had a terrible temper. She had only seen him get mad a couple of times since they'd been together and fortunately neither time had been directed at her. She didn't believe he was capable of being mad at her and she was glad. His temper was vicious, and she wouldn't want to be on the receiving end.

The one thing she didn't need was him going after grocery store guy and getting into trouble. They'd both already had their fair share of that.

* * *

He sat on the far side of the room, his face hidden behind a copy of the student newspaper that he'd bought on the way in. She hadn't seen him; he was sure of that. A couple of times she had glanced round the room and on one occasion both Alison and Donna had also looked, but evidently they'd been satisfied that no one was watching them, and they'd once again become engrossed in conversation. Even Kylan, who looked more than a little jumpy, had joined in and eventually started to relax.

He too relaxed behind his paper as he sipped his acidic coffee and watched.

After ten minutes the three girls got up, cleared their cups away and left the room. He gave them a thirty-second head start then, not bothering to clear away his own cup, he followed. As he crossed the cafeteria, he caught sight of Kylan through one of the large windows. Alison and Donna were no longer with her, and she was heading towards one of the older buildings on the campus.

Licking his dry lips, he stepped through the swing door and started to follow her.

* * *

Kylan had literature twice a week, both times in Room 331; it was the only class she had in the old building. Often, she would bump into one of her classmates on the way in and have company walking down the dark corridors. Today she recognised no one and guessed they must already all be in the classroom or running late.

She wished that wasn't the case. Room 331 was downstairs, one of four classrooms that had been built into the basement, but the only one currently in use. The lighting in the main part of the old building wasn't good, but downstairs in the basement the dull bulbs flickered on and off at regular intervals.

Telling herself she was stupid for getting spooked so easily, Kylan turned the corner in the corridor, passed the familiar row of red lockers and descended down the stairs that led to the basement. There were twenty-six steps: one flight of twelve, a short corner flight of four and then a final flight of ten that led straight into the basement corridor. She knew how many steps there were because, on the odd occasion she was alone, she always counted them to try and take her mind off the approaching dark basement.

The lower she climbed, the more echoing her footsteps became.

Clack, clack, clack.

Another reminder of the high ceilings and empty walls that awaited her.

She reached the bottom of the stairs and, trying to keep her mind focused on her literature class, walked down to the fork at the end of the corridor. Off to the right, the long corridor led to the boiler and maintenance rooms, and Kylan could hear the faint sound of banging pipes and clattering machinery. She turned left, knowing that once she had passed the three empty classrooms, she would arrive at room 331.

As she passed the first empty room, she realised that there was no noise coming from her literature class. Normally the students were deep in conversation before the lesson began and, even if they weren't, it was unusual not to hear the odd cough or the sound of shuffling papers.

It was then that she heard the soft thud of footsteps in the corridor behind her.

Expecting it to be a fellow student or maybe her lecturer, she turned and peered into the shadows.

No one was there.

Clutching her books to her chest, Kylan increased her pace and hurried past the other empty doors to Room 331. Not stopping to look behind her, she twisted the knob, pushed the door open and stepped inside.

The classroom was empty.

There were no books or pens on the desks, and the seats were free from discarded coats and sweaters. No one was there and it looked as though no one had been there for quite some time.

Where the hell is everybody?

She wondered for a brief second if maybe her classmates were playing a trick on her, if they were perhaps all hiding somewhere, waiting to jump out. The idea was stupid, and logic told her they wouldn't do that. She checked her watch, making sure she had the right time. It was eleven thirty. She was right on schedule. Thinking that maybe she was going crazy, she reached inside her top book for her timetable and scanned the page. Monday, eleven thirty, English Literature... Even as she read the words, she remembered.

In her Thursday class they'd been told that the lesson was being temporarily moved to a different block. No wonder there was no one there. She was in the wrong building. How could she have been so stupid to forget?

The realisation that she was all alone in the basement dawned on Kylan and a feeling of fear gripped the pit of her stomach. Suddenly the clanging of the pipes in the boiler room seemed louder and for the first time she noticed how the dusty bulb overhead was flickering dangerously on and off, the light threatening to cut out completely.

Recalling the footsteps she'd heard a few seconds earlier; she felt a shiver run down her spine.

She tried to rationalise that it was probably just one of the caretakers or another student who'd forgotten the change of classroom. Nonetheless, she didn't want to hang around. Tucking her timetable safely away inside her book, she turned and walked out of the classroom and straight into the guy in the corridor. Startled, she let out a yelp and stepped back, crashing into the wall.

The guy in front of her looked equally surprised and as she looked at his wide eyes and open mouth, she immediately recognised him.

It was the guy from the grocery store.

Screaming, Kylan dropped her books and ran.

29

Luke Williams had arrived back at the college late Monday morning and, still tired from his bus journey, had spent most of the afternoon in bed.

Knowing that Justine's last class finished at four, he set his alarm to wake him at three forty-five and, stopping long enough only to wipe the sleep from his eyes, he ran across campus to the English building to meet her. His weekend had been good. He had returned to the family home in Seattle for his parents' thirtieth wedding anniversary party and there was a lot of news he wanted to share with her.

Leaning back against the lockers that faced Justine's classroom, he watched the students disperse, wondering if he should tell her first about the Corvette that his older brother Steve had bought and fixed up for him or about the vacation to Mexico that his family were planning for July and that they'd asked him to invite her along to. As the last students left the room, followed promptly by Mr Parker, he stepped up to the door and peered inside, knowing that Justine often dawdled and expecting to see her still gathering her books together.

The classroom was empty.

Luke frowned, wondering where she was. He knew that she had stayed on campus all weekend and it was unlike her to miss one of her classes. Feeling a pinch of concern, he decided to go over to her dorm and see if she was in her room.

As he crossed the campus, his mind turned over various possibilities, and he wondered if she was sick or had perhaps decided to go home after all.

The murders had scared a lot of people, and he knew that a few of the students had decided to pack up and return home until the killer had been caught. Maybe Justine was spooked and had decided to do the same. Even so, he thought it a little odd that she hadn't called him or slipped a note under his door. He pushed open the main door to her dorm, quickly ascended the three flights of stairs to her floor and followed the hallway along to her room at the end of the block. Unlike most of the other students on campus, Justine was lucky enough to have a room to herself, the girl who she was supposed to have shared with, becoming homesick three weeks into the first term and deciding to drop out. Luke liked her having her own room. It meant that they always had somewhere to go where they knew they wouldn't be disturbed.

He rapped his knuckles against the door, aware there was no noise coming from the other side. He wondered if she had perhaps caught the bad bout of flu that had been going around the campus a couple of weeks back and was doing what he himself had done earlier, getting a few hours' sleep. There was a slightly pungent odour in the air that reminded him of sickness and he guessed he was probably right.

Getting no answer, he knocked again, this time louder. 'Justine? Justine? Are you in there?'

Still no answer.

Luke shrugged to himself, guessing that she couldn't be in her room after all.

Instead of walking away, though, his gaze slipped to the door handle, and he found himself questioning if the door was locked. It was silly really. He had knocked and Justine hadn't answered. There was no need to believe she was in her room and certainly no need for him to look. Still, he found his hand pushing down the handle to check the lock.

There was a slight creak and the door swung open.

Luke glanced into the room, taking in the open curtains, the two neatly made beds and the stack of books piled up on top of the dresser. In the middle of the floor was Justine. She was lying face down on the carpet, completely naked apart from a black-and-green checked tie that was wrapped around her neck. The skin beneath the tie looked as though it had been cut and the carpet beneath her was covered in crusts of dried blood.

Luke blinked hard and took a step back, not really registering what he was seeing. Suddenly finding his voice, he turned and ran screaming down the hallway.

* * *

Unlike the other victims, Justine Orton had been killed in her room and, with the exception of Emma Keeley, her body had not been dumped in the sewer.

Either the killer was changing his pattern, or he had been unable to get the body off campus without being seen.

Neither theory seemed likely. So far, all of the victims had been found in water; both Rodney Boone's and this guy's. There was absolutely no reason to suggest why he would suddenly decide to change location.

Justine's body had been found by her boyfriend, a freshman

called Luke Williams, who had gone to her room looking for her and discovered her lying dead on the floor. Within seconds of finding her most of the dorm knew what had happened and a couple of the students had gone running across campus to find Joel and Angell, who were busy taking prints in the main block. Joel had sent Angell on ahead of him to secure the crime scene before calling Max and then Greg Withers, telling both men to go get the team together and meet him over at the dorm. When he arrived at Justine Orton's room five minutes later, Angell had closed the door and was standing guard outside, trying to prevent the growing number of students that had already gathered outside from getting any closer.

Greg Withers arrived ten minutes later and quickly confirmed what they both already knew, that the killer had claimed his sixth victim. He also pointed out an inconsistency with the other killings: Justine Orton appeared to have put up a struggle.

So far, all the victims had been either drugged or knocked unconscious with a blow to the back of the head before they were killed. Justine Orton had been wide awake at the moment the tie was slipped around her neck. Joel wondered why this time the killer had decided to leave the murder weapon behind. The green and black checked tie had been bagged and taken to the lab. He doubted they would get any prints, but it would be interesting if they could find out who it belonged to.

Maybe Justine? Maybe a friend? Maybe her killer, though it was unlikely. Their killer might be inconsistent, but he had already proved that he wasn't stupid.

Once the pathologist and the photographer had finished and Justine Orton's body was zipped up in a bag and taken back to the lab, Max returned to the precinct with the unenviable task of calling her parents back in Missouri, leaving Joel and Angell to question Luke Williams and the students who shared her dorm.

Joel suspected that none of them would be able to help shed any light on Justine's murder and he was right. Nobody had seen her since early Saturday evening. She hadn't told anyone of any plans she had had, and not one person had seen or heard anything strange in the dorm over the weekend. Their killer was managing to be extremely elusive. The lock on the door to Justine's room had not been broken or tampered with at all, so it appeared that either she had let her killer in willingly or had opened the door to a stranger who had then forced his way into the room.

If it was someone she'd let in willingly, it was likely to be someone she knew, someone who was probably in attendance at the college; if that was the case then the list of suspects would be narrowed considerably.

Unfortunately, the process of taking the prints was going to run over several days, which allowed the killer plenty of time to pick off another victim.

Following the discovery of Rufus Lind's body, the beach entrance of the sewer had been put under twenty-four-hour surveillance, in the hope that the killer might return to the scene of his original crime. There were two other main sewer entrances, though, not to mention the myriad manholes throughout the city, and he had been smart enough to change location each time. He had also been smart enough to know how to get his victims, which fuelled the theory that each of them had probably already known him.

Catherine Maloney's alleged date, Aidan Reilly, had a solid alibi and claimed to know nothing about their supposed rendezvous. If he was telling the truth, and after having spoken to him at length, Joel didn't doubt he was, then who had Catherine been going to meet the night she was murdered? Had she planned a date with the killer? It was the same pattern as with

Emma Keeley, who had also been killed after she'd gone out claiming she had to meet somebody.

Had Catherine and Emma arranged to meet the same person?

Both girls had received a sharp blow to the head with a blunt instrument before they were killed. The pattern was consistent between the male students as well: Scott Jagger, Rufus Lind and Kevin North had all been drugged with a concoction of vodka and sleeping pills. Had they believed they were sharing an innocent drink with a friend, not realising the bottle had been laced with narcotics?

Rodney Boone had liked to feed off his victims' fear. He had enjoyed watching them suffer as he choked the life out of them. This killer, until he murdered Justine Orton, had seemed to want to spare his victims the agony of dying, preferring instead to render them unconscious first.

Why had he chosen to differ from Boone? And why had he now decided to change his pattern?

It was close to midnight when Joel and Angell finally wrapped things up at the college, and still they didn't have an answer to any of these questions.

They walked to their car in silence. Angell looked tired and Joel had too much on his mind to want to argue. Between them they had managed to interview all twenty-eight of the students who lived in Justine Orton's dorm, and had spent the evening asking the same questions and receiving the same answers.

Joel toyed briefly with the idea of asking Angell if she wanted to stop off for a drink. They could both use one, and it would give them the opportunity to talk over the evening's events. Remembering Saturday night, he rejected the idea. It had been a dumb move going to her apartment, especially after he had already warned himself to stay away from her. She had known what was going on in his mind. It had been obvious from the look in her eyes and he strongly suspected that had he made a move she would have reciprocated.

He hated to think how they would have coped working with each other had they ended up in bed together. There was no way he wanted any more than a one-night stand and, while it wouldn't surprise him to find that she didn't want or expect anything more either, it would have still made things unnecessarily awkward between them. Rebecca Angell's opinion of him was already not particularly high and although, after the way he had treated her, Joel guessed he deserved it, he didn't need her thinking any worse of him. If he could just keep his mind on the job, they would hopefully catch their killer and then he wouldn't have to see her again.

Hopefully, though with the lack of leads they had at the moment, he didn't think so.

30

TUESDAY 6 MAY 1997

Yesterday had been breaking point.

Seeing the man from the grocery store standing outside her classroom had pretty much ripped what was left of Kylan's nerves to shreds and was proof enough that she was definitely being followed. She didn't know why and didn't want to know why. All she did know was that this man had scared the hell out of her and, considering the circumstances, she didn't think anyone could blame her for her reaction.

She had considered going to the police and telling them about him, but soon realised it would be futile. After all, what would they be able to do? They could hardly arrest the guy for being in the same place as her on a handful of occasions and, even if they could, they would have to find him first and she wouldn't have any idea to tell them where to look.

It was no good. The police couldn't help her, and she wasn't about to risk putting herself in any kind of danger. What she needed to do was get out of town for a while. She needed to go somewhere quiet where she could relieve the pressure building up inside her head. She wondered if she should call Dr Slevin.

Maybe she could go back for a session and he would be able to help her. He would want to know that she was still taking her medication, though, and then what would she tell him?

No, what she needed was somewhere where she could be alone. Somewhere where she could regroup and somewhere where she would feel safe.

Glancing at her half empty closet and checking that she had everything that she needed, Kylan Parker picked her case up from the floor and made her way out of the bedroom.

* * *

Lawrence Parker was being uncooperative.

Not that it particularly mattered. He had been arrested late Tuesday afternoon and Joel had taken great pleasure in entering his classroom and reading him his rights in front of the class full of students.

It was very likely he would be charged with Justine Orton's murder. Not only had they found his prints all over the black and green tie that had been used to strangle her, but the tie actually belonged to him. Sloppy, Joel thought, and tried to push the niggling doubt to the back of his mind as to why Parker would leave such an obvious clue and also openly admit that the tie was his.

Right now, the most important thing was getting him to confess, not only to Justine's murder, but also to the murders of Scott Jagger, Emma Keeley, Rufus Lind, Catherine Maloney and Kevin North.

Of course, they still had the mystery print on the vodka bottle found at the crime scene of Scott Jagger's murder, but the evidence found in Justine Orton's room was so overwhelming it was easier to believe that the print had belonged to someone completely unrelated to the killings than the idea that Lawrence Parker had been set up.

There was other evidence that also pointed to Parker. All six dead students had taken his English class. The police already had the letter that Emma Keeley had sent to him, and Parker himself had admitted that his relationship with Emma was more than just student–professor. Going through Justine Orton's room suggested that she too had a 'special' relationship with him. There was no hard proof of this, but the drawings in her books and the picture of him cut from a student paper went a long way to confirm their suspicions.

Never one to forget a face, Joel could remember seeing Justine Orton in the classroom the day he had first met Lawrence Parker. He had come to the conclusion back then that she'd had a crush on him. Had Parker returned her advances? Or perhaps, knowing how she felt, had he used his charms to get himself invited into her room?

Parker wasn't as forthcoming about Justine as he was about Emma, claiming that he had never had anything to do with her outside of class. Joel guessed he was just being difficult because he knew they had him cornered. If he and Max both kept putting the pressure on him, he would eventually start to crack.

Staring coldly into Parker's eyes, he asked for the fifth time, 'So, if you didn't kill Justine Orton, how did your tie get in her room?'

Parker glared back. 'The answer is still the same as the last time you asked, Agent Hickok. I don't know.'

Although he'd been in the interview room for nearly two hours, his posture hadn't changed at all. Normally, by the second hour, suspects would start to crumble, become restless and lose their cool. Not Lawrence Parker. He was still sitting relaxed in his chair, legs crossed, eyes shifting from Joel to Max as each of them asked questions, answering them calmly and only raising his voice when he wanted to stress a point. Right now, his attention was focused on Joel. 'Have you decided if you're going to charge me yet, Agent Hickok?'

'No, we haven't.' Joel raised his eyebrows questioningly. 'Why? Think maybe it's time to call your lawyer?'

Parker shook his head. 'I've already told you; I have nothing to hide.' He had been offered a lawyer at the beginning of the interview but had refused, claiming he was innocent and could take care of things by himself. 'I just wondered when you were going to start believing me.'

Joel let out a sardonic laugh. 'Maybe when you start telling us the truth, pal.'

'I am telling you the truth.'

'Well, seeing as you're being so truthful, do you mind telling us where you were Saturday night?'

Parker nodded. 'Sure. I was home all evening with my wife.'

'How about the Saturday before?'

There was a brief silence while Parker cast his mind back. He smiled. 'We were out for the evening with friends. One of them is an officer who works here,' he added dryly. 'Vic Boaz. You know him?'

Joel exchanged a glance with Max before continuing. 'What time did you get home?' he asked, ignoring Parker's question.

There was another pause. 'It was early. Kylan had a headache, so before eleven.'

'And you were home all night?'

'I was.'

Joel nodded to Max who was making notes. 'We'll have to get your wife to verify your story.'

'That won't be a problem.'

'Do you want us to call her for you, Mr Parker?' Max asked. 'Maybe we should let her know where you are.'

Parker looked hesitantly at him for a moment. 'I think that would be a good idea,' he answered eventually. He gave Max the number.

Joel waited until Max was out of the room before getting up himself. He walked round to the side of the desk where Lawrie Parker was sitting and leant against the edge. Folding his arms, he stared into Parker's eyes.

'So, Lawrie, does your wife know you mess around with your students?'

'I don't mess around with my students.' Parker's tone was sharp. 'I have already told you that.'

'Of course you did, I'm sorry. Does she know you get your kicks out of killing them and cutting them up?'

Parker didn't answer. He leaned back in his chair and glared at Joel through black eyes. 'Pretty wife, you have. Kylan, that's her name, isn't it?' Joel watched him carefully, hoping to provoke some kind of reaction. 'Still, with a face like that, I doubt she'll be lonely for long. Not once you've been locked away.'

'Leave Kylan out of this,' Parker snapped.

'Hey, you're the one dragging her into it. This isn't gonna go away, buddy. You keep refusing to accept responsibility for what you've done and there'll be a big, nasty trial. You think Kylan wants to be dragged through all that? Why don't you just do everybody a big favour and come clean? It'll save us all a lot of trouble.'

Parker gave an icy smile, still refusing to bite. 'What part of "not guilty" don't you understand, Agent Hickok?'

'I'm not the one having a problem understanding...'

Joel was interrupted by Max as he re-entered the room. He looked up at his partner. 'So, what did Mrs Parker have to say?'

'Not a lot,' Max said, sitting down. 'She wasn't home.'

For the first time during the interview, Parker looked anxious. He leaned forward and narrowed his eyes. 'What do you mean she wasn't home?'

Max gave a casual shrug. 'She wasn't there. No answer.'

'She must be there. Are you sure you dialled the right number?'

'Hey, buddy, I know how to use a phone. Maybe she went shopping or something.'

'She wouldn't have gone shopping. She has to be at home,' Parker persisted.

'Look, I'm telling you, pal, there was no answer.'

'Then drive over there and check that she's okay.'

Max rolled his eyes, looking a little irritated. 'I'm sure she's fine. There's no need to get all jumpy just because she doesn't answer the phone. Maybe she's in the tub and didn't want to get out.'

Parker's black eyes were cold and scowling.

'Go and check,' he demanded.

'Look! Listen here, pal—'

'Hey, Max, calm down. I'll go. It's no big deal.' Joel got up, shaking his head, annoyed that Max had lost his cool and let himself get drawn into a fight with Parker. 'You stay here with our pal, Lawrie, and see what else you can squeeze out of him. I'll go check up on Mrs Parker. Let her know what her husband's been up to.' He winked at Parker and received a glare back. 'Hey, you want me to check she's okay or not?'

Parker scowled, ignoring him. 'You'll need my keys to get in.'

'Not a problem. I'll get them from the front desk.'

'What about the address?'

'I already have it.' Joel pushed back his chair and got to his feet. Patting Max on the shoulder, he grinned at Parker. 'I'll see you guys later.'

* * *

Lawrence Parker lived in a nice neighbourhood at the end of a quiet, tree-lined road. The houses were decent sized, though all red brick and nondescript, and all of them had large, neatly manicured lawns shrouded by trees and bushes. Not bad for a college professor and his student wife, Joel thought as he pulled the Lincoln to a halt outside Parker's house.

He glanced at Rebecca Angell, sitting in the passenger seat beside him.

'You ever been here before?' he asked.

She shook her head. 'No. I've only ever met Kylan Parker once and that was a couple of weeks back.'

Joel nodded and pushed open the car door. 'Come on, then. Let's go see if she's home.'

It hadn't been necessary for him to bring Angell along. She had spent the whole day at the college again, this time with Boaz, overseeing the collecting of the prints. The two of them had arrived back at the precinct just as Joel was leaving to go to Parker's house and when she enquired where he was going, although he should have known better, he had asked her if she wanted to tag along.

He kidded himself that it would be good to have her there when they told Kylan about Lawrie's arrest. If the two of them knew each other, Angell might be able to offer her some support. In truth, though, he knew that the reason he had brought her with him was the sole, selfish fact that he liked having her around.

Joel pushed open the front gate and together they walked up the path to the front door. The house seemed empty and there were no vehicles parked in the driveway. It might be that the Parkers only had one car between them, in which case it was probably still parked over at the college, where it had been left after Lawrie Parker's arrest.

Joel rang the bell twice and waited for a couple of minutes. When he didn't get an answer, he pulled Lawrie Parker's key ring from his pocket and let them both inside. Closing the front door behind him, he called down the hallway. 'Mrs Parker?'

There was no answer.

'Mrs Parker, this is the FBI. Are you home?'

Still no answer.

'I don't think she's here, Hickok.'

Joel pushed open the door to the left of him. It led into a spacious kitchen. Everything looked normal. All the drawers and cupboards were shut, and a pile of red and yellow dish towels had been neatly folded and left on the side. With the exception of a cup and two plates that had been washed up and left to drain, everything appeared to be in its correct place, and it looked as though nobody had been in the room for a while. He was about to pull the door shut when Angell caught hold of his arm.

'What's that?' she asked, pushing her way past him. She went straight to the kitchen table on the far side of the room and pulled at the sheet of paper that had been folded once and slipped half under the fruit bowl.

Joel went after her.

'Here, let me see that,' he demanded, reaching for the piece of paper.

Angell gave him a smug grin and lifted the paper out of his reach. 'Is that a good idea, Special Agent Hickok. Do you really think you should snoop?'

Joel scowled at her and snatched the paper from her hand. 'It's my job to snoop,' he told her, unfolding the letter and reading it to himself.

Lawrie,

I have to get away for a while and get my head together. I'll call you in a couple of days and explain.

Love, Kylan

He reread the note, then folded it up and put it in his jacket pocket. Angell looked at him, her green eyes wide with interest. 'So?'

'So what?'

'Don't be a jerk, Hickok. What did the note say?'

He gave a nonchalant shrug. 'Just that she's decided to skip town for a while.'

'You're kidding?'

'No kidding.' Joel picked up the phone on the wall and called the precinct. It rang twice before it was answered.

'It's Hickok,' he said brusquely. 'Put me through to Agent Sutton.'

There was a pause while his call was transferred, then he heard Max's gravelly voice.

'Hey, buddy! How'd you get on? The little lady home?'

'Nope,' Joel told him. 'Seems like the little lady decided to take a vacation.'

'Say what?'

'She's skipped town, Max. Left a note on the kitchen table for Parker telling him she needed to get away and she'll call in a couple of days.'

Max let out a low whistle. 'Oh boy, is he up shit creek without a paddle. Boaz can give him an alibi for the early part of the evening, but for later on, you know that without her he doesn't have any kind of alibi?'

'I know.'

'Do you have any idea where she went?'

'Are you kidding? We don't even know if she's still in the country.'

'Guess I'd better go break the news to him, huh?' Max said, not sounding at all disappointed.

Joel wondered if perhaps he'd been having a hard time with Parker since he'd left.

'I guess so,' he muttered. 'Well, I'll lock up here and be back in a short while.'

'Okay, pal. See you shortly.'

Joel hung up the phone.

'What did he say?' Angell asked, an expectant look on her face.

Ignoring her question, he pushed his way past her and out of the kitchen. All the doors leading off the hallway were closed, and he made his way along the wall, opening them one by one. Angell followed him.

'What are you doing?' she questioned, her tone suspicious.

'Looking,' Joel told her curtly.

'Looking for what?'

Opening the door of what appeared to be Parker's study, he stepped inside and went straight over to the desk. He pulled open the top drawer and started to sift through the contents.

'You can't do this,' Angell said, giving an incredulous laugh. 'In case you've forgotten, Hickok, you don't have a search warrant.'

He glanced up and met her eyes. 'So, I'm just having a quick look to see if we need one.'

'I can't believe you're violating Lawrence Parker's rights like this.'

Joel rolled his eyes, wondering why he'd bothered bringing her along. 'Jeez, Angell, you know what? You're a pain in the ass. Go and wait in the car if you've got a problem. If not, get over here and give me a hand.'

Angell glared at him and he wondered which side of her personality was going to win the battle obviously going on inside her head. Would it be the overly conscientious, law-abiding cop she was trying so hard to mould herself into, or the spirited tomboy who he knew lurked beneath the surface? As she made no move to leave or come into the room, Joel turned back to the task at hand, ignoring the frosty look on her face.

He found the library books in the bottom drawer of the desk.

They were hidden in a box and there were three of them, one on forensic evidence, one on serial killers and one on how to commit the perfect murder.

Beneath the books was a folder filled with several pages of handwritten notes.

Joel let out a low whistle. Angell watched him carefully, her look of anger having melted into one of curiosity, and he suspected that she was dying to know what he had found but was too stubborn to ask.

Closing the drawer, he made sure everything was exactly as he'd found it. Then he got up from behind the desk and ushered her out of the room.

'You're done, then?' she asked, her tone sounding deliberately uninterested as they left the house.

'Oh yes,' Joel told her, not prepared to share with her what he'd found unless she begged him. She didn't, though, and they walked down the driveway in silence.

Inside the car, Joel made another call to Max.

'I think we might want to go ahead and get a search warrant on Parker's house,' he told his partner when he came on the line, blatantly ignoring the look Angell was giving him. 'Things are starting to look interesting.'

31

When Rebecca and Hickok arrived back at the precinct, Sutton had already decided to call it a night with Lawrence Parker and the English professor had been escorted down to the cells. Vic was still there, busy coding the prints that had been taken throughout the day. He didn't look overly happy with the idea of having to work late and Rebecca wondered how Sutton had managed to persuade him to stay.

The older Fed looked up as they walked in the door, a wide grin spreading across his ruddy face. 'I thought you two were never coming back,' he said, giving Hickok a knowing look.

Rebecca narrowed her eyes suspiciously, not quite sure what he was implying by the comment. She decided not to analyse it and take it at face value.

'Yes, I was a little surprised at how long it took us to lock up,' she muttered, throwing a stony look back at Hickok.

He seemed unperturbed by her remark and moved closer to her, close enough that she could smell the faint scent of his cologne and was aware of the sudden charge of electricity that passed between them. Unsettled, she took a step back. He smiled at her, knowing, and a blush crept into her cheeks.

'I took a quick look around while we were there,' he explained to Sutton, as though it was no big deal.

Rebecca waited for the older agent to sound off at him, but instead, he simply nodded.

'I hope you were careful. We don't want to go losing this guy on a technicality.'

Hickok grinned cockily. 'Aren't I always.'

Always? So, he had done this sort of thing before.

Rebecca's jaw dropped, though she wondered why that surprised her.

Hickok nudged her. 'Close your mouth, Angell. You're catching flies.'

She scowled at him. 'Just get off my case, Hickok,' she snapped, fed up with how he always seemed to come up smelling of roses.

'I'm not on your case, Angell. I'm just trying to make you understand that sometimes you have to bend the rules a little to catch the bad guys.'

'You weren't bending the rules. You were breaking them.'

Hickok shrugged nonchalantly. 'Now you're just being picky.'

Rebecca rolled her eyes in frustration. 'I'm going home,' she muttered, crossing the office to the locker rooms, too tired to keep up the fight.

'Good idea,' Hickok agreed. 'You're gonna need all the sleep you can get. We'll be busy tomorrow.'

'Why is that? Planning on breaking a few more laws?' she remarked dryly, stepping into the locker room before he had a chance to retort.

She wondered what her family would think if they knew what kind of people she was working with. Vic the lazy cop, whose first concern was always for himself, and Hickok and Sutton, both dedicated to hunting criminals, but willing to break the law to catch them. Her parents would be shocked, especially her mother. Uncle Lou would probably approve of them; never one to back away from scandal, he would tell her to quit being so uptight.

'Nobody's perfect, Rebecca.'

'The law isn't necessarily always right.'

He would probably use her mother as an example of the last comment. Sarah and Lou had never seen eye to eye. She thought he was a rogue and he found her a little too virtuous.

Sarah Angell, the prude; Sarah Angell, who always did the right thing; Sarah Angell, only ever seeing black and white and not prepared to accept that there was a whole lot of grey in between.

God! That's it. I'm turning into my mother!

Maybe that was it. All along, her tomboy ways, the rebellion against her parents, the drinking and hanging out with Uncle Lou, perhaps it had been a subconscious act. Maybe she had been in denial all these years because she didn't want to accept the fact that she was an exact copy of her mother.

No! It wasn't true. She was just tired and letting her imagination get carried away. She was nothing like her mother. The reason she was so pissed at Hickok for illegally searching Lawrence Parker's house was because she still couldn't convince herself the man was guilty. It was stupid, she knew. The evidence against Parker was overwhelming. But she had a nagging doubt that he wasn't responsible; that she had missed something in the files that she'd read on Rodney Boone. Boone couldn't have escaped from the fire after he had been stabbed and left for dead on the cellar floor, but why hadn't the police recovered his body? There had to be a logical explanation of what had happened to

him and Rebecca had a sudden determination to find out what
it was.

* * *

Instead of driving home, she followed the road left out of the
precinct, driving past the college and out of the city towards the
coast. Until his disappearance, Rodney Boone had remained
living in the house he'd inherited from Cedric and Phillipa
Boone. Rebecca had never been to the house, but she did have
the address etched in her memory after meticulously studying
the files on Boone, and she found the dilapidated old building
without too much difficulty. The house was set back off a narrow
country lane about two miles from the coast and hadn't been
lived in since the fateful night when Jennifer Isaac had managed
to escape from his cellar. Rebecca had heard rumours that the
land had recently been purchased by a hotel group that planned
to rebuild the place and use its grisly history to draw tourists. As
yet, nothing had been done and, pulling her Jeep to a halt in the
driveway, she could see where what was left of the once white
walls had darkened to a charcoal grey.

She spent a moment staring at the house, trying to imagine
how it had looked before the fire. Old and imposing, probably
with many hidden rooms, isolated enough that no one would
ever hear Boone's victims scream. Her mind sifted through the
files she had read.

Jennifer Isaac had been down in the cellar with Boone. The
police report said that she had stabbed him twice; once in the
stomach with a screwdriver and then in the back with a butcher's
knife. Boone had fallen into a candle knocking it to the floor and
Jennifer had left him on the cellar floor believing he was already
dead. She hadn't stopped to look for a phone, running straight

out of the unlocked front door. She had tried the doors of the car parked in the driveway, hoping to use it to make her getaway, but they had been locked, so she had made her way on foot to the nearest farmhouse just over a mile away.

Rebecca tried to picture the scene in her mind: Jennifer running out of the house, trying the car then heading down to the road in search of help, leaving the burning building behind her.

The police hadn't been called until an hour later, which would have allowed Boone time to escape, but how had he managed to get out? When the police and the fire crew arrived at the house, the building had been pretty much devastated. The reports said that the cellar, all of downstairs, the car in the double garage, much of the main staircase...

The car in the garage!

Jennifer Isaac had said in her report that the car had been parked in the driveway. Yet the police report stated that it had been in the garage, gutted by the blaze.

Had there been two cars?

Rebecca felt her heartbeat quicken. If a car had been parked in the driveway, it wouldn't have been touched by the fire. Had the police seen it when they arrived? The report hadn't said so. Was it possible that the car hadn't been there when they arrived? That Boone had used it to make his escape?

The idea of a badly injured man crawling from the fire, finding his car keys and then managing to drive to safety was still a little far-fetched. But then it hit her. What if the car hadn't belonged to Rodney Boone? What if there had been someone else in the house with him? Someone whom Jennifer hadn't known about and who had pulled Boone from the fire then used the car to escape in?

Certain that she was onto something, Rebecca reached into

her purse on the seat beside her and pulled out her cell phone. She called Hickok.

* * *

The two Federal Agents had already pulled the files and made several calls by the time Rebecca arrived back at the precinct.

She saw Hickok glance in her direction as she walked through the door, an almost sheepish look on his face, and realised she had been presented with a perfect opportunity to gloat.

The truth was she was too damn excited to want to bother.

'The car outside wasn't Boone's,' Sutton told her without preamble. 'It was a silver Plymouth. Boone only had one car, a red Ford. That was the only car there when the cops arrived, and they found it sitting in the garage burnt to a cinder.'

'So you think that there was someone else in the house with Boone?' Rebecca asked, trying hard to maintain a professional tone.

'It's looking likely.'

There was a brief silence.

'So what happens now?' Rebecca asked, noticing that neither agent seemed prepared to give much away.

Hickok glanced at his partner. 'Max is going down to San Palimo tomorrow to talk with Agnes Barnes.'

'Really?' Rebecca asked, pleased that all her hard work from Saturday wasn't going to waste. Now they believed it more likely that Boone was alive, it seemed they were prepared to check out her theory about Boone's brothers.

'He and Boaz are leaving in the morning.'

Boaz?

'What?' Rebecca fought hard to keep the look of surprise from her face. She lost. 'Vic's going? Why?'

Sutton came over and squeezed her shoulder in a gesture that reminded her of Uncle Lou. 'Don't take it personally. You've done a really good job, and I intend to recommend you to your captain. Officer Boaz, though, has seniority and he tells us that he's familiar with the area. It makes sense to take him along.'

'Sure, I understand,' Rebecca said, trying her hardest not to sound disappointed.

Truth was, she didn't understand, and she didn't think it was fair either. Vic might have seniority, but that didn't change the fact that he was lazy and couldn't care less. What the hell had he done to help this investigation, except whine like a baby and try to make out in front of anyone stupid enough to listen that he was some kind of hero?

It wasn't fair, and it pissed her off.

She watched her partner get up from behind the desk and yawn loudly.

'Guess I ought to go home and get some shut-eye,' he said, talking to Sutton, but grinning at Rebecca. He slapped her on the back as he passed her. 'You did a good job, sweetheart,' he muttered, his tone patronising. 'But it's time now to step back and let the professionals take over.'

Rebecca clenched her fists together, fighting to keep them by her side. She wasn't going to let Vic Boaz see that she was upset by the decision.

'Have a good trip, Vic,' she told him, forcing a smile.

She glanced at Hickok, meeting his eyes, expecting a sarcastic comment. He didn't make one though, and she got the impression from the way he gave her a half shrug, and what appeared to be a sympathetic smile, that the decision to send Vic hadn't been his.

Maybe he wasn't such a jerk after all.

Watching Vic slip his jacket on over his uniform, whistling

loudly as he fished out his car keys and headed out of the door, Rebecca half wished something would happen to him so he couldn't go with Sutton.

Nothing serious. Just a little accident. Perhaps he could break a leg.

Perhaps break both legs!

She smiled to herself, knowing her wish was unlikely to be granted and knowing that her parents would be appalled if they ever found out about the devious thoughts that sometimes went on in her mind. She guessed that at least it proved one thing. Maybe she wasn't so much like her mother after all.

32

Vic couldn't believe his luck.

So far, it had been Rebecca Angell, his rookie partner, who had been allowed to do all of the good stuff like the college interviews and, while he didn't doubt that it was because Hickok fancied her, it was still about time that he got to see some of the perks of the job. A trip down to California would do very nicely.

He was familiar with the area. His parents had raised him and his sisters in a town less than thirty miles from San Palimo and he had served ten years with the San Francisco Police Department before being transferred up to Juniper. Driving through the familiar hilly districts, a heavy fog rolling in from the ocean, he realised just how much he'd missed it.

His family no longer lived locally. Cynthia, his oldest sister, had moved to Phoenix years ago with her husband, Drake, and the twins, Annie and Shelley, were both working down in Los Angeles. His parents had sold up two years back, claiming the house was too big and empty for just the two of them, and bought a retirement home down in Florida. Vic had visited them a few times since they'd been there, though it was usually because he wanted a vacation rather than to check on their well-being.

A little like now, he guessed. Although they were supposed to be down here to work, he couldn't help thinking of it as more of a vacation. Sutton wasn't going to uncover anything. Rebecca Angell might have thought she'd found all the answers, but she was wrong. San Palimo would provide nothing more than a pleasant distraction.

The words pleasant and distraction sprang to mind again as he laid eyes on Karen Harris, the librarian with the husky voice whom he had spoken to earlier that morning to let her know they were coming. Although he had hoped she would have a body to match her voice, Vic knew his chances weren't good, especially since she worked in a library. So, his face lit up like a Christmas tree when on arrival at the library they were greeted by a tall, vibrant redhead with a curvaceous figure and startling blue eyes. Karen Harris didn't seem too disappointed when she laid eyes on him either.

'It's a pleasure to meet you in the flesh, Officer Boaz,' she said, smiling at him warmly.

Vic glanced at Sutton and raised his eyebrows, then he looked back at Karen. 'Oh, believe me, the pleasure is all mine.'

Boy! Have I lucked out here.

All thoughts of Jill Boleyn went out of the window as he locked his sights on Karen Harris, treating her to his most dazzling smile.

'Would you like a cup of coffee before I take you in to meet Agnes?' Karen asked, a hopeful tone to her voice. Vic nodded, wondering what the librarian looked like naked. Forget Rebecca Angell. This was a woman who obviously knew how to treat a man with respect. 'Coffee would be terrific, Karen. Really terrific.'

'Actually, I think we'll save coffee for later, thank you, Miss

Harris,' Sutton said, butting in. 'Right now, I think we should go have a chat with Ms Barnes.'

'Oh, okay.' Karen looked a little disappointed but didn't say anything. She turned and led the way into the library.

Vic let out a loud sigh, flaring his nostrils. 'What'd you go and do that for?' he hissed at Sutton. 'Couldn't you see that she really liked me?'

Sutton arched a brow. 'I thought you had a girlfriend, Officer Boaz?'

'I do,' Vic muttered, looking at his feet. 'That doesn't mean I can't shop around though, does it?'

'Why, do you think you're too much for one woman?'

'I never said that.'

Sutton gave him a toothy grin. 'You just don't understand commitment, do you, buddy?' he said, patting him on the back. 'Come on. Work first and I'm sure you'll have time to play later.'

Vic grunted, but let the matter drop. Sutton had let him come along. He didn't want to screw up, or the Fed might regret his decision. Work first and play later. Determined that he was going to get to play later, he turned and followed Karen Harris through the swing door.

She led them through the maze of bookshelves to a room at the back of the library, opened the door and motioned for them to go inside. The room was small and piled with books. On the floor in the midst of the chaos sat an elderly woman whom Vic guessed had to be Agnes. She was dressed in navy and her grey-black hair was scraped back into a tight bun, making her face seem somewhat gaunt. A pair of glasses hung on a silver chain around her neck; she perched them on the end of her nose as she looked up to see who had entered the room. She glanced at Sutton first through the tinted rims, then at Vic and then at Karen.

Karen smiled at her. 'Agnes. These are the policemen I was telling you about this morning. They've come to see what you can remember about Helen White.'

Agnes nodded, suddenly interested. She finished stacking the pile of books she had on the floor and smiled up at Sutton, nodding.

'You're here at last,' she said, matter-of-factly. 'Good. I've been waiting for you.'

* * *

The three of them sat in a booth in the Cloistered Oyster, a secluded diner set high on the cliff top overlooking the ocean, which Agnes Barnes claimed sold the best fresh seafood for miles. Despite her recommendation, none of them had seafood, Max ordering a black coffee, Agnes choosing a pot of tea and Boaz stuffing his face with a box of the diner's speciality dough-nuts and a large chocolate milk shake.

'I understand you knew Helen White, ma'am?' Max asked, having made small talk for a couple of minutes and now feeling it necessary to move onto the reason they were there. Agnes nodded slowly. 'Oh yes, I remember Helen White. She was the widow of Professor White, you know. Completely threw her life away.'

'She did? How?' Max asked, curious.

'Her husband was an English professor over at the local college. After the accident, Helen couldn't cope by herself, not with the three boys to look after. And then of course there was her little problem.'

'What problem was that?'

'She had a drug problem, Mr Sutton,' Agnes said nodding, as though to confirm the fact to herself. 'Tried to pretend that she didn't. But everyone knew it was a lie. You could tell just by looking at her. That, of course, is why she turned to prostitution. You know, to pay for her little habit.'

'Prostitution, hey? She sounds like the perfect mom.'

Agnes snorted loudly through her nose, causing a couple of the other customers to look in her direction. 'Hardly!' she told Max, misinterpreting his sarcasm. 'When she had the overdose, her three little boys were taken into care. Rumour has it that they were found nearly starved to death. She used to beat them as well, you know, Mr Sutton. I remember that poor little boy of hers, he was slower than most other children of his age. Helen used to punish him for it. She thought he was letting down the family. The poor child was always filthily dressed.'

'That would be Rodney you're talking about, wouldn't it?' Max asked.

Agnes frowned at him slightly. 'I'm not good with names, Mr Sutton. Was he the oldest boy?'

'We believe so.'

She nodded. 'Then yes, it was Rodney.'

Max started making a few notes, trying to ignore the noise Boaz was making beside him as he sucked out his milk shake through the straw. 'Do you know much about what happened to the three boys, Ms Barnes?' he asked, trying to concentrate on the task at hand.

'Not really.' Agnes shook her head, opening another sachet of sugar to pour into her already overly sweet tea. 'They were all put into foster care and eventually adopted.'

'By different families?'

'Yes, I believe so.'

Max paused to take a sip of his coffee. The black liquid was strong and tasted good. 'Do you know what happened to

Rodney's two brothers? Who they were adopted by? Whether they still lived locally?'

'I'm sorry, Mr Sutton,' Agnes apologised, stirring her tea. 'I'm afraid I wouldn't know.'

'What were their names?'

'Oh, now you've got me.' She bit down on her bottom lip, staring intently past Max's shoulder. 'One of them was Clint or Clive. Something like...' She paused mid-sentence as the old-fashioned bell rang above the door and a tall, blond man entered the diner.

'Doctor Turner!' she cried, getting to her feet.

The man ambled across. He appeared to be in his late thirties, not unattractive, with a broad forehead and a strong jawline, and he was smartly dressed in a grey suit and a conservative pale blue shirt that matched his eyes.

'Agnes,' he greeted her, his voice soft and reserved. He took hold of both her hands. 'How are you doing?'

'I'm very well, Doctor Turner.' She turned to look at Max and Boaz, and then back at the doctor. 'I'm having coffee with these nice policemen.'

'Policemen?' Doctor Turner's eyebrows rose slightly as he turned to study Max.

Max nodded to him. 'Agent Sutton with the FBI. This is Officer Boaz,' he said, waving a hand in Boaz's direction.

'Boaz?' The doctor smiled faintly. 'I knew some people called Boaz once.'

'Yeah?' Boaz slurped up the rest of the milk shake and wiped his mouth with the back of his hand. 'Well, my family used to live out this way. Maybe it's them.'

'Maybe.'

'Mr Sutton and Mr Boaz are in town doing some investigat-ing,' Agnes explained, not wanting to be left out of the conversation. 'They are following up a lead on a lady I used to know, Helen White. They're trying to find her sons.'

'Really?' Doctor Turner looked from Max to Boaz and back again. 'I'm afraid I don't know anyone by that name.'

Agnes shook her head. 'You wouldn't, Doctor. This was a long time ago, a long time before you moved to town.'

'I see.'

'I was just trying to remember what their names were. Rodney, Clive...' She knitted her brows together as she struggled to remember. 'I think it was Clive. And then there was the baby. Now what was his name?'

'It would really help us, Ms Barnes, if you could remember,' Max pushed.

Agnes nodded, sitting down.

'I'm sorry, Mr Sutton. It was a long time ago and my memory's not what it used to be.'

'That's okay,' Max told her. 'Take your time.'

'Do you mind me asking why you're looking for these gentlemen,' Doctor Turner asked. 'Are they criminals?'

Max had no intention of telling the doctor or Agnes Barnes exactly what leads they were following up. Before he had the chance to politely foil the question, Boaz piped up.

'We think these men might know the whereabouts of a serial killer,' he said brightly, ignoring Max's scathing look.

Not for the first time, Max wished he'd never brought the loud-mouthed officer with him.

'Really? A serial killer,' the doctor mused.

'We're investigating...' Boaz started to explain but was stopped mid-sentence by Agnes Barnes who was waving her hand in the air like a schoolgirl who knew the answer to a question.

'Mr Sutton, Mr Sutton. I think I know a way to find out the names of those children.'

Max looked at her, glad for the reprieve. 'How is that, Ms Barnes?'

'The old news files in the back room of the library. Helen White's case was well publicised. I'm sure if you go through the back copies of the old newspapers, you'll be able to find out the names of her children. There might even be some news about the adoptions.'

Max grinned broadly at her. 'Ms Barnes, you're a peach.'

Agnes smiled, flattered. 'Why, thank you, Mr Sutton.' She glanced up at Doctor Turner, patting the empty red vinyl seat beside her. 'Are you going to join us for coffee, Doctor?'

Doctor Turner shook his head. 'No thank you, Agnes. I have patients to see. In fact, I really should be going.' He glanced briefly at both Max and Boaz. 'Gentlemen.'

Max nodded to him, watching him exit the diner.

'Well, that's strange,' Agnes said, furrowing her brow.

'What's strange, Ms Barnes?' he asked, turning back to look at her.

'Doctor Turner running off like that. He came into the diner, but he didn't order anything.'

'Maybe he lost his appetite,' Max suggested, looking at the big glob of blueberry jam that had just dribbled out of Boaz's mouth and down onto his chin.

'Maybe.' Agnes looked thoughtful for a moment as she stared out of the diner window at the crystal blue water in the bay below. 'Very peculiar,' she muttered. 'Very peculiar indeed.'

Eager to get back to the library and hunt out the newspaper reports, Max reached into his wallet and pulled out a twenty. 'Come on, Officer Boaz, eat up. We have work to do.'

'You're going back to the library already?' Agnes asked, her grey eyes wide with surprise.

'That's right, Ms Barnes. We need to make a start on those newspapers.'

'But we haven't talked about Myron White yet.'

Max looked at her, curious. 'Myron White?' he questioned.

'Helen's husband,' Agnes elaborated.

'What about him?'

'Well, I thought that was what you wanted to talk to me about. I thought you wanted to know what happened to him.'

'You said he died, right? In some kind of accident?' Boaz piped up, cramming his mouth full of doughnut.

Agnes nodded. 'That's right, Mr Boaz. He was hanged.'

'You mean it wasn't an accident?' Boaz said, spitting dough across the table. 'He killed himself?'

'No, he didn't kill himself. It was an accident. Some of the students put a noose around his neck. They were just trying to scare him. But he slipped and fell.'

'Really?' Max said, becoming interested. 'And why were his students trying to scare him?'

Agnes Barnes signalled to a passing waitress.

'I think we're going to need another pot of tea over here, Lucinda. And another coffee and milkshake for the gentlemen.'

Lucinda, a middle-aged woman with a honey-coloured beehive and a bright red lipstick smile, gave her a wink and a nod.

'Coming right up, Agnes.'

Watching the woman walk away, Agnes leaned back in her seat, hands folded across the table, and smiled at Max. 'Why don't I tell you all about it.'

33

SAN PALIMO, CALIFORNIA. NOVEMBER 1963

Good grades were something which Carolyn Mayo usually had to work hard to achieve.

Some of the kids on her course seemed able to get an A by putting in the minimum amount of effort. Others couldn't be bothered and were happy enough if they managed to get a D. Carolyn didn't want Ds. She wanted As, and she found that these days she was starting to get them, though she had to work twice as hard as any of the other students to do so.

This didn't bother her. She planned on becoming a newspaper reporter and knew that in order to fulfil her ambition she needed to pass her English class with good grades.

Her boyfriend, Bobby, thought that she was nuts wanting to become a reporter. His cousin was a photographer, and he was always going on about how Carolyn should try modelling. Although she was secretly flattered that he thought she was pretty enough to be a model, she had her heart set on the world of journalism, and deep down she knew that Bobby was proud of her trying to get ahead in what was still a man's world.

On the whole, life was good: her grades, her relationship with

Bobby, she had plenty of friends and a great social life. Back in the early part of 1963, Carolyn Mayo didn't have a problem in the world.

Then shortly after she returned from summer vacation, ready for her second year, Professor Hayes, who tutored her in English, was killed in an automobile accident and his classes were divided between the other professors in the department. Carolyn's class was taken over by Professor Myron White, an affable man whom, until now, she'd had little to do with.

The classes had started fine. White quickly became popular among the students. He was a handsome man in his late thirties, with thick wavy brown hair and a rugged jaw, and many of the female students found him attractive. He was the perfect professor, often making jokes during lectures and always telling them that his door was open should they ever need to talk.

Carolyn got on fine for the first few weeks. Unlike some of her female friends, she didn't have a crush on the new professor, but she believed him to genuinely care about whether or not his students passed the course.

It was on a Thursday afternoon that she first noticed him paying her extra attention. It seemed that every time she looked up, he had his eyes on her chest and when, at the end of the lecture, she was leaving the room, he brushed past her, his hand drifting down to caress her on the ass.

At the time she tried to tell herself that it had been an accident. It was silly to think the man had done it purposely.

Although the incident remained in the back of her mind, she chose not to mention it to Bobby or any of her friends and she went to her Tuesday lecture thinking nothing more of it. It wasn't until a week later, when White handed her back a paper he'd marked, that she realised she had a problem. Over the past few months, she had managed to consistently achieve As. Although she had worked just as hard on this particular paper and knew it to be worthy of an A, it came back graded with a D.

After the lecture Carolyn stayed behind to confront White and find out why she had been marked down. When she left the room twenty minutes later, she went straight to the bathroom, locked herself in the toilet and burst into tears.

Professor White had made it clear to her that he did not believe her paper to be worthy of anything more than a grade D. He told her that he felt her level of work had been slipping since the death of Professor Hayes and he suggested that she might wish to come back on Thursday evenings for extra help with the work. While there had been nothing overtly threatening in the words that he had used, the tone of his voice and the way in which he had allowed his hand to brush over her breast had left her in no doubt as to what he meant.

If Carolyn Mayo wished to achieve good grades again, she was going to have to offer the professor a little incentive.

Her initial reaction had been to report White to the College Dean. There was no way that he could get away with blackmailing her this way. Surely, if she reported him his contract with the college would be terminated.

It didn't take her long to realise that if she did report him nobody would be likely to believe her. Professor Myron White was held in high esteem by all of his work colleagues and practically worshipped by the student body. Why would they take the word of an average student over his? Carolyn could just imagine what would happen if she tried to report him. White would probably turn the tables around, maybe even make out that she had a crush on him and that she became nasty when he didn't reciprocate her advances. She would not only be risking her grades, but also her future with the college. What newspaper would want to hire her if she was kicked off her course?

She didn't sleep for worrying for the next two nights, knowing that if she said nothing and didn't comply with his requests, her grades would continue to slip. During her Thursday lecture she couldn't bring herself to look the man in the eye and, when he called her back after class and asked if she had decided to take him up on his offer, she told herself she was thinking of her future before answering the one word that was about to ruin it.

Yes.

They met in the classroom at half seven that evening. Carolyn lied to Bobby, telling him she was feeling ill and planned on going to bed early, before leaving her dorm and making her way across campus to the building that housed the English Department.

White was already in his classroom, waiting for her, looking like the cat that had got the cream as he sat behind his desk, his elbows resting on the arms of his chair and his two index fingers pressed together in front of him.

He looked at her and smiled. 'I'm glad you came, Carolyn. It's nice to know you care enough about your grades to put in the extra work.'

Carolyn swallowed back the bile that was rising in her throat and clutched her purse tightly. Her eyes flicked nervously around the room. The overhead light was on, and White had drawn the blinds at the windows to prevent anyone being able to see inside the classroom. As she had entered the building, she had noticed that no one else seemed to be around and it made her apprehensive, knowing she was all alone with him. White moved past her to the door, pushing it shut before pulling the blind down and turning the key. Noticing the fearful look in her eye, he gave her what she supposed was meant to be a reassuring smile.

'We need a little privacy, Carolyn,' he explained. 'I wouldn't want anyone to come in and disturb us while we work.'

Carolyn felt a little of her fear subside as he stepped away from the door, noticing that he'd left the key in the lock. He came to stand before her, placing his hands on her shoulders. Slowly he began to massage them.

'You're so tense, Carolyn. You need to learn to relax. We will work better together that way.'

Slowly he eased the strap of her purse off her shoulder, letting it slip down her arm to the floor. He pulled her closer and allowed his hands to drop off her shoulders and down onto her back.

Carolyn closed her eyes, wishing she could block out the peppery scent of his aftershave.

You're doing it for your future, she reminded herself.

She felt White's hands untuck her blouse from her skirt and she winced as they touched the bare skin of her back, moving up and down and beneath her bra strap.

He removed one hand and brought it up to caress the side of her face, pushing her head back so he was looking her directly in the eye. His breath was warm on her face and smelt strongly of coffee.

'You're doing very well, Carolyn. I think your grade might have already just improved to a C.'

His gaze dropped down to the neckline of her blouse and with impatient fingers he pulled the buttons undone. Carolyn stared past his head at the locked door, tears pricking against the back of her eyes.

How could she let him do this?

Pulling the strap of her bra off her shoulder, he slipped his hand inside the white lacy cup, his fingers greedily squeezing the tender flesh of her breast.

Carolyn tried to pull away.

'*No!* I can't do this!'

White stopped. His eyes met hers and she saw a flicker of uncertainty pass through them. 'You can do it and you will do it,' he answered coldly. Clamping a hand across her back he pulled her towards him, pushing his face against hers and forcing his tongue into her mouth. Carolyn struggled in his arms, choking back a sob. Reaching down she grabbed hold of the front of his trousers and squeezed hard.

White screamed loudly into her mouth, relinquishing his grip and stumbling backwards.

'You little bitch! What did you go and do that for?'

Brushing the tears from her eyes, Carolyn reached down and grabbed her purse.

'The lesson is over, Professor. I'm not sleeping with you, ever!' She spat the last word in his face and pushed past him to the door.

White grabbed hold of her arm. 'You think you can just walk away and forget about this?' he asked, his tone low and threatening. 'If you leave this room, I promise I will ruin your reputation. I can make you flunk this course if I want. Hell... I can even get you kicked out of the damn college.'

Carolyn closed her eyes, knowing that he was telling the truth. This was it. This was where her life ended. Mustering all of her courage, she pulled herself free from his grip and continued to the door. With a shaking hand, she turned the key, feeling a small surge of relief as she heard the click of the lock.

Pulling open the door she turned around to face him, staring at him through a sheen of tears, and forced a smile. 'Go to hell, Professor!'

She allowed herself a moment to register the look of shock on his face before she turned and, holding her head up high, left the room.

* * *

Her plan had been to tell no one.

If White planned to flunk her or get her kicked out of college, Carolyn decided she would go quietly. Nobody was ever going to know about what happened in his classroom on that Thursday evening in November.

What she hadn't counted on was finding Bobby waiting for her outside her dorm room. Believing her to be sick, he had come across to cheer her up and immediately became suspicious when he'd found that she wasn't there. Caught by surprise, Carolyn didn't have time to come up with a believable story, and he wasn't going to give up until she told him the truth. Half an hour later he knew everything that Myron White had done, and he was hell bent on revenge.

Carolyn begged him to let the matter drop. Bobby had a vicious temper and seemed unable to stay out of trouble for longer than five minutes. He wouldn't hear of it, though, and when he left her that night, he looked her in the eye and made her a promise.

'Don't worry, honey. I won't do anything to hurt him. I'll just scare him a little.'

And as she stood and watched her boyfriend disappear down the hallway, Carolyn Mayo really believed that he was telling her the truth.

34

SAN PALIMO, CALIFORNIA. WEDNESDAY 7
MAY 1997

Max listened as Agnes Barnes finished recounting her story, then he leaned back against the red vinyl seat and let out a low whistle. 'Oh boy,' he murmured, shaking his head. 'Sounds to me like Professor White was a bad man; that's why his students decided to teach him a lesson, right?'

Agnes nodded; her eyes having turned a stormy grey. Max noticed that her mouth was pulled into a tense, thin line. 'They didn't mean to kill him. Bobby just wanted to scare him a little. Get him back for what he'd done to Carolyn.'

Max picked up his spoon and began to idly stir the black liquid in the coffee cup. 'It would sure explain where little Rodney got his screwed-up genes from: an abusive mother, a father who blackmailed his students into having sex.' He glanced up at Agnes. 'You said they hanged him, right?'

'That's right, Mr Sutton.'

Max thought of Boone's victims, all of them killed by asphyxia. Several of them had been strangled. Had he chosen this particular method of death because of what had happened to his father or was it just some sick coincidence? His mind turned to

Lawrence Parker, currently being held in custody back in Juniper, suspected of murdering six students. He was also suspected of having affairs with at least two of them.

Another coincidence, or had Lawrence Parker inherited rogue genes from a father he probably never knew existed? It was a far-fetched theory: Lawrence Parker, son of Myron White and brother of Rodney Boone.

Agnes had said that Myron White was killed back in 1963. That would mean all three sons would have to be at least thirty-four.

How old was Parker? Thirty? Thirty-five?

Maybe it would be a good idea to call Joel and check. If the age was right then they could look into his background, see if he was adopted.

Max sighed deeply and rubbed his palms across his face. It all sounded good, but wasn't he getting a little carried away? It seemed at the moment that all he had was an old lady with a story and a whole bunch of coincidences.

He glanced up at Agnes. 'This stuff about Rodney's father, it's all definitely true, isn't it, Ms Barnes? I mean, it's not like one of these dumb folklore stories that gets passed around town?'

Agnes narrowed her eyes, looking a little offended at the insinuation.

'It's all quite true, I can assure you of that,' she told him, smiling thinly. 'I should know better than anyone. You see, Mr Sutton, Carolyn Mayo is my younger sister.'

35

JUNIPER, OREGON. WEDNESDAY 7 MAY 1997

Rebecca had awoken on Wednesday morning expecting to spend the day over at the college helping to collect prints, but when she arrived at the precinct, Hickok had already dispatched a couple of the other officers, and instead he asked her to sit in on the Lawrence Parker interrogations with him. She was pleased, knowing the job would be far more interesting, but she also suspected he was trying to make it up to her for losing out to Vic on the California trip.

She wondered how her patrol partner and Sutton were getting on. They had left at seven that morning so should have arrived in San Palimo around lunchtime.

Had they spoken with Agnes Barnes yet?

Her own morning ended up being pretty uneventful. Hickok had been down to the courthouse first thing to apply for a stay of arrest on Lawrence Parker. Both agents had decided to put off applying for the search warrant on the house until Sutton had a chance to see what he could uncover in San Palimo, but they were keen to prevent Parker from going anywhere.

When Hickok returned, he had Parker brought up from the

holding cells and, with Rebecca looking on, had started to thoroughly grill the professor. She had watched his relentless attack of blunt and aggressive questions, a little surprised by the cool façade Lawrence Parker was managing to keep up, while trying to ignore the long, lingering, almost flirtatious looks he kept giving her across the large wooden desk.

Hickok didn't seem to notice and, while it was probably because he was on a mission to break Parker into confessing, Rebecca preferred to put it down to her own paranoia. It was stupid to believe that this mild-tempered married man, who might not even be guilty of anything, was flirting with her. He was being held on a possible charge of murder. Why the hell would he want to do anything that might jeopardise his chances of leaving this room a free man?

Admittedly, things weren't looking too good for him at the moment. Aside from the black-and-green check tie that had been used to strangle Justine Orton, he wasn't having much luck with his alibis. Scott Jagger had been murdered on a Friday night and Parker claimed to have spent the entire evening marking test papers in his classroom at the college. Unfortunately, he had no witnesses to collaborate his story. On the two Tuesday nights when Rufus Lind and Kevin North had been killed, Kylan Parker had been out with friends, and he swore blind he had spent both evenings home alone. Again, there were no witnesses. And when Emma Keeley had been murdered, Parker claimed he couldn't remember what he had been doing. The two Saturdays when Catherine Maloney and Justine Orton had been killed were looking his best hope at the moment.

Well, they would do if his wife could be found.

Parker insisted that Kylan would be able to confirm his story that the two of them had been together on both nights. Unfortunately, until she returned, he was left dangling by a thread.

Hickok insinuated that she might not be coming back, that perhaps Parker might have killed her.

Rebecca thought the idea pretty stupid, believing that if Parker was their killer he would have enough sense not to kill the one person who could provide him with a solid alibi. Even so, she had to admit that the evidence piling up against the professor was beginning to look fairly overwhelming. Maybe she was wrong about him. After all, what would she, a rookie police officer, know? Hickok had experience and, as he had already proved to her, he also had pretty good hunches.

After two hours of solid questioning, Hickok decided to go and get coffee – and, Rebecca guessed, to go bang his head against the wall. Cracking through Parker's hard exterior was proving to be harder than she had imagined and, whilst Rebecca was still unsure about him being a murderer, she didn't doubt for a second that he was hiding something.

But what?

He swore blind that he and Emma Keeley were no more than friends, claiming that the note Hickok had found in his desk drawer was completely innocent. Then there was the tie that had been used to strangle Justine Orton. It was his and he didn't try to deny it. What he did do, though, was insist that the last time he'd seen it had been over a week ago, sitting in his closet.

Was he telling the truth?

Alone in the room with him while she waited for Hickok to return with his coffee, she studied Lawrence Parker's face, wondering what was going on behind the calm, impassive mask he wore.

He glanced up, startling her with hooded black eyes that seemed to bore right through her.

'Have you been working here long, Officer?' he asked, almost conversationally. His gaze remained on her and Rebecca struggled not to look away.

'We're not here to discuss me,' she told him, keeping her tone cool.

'You're new to this profession, aren't you? I'll bet you've only just graduated from the academy.' He smiled at her, teasing, almost seductive. 'In fact, I'll bet this is the first investigation you've been involved in.'

Rebecca narrowed her eyes, wondering what he was trying to insinuate. Was he trying to intimidate her, she wondered, coming out with all that crap about her being new to the police force, trying to make her think he had the upper hand?

She imagined that he could easily make a lot of people feel intimidated. He was powerfully built and incredibly handsome, with dark chiselled features and those intense black eyes that seemed to blink less than a cat, and he radiated a strong aura of power. It was difficult not to feel vulnerable in his presence. He continued to stare at her, almost challenging her to hold his gaze. Rebecca managed for about fifteen seconds before she had to break away. She focused instead on her hands in her lap and cursed herself under her breath.

He was getting to her, and it pissed her off.

'Officer Angell, isn't it?' he asked suddenly, drawing her attention back up to his face.

'That's correct.'

'Angell. I like that name. It's very pretty. Do you have a first name, Officer Angell?'

'Not one that you can call me by,' Rebecca told him laconically.

She was a little surprised that she was able to keep her own mask of calm composure from slipping, considering how her stomach was twisting knots inside.

Instead of being deterred by her put down, Parker's smile grew into a broad grin.

'You're feisty. I do like that quality in a woman.' His gaze dropped slowly to her breasts, lingering there for a moment before coming back up to meet her eyes. 'I like that quality in you, Officer Angell.'

Rebecca let out an inelegant snort, her mouth dropping open. She pushed her chair back and got to her feet, so she at least had the advantage of height over Parker. She glared down at him.

'Are you coming on to me?' she demanded, feeling her temper boil.

Parker stared back at her, still calm, still composed, and looking amused at her outburst.

'Is that a problem?' he asked, a suggestive glint in his eye.

Hickok chose that moment to return to the room. He glanced first at Rebecca, then at Parker, a look of thunder on his face.

'What the hell's going on here?' he stormed, slamming his cup down on the desk hard enough to slosh coffee over the sides.

'This jerk just made a move on me,' Rebecca snapped angrily.

Parker gave Hickok an innocuous smile.

'I think Officer Angell just misinterpreted the situation.'

Rebecca glared at him. 'I did not, you lying son of a—'

'Angell! Outside, now!'

She glanced at Hickok, seeing the warning on his face. Drawing a deep breath, she scowled at Parker and stormed from the room, slamming the door shut behind her. She expected Hickok to follow, but he didn't and that irritated her even more.

Although she knew she was in the wrong for losing her temper with Parker, now she was mad, she needed to vent her rage on someone, and Hickok was the perfect choice.

Sullenly, she skulked back to her desk, knowing that by the time he was finally through with Parker and ready to sound off at her she would have calmed down and be in no mood for a confrontation.

Stupid jerk! That's probably why he did it.

'Hey, Angell?'

Rebecca looked up to see Wayne Hankins waving the phone in her direction.

'Who is it?' she asked, crossing the room.

'It's Peterson, wanting Hickok. Can he be disturbed?'

Rebecca thought back to the situation she'd just left, Hickok angrier than she'd ever seen him and Parker smugly knowing he had got one up on her.

'I'll take it,' she said, snatching the receiver. Hankins pulled a face at her, and she turned her back on him. 'Hal, it's Rebecca.'

She heard Hal Peterson's voice on the other end of the line. 'Where's Hickok?'

'He's busy. What do you want? I'll give him a message.'

The line crackled and Rebecca heard what she thought was a snort. It didn't surprise her. Vic Boaz wasn't the only officer who seemed to think she'd landed herself a cushy number since the Feds had arrived. She waited patiently for Peterson to speak.

'You'd better make sure he gets this, Angell. It's important.'

'Gets what?'

'One of the girls whose prints we took earlier...' He paused and Rebecca heard the flutter of pages as he consulted his notes. 'Renee Lewis,' he confirmed. 'Turns out she was real good friends with Emma Keeley. She was telling us all about how Emma was totally infatuated with this guy. Even gave her the key to her room so they had somewhere private to go.'

'Really?' Rebecca felt her heartbeat quicken. 'Did this guy she was seeing have a name?'

Peterson let out a gruff laugh. 'Yup... Want to know who it was?'

Rebecca glanced in the direction of the room where Hickok was still hounding Lawrence Parker. She felt a smile crease the corners of her mouth.

'I think I've already got a pretty good idea.'

* * *

Parker fixed Joel with a bored look. 'Okay, so I slept with Emma Keeley. Happy now?'

Joel, sitting instead of pacing now he had the upper hand, ran his hands back through his hair. 'Why didn't you tell us this before?'

'Because I didn't want my wife to find out.' Parker shifted forward slightly. 'I still don't want my wife to find out, Agent Hickok. Are we clear on that?'

'Are you threatening me?' Joel asked, amused.

'No, I am merely making sure you're aware of the delicate situation.'

'Delicate situation?'

Parker nodded. 'Kylan is... how can I put it. She's fragile. And she doesn't need any unnecessary trouble.'

'She doesn't need you screwing your students behind her back either,' Joel added.

Parker glared at him and leaned back in his chair.

'So, Lawrie, Emma's dead, you wanted another fling. Is that when you took up with Justine Orton?'

'I never had anything to do with Justine Orton outside of class.'

'Really?' Joel pulled a face. 'Funny that, because Justine Orton seemed to have a lot to do with you outside of class.'

'Implying what?'

'Did you know that she kept your picture in her room?'

'My picture?' Parker looked almost pleased. 'So one of my students had a crush on me, that doesn't mean anything.'

Joel flipped open the notepad that sat on the desk. He studied the page and regarded Parker with a dry smile. 'Let's go back to your alibis.'

He watched Parker roll his eyes, the frustration finally beginning to show, and felt a sense of satisfaction that he might finally be getting somewhere.

'The night when Scott Jagger was murdered, you weren't really marking papers in your classroom, were you?'

'No,' Parker admitted with more ease than Joel expected.

'So, what was the deal, Lawrie? Did you meet Scott Jagger in a bar, make out you're his buddy and buy him a few drinks?'

Parker shook his head, looking Joel straight in the eye.

'I wasn't with Scott Jagger. I was with Emma.'

His admission stunned Joel into a moment's silence. He studied Parker carefully through narrowed eyes, trying to figure out if he was telling the truth or, now they'd found out about his affair, if he was trying to use Emma Keeley as an alibi.

'You were with Emma?' he said eventually.

'That's right.'

'And where were you the night Emma was killed?'

Parker gave a twisted smile.

'Waiting to meet her.'

'What?'

'The note you found, Agent Hickok, I received it the day she... the day she died. I turned up to meet her, but she never showed up.'

'And why would I believe that?' Joel asked, his tone sardonic.

Parker's lips thinned. 'Because it's the truth.'

36

He couldn't believe that he had lost her.

All of this time he'd been watching her so carefully, probably more often than he should have done, and she'd managed to give him the slip.

He guessed he was partly to blame. Kylan had run into him three times and it was inevitable that she would eventually get spooked, especially after the Feds had decided to go public about the murders. The poor girl probably knew the killer would be looking for her. He should have been more careful. He should have watched her day and night.

With no clue as to where she had gone and at a loss what to do next, he made the call to his employer. He expected to get an angry reaction, and he was right.

'You've lost her! How the hell did you manage to lose her?'

'I guess she got spooked and decided to get out of town.' He knew his excuse was feeble, but it was the only one he had. The truth of the matter was, he'd been sloppy all along. Sloppy because he'd wasted so many victims, so many chances; sloppy because when it came down to getting Kylan, he hadn't been careful enough.

'What do you intend to do about this mess?' the voice asked huffily.

'There's nothing we can do until she returns.'

'If she returns...'

'You said yourself it definitely has to be her. She'll have to come back eventually and when she does, I'll pay her a visit.'

There was a long pause before the voice answered.

'You'd better be right. You've missed every opportunity so far. Kylan Parker is our last chance. Without her we have nothing. Without her, this whole thing is a waste of time.'

'Don't worry. I'll find her.'

'I hope you're right.'

He hung up the phone, pondering for a moment, not sure what to do.

Things with his employer were supposed to be kept top secret and that had been fine in the beginning. Now, it seemed as though the whole situation was spiralling out of control.

He climbed into his Buick, started the engine and swung the car out onto the road. As far as he could see, he only had one choice left. Seeing the police precinct on the road ahead, he began to indicate.

* * *

The man entered the police precinct late in the afternoon and asked to speak to whoever was dealing with the Juniper College murders. Hickok was still interrogating Lawrence Parker and, instead of disturbing him, Rebecca agreed to speak with him.

He was young, probably no older than thirty, with pale blond hair and acne, and he seemed nervous. As she approached the front desk, the thought crossed her mind that maybe he was a crank coming to confess to the murders. He wouldn't be the first one they'd had.

She smiled politely at him. 'Hello, I'm Officer Angell. I understand you have some information on the Juniper College murders?'

'That's right, I think I do.' He glanced around the room. 'Is there somewhere private where we could go talk?'

'Yes, sure. Okay.' Rebecca stepped out from behind the desk and led the way down to the office that Hickok and Sutton had been using.

'We can talk in here,' she said, following him inside the room.

He glanced around again before sitting in one of the two chairs at the desk. Rebecca shut the door. She stepped round to the other side of the desk and took a seat.

'Can I take your name, please?'

The man nodded, looking a little more confident now that they were alone.

'Yes, it's Richard Lamb.' He smiled at her. 'I'm a private investigator.'

37

SEATTLE, WASHINGTON. WEDNESDAY 7
MAY 1997

The nightmare had begun almost eight years earlier and now, just when it seemed she had finally found a way to deal with what had happened, the shadows of the past were returning to haunt her.

Jennifer Isaac was Rodney Boone's one surviving victim, the only one who had managed to get away. What she hadn't counted on at the time was that Rodney Boone would get away too.

The police had tried to reassure her, telling her he was more than likely dead. The house had burnt to the ground. It was unlikely he could have survived. It didn't matter that they had never recovered his body. He would never be able to harm her again.

Of course, she hadn't believed them. She had stabbed him. She had left him to burn in the cellar. So why hadn't they found him? It was at that point she realised that he was no different to the movie monsters. He was alive and he was invincible. Knives and fire couldn't destroy him. He would always be out there, always searching for her. Always looking forward to that moment he would find her and take revenge on her for ruining his alphabet.

After her ordeal at the hands of Boone, Jennifer had dropped out of college and moved back east to be with her family. She lost contact with all of her college friends, including Miranda, preferring to leave behind everything that reminded her of what had happened. The last time she had seen Miranda had been in hospital, when her old roommate had come to visit. Neither of them had much to say to one another. Jennifer knew that Miranda felt guilty about what had happened and was uncomfortable being around her. When she left, she'd promised to come back again the next day, but had never shown. Not that it mattered, because Miranda was part of the past, the part she would rather forget.

It had taken years of therapy for her to start putting the pieces of her life back together. For the first six months she suffered badly from agoraphobia and didn't leave the house. Gradually, she learned to deal with her fears, and she eventually reached a point where she knew she was as well as she could ever again hope to be.

The first year was understandably the worst. Her father suffered a heart attack as a direct result of what had happened to her, and her older sister gave up her job and moved back home to help with both his and Jennifer's recovery. The second year was a little easier. They moved to a small fishing village in South Carolina where they could all make a fresh start. Her parents bought a restaurant in town and the four of them concentrated on building a new life together.

Following the move, Jennifer had decided she would reinvent herself. Her sister went with her and together they shopped for a new wardrobe: for clothes that were different to those she had worn before, that showed she was a new person. Then she went to the hairdressers and had her long brown hair cut shorter and lightened to blonde.

She started working part-time, waitressing for her parents in the restaurant on the days when she didn't have therapy, and after eighteen months of working there she bumped into the one person from her past whom she had never quite forgotten.

Lawrie.

He recognised her instantly, despite the changes she'd made, and they got talking. About college, about what they were both up to and about what had happened to her. He had moved east to complete his teaching degree after graduating from Juniper and was living locally. He came to the restaurant every day that first week and it was on his fifth visit that he asked her out.

She was still pretty screwed up and at first it was difficult for her, seeing a face from the one time she wanted to forget. Lawrie was persistent about wanting to see her again, and his concern for her seemed so genuine. She finally relented and agreed to go out with him.

Since the Boone incident she hadn't dated at all. Now, with her image change and knowing that she could trust Lawrie, it seemed like the perfect time to restart.

The date was successful. They went to a seafront restaurant and ate clams, then walked along the beach and spent a lot of time talking. They got on well together and over the following months began to see each other on a regular basis.

Although he originated from California, Lawrie liked Juniper and had made it clear that one day he intended to move back there and get a teaching job. She had accepted his decision at the time, hoping he would change his mind, and not realising how hard she would fall for him. Another year passed and a teaching position came up. When the time came for him to leave, she didn't want him to go, and he surprised her by asking her to marry him.

It was a tough decision. She didn't want to lose him, but she wasn't sure if she could ever bring herself to move back to the place where she had nearly been murdered, especially knowing that Boone had never been caught. The only people who knew what had happened to her were her parents, her sister and Lawrie. If she went with him, she would have only him to rely on. At first, he went alone and during those first few weeks that she realised just how much she missed him.

Her doctor told her she had made the right decision in staying. He said that she was still too traumatised by the incident and there were a lot of buried feelings that she had to learn to deal with. If she went back to Juniper, it was possible she might have a nervous breakdown. She accepted the diagnosis and agreed to stay with her family, but then Lawrie came to visit her, and she knew that she couldn't let him leave her again.

She told him how she felt and within three weeks they were married.

Jennifer Isaac had stopped existing the day she had decided to reinvent herself and start going by her middle name, Kylan. Now she had become Mrs Parker she was finally able to shake off the one piece of her past that still haunted her, her maiden name, Isaac.

Things had gone okay at first. It was scary returning to places that held such bad memories, and she regularly suffered from nightmares in which Boone was coming to get her. She had Lawrie for support, though, and her records had been transferred to one of the therapy groups in the city. The sessions she attended helped and her new doctor gave her pills to help her sleep through the nightmares.

She convinced herself that she was safe. Eight years had

passed. If the serial killer was still alive and looking for her, surely Juniper was the last place he would expect to find her.

Lawrie had his teaching job, back at the same college where she had been attacked. At first Kylan refused to go near the place, but with time she gradually grew more confident and eventually gave in to his wishes and went back to finish her college degree.

Living off campus made it easier. Stepping inside the dormitories was something she didn't think she would ever be able to do again, but the day-to-day routine of attending her lectures helped and, if anything, made her learn to deal with what had happened. Of course, she was always more on guard than before. She avoided going places alone and often found herself glancing over her shoulder to check that she wasn't being followed, but it helped knowing Lawrie was close by. If she ever needed someone to talk to, he would be there for her.

Or so she thought.

It was the day in the grocery store when things had taken a turn for the worse, when she had first noticed the man watching her. Then, of course, she had seen him at her kitchen window. He had something to do with Rodney Boone. She knew it. Did he have spies out there looking for her? Keeping an eye on her, until he was ready to make his move?

She tried to ignore it, tell herself she was safe and that the whole situation had nothing to do with Boone. She needed Lawrie more than ever, but she didn't dare talk to him. It was almost as though he was so preoccupied with his work that he no longer had time for her.

She had changed her name, her looks, her whole identity, but still she felt vulnerable. Now she wasn't sure if she could even trust the man who had promised to look after her. Feeling desperately alone and scared of being attacked a second time, she wasn't willing to take any chances. That was when she had packed her case and left.

Her sister, Tania, lived in Seattle; Kylan knew it was a place she could go and feel safe, to get away from the pressures that were building in her head. She needed to be alone for a while, to make some decisions about what was happening to her and to the people around her. Her plans to make things better were not working and she was terrified that if she wasn't careful, Boone might be granted a second chance to kill her.

Figuring that if Lawrie really loved her, he would understand, she had caught a cab to the bus station and booked herself a ticket on the next Greyhound.

Now she was in Seattle, in Tania's house. Her sister wasn't home, so she had let herself in with the spare key kept in the barbecue, but she was feeling more alone than ever. In an attempt to obliterate her fears, she took the bottle of gin from the liquor cabinet and went upstairs, where she sat in her sister's bedroom drinking it neat from the bottle, the curtains drawn shut to keep out the demons.

Eventually, too exhausted to think any more and too drunk to care she fell back on the bed and closed her eyes, hoping to fall into a deep, dreamless sleep. Instead, she dreamt of a faceless man who held a playing card out to her and when she took the card from him and studied it close, she realised that the joker in the picture had the smiling face of Rodney Boone.

38

SAN PALIMO, CALIFORNIA. WEDNESDAY 7TH
MAY 1997

The old newspapers stacked high in the back room of the library showed Max that he and Boaz had a mammoth task on their hands.

Most libraries now had up-to-date computer equipment, but San Palimo was only a small town and not yet able to afford such luxuries. Agnes Barnes had explained that the library hadn't been set up long and, due to a staff shortage, nobody had really had time to sort out any kind of filing system or date order for the papers. She had pointed a long finger towards the back of the room, telling them that was where they were likely to find most of the papers from the early sixties, and Max and Vic had gone to work.

They worked through the rest of the afternoon and into the early evening, then Max suggested they take a night shift each, so they could both get some sleep. He agreed to take the first shift and Boaz left at ten to book them a room at the motel across the street, arranging to come back at two to take over.

As Karen Harris had still been hanging around in the library after hours, Max suspected that Boaz wouldn't actually use the room for sleep. He just hoped that the two of them wouldn't leave the bed in too much of a mess and, of course, that Boaz wouldn't forget to come and relieve him. Looking at his wristwatch, he saw that it wasn't quite midnight and he cursed having over two hours to go. His eyes were sore, and his back ached from leaning over the papers. He stood up and stretched, trying to ease his aching muscles. What he wouldn't give to be back home right now, his back rested against the plumped-up pillows, a large glass of scotch on the nightstand, and Rita in bed beside him.

When he was actually home, and that was seldom these days, the two of them liked to spend the evening in bed, either reading or watching re-runs of old TV shows on cable. He guessed the idea would seem boring to a lot of people, but to him it was heaven.

He knew he shouldn't complain. Max loved his job and he would hate it if he ever got stuck behind a desk. Now the boys were grown-up, Rita had more spare time, and she sometimes flew out to meet him if he had a free weekend. But when he was stuck in a small-town library in the middle of the night, rummaging through old copies of newspapers, it was difficult to be appreciative of these things.

So far, he had gone through all the papers from April 1963 to mid-November. He hoped that Agnes Barnes was right about the year of Myron White's death. It would be unlucky if they were wrong by one year. Glancing at the large pile of papers that he had already gone through, he hoped that wouldn't turn out to be the case.

Max made himself as comfortable as possible on the floor and opened the yellow-stained front page of the *San Palimo Press* for 21 November. The paper had closed its doors back in 1972 and was now a derelict building on the outskirts of town. Agnes Barnes had told him and Boaz that there had been plans for the last ten

years to turn the old press building into an apartment block. As
yet, nothing had been done.

He scanned the page before him and turned over, disturbing a
thick film of dust on the page beneath. Sneezing loudly for about
the twentieth time since he'd been in the room he swore at his
dust allergy.

*Well, look at you, old buddy. Twenty years with the Bureau and
you find yourself shuffling papers in a dusty old library. Is life the pits
or what?*

He laughed to himself, thinking he should have cajoled Joel
into coming down here instead. Had he known what the visit to
San Palimo would entail, he would have given it his best shot.

Maybe he had been foolish in letting Boaz off so lightly.
Instead of allowing the lazy officer the chance to go partying with
some babe he'd picked up, he should have made him stay at the
library all night and search through the papers while Max
supervised.

*Too late now, buddy. You've taken the job on, so you might as well
get on with it.*

He flicked over the next page and read the headline.

LOCAL PROFESSOR KILLED IN PRANK

He read the beginning of the story.

San Palimo Police were today questioning three local youths
about the death of a San Palimo College Professor who was
found hanged in his classroom. It is believed that Professor
Myron White, who taught English at the college, was killed
when a prank went wrong.

Max read the rest of the story. It went on to say that the police had not yet decided whether they would press charges and that White had left a wife and three young sons. No details were given of the children's names. Quickly Max found the paper for 22 November. He flicked through twice but was unable to find any further developments on the Myron White case.

The next story was on the 26th of the month and much longer than the previous article. He scanned through, looking for the names of the children.

A loud bang came from out in the library, throwing his concentration.

He jumped and looked up.

'Hello? Who's there?'

There was no answer.

Not wanting to leave the newspaper now he had found what he wanted, Max ripped the page out, folded it up and stuffed it in the front pocket of his jeans. Then he reached for his revolver. The library had closed at ten when Boaz had left and Agnes Barnes had locked the door, leaving Max inside with a set of keys. Logically, he knew that any disturbance would have to be caused either by one of the library assistants coming back (unlikely), or Boaz banging on the front door, having decided to come across early to help (even less likely). Whatever or whoever had caused the noise, he wasn't prepared to take any chances.

He waited a second before gently easing down the handle of the door to the back room, listening for further sounds. Then, satisfied there was no one waiting on the other side, he stepped through into the room with the books and pulled the door shut.

The room was dark and not wanting to turn on the light he stepped carefully around the books so as not to make any unnecessary noise. The next door separated him from the main library. Back against the wall and his revolver ready, Max eased down the handle and pushed the door open.

There was no one there.

He considered calling out again, before he scared the shit out of one of the library assistants with the loaded gun. But he couldn't take the risk.

Just in case.

The room was filled with high bookshelves, offering any intruder a hundred places to hide, but they were as much an advantage as a disadvantage. Whilst an intruder could hide from him, Max could hide from an intruder.

His revolver raised and ready, he crept around the bookshelves, keeping his footsteps quiet and his breathing as shallow as possible. At the end of each shelf he stood with his back against the books and cautiously peered around the corner to make sure the coast was clear before crossing into the open.

He saw no one and he heard no one.

It's probably all a false alarm. Jeez, old man! You're running around an empty library, waving your gun in the air. You look like a damn fool.

Feeling it probably was a false alarm, Max relaxed slightly. He loosened his grip on the revolver.

Then he saw the broken glass on the floor.

He was over on the left-hand side of the library, standing between the wall and an end bookshelf containing children's titles. Looking up at the window he could see that the pane of glass had been completely smashed. It was only a small window, but just big enough for an intruder to climb through.

So much for imagining things. He'd been right about hearing a noise after all.

He took a step closer, wondering why someone would want to break into a library. Maybe to steal a copy of *Moby Dick* or *The Catcher in the Rye*. He laughed quietly to himself, not seeing the approaching shadow on the wall in front of him.

The wooden club smashed down, crunching hard against the

back of his head and knocking him to the floor. Max rolled over just in time to get a glimpse of his attacker's face, before the club smashed down again, hard against the side of his head, knocking him unconscious.

He was still unconscious five minutes later when the library, strong with the smell of gasoline, started to fill with smoke and flames began to tear through the newspapers in the small room out back, destroying the last remaining records of San Palimo's history.

39

JUNIPER, OREGON. THURSDAY 8 MAY 1997

By the time Rebecca finally located Kylan Parker, she had just about managed to piece everything together.

Richard Lamb had been a great help at filling in the gaps when he'd come in the day before; she only wished he had decided to come to them earlier. She had listened to everything he had to say, shocked that people could be so callous. Then she had called Hickok and made Lamb repeat his story.

The private investigator had been hired by a woman called Barbara Hyde, whose only son, Marcus, had been Rodney Boone's eighth victim. Marcus had spoken with his mother only hours before he was murdered, and she remembered how he had mentioned to her that he'd found an envelope stuffed into the door of his locker that contained a playing card of a joker. At the time they'd both found it strange, but neither of them had thought any more about it. After Marcus's murder, Mrs Hyde became convinced that the playing card must have been some kind of calling card sent by the killer. When she learned about Scott Jagger's murder, she was convinced that Boone had returned to his old hunting ground to finish his alphabet. Not trusting the police to catch him, she had asked Lamb to help her trap the killer, using the intended victims as bait.

She told the investigator that she suspected the new killer would send his victims the playing card once he had made his selection and asked Lamb to try to find out who had been chosen. The plan was to use the victim to lure Boone out of hiding, catching him when he attacked so Mrs Hyde could personally avenge her son's death.

Lamb had researched the original killings thoroughly before undertaking the task, but it wasn't long after arriving in Juniper that he got side-tracked by a pretty, blonde student called Kylan Parker. A little personal research of his own revealed that she was Jennifer Isaac, Boone's one surviving victim.

When he told Mrs Hyde this information, she became convinced that Boone knew Kylan's true identity and would go after her again, only this time as victim P. Although she still wanted Lamb to try and catch Boone through one of the earlier victims, Kylan Parker became her safety net and she believed that if all their other chances failed, they would definitely be able to catch the killer when he went for her.

Unfortunately, the whole plan fell apart when Kylan got spooked and left town. Lamb admitted that it was his fault, because he had spent most of his days following her around instead of concentrating on finding the killer's other victims.

Rebecca had asked him if Barbara Hyde had been right about the killer's calling card and whether he had known of any victims who had received a joker playing card.

It was then that he told her about Justine Orton. About how he had seen her by her locker with the playing card the day before she was killed, and how he had followed her when she went shopping and talked her into meeting him under false pretences. They had met Saturday evening and he had been taking her to meet Barbara Hyde when Justine had gotten spooked and jumped from the car.

Lamb claimed that he tried to find her, but to no avail.

Rebecca suspected he wasn't telling her the whole truth but decided not to push. Hickok wasn't as easy on him and grilled the investigator until he finally broke down and confessed that he had returned to the college. He had gone to Justine Orton's room, only to find that someone else had beaten him to it.

Hickok had gone nuts at Lamb for not calling them, before finally placing him under arrest for withholding evidence and obstruction of justice. There was every possibility that Richard Lamb had not just seen Justine Orton's dead body but had been the one who had killed her. Rebecca didn't think it likely, though, and she suspected that Hickok didn't either.

His whole story was so crazy it had to be true.

At least he had decided to come forward now and tell them what he knew. She suspected it was because of the crush he had developed on Kylan Parker and that he was scared that she really was in danger.

Given Kylan's past, Rebecca had a feeling that he could be right. After throwing Lamb in the holding cell, Hickok had spent twenty minutes with Lawrence Parker. Again, it seemed that Parker had been holding back on them. He knew all about Kylan's change of identity and all about how Boone had attacked her.

When Hickok demanded to know why he hadn't mentioned any of this before, he had given a bored smile and casually explained that it was a matter between himself and his wife and one that they preferred to keep private. He did give them a list of numbers where Kylan might be, and Rebecca spent Wednesday evening trying to track her down. Having had no luck, she went home to get some sleep and then tried them all again first thing Thursday morning.

When she called Kylan's sister, Tania, again at the number she had in Seattle the answer machine clicked on. Rebecca hadn't left a message the night before, as there were several other places to try, but having exhausted them all she decided this time to leave a message for Tania Isaac asking her to call. Even if Kylan wasn't with her, it was possible that she might know where her sister was.

She waited for the beep and spoke into the receiver.

'Hello. My name is Rebecca Angell, and I work for the Juniper Police Department in Oregon. We're trying to locate your sister, Kylan Parker, and wondered if you had any idea where she is. I'd appreciate it if you could call me. My number is...'

Rebecca paused, hearing the sound of the phone being picked up. A voice came on the other end of the line.

'Hello? Rebecca? It's Kylan.'

Rebecca caught her breath. 'Kylan? Are you okay?'

'How did you know I was here?' Kylan asked, ignoring the question.

'Your husband, Lawrie, thought you might be. He gave us the number.'

There was a long pause. 'Why? Is he okay?' Kylan's voice sounded shaky.

'He's okay.' This time it was Rebecca's turn to pause, as she decided the best way to break the news to Kylan. 'He's at the police precinct with us,' she explained, having concluded it best just to be truthful. 'We've been questioning him about the Juniper College murders.'

'You've arrested Lawrie?'

'He's a suspect, Kylan. We have evidence that suggests he's guilty.'

'My husband is not a killer,' Kylan said, her voice carrying an edge of uncertainty that didn't make her words convincing.

'We need you to come back, Kylan,' Rebecca said hastily. 'Lawrie said he was with you on the nights of two of the murders. If that's true, then we can release him.'

'What nights?'

'The twenty-sixth of April and the third of May,' Rebecca told her, consulting the notes on her desk. 'That's last Saturday and the Saturday before.'

'He's telling you the truth. We were together both nights. Last Saturday we spent the evening in and the Saturday before we were out for a meal with friends then we were home together.'

'You're sure about that?'

'I'm sure.' There was a brief pause. 'Will you let him go now?' Kylan asked, sounding hopeful.

'We really need you to come down to the precinct,' Rebecca told her.

'I can't!' There was panic in Kylan's voice. 'I need to be away for a while. I need some time to think.'

Rebecca bit her bottom lip, deliberating over whether or not she should tell her that they knew about her past.

'We know about what happened, Kylan,' she started hesitantly. 'We know about Rodney Boone.'

When Kylan spoke, she sounded wary. 'What do you mean?'

'We know what he did to you. We know that you're Jennifer Isaac.'

For a long time, Kylan didn't answer. 'I can't come back,' she said eventually, neither confirming nor denying what Rebecca had said.

'Lawrie needs you, Kylan. Why don't we send someone to pick you up?'

'I'm not coming back!'

'No one will hurt you,' Rebecca tried again. 'If you come back to Juniper, we can protect you.'

'No!'

'Please! Kylan, just listen to—'

Before she had the chance to finish her sentence the line went dead. Putting the phone down Rebecca let out a deep sigh. She dropped her head into her hands, combing her fingers back through her hair.

'You found her, then?'

She glanced up to see Hickok watching her from the door of his office, a cup of coffee in his hand.

'Yeah, I found her,' she grumbled. 'But I don't think she's coming back to Juniper any time soon. She hung up on me.'

Hickok gave a half-smile. 'I guess it must be the effect you have on people, Angell,' he said dryly.

* * *

Max awoke to see the smiling face of a young blonde nurse looking down at him. It took him a second to recollect what had happened, but everything came back with the raging pain that thumped in his head.

'Nasty fire,' the nurse commented, a solemn expression on her face. 'You were very lucky to get out alive.'

Fire? What fire?

He stared at her blankly and then at the four white walls of the small hospital room, not quite sure how he'd gotten there.

'I guess you must have knocked yourself unconscious trying to escape from the flames. You were very lucky to get out alive,' she repeated.

He narrowed his eyes. 'There was a fire in the library?'

'You don't remember?' The nurse shook her head frowning. 'It was pretty bad. The whole building was devastated.'

'What about the newspapers in the back room?'

'All gone. The books too.'

'Jeez!'

She looked at him concerned. 'Do you remember anything that happened?'

Max thought hard. He remembered how he had been sitting in the back room of the library looking through the newspapers. He remembered how he had heard a noise and had gone to investigate. He remembered standing by the window and wondering how the glass had been shattered.

In a flash it all came back to him. How he had been hit over the head and how he had seen the face of his attacker.

Shit!

Although he had awoken in a hospital bed, it still surprised him when he looked down and saw the pale blue robe he was wearing.

'Where are my clothes?' he demanded.

'Clothes?' The nurse shook her head. 'You can't go anywhere. You took in a lot of smoke before they pulled you out. You're going to have to stay here for a while and get some rest.'

'You don't understand. I need to find my clothes.'

Climbing from the bed and pushing her out of the way he opened the small grey locker beside the bed. Inside he found his jeans on a hanger beside his shirt. In the pocket of the jeans, he found the newspaper page he had ripped out in the library. Quickly he scanned the page, looking for the Christian names of Helen White's three sons. He found them mentioned at the bottom of the page, together with their ages.

'Shit! Shit! Shit!'

'Mr Sutton, I really do wish you would get back into bed,' the nurse pleaded, trying hard but failing to keep an authoritative tone to her voice. Max smiled at her, his mind working overtime as he tried to fit the puzzle together in his head.

'Oh, Mr Sutton?'

He glanced up to see Agnes Barnes entering the room, a pot plant under one arm. Seeing his state of undress, redness crept up her neck.

'Ms Barnes, just the lady I need to see,' Max exclaimed, treating her to a wide grin and grabbing hold of her free arm to pull her further into the room.

Agnes seemed pleased at his enthusiasm. 'I'm glad to see you're back on your feet, Mr Sutton. You had us all worried. Are you feeling okay now?'

'Ms Barnes. Help me out here,' Max said, ignoring her question. 'Your Doctor. Turner, wasn't it?'

'Yes, Doctor Turner, that's right. Such a lovely—'

'Ms Barnes. Concentrate. What is Doctor Turner's Christian name?'

Agnes frowned at him, looking concerned. 'Are you sure you're okay, Mr Sutton? You look a little flushed.'

'Please, Agnes. This is very important. What is his name?'

'Clifford.' She nodded and smiled. 'It's Doctor Clifford Turner.'

Clifford. Rodney's younger brother.

Max beamed at her, watching the first piece of the puzzle slot into place. Now it was time to fit the second piece.

'Do you know where Officer Boaz is, Ms Barnes?'

'Officer Boaz? The gentleman you were with?' Agnes shook her head. 'I'm sorry, Mr Sutton, I haven't seen him since yesterday afternoon.'

Max gave a grim smile, not surprised. Of course, it was only a hunch, but having seen the name in the paper and remembering what Doctor Turner had said in the diner the day before – *I knew some people called Boaz once* – he knew there was a chance it could be true.

A hand took hold of his arm, and he turned to see the blonde nurse. 'Please, Mr Sutton. You have to get back in bed,' she said, her brows knitting in frustration.

He gave her a toothy grin, easing himself free from her grip. 'I just need two minutes, honey, then I'm all yours. First though, I need to make a very important phone call.'

40

JUNIPER, OREGON. FEBRUARY 1968 – JULY 1989

As the author of over a dozen bestselling crime novels, Cedric Boone had enough money to ensure his family were provided for. He lived on the outskirts of Juniper with his wife Phillipa – Pippa to her friends – just two miles from the coast in a sprawling country house that allowed him the privacy to write and to raise a family.

While the Boones appeared to have everything they could possibly want, the one thing beyond their reach was the ability to have children. They had tried to conceive for over fifteen years and were ready to give up on the idea of having a family when a friend suggested adoption.

Rodney White hadn't been exactly what they were expecting. Both Cedric and Pippa had intended to adopt a baby, but when they met this sullen thirteen-year-old boy, and learned of his terrible childhood, their hearts went out to him.

They rationalised their decision: Cedric was forty, Pippa thirty-nine – did they really want to have a young baby at their age? Rodney White was without the love of a caring family and perhaps they could give him what he needed most, a chance at life.

The Boones gave Rodney everything he'd ever dreamt of and more. Like a fairy tale, his life went from rags to riches, and he found himself the central player in a warm, loving home.

They gave him new clothes and toys on his birthday and at Christmas. Each year they took two holidays, usually one in the country and one overseas. Then there was his education. Instead of having to worry about fitting into an overcrowded classroom where his teacher didn't even know his name, let alone that he couldn't spell, Rodney had private tutors who coached him to read and write and gave him lessons in history, French, German and music.

By the time he turned eighteen, Rodney Boone had far excelled his adoptive parents' expectations, proving to them that all he had really needed was someone to give him a chance.

He played Tchaikovsky beautifully on the piano and Pippa wanted him to continue his study of music. Rodney had other ideas and planned on becoming an English professor. He hadn't forgotten his childhood. Couldn't forget.

His father had been murdered and Myron's death had been the downfall of Rodney's family.

The Boones had been wonderful to him, giving him a chance to better himself, but still he thought of his mother, locked away in the institution, and of his two brothers living separate lives with other families, when really, they should still all be together.

He had worked so hard to improve himself and knew that his mother would be proud of him if she could see everything he had achieved. If he could just find a way to stamp out the bitter feelings of his childhood, then maybe he would finally be free to enjoy his life.

College proved to be a new learning experience: four years

studying a teaching degree, his first time away from home, inter-
acting with other students. It didn't take him long to realise that
he was different from the rest of them. More intelligent and more
important. He wanted to learn, to improve himself, but it seemed
that everyone else around him just wanted to get drunk and fool
around.

Back in the children's home, he'd learned to deal with things
by channelling his emotions into hatred and violence. Living with
the Boones had taught him how to cover those feelings with a
genial mask. Not wanting to show the other students that he was
different, he wore this mask to make them believe he was one of
them.

It wasn't difficult. He was smarter than they were and knew
how to fool them. By the time he had graduated, top of his class,
they looked up to him and respected him; all of the female
students wanted to date him, and all of the male students wanted
to be his friend.

Not once did any of them see beyond his mask and never did
they suspect that on the sporadic occasions when the pressure
got too much, he would take long drives to nameless towns,
picking up women or hitchhikers and brutally pounding the life
out of them, dumping their bodies in woods and ditches. He
could remember the first time almost as clearly as if it had
happened yesterday, even though it had actually been almost
fifteen years ago.

Her name had been Evelyn and he had picked her up while
driving down to Cedric and Pippa's holiday home in Palm
Springs. It was the beginning of summer vacation, and she had
been thumbing a lift, trying to get to her boyfriend's place in Los
Angeles. He had seen her standing on the edge of the road,
dressed only in a white bikini top and a skimpily cut pair of
denim shorts, her crimped blonde hair blowing in the breeze. He

had immediately been drawn to her. Although he had never picked up a hitchhiker before, he found himself pulling his car over to the side of the road and offering her a ride. Evelyn was an earthy person, sensual and free-spirited and she talked to him about love and peace and being at one with nature. As she talked, Rodney listened, hating the way that she tried to simplify everything, claiming to have a solution to every problem. What did she truly know about the mundane reality and hardships of life?

He hadn't set out to kill her. When she had first got into his car his intention had been to drive her to Los Angeles. The longer he spent in her company, though, the stronger the urge became to wrap his hands around her throat and crush the life out of her.

The deed was carried out on a quiet stretch of coastal road. Rodney had stopped the car, using the excuse that he needed to stretch his legs. Knowing there was nowhere for her to run, he had waited until the exact moment Evelyn realised his intentions before he took her life, enjoying the look of terror in her eyes as she finally understood not every story had a happy ending.

As he kicked her limp body over the edge of the cliff and watched it drop like a rag doll onto the sharp rocks below, he found a bitter irony in the fact that she had been named Evelyn. Eve. The life-giver, the first woman.

Eve had been his first victim, but having experienced such a high feeling of euphoria, he knew she would not be his last. The killings continued long after he had graduated college and long after he had taken up the post as one of the English professors at Juniper College. Six months into the first semester, Cedric and Pippa were killed in a car accident and left their vast fortune to Rodney; and it was six months after their deaths that he was finally reunited with Clifford.

Just as he had promised, his younger brother had tracked him down so they could be together again. It had been difficult. The home hadn't been helpful in giving out details but suspecting that Rodney was still somewhere on the West Coast, Clifford had started placing personal ads in some of the main papers. Three years, two months and twelve days after the first ad had gone in, Rodney saw one of them and called his brother.

Although they hadn't seen each other in several years the first meeting wasn't at all awkward. Both brothers had a lot to catch up on.

Clifford, adopted by Eric and Molly Turner, had spent his childhood in Seattle and after graduating high school he had gone on to study medicine, eventually becoming a doctor. Just a couple of years earlier he had moved back to their hometown, San Palimo, where he had made a fresh start as Doctor Turner.

Rodney was proud of his brother's achievements and Clifford, likewise, was impressed by how well Rodney had done. They became close, as brothers should, and when Clifford visited Juniper, they would spend their weekends together, sometimes talking, sometimes in mutual silence, but always playing cards just like they had done when they were children. Although he shared most secrets with his younger brother, Rodney still wore the mask that covered his raging hatred and he never told Clifford about the way he chose to cure it. Those feelings were not Clifford's concern. It was Rodney's job as head of the family to make sure all the problems were taken care of.

He had thought long and hard over the years about how he could bring closure to his pain and suffering; watching his students, with their flippant, puerile attitudes towards life, he came to realise that the only way to do it would be to truly avenge his parents.

Instead of randomly choosing victims who were unknown to him, he would instead take the lives of some of his students. He would commit twenty-six murders, one to represent each letter of the alphabet to show his mother how hard he had worked, and in doing so he would be cleansing the college of the students' selfish, carefree attitudes while at the same time freeing himself of the guilt that he had let his parents down.

He decided that Clifford couldn't know of his plans. If his brother found out, he would either try to stop him, or insist on helping. There could be no assistance. This was Rodney's job and with each student he killed, Rodney could feel the burden of responsibility being lifted from his shoulders.

He had already chosen the students, and he kept their names written in a diary that was locked in the drawer of his desk in the study. He always selected the louder ones. Some male, some female, but always the ones who were popular and stood out from the crowd. He liked to watch that moment between life and death when they finally realised they were not invincible and that their lives could be crushed out in the blink of an eye. Then when he'd killed them – usually he choked them, though the pretty ones he liked to watch suffocate – he would throw their bodies away into the sewer, damning them to eternal hell.

Everything was successful for a while, then, just after he'd claimed his fourth victim, his mother had died. She was still in the institution and had suffered a heart attack. Although Rodney hadn't seen her since the family had been split up, he still monitored her progress, often calling to see how she was.

He had decided that he wouldn't see his mother face to face until he had completed the killings. Then he would be able to tell her of his achievement, and she would finally love him, absolved from his guilt, the way he had always wanted her to. Now, with news of her death, he didn't feel love. Only anger. Anger at how she had denied him in life and anger that she had died before he had the chance to complete the alphabet. For a while he stopped killing the students, seeing no point in continuing. Eventually he realised that his pain was not going to go away and that he needed to kill, if not for his mother, for himself.

He suspected that Clifford knew what he was doing. Although the Alphabet Killings were headline news and the focal point of every conversation, his brother never said anything, and it was almost as though the subject was taboo. It didn't matter if Clifford knew. Rodney was sure that his brother understood his reasons and would never go to the police. He even took to killing the occasional victim in his cellar workshop while his brother was upstairs in the house.

One such victim was Jennifer Isaac. An English student who, together with her best friend, flirted and joked her way through her classes, never paying attention and having the nerve to not take the killings seriously.

He went after her on a Saturday, knocking her unconscious in one of the shower rooms and carrying her limp body out of the dorm to his car. The risk he had taken that night was incalculable. Any one of the students could have stepped out of their room and seen him. With each killing he had become stronger, more invincible, and the risks he took each time were greater. In his mind he had convinced himself that he was infallible and that no matter what he did, the police would never catch him.

That's why he had been so surprised when Jennifer Isaac had attacked him. Back in the cellar of his house he had watched her suffocate under a plastic bag and left what he believed was her lifeless body lying on the work bench.

Usually, he liked to cut his victims the instant they were dead, when the blood was still warm and running in their veins. This time was different, and he had foolishly decided to leave her body for a while, telling himself that there was no imminent hurry.

This one mistake was his downfall as, still alive, Jennifer had woken, attacked him and managed to escape. As he lay on the cellar floor, the blade of the butcher's knife wedged deep into the bottom of his spine and flames rising around him, he had truly thought he was going to die.

He was a failure. The alphabet would never be completed, and he would never be free from the burden of guilt and responsibility.

As he flitted between life and death, his mind and body barely conscious, someone was there to help him. Someone who had heard the noise and come down into the cellar to pull him free from the flames. What seemed like hours later, but was probably only a matter of minutes, he found himself outside, lying on the back seat of Clifford's silver Plymouth, the fusion of yellow and orange flames burning against the backdrop of the sky and his brother staring down at him with a look of concern on his face.

He realised then that he was not alone. He didn't have to shoulder the responsibility all by himself.

There were two of them now, two of them to share the pain, two of them to deal with the rage and, like he had always been there for Clifford, Clifford was now going to be there for him.

41

SAN PALIMO, CALIFORNIA. THURSDAY 8
MAY 1997

As soon as Max got off the phone from Joel, he called the San Palimo Police Department. Ten minutes later, Captain Trent and two of his best officers arrived at the hospital.

An APB was immediately put out on Vic Boaz. Although Max didn't know for certain that the officer was involved, they still had to try and find him. Then leaving Agnes Barnes and the still protesting nurse behind, the four of them went to make a house call on Doctor Clifford Turner, playing on a strong hunch that the man who'd knocked Max unconscious and set fire to the library was none other than Rodney Boone's brother.

* * *

Rodney heard the sirens before he saw the cars.

Drawing his eyes away from the attic window he glanced at Clifford's reflection in the dresser mirror. His brother looked scared, and Rodney sympathised with him. Clifford had been harbouring him from the police for the past eight years, nursing him back to health and looking after his every need. It hadn't been an easy job, and he admired his brother for never complaining, even though at times he had been able to see the strain and frustration in his eyes.

At first neither of them had truly believed their plan would work. Rodney had been badly injured when Clifford pulled him from the fire and, had it not been for his skills as a doctor, there was no way he would have survived.

It had been difficult for both of them: Rodney had to learn to live with the fact that he couldn't leave the attic and Clifford, in turn, had to deal with the few inquisitive townspeople who found it hard to believe he lived alone. Between them they created a fictitious elderly aunt and eventually the curiosity over the extra groceries and the face sometimes seen at the window had died.

They had worked hard to keep their secret and now it was almost over.

Rodney Boone, the infamous serial killer, could no longer run and it seemed he could no longer hide. He was going to jail, and it looked like Clifford would be going with him. He had known it was over from the moment Clifford had come running upstairs telling him about the cops in the diner, the ones who were in town trying to uncover details of his past.

In desperation, Clifford had gone to the library, planning to set it on fire and destroy all the town's papers and records. What he hadn't counted on was running into one of the cops. Panicking, he had hit him over the head and fled from the building hoping that before the cop gained consciousness he would be burnt in the flames.

The plan hadn't worked. Seeing the flames engulf the building, people had called 911 and a fire crew had arrived on the scene and rescued the cop. The cop who had seen Clifford's face and who had probably figured out why he had torched the library.

Hearing the sirens only went further to confirm his suspicions. Now it really was over.

* * *

Doctor Turner answered the door of his house protesting his innocence even before the police had the chance to charge him with anything.

Max watched two of the officers cuff Turner and escort him to one of the patrol cars, his mouth set in a grim line as he recalled how the man had left him for dead in the library. Hoping that his hunch was right, he unholstered his service revolver and followed Captain Trent inside the house.

* * *

Rodney heard the footsteps on the stairs, and he glanced at the wall at his chart of freedom. The seven years, ten months and twenty-seven days, all written in black and circled in red.

They were here; he knew it.

As the footsteps grew louder, he trained his eyes on the dresser mirror. The door opened and two men entered. One bulky and balding with close-set eyes and three chins, wearing a uniform. The other a blond-haired man of about fifty, dressed in plain clothes.

Both had their weapons aimed in his direction.

Rodney Boone wheeled round to greet them with a humourless smile, registering the looks of surprise on their faces.

The blond man blinked hard. 'Sweet Jesus!'

* * *

Max's jaw dropped as he stared at the man in front of the dresser. It was Rodney Boone; there was no doubt about that. He looked the same as his picture. A little older, hair a little greyer, but still the same.

What he hadn't expected was to find the infamous serial killer sitting in a wheelchair.

Captain Trent recovered quicker, stepping into the room, still covering Boone with his revolver. Max knew it was possible the wheelchair could be a trick, intended to lull them into a sense of false security.

'Rodney Boone?' Trent barked.

The serial killer nodded in answer.

'I'm placing you under arrest on eight counts of murder. You have the right to remain silent. Anything you say, can and will be used against you...'

* * *

Rodney listened as the policeman read him his rights, taking a final look around him, knowing he would never see the attic room again. They had seemed shocked to find him in a wheelchair, and he guessed that they probably believed it to be some kind of trick.

It was no trick though. Little Jennifer had hurt him badly when she'd rammed the butcher's knife into his back and Clifford had told him in no uncertain terms that he would never walk again.

That was why it was good that there was someone to finish the alphabet for him. Someone who wanted to see his work completed.

The police had caught him now, but in his heart of hearts, Rodney Boone knew that it wasn't over. Not by a long shot.

* * *

By the second time Max had called, Joel had already pulled out the files on Boaz.

The officer's birth year was September 1963, which would have made him two months old when Myron White was killed. A call to his parents at their home in Florida established that he had been adopted.

Mrs Boaz wasn't forthcoming with the information. She and her husband had wanted a son to add to their all-girl family and when they adopted Victor, they'd decided to raise him as their own. She claimed that as far as Vic was aware, they were his birth parents, and she made it clear that she wanted to keep things that way if at all possible.

Although she didn't know the names of Vic's real parents, she did confirm that they had adopted him from the Wyefield Children's Home.

Could it really be true? Was Victor Boaz really the baby brother of Rodney Boone?

Max's second call was to tell Joel that they'd arrested the serial killer. As suspected, he was being hidden by Clifford Turner, the other brother. Was it possible that all three brothers were somehow involved in the Alphabet Murders, past and present?

Until they found Vic, they really had no way of telling.

During his conversation with Max, Joel had discussed Lawrence Parker. The man had now been held for almost forty-eight hours, and they had to make a decision about whether or not they were going to charge him.

If Kylan Parker was telling the truth, her husband had solid alibis for two of the murders. Given the new evidence that had recently come to light about Boone, the decision was made that for now they would release him, and after getting off the phone, Joel went down to the holding cell to tell him.

As he expected, Parker took the news with a knowing smile.

'You finally decided to believe me, Agent Hickok?' he said mockingly, as he stepped from the cell.

Joel scowled at him, wishing he could leave the man in there and throw the key away. 'We're not done with you yet, Lawrie. Just think of this as a temporary reprieve.'

'Have you found my wife yet?' Parker asked, ignoring his comment.

'Yes, she's safe.'

'Where is she? In Seattle?'

'That's not for you to worry about and don't start getting any smart ideas about trying to find her either. I don't want you to leave town until we've cleared up our enquiries.'

Joel escorted him to the front desk and watched him collect his belongings. From the corner of his eye, he saw Angell looking on in disgust at the whole proceeding.

Although she had initially been on Parker's side, her opinion of him had changed drastically after he'd come on to her. Then when the call came in from Emma Keeley's friend, Renee Lewis, she had finally started to believe that he could be responsible for the murders. Unfortunately, they didn't have enough to charge him with, especially since his wife had just provided him with two alibis. Joel hoped for Kylan Parker's sake that she was telling the truth. If by chance her husband was the Alphabet Killer, then it was very possible that she had just signed her own death warrant.

42

When Lawrie arrived home, Kylan wasn't there, though given the circumstances that didn't surprise him. Poor Kylan, she'd been lucky enough to evade death once and now she was being forced to look it in the face again. The cops dragging him in to be questioned had been a mistake. How was he supposed to keep an eye on her when he was locked in a prison cell?

Kylan had come through for him though, providing him with two rock solid alibis. He had known he would be able to count on her if the going got rough. She hadn't yet discovered the truth, which meant she must still trust him. Now, all he had to do was find her.

The rude Federal Agent, Hickok, hadn't confirmed her whereabouts, which meant that they probably still suspected him. Of course, they couldn't prove a thing. As for Kylan, if he knew her as well as he thought he did, she had probably gone to her sister's place in Seattle, thinking she would be safe there.

Upstairs in the spare bedroom, he pulled the suitcases out from under the double bed. Finding one that was bulging with clothes, he dropped it onto the mattress and unzipped it.

Inside, lying on top was Emma Keeley's short, figure-hugging blue dress; the one that she had liked to wear to tease him. The one she had been wearing on that last night.

He stared at it for a long moment before dropping to his knees. Burying his face in the dress, he inhaled the scent of the still perfumed fabric and allowed himself to remember the way she had looked with her shiny dark hair and her milky-coloured complexion, ice-blue eyes and blood-red lips.

Realising he was wasting time, he tore himself away from the memory, dropped the dress back into the case and left the room, stopping only to collect his wallet and keys before he left the house.

As he started the car engine he thought again of Emma. And then briefly of Scott Jagger, Rufus Lind, Catherine Maloney, Kevin North and Justine Orton. He wiped the images of their faces from his mind, trying to concentrate fully on the present.

He had to find Kylan, darling sweet Kylan.

* * *

Hickok had been reluctant when Rebecca told him she wanted to go to Seattle.

He had decided after Lawrence Parker had been released that it might be safer to put Kylan under police protection until the killer had been caught, but when Rebecca had volunteered to go and collect her, he hadn't been at all keen on the idea.

'You're really sure you want to drive all that way?' he asked her, pulling a dubious face.

'Sure, why not?'

'Well I could easily get someone else to go pick her up.'

Rebecca narrowed her eyes suspiciously. 'Are you trying to say that you don't trust me, Hickok?' she snapped. 'Don't you think I'm responsible enough for the job?'

'Hey, I never said that.'

He looked a little taken aback, and Rebecca felt guilty. She had been blowing hot and cold with him ever since he'd been over at her apartment on Saturday night, not sure how to deal with the way she felt. Lawrence Parker's release from jail had just put her on edge.

'Look, I'm a big girl,' she added, her tone softer. 'I'm perfectly capable of driving to Seattle and collecting Kylan.'

'Okay, fine,' Hickok nodded. Still, he looked unsure. 'There are plenty of other jobs you could be doing around here, though,' he said with a smile. 'For starters, my coffee cup is getting empty.'

Rebecca gave a sarcastic laugh, wondering why she had bothered feeling guilty. 'Ha ha, you're so funny, Hickok. Well, I guess you're going to have to get it yourself, because I've got better things to do.'

'Like driving to Seattle?'

She gave him a sharp look. 'Why do you have such a problem with that?'

He backed off, hands in the air. 'No problem, no problem.'

'So I can go?'

From the scowl on his face she could tell he still wasn't happy. 'If you have to,' he grumbled, evidently not having a good enough case to make her stay.

He watched her slip on her leather jacket. 'Hey, Angell, what's the big deal here anyway? I mean, why do you want to go so bad?'

Rebecca shrugged, not really sure that there was one particular reason. It was just something she felt she ought to do. 'I don't know,' she muttered. 'I guess Kylan knows me. Well... sort of knows me, and it will probably help having another female around. I would imagine after everything that has happened to her, the last thing she needs is a man.'

Hickok grinned at her comment. 'Hey, we're not all bad.'

They locked eyes and for a second Rebecca felt another surge of electricity pass between them. Quickly she broke the contact.

'I have to go,' she mumbled, hunting for the keys to her Jeep amongst the paperwork piled high on her desk.

Hickok nodded, watching her. 'Hey, Angell, you want me to get someone to go with you?' he asked, his tone sober.

'I'll be fine. I have the address of Kylan's sister. I'll go straight to the house, have a chat with her and tell her we're gonna put her into police protection, and hopefully we will be back tomorrow morning.'

'Okay.'

Rebecca could tell from his tone that although he still didn't want her to go alone, there weren't any more arguments he could use to make her stay.

'Well, I guess I'll be seeing you later,' she said, heading for the door.

Hickok caught hold of her arm. His voice was serious. 'Be careful, okay? Just in case.'

Glancing up Rebecca met his eyes. She saw concern in them. 'Don't worry about me,' she reassured him, forcing a grin. 'I drive a lot slower than you do.'

* * *

Before leaving for Seattle, she returned to her apartment for a quick shower and changed from her uniform into a T-shirt and a pair of jeans. She fed Sabrina and found her road map in one of the kitchen drawers. Certain that there was nothing else she needed to do, she took two cans of Pepsi from the cooler box of the refrigerator and grabbed her Jeep keys from the work top. Saying goodbye to the cat, she left her apartment.

Outside, she crossed the road to where she had parked her Jeep. She deposited the Pepsi cans in the glove compartment, selected a Chili Peppers cassette and slid it into the tape player. As she started the engine she glanced at the clock on the dashboard, estimating how long it would take her to drive to Seattle. It was already past six and it was unlikely that she would get there much before midnight.

Hoping the killer hadn't followed Kylan Parker, she shifted into drive and pulled away from the curb.

* * *

Joel had been worried about Kylan Parker being attacked ever since they had learned her true identity. Now, and for more selfish reasons than he cared to admit, he had more cause for concern. He kept telling himself that Kylan would be fine, that Angell would be fine. Much as he didn't like it, it was looking increasingly unlikely that Lawrence Parker was their killer. There was no need to worry.

That didn't stop him from picking up the phone later that evening and dialling Parker's number.

He let it ring twelve times without getting an answer.

Maybe he's asleep.

Despite his best efforts to convince himself that there was nothing wrong, Joel was still uneasy. Knowing how much he hated those niggling questions that began with 'what if', he grabbed his car keys. Ten minutes later he found himself knocking on Parker's front door. There was no car in the driveway, and it looked as though no one was home. Knowing better, but also knowing that he had to put his mind at rest, Joel tried the front door, surprised when it opened.

Hesitantly, he stepped inside.

'Lawrie? Lawrie? It's Special Agent Hickok. Are you home?' There was no answer.

Closing the door, Joel unholstered his weapon and conducted a quick search of the house.

When he stepped into the guest bedroom his attention was immediately drawn to the case that was open on the bed. It was filled with clothes, all of them packed neatly with the exception of a blue dress, which was draped across the top of the pile. Was someone planning a vacation?

He took a step closer and picked up the dress. It looked familiar, but he couldn't immediately place it.

The other clothes in the case were both male and female: jeans, sweaters, another dress...

He looked at the blue dress again, frowning.

Short, silky, midnight-blue, patterned with tiny white flowers, he remembered with a start that he had seen it before on Emma Keeley. She had been wearing the dress in the picture that Mindy Tyson had given him. Furiously he started to pull the other clothes from the case: the jeans and sweaters, jackets and sneakers, the dress. A black leather wallet dropped from the pocket of a black denim jacket and Joel stooped to pick it up.

Inside was a photo ID. The smiling face in the picture was Scott Jagger.

He thought of Angell on her way to Seattle and he realised there was a strong possibility that Lawrence Parker might already be there.

* * *

When Agnes Barnes told Max that Karen Harris hadn't shown up for work at all on Thursday and hadn't answered her phone when she'd called, he felt his stomach start to churn. The last time he had seen her had been Wednesday evening when she had been waiting for Boaz to leave the library. Now she was missing and so was he.

Assisted by Agnes and one of Captain Trent's officers, Pete Bakerman, he drove over to the librarian's house, hoping against hope that the feeling he had about Boaz would turn out to be wrong.

Agnes directed them to her colleague's house, a neat two-bedroom property that overlooked the bay, repeatedly telling them that Karen was always reliable and never took sick days. Her words didn't offer Max much comfort as he climbed from the patrol car, telling her to wait in the back.

As he crossed the neatly maintained lawn, he felt his legs start to shake. If he opened the door now and found Karen Harris lying dead on the floor, how would he live with his guilt, knowing that he'd been responsible for bringing her killer to the small town?

Tentatively he knocked on the front door.

There was no answer.

Service revolver raised, he gave it a sharp kick, sending the door flying back on its hinges. With a nod to Bakerman to follow, he stepped inside. The light was on and the room they found themselves in was open-plan, serving as both a living room and a dining room, with the kitchen sectioned off to the rear.

The walls were painted in a bright lemon and the place was filled with colour, with several prints, and vases of blue and orange flowers sitting on the glass coffee table and the breakfast bar.

Max noticed that the room smelt fresh: a mixture of furniture polish and floral air freshener. There was no scent of death lingering in the air. Hoping that was a good omen, he crossed the room to the two doors on the far wall. Choosing the one on the left he waited for Bakerman to join him before slowly pushing down on the handle and easing the door open.

At the sight on the bed before him, Max dropped his revolver. He let out a low groan and closed his eyes.

'What the fuck?'

Daring to open them again he took in the scene before him. Karen Harris had disappeared beneath the sheets, giggling girlishly, and he could just see a few of her red curls poking out onto the pillow. Boaz sat beside her wearing no more than a blush, his hands clutched defensively between his legs as he eyeballed Max.

Max shook his head, not sure if this was better or worse than he had expected.

'Buddy,' he said with a deep sigh. 'You have got a lot of explaining to do.'

* * *

Joel spent five minutes on the phone to Max before he left the precinct, learning about Boaz's sexual exploits and warning his partner about the clothes he had found in Lawrence Parker's house.

He had already tried to call Angell on her car phone, only to find the line engaged, and had immediately made arrangements to charter a plane from one of the local airfields. Hanging up from his partner, he tried Angell again, found her still engaged, grabbed his keys and headed for the door.

43

Tania Isaac lived in a leafy suburban neighbourhood at the end of a wide street that was lined by cedar trees and Victorian style street lamps. Her house was large and appeared to be well designed but, like all of the others in the street, it was a nondescript, grey brick, two-story box. The front door, like the framework of the windows, was painted white and set back into an open porch flanked by pillars, and two brass lanterns hung overhead emitting a warm welcoming glow across the front path.

Rebecca left her Jeep parked on the street and stepped up to the wrought-iron gate for a closer inspection, rubbing at a tender spot on the back of her neck. She was tired from the drive and longed for nothing more than a relaxing soak in a tub full of bubbles.

During her first hour on the road, she had received four phone calls from her mother. The first had been just to check that she was okay after her mother hadn't been able to reach her at home.

Rebecca had told her she was fine and explained that she was on her way to Seattle on police business. It had been a foolish thing to say because her mother had then proceeded to call her every ten minutes, worried that she might be involved in something dangerous. Despite Rebecca telling her that the only danger she was in was of crashing while she was on the phone, her mother hadn't listened. After the fourth call Rebecca had given up arguing and switched the phone off.

She wondered now if perhaps she should have left it on. If Hickok had needed to call her, he wouldn't have been able to get through. Not that she could imagine he would have any need to call her.

She remembered his concern before she had left, how he had told her to be careful, and thought it was sweet. Unnecessary, but sweet.

There was no need to worry about Lawrence Parker. She could see from the empty driveway that he wasn't here. More than likely, he was waiting at home for his wife. Or out screwing more of his students, she thought, remembering how he had come on to her in the interview room back at the police precinct.

Did Kylan know about his infidelities?

Pushing the question to the back of her mind, telling herself it was none of her business, Rebecca let herself in through the front gate and walked up the driveway to the front door, the crunch of her sneakers against the stones sounding loud against the quiet night.

She rang the bell, jumping back at the sonorous chime that vibrated into the house.

A moment of silence passed as she waited, listening for the sound of approaching footsteps.

They didn't come and she rang again, certain that Kylan must be there. When they had spoken on the phone, the woman had been spooked. But had she really been spooked badly enough to run away again? Rebecca had tried Kylan's sister's number a couple of hours back, but the phone hadn't been answered. At the time she hadn't thought anything of it. Kylan could have gone out, or was maybe just ignoring the phone, knowing who it was. Thinking about it now, the house appeared empty, the only light coming from the porch. Perhaps she had packed up and moved on.

Another minute passed. Still no answer.

Rebecca stared at the door, not sure what to do. She had driven for nearly five hours to get there. She couldn't just leave. Maybe she should go back to the Jeep and call Hickok.

She was about to walk away, when she heard a muffled sound coming from inside.

Could be a cat, or a dog, though she'd heard no barking. She contemplated ringing the bell again but, as whoever was home wasn't answering, she decided against it. Maybe it would be better if she had a quick look around out back, just to see if there were any lights on.

The house had a generous-sized plot that was filled with a variety of trees and shrubbery. She could see a pathway of paving stones leading across the lawn, through long grass that looked damp and overdue for a cut.

The backyard was secluded. There were no lights on inside, only an overhead wall lantern, brass, like the two out front. The dim glow it cast created the illusion that the black shadows of the surrounding trees and bushes were dancing together on the lawn. There was a large pond at the far end of the yard and the leaves of the willow tree that hung above drooped down into the water. A patio table and chairs were set up close to the house, though the umbrella and cushions had been removed and she guessed they were probably in the small wooden shed that stood near the pond. Like the house, it suggested that no one was home. Maybe it was a cat she'd heard after all.

She was about to make her way back to the front of the house and call Hickok, when a shrill, high-pitched scream cut through the air, and her heart lurched into her mouth. Stopping dead in her tracks, Rebecca stared at the house; the sound had come from inside.

Shit! Shit! Shit!

She ran to the back door, tugging on the handle, knowing she should stop and assess the situation, but not wanting to waste time.

The door was locked.

Cursing under her breath for believing she would be lucky enough to find it unlocked, she took a step back, wondering if she should go back and try the front door. It was then that she noticed one of the back windows had been left ajar. A small sliding window on the ground floor that had been pulled down, exposing what was probably no more than a ten-inch gap.

She doubted that she'd be able to get through such a narrow space but dragged one of the plastic chairs across the patio, placing it beneath the window. Standing on tiptoe on the seat of the chair, she peered through the crack and found herself looking into some kind of laundry room. Despite the darkness, she could make out a washer and dryer on the opposite wall, and a shelf that contained fabric conditioner and soap powder.

Forcing the window down another inch, Rebecca debated as to whether or not there was enough room for her to get through.

Nothing ventured, nothing gained.

Remembering the scream she'd heard and wondering if it was Kylan, she climbed up from the chair, onto the brick ledge, and lowered herself enough to squeeze her head, shoulders and arms through the open space. There was nothing inside the room to hold on to except for the window frame and she gripped on to it tightly as she attempted to pull the rest of her body through.

She was halfway through when her ass got jammed.

Shit! Goddamn it!

Dangling precariously, half in and half out of the window, she wiggled from side to side, ignoring the cutting pain of the frame digging into her stomach.

Damn my big fat ass.

She cursed herself, wishing that she'd had more willpower when it came to resisting unhealthy food. Clenching her teeth together, she pressed the palms of her hands against the inside of the glass and gave herself a hard push.

As she came unstuck, her ass went flying through the window, followed by her flailing legs, and she reached out, frantically trying to grab hold of something to break her fall. Directly below the window was a heaped basket of washing and she fell into it headfirst, her legs flying over her head and crashing loudly into the door of the dryer.

Rebecca lay dazed for a moment sprawled half in the basket, half on the floor. Her ankles hurt where they'd caught the dryer door and she reached down to rub them, wondering if anyone had heard her.

Of course they did, you dip shit! And so did probably half the neighbourhood.

Picking herself up from the floor, she stared cautiously at the closed door. What if the killer was waiting on the other side for her?

She wished for the first time that she had her sidearm with her. Not having realised that the trip to Seattle could be potentially life-threatening, she had left it back in her apartment.

Talk about always be prepared. You screwed up good this time.

Gingerly, she reached out for the door handle and slowly pulled the door open.

The laundry room led directly on to the kitchen. The room

was dark and filled with shadows, but no one appeared to be waiting on the other side of the door for her. Being careful not to make any more unnecessary noise, she stepped into the kitchen and took a quick glance around. The units were white and clean. There was no food or dirty dishes on the side to suggest that anyone was there.

What about the scream you heard?

Rebecca peered cautiously over her shoulder at the open door that led into the hall. If she was going to explore the house, she needed some kind of weapon. Noticing the wooden knife block that stood on the sideboard, she tiptoed across the room and selected herself a carving knife. The blade looked sharp, and she didn't doubt that it would do the job should she need to use it. Hopefully she wouldn't. It was possible that she was jumping to the wrong conclusions and there was a perfectly logical explanation for the scream she'd heard.

Before she'd even finished reassuring herself, she found her attention drawn back to the knife block and the two empty slots.

One which her own knife had occupied and one where there didn't seem to be any knife at all.

You know what the Alphabet Killer likes to do to his victims.

Rebecca pushed the thought from her mind. Maybe the knife had been missing for some time. Maybe it had been stashed away in a drawer by mistake.

Or maybe there is someone else in the house who is already using it.

Drawing a deep breath, Rebecca peered around the kitchen door into the hallway. Whatever the explanation was, she knew there was only one way to find out. With the knife clasped tightly in her hand she began to explore the downstairs rooms of the house. Everything seemed incredibly still and, with the exception of the perpetual ticking that came from the large oak grandfather clock that stood in the hallway, eerily silent. Constantly reassuring herself that there was probably nothing foreboding in the house, while fighting to control her growing sense of unease, she stepped into the dark shadows of the living room.

Heavy green velvet curtains were draped across one wall, concealing the window and blocking out any light that might have come from the moon.

Rebecca peered into the darkness briefly, taking in the furniture, wondering if perhaps she should venture further into the room and check behind the two dark leather couches.

Jeez! What do you expect to find? A dead body?

She had just taken a tentative step forward, when the grandfather clock chimed loudly. Jumping, she stifled a scream as the knife slipped from her shaking hand.

Christ, Rebecca! Get it together.

She remained standing for a moment in the shadows of the living room doorway, trying to keep her breathing quiet and wishing that her heartbeat would slow down. There was no one downstairs and, so far, she had found nothing to suggest that there was anyone else in the house. She thought about the missing knife and about the scream she had heard. They probably both had perfectly good explanations. Maybe she should just go out to her Jeep and call Hickok.

What about upstairs though? You haven't checked upstairs yet.

She stooped down to retrieve her own knife then cautiously she stepped out into the hall. As she tiptoed towards the front door, half expecting someone to jump out from behind the grandfather clock and grab her, she thought again about the scream she had heard.

Shit, Rebecca. Who are you trying to kid? The scream came from inside this house, and you know it.

Tentatively, she glanced over her shoulder at the staircase. The landing at the top was a mass of black shadows and seemed almost too quiet. Only a fool would venture up there alone. She knew that the wise thing to do would be to go out to her Jeep and call for backup.

What if there isn't time to wait for backup?

Summoning up all of her courage, and cursing at herself under her breath, Rebecca began to climb the staircase, using her free hand to steady herself on the banister. If anything happened to her now, it would be her own fault.

She imagined her obituary. The stories in the press. *Rookie cop killed exploring house. Foolish decision loses cop her life.*

She wondered what she would find upstairs.

Would Kylan be lying dead in one of the bedrooms?

The landing at the top of the stairs was long and wide with a high-beamed ceiling. The cream-carpeted floor led off in both directions and the first door on the opposite wall was ajar.

The curtains were drawn shut, but the light was on, and Rebecca could see the motionless figure sitting at the foot of the bed.

She caught her breath sharply.

Oh my God!

Cautiously, she pushed the door open and stepped into the room, her eyes taking in the scene before her.

Lawrence Parker was slumped with his knees bent, head falling back against the floral duvet. His black eyes were wide and staring up at the ceiling and both his hands clutched at the knife buried deep in his chest.

On the floor in the corner of the room sat Kylan. Her pale face was covered with blood and she was hugging her knees to her chest as she shook uncontrollably.

Rebecca stared at her for a moment, too shocked to speak. Finally, Kylan looked up at her through a sheen of tears.

'I killed him,' she murmured, her voice trembling. 'Oh my God! I killed Lawrie.'

Rebecca stared at Parker, and then back at Kylan. 'Did he hurt you?' she asked, finally finding her voice.

Kylan nodded numbly. 'I killed him,' she repeated, this time her voice even quieter, almost a whisper.

Rebecca set down her knife and eased herself down onto the floor, wrapping her arms around the girl. 'It's okay, Kylan,' she soothed. 'He tried to hurt you. You had to protect yourself.' She glanced at Parker's body. 'It's okay now. It's all over.'

She thought about Hickok. He had been right all along, suspecting Lawrence Parker from that very first meeting. She should call him. Tell him that Parker was dead.

Sick bastard. Trying to kill his own wife.

She wondered if he had intentionally married Kylan because of who she was. Had he planned to kill her all along?

The thought made her sick.

'Come on,' she said, squeezing Kylan's shoulder. 'Let's get you out of here.'

Being careful not to rush her, Rebecca led Kylan down the stairs and into the kitchen. Now that she knew there weren't any demons waiting to get her, she felt a lot more at ease. She flicked on the light switch, casting a warm glow onto the room, and sat Kylan down in one of the kitchen chairs. Finding a glass in one of the overhead cupboards, she poured her some water, telling her to sip it slowly. Then she picked up the phone that hung on the wall.

The line was dead.

Certain that she had seen a phone up in the bedroom, she left Kylan sipping the water and went back upstairs.

As she stepped back into the room with Parker, Rebecca screwed up her nose. Although she knew that he was dead, she was still hesitant to go near him, half expecting him to suddenly jump up and grab her, like in the movies.

She studied his face. Lawrence Parker had been a handsome man alive, but in death, his dark features only seemed to make him look ghoulish. Her eyes drifted down to the knife embedded deep in his flesh, and the blood spilling out onto his grey T-shirt.

Yuck! That had to have hurt.

Tearing her gaze away, she spotted the cordless phone on the far side of the bed.

Typical. To get to it she was going to have to pass him.

Coward!

Ignoring her inner voice and telling herself she had every right to be a little spooked after what she'd just seen, she sidled alongside the bed, choosing to get to the phone by clambering across the mattress.

As she picked up the phone, Parker suddenly gave a loud groan and lurched forward, his head dropping between his knees. Rebecca let out a yell, her heart pounding loudly in her chest. Dropping the phone, she scooted back across the mattress. She stared at Parker, expecting him to move again. He didn't and she suddenly found her attention focused on the cut in the back of his neck.

Rough and jagged, covered by a film of blood. Carved in the shape of the letter P.

What the fuck?

From somewhere in the house came the sound of whistling. At first soft and distant, but gradually getting closer and louder.

Rebecca recognised the tune.

Tchaikovsky's 'Scene' from *Swan Lake*...

For a moment she found she couldn't move. Sitting on the bed listening to the familiar whistle and the approaching footsteps on the stairs, she tried to rationalise with herself.

It wasn't possible. It couldn't be.

Her legs unsteady, she climbed to her feet and took tentative steps towards the door. In her mind she replayed the scene she had discovered in the bedroom. Kylan huddled on the floor and Lawrie dead, stabbed with the knife. Self-defence. That was what Kylan had told her. Lawrie had attacked her, and she had protected herself. It had been self-defence.

Thinking about it, Rebecca realised that Kylan had never actually claimed it to be self-defence, not until Rebecca had put the words in her mouth for her.

'It's okay, Kylan. He tried to hurt you. You had to protect yourself.'

If Lawrie had attacked Kylan, how come she had been the one holding the knife?

Shit! This is insane. It can't be Kylan. It doesn't make sense.

Even as the thoughts passed through her mind, she realised that it did make sense. Everything that pointed to Lawrence Parker being the killer made sense. The tie. Kylan was the one person aside from Parker who would have easy access to it. The affair with Emma Keeley – a jealous wife. The alibis. Kylan had provided them for Parker, but would he have been able to provide them for her?

But what about Richard Lamb? He'd been watching her, following her. He must have known.

Not necessarily. The private investigator claimed to have followed her only during the day. At night he had been out hunting for the killer.

A killer who nobody would have suspected in a million years.

Realising that if she was right then her life was in danger, Rebecca glanced desperately around the room, looking for some kind of weapon to use. The knife she'd earlier brought upstairs was now down in the kitchen, in plain sight of Kylan. No use to her now. As she cursed herself for being so stupid, her eyes dropped to the knife embedded in Lawrence Parker's chest.

Could she really bring herself to pull it free?

Do you have a choice?

If she touched the knife, she would be tampering with evidence.

Screw evidence! This is a matter of life or death.

Bending down over Parker's body, she placed both hands firmly on the wooden handle and pulled hard, trying to wrench it from his chest. The blade made a wet sucking sound as it started to tear free from his flesh and Rebecca grimaced, feeling the urge to throw up.

She looked down at the knife. What was visible of the blade was red and shiny, dripping with his blood. Could she do this?

Do you have a choice?

As she started to give the blade a second tug, she heard a noise coming from behind her. She turned to face the door and caught her breath sharply as she saw Kylan standing above her with the knife from the kitchen in her hand. There was no malice in the girl's eyes. They were wide and glazed, staring at Rebecca as though she didn't know who she was.

As the knife came towards her, Rebecca tried to duck to the side, but she was unable to miss the penetrating blade as it drove into the back of her shoulder. Screaming loudly, she toppled forward, landing against Lawrence Parker's corpse.

The pain was blinding and, as she slid off his body, landing in a heap on the floor, she struggled to keep hold of consciousness, knowing that she had to get out of the house.

Nobody knows. They'll never believe it's Kylan. I have to tell Hickok. I have to get out of here before she kills me.

Finally, unable to hold on any longer, her eyes dropped shut.

* * *

Joel arrived in Seattle a little after midnight.

He had called the local police department just before landing and when he arrived at the airfield two patrol cars were waiting to greet him. As they made their way to Tania Isaac's house, he thought back to Parker's house. To the clothes he'd found in the bedroom.

Kylan?

As they approached the house where Rebecca Angell was planning to meet her, he hoped to hell he was wrong. Hoped, but knew it was unlikely.

* * *

Kylan stared at Rebecca Angell, lying sprawled across the bedroom carpet, and wondered if she was dead. She hadn't meant to kill her. Hadn't wanted to hurt her. Unfortunately, she hadn't had a choice. Rebecca Angell knew the truth, and if she survived then everyone would find out the truth. They would come and take her away. Lock her up and force her to see all the doctors and therapists again. The ones who made her take pills and thought they could cure her.

What they didn't understand, what nobody seemed to understand, was that they were wasting their time. Instead of trying to analyse her every thought, they should be out there hunting for Boone. He was the one who was dangerous. They had told her that he was probably dead, but she knew different. Rodney Boone was still alive, and she knew that one day he would come for her.

Lawrie had said he would protect her. He had promised that if they moved back to Juniper, he would be there for her. And, at first, he had been. Then he had started working late. Always too tired to talk when he got home. Never reassuring her. No longer telling her that things would work out okay. Kylan had suspected he was seeing Emma Keeley. She had seen the way the two of them acted together when they thought she wasn't watching. The lingering looks they shared. The secret touches. Lawrie was slipping away from her, and with him he was taking all of her strength. When Boone came back for her, when he came to take revenge for what she had done to him, how would she be strong enough to fight him off?

Then it had occurred to her that maybe she could save herself. If she helped Boone finish his alphabet, perhaps he would leave her alone. After all, that was what he had wanted, wasn't it?

Twenty-six students. Twenty-six letters. All she needed to do was take up from where he had left off.

She knew the drill. The joker playing card. The initial carved into the back of the neck. She could finish the murders for him and then it would finally be over.

The first time had been easy. Lawrie had been working late and her selected victim, Scott Jagger, was a flirtatious football player who'd just broken up with his girlfriend. Kylan knew that he liked her, and it wasn't difficult to persuade him to go for a drive out to the coast, or to have a few drinks from the vodka bottle she'd earlier laced with sleeping pills. When he finally passed out, she wrapped her belt around his neck and pulled tightly until he stopped breathing.

She dumped his body in the beach entrance of the sewer, just half a mile from where she had killed him, sensibly waiting until she had dragged his body out of the car before she cut the back of his neck with the kitchen blade she'd brought from home. By the time Lawrie returned, later that night, she was in bed, the car was in the garage, and the knife she had used was washed up and returned to the kitchen drawer.

The second victim hadn't been a difficult choice. If Emma Keeley was having an affair with her husband, she would be able to deal with two problems at once. Playing on her hunch, she had sent two typed notes, one to Lawrie pretending it was from Emma, asking him to meet her at The Coven; another to Emma inviting her to the house. When the girl arrived, she used Lawrie's baseball bat to hit her over the head then, after strangling her, she dragged her out through the side door to the car in the garage. Not sure how much time she would have before Lawrie returned to the house, she decided not to use the sewer, and instead dumped Emma's body in the river, which was less than a five-minute ride away.

It hadn't taken her long to work out that the male victims were easier than the females. Kylan knew she was attractive, and she had no problem enticing Rufus Lind or Kevin North to their deaths. She made sure that they were blind drunk or had passed out before she killed them. Aside from being physically stronger than her, she didn't want to see them in pain. The only reason she was doing this was to stop Boone.

Catherine Maloney had been risky. She hadn't known for sure that the girl would show up at the bridge. Catherine had talked non-stop about Aidan and about how much she liked him. Did she like him enough to meet him in the middle of the night, though? Feigning a headache, Kylan had persuaded Lawrie to return home early from their date with Vic and Jill, and she had dropped a couple of her pills into his coffee to make sure he slept like a baby. When she was certain he was zonked out, she had taken the car and gone down to the bridge to find Catherine.

Justine Orton was the only victim who had proved to be a problem. Not knowing enough about her, Kylan was unable to come up with a plot to lure her away from the campus, so using Lawrie's keys she had let herself into the caretaking block, stolen the master keys to the dorms, and gone into Justine's room to wait for her. While she'd been in there, she had found Lawrie's tie. Her mind had worked overtime as she'd tried to figure out if her husband was having an affair with Justine Orton and, when the girl finally returned, it seemed only fitting that she use the tie to strangle her. Killing Justine Orton in her room made it impossible to get the body off campus. Kylan didn't think Rodney Boone would worry about technicalities though. As long as she completed the alphabet, she figured she would be home and dry. At least that was what she had thought before running into the guy from the grocery store outside her English classroom. Initially she had assumed that he was there to keep an eye on her. Probably working for Boone to make sure she finished the alphabet. Then it had occurred to her that maybe her plan wasn't working. That maybe Boone was going to kill her anyway. She had panicked and come to Seattle, to get away from everything that was happening and figure out the best course of action.

What she hadn't counted on was Lawrie showing up on Tania's doorstep earlier that night, saying that he'd found the case full of clothes. The clothes she had taken from the victims and, not knowing what to do with them, had hidden under the bed in the spare room. Lawrie told her she had to go to the police, that they would help her get psychiatric treatment. Kylan didn't want treatment, though, she just wanted to be rid of Rodney Boone and in a moment of rage she had stabbed her husband in the chest.

When he didn't get up again, she realised that there was only one thing to do. Lawrie would have to become the next victim.

Looking down at Rebecca Angell, Kylan wondered what she should do with her body. She was the wrong letter to be part of the alphabet. What was she supposed to do now? Take her body and dump it somewhere? Leave it in the house? As she turned the various possibilities over in her mind, Kylan heard the sound of a car engine. Her whole body still trembling, and her heart caught in her throat, she crossed the room to the window and pulled back the curtain.

In the light of the street lamp, she saw two police squad cars. Men – she could make out five of them, four in uniform, one in plain clothes – were heading up the driveway.

They knew. Lawrie or Rebecca must have tipped them off.

Wrenching the knife out of Rebecca's shoulder, she gripped the handle tightly in her shaking hand, stumbled across the two bodies and out of the room. What was she going to do? How could she complete the alphabet? If they caught her and put her in jail or hospital, did they really think that Rodney wouldn't be able to get her?

The doorbell chimed, and she stepped back against the wall, her mind racing, as she searched for an answer. She couldn't think straight. Everything was a blur. They were coming to get her. They would find Lawrie and they would find Rebecca, and they would know. There was nowhere for her to escape to.

The bell chimed again, the vibrations shuddering through her.

Kylan looked at the knife in her hand, still wet and shiny with Rebecca's blood, and in that instant, it came to her. There was a way of escape. One thing left that she could do. Hearing the sound of a gunshot hitting the lock on the front door, she raised the knife high in the air and poised the blade, ready to end her nightmare.

* * *

Aware of the floorboards vibrating beneath her, Rebecca forced her eyes open and tried to look up.

She immediately wished she hadn't. The pain in her shoulder was excruciating and the black dots crowding her vision were making her feel violently sick.

For a second she wondered where she was. She wondered why she was on the floor and what had happened. Then hearing a loud chime, and feeling the floorboards vibrate again, it all suddenly all came back to her.

Kylan.

Kylan had killed Lawrie. Kylan had killed Emma and Scott and...

Oh God! Kylan tried to kill me!

Hearing a noise coming from outside the bedroom, Rebecca struggled to get up. Her left arm had gone completely numb, and she held on to the bed for support as she tried to pull herself to her feet. She felt dizzy and disoriented; glancing down at the floor she saw a large crimson puddle from where her shoulder had been bleeding.

Shit! I'm fucking dying.

She wondered where Kylan was. Had she gone downstairs? Or even left the house?

God! What if she comes back?

Knowing that she had to get help, Rebecca stumbled towards the door, clutching her shoulder with her right hand as she tried to stem the flow of the blood.

A loud shot rang through the air. A gun shot.

She jumped, gripping her shoulder a little too tightly, and yelping loudly in pain. Who had fired? Kylan? Did she have a gun?

Is she planning to make sure I'm dead?

There was a crash. Like the sound of someone breaking the door, and then she heard voices. First, one she didn't recognise.

'Shit! What's she doing!'

Then one she did. 'Kylan. Put the knife down.'

Hickok!

Rebecca stumbled through the door just in time to see Kylan standing at the top of the stairs, the bloody knife in her hand, poised in the air, ready to stab herself in the chest.

Oh my God!

'No!'

Forgetting all thoughts of her own safety, Rebecca gritted her teeth against the pain and using all of her remaining strength, hurled herself forward. She hit Kylan side on, knocking the knife from her grip. The two of them fell to the floor: Kylan, kicking and screaming, trying to reach for the knife; Rebecca desperately clinging on to her, all the time trying to hold on to her own consciousness.

She heard footsteps on the stairs, growing louder and louder as she slipped closer to oblivion. Blurred voices spoke words and sentences she couldn't understand, and then she felt the pull of arms around her waist, easing her off the struggling Kylan. She heard a voice.

'Rebecca? Rebecca? Come on, Rebecca, talk to me.'

Her lids were heavy and as she struggled to lift them a million black dots clouded her vision. She blinked hard, trying to focus, fighting the burning pain in her shoulder that was threatening to engulf her.

Joel Hickok was looking down at her. His face looked strained, and his dark eyes full of concern.

'Come on, Angell. Hold on just a little longer. You're gonna be fine. There's an ambulance on its way.' His tone was warm and soothing as he talked to her, and Rebecca managed a smile, wondering if he realised that he'd let his guard slip. As a second, much stronger wave of pain surged through her, trying to pull her down, she made a mental note that she would have to tease him about it later. Right now, all she wanted to do was sleep. She started to let her eyes drop shut.

Hickok slapped her face gently. 'Come on, Rebecca. Stay awake. Stay with me.'

Easy for him to say. He wasn't the one feeling so damn tired. She wouldn't go to sleep, but she had to close her eyes. Just for a short while. Giving up the battle, Rebecca allowed her lids to drop shut. She let the wave wash over her, pulling her under, deeper and deeper, until finally she felt herself disengage from her body and she found herself in a warm and pleasant place where she was finally free of the pain.

EPILOGUE

SEATTLE, WASHINGTON. SATURDAY 10 MAY 1997

Rebecca spent the best part of two days slipping from consciousness to oblivion and back again.

During that time, she had several visitors. Some she could remember; others who came while she was asleep left flowers and cards in their wake. Martin and Sarah Angell had flown to Seattle as soon as they heard the news and were taking it in turns to keep a vigil by their youngest daughter's bedside.

Unable to escape from her hospital bed, Rebecca had no choice but to lie there and listen to her mother as she lectured, scolded and blamed her for a situation that had been beyond her control and, as the periods of consciousness grew longer, she began to wish she could return to the dream world from which she had just escaped.

By Saturday afternoon she was getting restless with being confined to her bed and longed to return home. Her doctor, a friendly woman, who didn't look much younger than her mother, promised she could be discharged on Monday and as far as Rebecca was concerned it wouldn't be a moment too soon.

She tried time and time again to persuade her mother to

return to Swallow Falls, assuring her that she was now fine. Sarah Angell hadn't relented, though, insisting she stay with her daughter until she returned to Juniper.

One person Rebecca had expected to see more of was Joel Hickok. He had been to see her once, together with Max Sutton, and they had given her an update on everything that had happened.

Kylan Parker had broken down and confessed to the murders the moment she had been arrested. The final threads of her sanity had pretty much snapped with the murder of her husband, and it was highly unlikely that she would ever stand trial. She was currently under heavy sedation in a psychiatric hospital in Oregon following two suicide attempts, while the doctors decided the best possible course of treatment for her condition.

Despite everything that had happened, both to her and the victims, Rebecca felt sorry for Kylan. Nothing could condone what she had done, of course, and because of her actions seven families were now mourning the loss of loved ones. Ultimately, though, the fault lay with Rodney Boone. If he had never attacked Kylan, then the aftershocks of his crimes would not have reverberated through her actions years later.

By an almost sick twist of fate, one of Lawrence Parker's colleagues had come forward following his murder, shedding light on the books Hickok had found in his study. It turned out that the two men had been in the process of writing their own investigative book on serial killers, little knowing that Parker was actually living with one.

Vic Boaz had also received a rude awakening when he'd learned the identity of his blood relatives. His parents had never told him that he was adopted and to find out that he shared genes with the infamous Rodney Boone had apparently, according to Sutton, knocked the stuffing out of him.

Suffering from a severe identity crisis, he had taken vacation time and gone down to Florida to talk things through with his adoptive parents.

One person who did get what was coming to him was Rodney Boone himself. It was satisfying to know that the murderer had been confined to a wheelchair, but not as satisfying as knowing that he had finally been caught and would be standing trial on eight counts of murder.

His younger brother Clifford had also been arrested, and it looked likely that he too would be spending time behind bars for aiding and abetting.

All's well that ends well, Rebecca guessed. Though she wished there could have been a happier outcome for Kylan.

And what about you Rebecca? How are things going to end for you?

The murder investigation over, it was unlikely that Special Agent Joel Hickok would be staying in Juniper. Although she didn't want to admit it, Rebecca didn't really want him to go. They were both stubborn and had too much pride, but it was foolish to keep on pretending that there was no spark between them.

With that thought on her mind, Rebecca was surprised, and secretly pleased, to see him enter the room, half hidden behind a vase of tall lilies. She looked at him, eyebrows raised, as he placed them down on the table beside her bed.

'Hey, nice flowers. I'm touched.'

He gave a teasing grin. 'Well, don't get too flattered. They're from the guys down at the precinct, not me.'

'Then I'm touched that the guys down at the precinct thought of me.'

She watched him glance warily around the room. 'Where's your mother gone?' he asked in a low voice.

'My mother?' Rebecca asked, surprised. 'She went down to the cafeteria. Why?'

Hickok nodded, looking a little relieved. He pulled up one of the two visitor chairs and sat down.

'I think she's got me lined up as prospective boyfriend material,' he told her conspiratorially, pulling a face.

'Oh.' Rebecca felt herself redden. 'She does that. You just have to ignore her.'

'I'll keep that in mind,' Hickok said, giving her a knowing grin. There was a moment's silence as he studied her face. 'So, how are you doing, Angell?' he asked eventually.

'Well, I've been better.'

'Yeah? I guess that's because you haven't had me around to cheer you up.'

Rebecca stifled a laugh. 'You reckon?'

'Of course.' He smiled at her, though his eyes stayed serious. 'That's why I figured you're gonna want me to come and keep you company next week when you get out of hospital.'

Rebecca raised her eyebrows slightly, resisting the urge to make a sarcastic comment. This was what she wanted, wasn't it? 'Don't you have to be somewhere else?' she asked. 'I'd have thought that you and Sutton would be off solving murders in the Deep South or something.'

'Nothing quite as pressing as that.' He turned his grin up a notch. 'So, what do you say? Your place, Monday night. I'll even bring the pizza seeing as I know you can't cook.'

'Really? How would you know that?'

Hickok shook his head. 'You'd be surprised to know the things your mother's been telling me about you.'

'My mother!' Rebecca grumbled, guessing she should have known. 'I hate to think what else she's been saying.'

'Yeah, I'll bet you do,' he agreed. 'So, what do you think then, Angell? Pizza? Monday night?'

Rebecca pulled a face, pretending to mull the idea over. 'Pepperoni and mushroom?' she questioned.

Hickok grinned and nodded. 'Okay, you've got yourself a date.'

* * *

MORE FROM KERI BEEVIS

Another book from Keri Beevis is available to order now here: https://mybook.to/KeriBeevis14